THE DOG WALKER

THE DOG
WALKER

LIZ
  Hope that you
enjoy. I am sure that
you will understand.
          John Hope

JOHN HOPE

ISBNs
Paperback: 978-1-80541-126-0
eBook: 978-1-80541-127-7

CHAPTER 1

Eleanor McLoughlin's hands shook as she removed the stopper from the crystal decanter and then cursed loudly to herself as she over-filled the sherry glass, spilling a small amount of the rich liquid onto the green-topped cover of her desk. Her faithful dogs, the white standard poodle, Marilyn, and the small mongrel, Rags, watched intently as she snatched a Kleenex from a box and rubbed vigorously until she was sure there would be no stain on the coated vinyl, much more practical than leather and a fraction of the cost.

Not feeling very lady-like, she stooped down to sip from the edge of the glass in order to avoid further spillage, glad that, apart from the dogs, no one could witness her performance.

Still trembling hands lifted the glass to her lips and she drained half of the contents before placing it on a coaster next to her laptop.

Eleanor's nervousness was caused by the fact she was planning a murder and she had important emails to send and equally important telephone calls to make. Timing was of the utmost importance if her plan was going to work. So much depended on her activities over the next few minutes.

Switching on the machine, she began typing slowly and carefully to ensure no mistakes.

The murder being planned by Eleanor was her own.

CHAPTER 2

1989

Eleanor Robinson was just a week away from her twenty-fifth birthday when she met Gerald McLoughlin and there was no way she could guess how the meeting would transform her life forever. The encounter had taken place in the office of her boss Vincent Montgomery, general manager of a company which manufactured paper and had been doing so for over two centuries.

Eleanor had been amazed, on joining the organisation straight from university, how complicated the paper business was. Like the majority of people, Eleanor accepted everyday use of paper in all its forms and whilst she knew it originated from wood, had not a clue regarding the different materials used and for what purpose. She certainly had no idea how it was made. She was surprised and delighted when taken on a tour of the factory on the borders of Yorkshire and Lancashire. Unlike some of her colleagues, she had already appreciated the scenery of the area with the huge mills overlooked by hills, but the introduction to the world of paper was extremely educational.

Her induction covered the fact that the Chinese made paper in the first century and printed books in the ninth. Whilst machinery, invented a hundred years later, resulted in the majority of paper being made of wood pulp, she learned

that cotton and other textiles were used for better quality finishes. Her company had been using some of these other materials for over a century and now specialised in the better quality end of the market and she learned how they used cotton and wool as base materials. Cylinder mould machines meant nothing to her, although the claim that the papers would last for hundreds of years made an impression. She heard about the significance of small grain, the importance of being acid-free and the advantage of buffering each sheet with calcium carbonate in order to protect against discolouration caused by acid in the atmosphere. The instructor emphasised the popularity of their products, with artists and printers requiring the best. Using a network of various distributors, their products sold in many countries throughout the world.

The company had decided it required an upgrade to its computer system and had selected three possible suppliers to provide a solution to their requirements. Presentations were made to the general manager, the company accountant and the general sales manager. A competent shorthand typist, Eleanor attended the meeting in order to take notes and to ensure coffee, tea and biscuits were in plentiful supply.

The first two bidders made their pitch in the morning, with Gerald and his boss attending in the afternoon. Although no stranger to computers, Eleanor found difficulty in following some of the jargon which had been spoken in the two morning sessions and hoped her notes would make sense. She had been relieved to see her colleagues also making notes so hoped they had a better understanding of some of the things than she did. The afternoon session was totally different as the company owner, a man in his late thirties, briefly presented his company then handed over to

his youthful assistant, explaining that, should their bid be successful, Gerald would be writing the computer programs.

The gangly young man made the impersonal technical details come alive. Speaking in a language which everyone understood, he carefully explained how computers worked, asked each member of the buying team what their requirements were and came up with solutions. Sketches on sheets of paper were used to illustrate how information was transferred from one part of the machine to another and how he could write programs so everyone would get the information they required, all in a format which was clear and concise. He listened to every question asked of him, thought carefully then explained the options available. Clearly, he understood accounts and satisfied the accountant that the system would provide everything he needed. The sales manager was advised he would receive comprehensive sales reports provided for him as opposed to accounting reports. The general manager would have full information on stocks in and out and a system of stock control which would prompt order placing.

Whatever questions were put to the youngster, he came up with an acceptable answer, several times emphasising that the system would be tailor-made for the company. Having listened to his young employee, the computer company owner assured his small audience that they would be getting a 'Saville Row suit at an off the peg price'. The group discussed installation, training, data input and lots of other small details, many of which had not been aired during the morning sessions. Eleanor got the feeling that the dark-haired young man whose curly hair and horn-rimmed glasses gave him a look of the late Buddy Holly, the American rock and roll idol, and who looked no older than she did, had convinced her superiors he was the man for them.

She met him again two days later when she went down to the ground floor reception area to escort him up to the office of the general manager. The purpose of his visit was hand delivering a quotation and detailed specification of the work to be carried out. Unfortunately, the general manager was in a meeting which had gone on longer than expected, so she had to entertain the visitor. When not talking about computers, she found him shy, quiet and not easy to engage in conversation. She tried talking about television programmes, films and music with little response, although she did discover he was fond of pop idol David Essex and they shared a common admiration of Margaret Thatcher, the recently elected first woman prime minister.

A comfortable half hour passed before her boss telephoned from his meeting to disappoint the young man by asking him to leave the documents as he would not be back for some time. Gerald was unable to disguise his disappointment, explaining he had wanted to go through the points discussed at the meeting.

'If they're as clear as you presented them, I'm sure he'll understand,' she advised him then almost bit her tongue off as she tried to cheer him up adding, 'The others talked a lot of gobbledegook, but you explained everything in language which we could understand.'

She found herself blushing at his grateful smile.

Less than twenty-four hours later she saw him again, having taken a taxi to the modest offices near Victoria station, which housed the company's complete staff of five. She had to climb two flights of narrow stairs in the terrace building to the two small rooms which were home to the small organisation. Gerald shared the first room with two other men. Two large tables were butted together with Gerald

at one side and his colleagues at the other. A large window showed similar tables in an adjoining room where Gerald's boss, telephone to his ear, sat on one side and a young girl behind an electronic typewriter on the other.

As Eleanor tapped on the glass window of the door to the first office, Gerald leaped to his feet and hurried to open the door to welcome her.

'I've been asked to deliver this,' she told him, handing over a large brown envelope then added, 'There's a cheque and can I please have a receipt for it?'

'Sit down please.'

He removed his jacket from the back of the chair in which he had been sitting and waved her towards it as he put the jacket on over his pink shirt, red tie loose and top button unfastened. Hurriedly, he adjusted his clothing, straightened his tie and waved the envelope in the direction of the next office. She watched as Gerald's superior beckoned him through then kept him waiting until he had finished his call. Taking the envelope from the younger man, he tore it open, extracted the cheque which he raised to his lips then exchanged words with his employee which Eleanor could not make out. Gerald came back and told her his boss had suggested he take Eleanor for a coffee whilst the receipt was being typed out.

Descending to ground floor level, she allowed herself to be escorted to a Wimpy Bar where they sat for more than thirty minutes, during which time she drank a coke and a coffee as she learned one of the men with whom Gerald shared an office was the brother-in-law of his boss who looked after the accounts and administration and that the girl was his daughter, a niece of the business owner. The other man was described as a 'data input' person. Eleanor began to

realise the young man whose company she was sharing was the brains behind the organisation and he was key to the success of the contract which she had just delivered. As they sat, he explained the procedure and, as in his presentation to her managers, he spoke in plain language so she understood what would be happening. Gerald informed her that training was part of the arrangement and that, although his 'data input' colleague would be setting much of the information, it would be her and her colleagues who would be continuing the process once things were up and running.

Usually shy in the presence of girls, Gerald felt comfortable in the company of Eleanor who did not seem phased by the technical information with which he bombarded her. The hazel eyes showed interest and, as he talked, found himself studying the rest of her. Dark roots gave away the fact that the honey blonde was not the natural colour of the shoulder length hair. Her round face with a straight nose and flared nostrils had a healthy complexion, covered with very little make-up as far as he could tell and her full lips were of a pale pink hue. As she leaned on one elbow, her hand brushed sufficient hair back to reveal a small ear lobe pierced with a tiny gold ring. Bare shoulders exposed a light tan, emphasised by the white top displaying the beginning of cleavage. He noticed just a small signet ring on the little finger which he hoped signified no ties. At five feet ten inches, he was not unusually tall and the short walk showed that, even with heels, she was still half a head shorter than him.

Eleanor developed a feeling of self-consciousness under the appraisal but was reasonably confident with her own appearance as she returned his gaze. The earlier likeness to Buddy Holly still applied and his pale colouring hinted at more time spent indoors than out. Her Yorkshire mother

would have used the description 'as thin as a rake' and heaped large plates of food on him. The cheeks beneath the high cheekbones were quite drawn with a slightly pointed chin producing an elongated face.

Later, she could not remember how or why she had agreed to go to the cinema with the Buddy Holly lookalike to celebrate her birthday, but over the next few weeks they saw five films together and attended an office equipment exhibition at Olympia. He was allowed to feel her breasts outside her blouse as they watched the second *Back to the Future* movie, to venture inside her bra as Meg Ryan shocked Billy Crystal in *When Harry Met Sally* and put his hand up her skirt whilst watching Timothy Dalton making his second performance as James Bond in *Licence to Kill*.

Their first hurried 'all the way' experience occurred on Hampstead Heath on a summer's evening. Neither were virgins but Eleanor's strict upbringing had resulted in her having just three boyfriends at university whilst Gerald's experiences were even less having had one steady girlfriend until a year previously. Discussions about sex were vague. Apart from music, computers and the work he was doing dominated most of their conversation and she found herself more and more attracted to the subject as he explained things to her. On more than one occasion, and at Gerald's request, she ensured that instalment cheques were paid promptly and when her new young man let her know his wages were dependant on delivery of these, gave the envelopes containing payment cheques to him instead of posting them.

The new equipment arrived, the system was installed and Gerald started spending quite a lot of time at her employer's

offices as he began training Eleanor and two other girls on the mechanics of data input. Partly due to their relationship, she was the most proficient of the trio and would often be called upon to help the others when Gerald was not there.

As the months rolled by, the relationship between the couple grew as they spent more time together. From her part, she found it refreshing that he appreciated her intelligence, treating her as an equal, although he obviously admired her physical assets. As for Gerald, he had time for anyone who would share his fanaticism for computer technology. Exchanging information, he became aware that her company was a well-established successful manufacturer whilst she learned that, apart from a few small jobs, her organisation was keeping his employer's small business alive.

It was when the period of 'free back up' was due to end and she opened the quotation for the continuation that Eleanor came up with the idea which would have a huge influence on the lives of the youngsters. By this time, she knew all of the work on the contract was being carried out by Gerald and that the value of the contract for one year was ten times what her boyfriend would earn. It took her some time to make him accept his talents were being exploited and suggested she could persuade her boss to deal directly with Gerald if he set up on his own. The thought had not previously entered his head and it took a lot of talking before he would even contemplate the idea. Together they hatched a plot to try to see how they could ensure Gerald received a fairer deal, with a larger share of the cake for himself.

Discussing the matter at length, Eleanor convinced Gerald that, without him, it was unlikely the contract could be completed as he had written the program. Although confident that it was totally reliable with most problems

caused by user error, the young man admitted there may be the occasional 'blip' which would require his attention to rectify. Pressurised by Eleanor, he plucked up the courage to suggest to his employer that he changed his position to self-employed and quoted a figure to carry out the contract with Eleanor's company. He would still require use of the facilities in the office in Victoria, although the majority of the work would be carried out on the equipment situated at the paper company. Although the proposal would more than double his personal income, there would still be a handsome margin for his boss. What he did not realise was that whilst his employer was still very happy with the amount of profit he was making out of the contract, Vincent Montgomery was even happier.

Montgomery had been in the paper business man and boy, having served an apprenticeship in the printing department of a well-known London newspaper and progressed to the office as supplies clerk, buying inks and paper. Becoming chief buyer, he held the position for several years until applying for and obtaining the lucrative position of general manager of the present organisation. Using his experience as a buyer, he set about reorganising the supply chain with a vengeance, negotiating better deals, reducing suppliers where there were duplications, and harshly cutting out some smaller companies. One major area which attracted his attention was the supply of office equipment and ancillaries, discovering they had seven or eight places from which they purchased the items. In order to explain changes, he called in the suppliers in the reverse value of the amount of business for which they were responsible, concentrating initially on the bulky items of filing cabinets, office furniture and some

fixtures and fittings. The majority were bought from the London branch of a national well-known supplier but some were from a newer, independent outfit whose sales director came to see him when he advised that the company would be looking at competitive quotes from now on.

On being provided with a list of the items, when asked to quote, the man had looked Montgomery in the eye and blatantly asked the question, 'And what do I need to add on for you?'

Initially shocked, he advised the man it would be more than his job was worth, at which time the young man making the pitch apologised, but advised his client that what he was suggesting was not uncommon practice in the city.

When the quotations for the major items arrived, Montgomery noticed the organisation who'd offered a bribe was the most competitive in the majority of items for which they had been invited to quote. Having often mused over the initial proposition, he found the man's business card and telephoned, proposing lunch at an expensive restaurant in the city and suggesting the sales director brought a copy of his quote.

Montgomery waited until the waiter had taken their order before opening the conversation, pulling no punches as he blatantly asked the man, 'What kind of percentage were you talking about the other day?'

The salesman, who looked very young to hold the position as a director, although very smartly dressed in a dark three-piece suit, smiled. 'Whatever suits you, governor. I make more profit on some items than others. But, of course, there are opportunities to inflate the price a bit to ensure you get your cut. Also, I'd like you to come to our warehouse where we have a showroom and to meet my boss.'

Montgomery looked at him. 'We'll need to do it quickly. Some of the items for which you've quoted are slightly over the top and others you're very competitive so we may need to swap some around to ensure yours is the best price should it be queried.'

As they talked during the meal, Montgomery learned that, although the company the young man worked for had only been operating for three years, they had a large turnover on the office equipment side. He was advised they also supplied ancillaries including paper, carbon paper, paper clips and a full range of items. The sales director, reminding Vincent he was called Paul, went on to explain that the company used incentives to persuade people to buy and the target for these was varied. He boasted he had a team of five young ladies who toured the city, offering shopping vouchers in return for orders for the smaller items, the purchasing of which was often left to office juniors. Montgomery was aware his own company appeared to buy only a nominal amount so far, but were on his list for investigating later. Whilst Vincent found the young man to be a little brash and arrogant, he allowed him to pick up the bill and made the effort to be pleasant, aware of the possible rewards of working with the company.

The meeting took place in an evening with the owner of the business, an Iranian, showing the considerable stocks he held, explaining they came from several parts of the world including India, Taiwan and the Philippines. They spent some time looking through and adjusting the figures, which they had already quoted, making the necessary alterations by calculating the percentage that would be creamed off the top for the general manager, increasing some prices and reducing others in order to ensure they would be the most inexpensive

in all areas. A young very pretty girl, hair covered by a black headdress, took the papers away and the men chatted for the fifteen minutes required to retype the quotation, during which time the Persian educated his visitor about offshore trusts which he had used to get monies out of Iran. Feeling a little out of his depth but not wishing to appear naïve, Vincent agreed to let the other set up a meeting with an accountant in the Channel Islands who would explain the situation to him and even offered to pay the fare once the initial order for equipment had been received.

Two weeks later, they flew from a small airport in Cambridge to Guernsey where he was taken to a large office block, housing the headquarters of the Channel Islands-based accountant. He was advised that the trust should be set up to benefit his children but he would be free to take out any amount he required at any time. When asked to come up with a name, he could only offer 'Danart' using three letters each of the names of his daughter Tracey and son Daniel. He was then invited to sign some papers, advised that an account with a Spanish bank would be opened with the name of the trust and which he could use to draw cash or pay bills. He had been helped by the Iranian to produce letterheads, which were used to invoice the supplier company for an introductory agency fee.

Kacpur, preferring to use the pseudonym Ken, would make payments into the account on a monthly basis, agreeing to send a statement to his home address.

The explanation of his absence to his wife was a visit with a colleague to the horse racing at Newmarket and thankfully she accepted the lie.

One week later, the cheque book arrived in an envelope marked private and confidential at his home address. Whilst

feeling guilty at keeping things from her, he decided to pretend to take an interest in the sport of kings. He would occasionally cash a cheque at the London branch of the Spanish bank followed by a trip to Kempton Park, returning home to produce cash which he claimed had been from winning bets on the horses. Already making thousands of pounds from the original venture, he sensed an additional opportunity to benefit from the installation of the new computer system.

It did not go unnoticed that Gerald was the only contact from the computer company during the next few months, a matter Eleanor brought to the attention of the general manager when it was decided that some of the work at the mill could be computerised. Although not openly admitting the computer wizard was her beau, Eleanor let her boss know he was now operating freelance and suggested he be allowed to quote for the work independently.

Montgomery was nobody's fool and appreciated the fact that the youngster was the brains behind the firm providing the computer work and that by dealing with him direct he could save a considerable amount of money for the company. He was also aware the young man would not have the financial clout to buy the relevant hardware for the new project. Unknown to Gerald, he was already receiving a payback from the computer company for the existing contract but Montgomery was quick to see an opportunity to make even more on the new project.

Eleanor was excited when her boss advised her that the pair of them were going to make a visit to the factory for discussions with the operations manager on what was needed. Whilst Gerald was disappointed she would be away for two nights,

she reminded him of the wonderful opportunity they were being presented with and the influence which it could have on his earnings.

The general manager used the stop for lunch on the drive north and dinner at the hotel where they were staying to question her about her relationship with the computer man. His charm relaxed her, aided by her share of the red wine which accompanied dinner so that she confessed to Gerald being her boyfriend.

The following day, Eleanor was made to feel important, being involved in the discussions regarding requirements and charged with making lots of notes dictated to her by both the operations manager and the general manager. The pair took her for lunch at one of the local hostelries then it was back to the factory where she was allowed use of a typewriter to record details of the notes which she had compiled. Glowing compliments from the two managers on her interpretation and understanding of the work required gave her a feeling of pride, satisfaction and elation. All of these feelings were quickly dispelled by the general manager over dinner. Having pointed out the value of a likely contract to carry out the work, Montgomery made it crystal clear he would be the person awarding the contract and she would have to be nice to him in return for the order being awarded to Gerald.

Although very tired, Eleanor slept fitfully after her boss left her room. Managing to put to one side her feeling of shame over behaving like a prostitute, she admitted to herself the experience had not been quite as unpleasant as expected. Vincent proved to be a considerable and very experienced lover, frightening, surprising and thrilling her as she was introduced to oral sex for the first time in her life. Using

fingers and tongue, he had brought her to orgasm prior to persuading her to return the compliment by using her mouth on him before he placed himself between her legs, assuring her a vasectomy ensured no protection was required as he penetrated her to achieve his own satisfaction.

She hoped guilt did not show on her face the following morning when they returned to the factory for further consultation before commencing the journey back home. He used the time to explain to her that his plan was to allow Gerald to write the software but that the expensive hardware would be purchased through an organisation who already supplied the company with office furniture and ancillaries. He also explained that he expected Gerald to accompany him back to the factory, armed with her notes, so he could actually finalise the specification required.

Gerald fitted the description of many southerners who had never ventured north of Watford and it was an eye-opening trip for him, leaving him marvelling at the landscape, totally unexpecting the views of beautiful green hills and fields as, like so many, he associated the north with Coronation Street and similar programmes portraying the area as a vast collection of chimney pots with no open spaces. As Eleanor had been on her introduction, he was intrigued with the manufacturing methods. Looking through the laborious way that production was organised, he was sure he could produce computerised systems to bring better control, ordering, costing and pricing systems which was exactly what the company were looking for.

Deciding on a direct approach, Montgomery indicated that the hardware would be very expensive and Gerald would not necessarily be in a position to finance the purchase of

that, but Vincent would be happy to make arrangements whereby he could benefit financially from helping to select and specify the actual equipment. He enlightened Gerald to the fact the company had an arrangement where they bought all their office equipment, which by this time had expanded to include photocopiers, electronic typewriters and word processors, from the organisation owned by the Iranian. The proposal was he would introduce Gerald to the company and liaise with them to inspect and recommend the various items. Software would be the subject of a separate service contract for which Gerald would be paid directly.

Without the backup of the small staff in the Victoria office, Gerald realised he would have to carry out much of the input of information himself, a matter which he raised with Eleanor later. Investment in a larger computer and server of his own would be necessary, so he could work longer hours on the project without the office time restrictions of the company. Also, he would need to spend some time in the north initially. With his new agreement for the original contract, he was doing very well financially, so the cost of the new machine would not be a problem. However, space might be as he lived in a bedsit and suggested he would need something bigger.

The following weekend, Eleanor accompanied him to view various options. First choice turned out to be a first floor apartment in a large terraced house in Holland Park but, despite his additional wealth, he balked at the amount of rent. Space was plentiful and he would be able to use one of the two very large bedrooms for an office. As they were already spending almost all of their spare time together, to Eleanor it seemed to make sense for her to move in with him,

assisting with finances by paying the savings on her own bedsit towards the rent. The proposal which she put forward seemed almost clinically practical with no emphasis on their personal relationship. Clearly, the fact that one bedroom would be used as an office suggested they would share the other and as they were already having sex, it was reasonable to assume it would be in the same bed. Gerald questioned this to be reminded that, although they had only actually spent four or five whole nights together, they seemed comfortable in each other's company. Neither of them had used the word 'love' during their times together and whilst the sex was very nice and important it was not a major driving force between them. They just seemed to get along very well, letting physical intimacy happen when they felt like it.

There did not seem any point in putting up much of an argument and they made arrangements to go and see the agent together on a Saturday morning. The smartly dressed middle-aged man advised them they would need to sign up for a joint tenancy in view of the fact Gerald was self-employed and references would need to be checked. Eleanor was a little concerned they would have to contact the accounts department of her firm and wondered if Montgomery would raise any issues. As far as she knew, there was nothing in her work terms and conditions which would prevent any liaison with a provider to the business, although she was aware it might be influential. She needn't have worried as her superior, fully aware of the transaction, provided an excellent reference and between them, they came up with the required deposit, moving in two weeks later.

Eleanor had mixed feelings when invited to accompany Gerald, the general manager and a young man called Paul

to go to the city showroom of the hardware suppliers. She found the young man to be confident to the point of arrogance, paying a considerable amount of attention to her, not having been made aware that Gerald was her boyfriend. The majority of the discussions took place between Gerald and the salesman of the equipment and although she did understand many of the terms used, a lot of the technical details went over her head.

When questioned about the facilities of his own organisation, Paul was very evasive, particularly when it came to technical backup. Seeing the young man struggling, Montgomery intervened, advising the salesman he was having discussions with the owner of the business with a view to recruiting computer experts. He also had the foresight to ask the computer supplier about the training which they were able to provide on installation. Gerald and Paul were tasked with going through the ordering process, the specification having been agreed, and there seemed to be a mountain of paperwork involved. Montgomery used the opportunity to talk to Eleanor.

'You do realise this could be a really large contract for your young man and that there needs to be a certain amount of flexibility. I'll need him to do some work with the people who are buying the hardware on our behalf but will make sure he gets rewarded for that.'

She blushed as he looked at her knowingly.

'This is a marvellous opportunity which I'm sure both he and you realise.'

Two days later, Gerald was invited by Montgomery to go to the premises of the company who would be factoring the transaction for the hardware in order to meet the owner.

The Iranian showed him round his warehouse, explained the operation which he ran and quizzed the young man about the possibility of installing a computer system. Over lunch at a steakhouse, where the warehouse owner demonstrated he did not follow all of the rules of being Muslim, he and Montgomery introduced the young man to the world of offshore trusts. More than competent at maths, Gerald understood the procedure, grasping the method by which high rates of tax could be avoided. The two older men emphasised the importance of planning now before his income became too high, thus attracting the attention of the taxman, whilst Gerald had a feeling of being swept along on a wave of enthusiasm in matters which he did not fully comprehend.

At the weekend, he explained to Eleanor that the Iranian had arranged for him to visit Guernsey in order to look at another possible software contract. In fact, he finished up with an overseas bank account and what appeared to be a very complicated arrangement of agency fees being both paid and received by him regarding the provision of the hardware to the paper business. It also involved him having to produce a copy of the software, which he had designed for the factory, suitably amended to fit the needs of the warehouse.

For three weeks, Eleanor and Gerald laboured every evening and all weekends, painting walls and doors in order to create a light environment. In addition to the two very large bedrooms, they had a huge lounge and a kitchen with enough space to hold a small dining table and four chairs. A bathroom and separate toilet completed the accommodation, apart from a small room which housed coats and shoes.

The computer, together with two monitors, arrived four weeks after they moved in and Gerald disappeared north

three days later to oversee the installation of the system at the factory. Eleanor was left alone in the double bed four nights a week for the next six weeks. He would return late on Thursday, work in his office for the next two days then drive back north on Sunday. Unable to contribute on the technical side of things, she busied herself with putting the finishing touches to the apartment and for the first time in her life, took an interest in cooking. When Gerald disappeared into his office, she would set about preparing different dishes which they would share later. Recipes were collected from magazines, carefully cut out, building up a library, which she saved in folders and also bought cookery books, following the directions meticulously. Wine also became a hobby and she used a wine shop near the office for one or two bottles and ordered the special offers from the Sunday paper magazines.

Gerald, whilst appreciative of her efforts, simply consumed whatever was put before him in respect of both food and drink, rarely commenting on either and only seemed interested in talking about his work in which he was totally engrossed.

It was during one of his periods away that Eleanor did fall in love, but this was with two dogs.

The couple's landlord, Ebenezer Cohen, lived at ground floor and basement level of the house. Not unattractive with well-groomed dark hair, straight nose, generous mouth, olive complexion and deep brown eyes, he would be the first to admit his five feet eight inches carried the bulk of someone who should be at least six inches taller. A divorcee, he made his money from property, which he owned in different parts of the capital. According to the story which he gave to the pair, he originally came into money when his parents died in a plane crash with Ebenezer and his sister being the only

living relatives. He inherited the house in which they all lived and several other properties including five out of a row of a ten-shop parade in Golder's Green, with his sister gaining the other five plus a house in Hampstead which she already occupied with her husband and children.

Ebenezer had two dogs which he bought to guard the property in his absence but which Eleanor soon discovered would have allowed anyone access. They were both black labradors, one dog, one bitch, and Eleanor's relationship with them progressed from letting them out in order to carry out their ablutions to taking them for walks which became progressively longer. The dogs adored her and the feelings developed mutually during long sorties around the vast fifty acres of Holland Park. Eleanor and the dogs preferred the northern part of the expanse with its semi-wild wooded area, where she very soon learned to trust them off the lead as she grew more confident they would return from their foraging in the undergrowth. When having to call them, she was a little relieved that the dog Abraham had got used to the abbreviation Abie and she did not have a problem with Mathilda. She treated herself to a sturdy pair of wellington boots so she too could enjoy the long grass areas.

On one occasion, she did have cause to change her mind about their ability to guard when a group of five boisterous teenage boys approached the trio. The labradors instinctively went in front of her, showing teeth and snarling at the youths who changed direction, passing by at a respectful distance as a relieved Eleanor fussed over the dogs whose tails wagged vigorously.

Dog walking helped her wile away some pleasant summer evenings when Gerald was away and she would occasionally

accept an offer of coffee or glass of wine from Ebenezer. Not the most active or energetic person, his rare walks with the animals were much more condensed than those of his tenant and he appreciated her taking the trouble to provide his pets with some much-needed exercise. She found the older man fascinating, listening to stories of unhappy and bullying times in early childhood spent in the East End, followed by even unhappier ones at boarding school. Without self-consciousness or embarrassment, he related tales of younger boys being expected to grant sexual favours to older colleagues, then apologised as he caught her blushing. Fearing he would stop his admissions which she enjoyed listening to, she assured him there was no problem and urged him to carry on his reminiscing. She learned of his studying architecture at university, early marriage to a 'nice Jewish girl' and subsequent divorce following her infidelity, although accepting much of the blame due to his lack of ambition and self-confessed laziness. Thankfully, there were no children.

Eleanor was not sure if it was loneliness, intrigue, boredom, too much wine or frustration which decided her to go to bed with the landlord on an occasion when Gerald was away in the north. She had been listening to Ebenezer's account of the sex life shared with his wife, describing his experiences as pleasant but admitting to his wife complaining about his unsatisfactory performance in bed. Three quarters of the way through the second bottle of wine, he explained that his wife's criticism resulted in his being unable to raise an erection during love-making. Half way through the third bottle and in a tipsy state, he realised he currently had an erection which he confessed to Eleanor.

In an equally tipsy state, she asked to look at it and out of curiosity, and for confirmation of his claim, went

on to suggest that, 'It would be a shame to waste it,' and accompanied him to his bedroom.

Waking up together, neither showed or discussed any remorse, shame or regret. They shared coffee and toast before she returned to her own apartment.

Gradually, Gerald spent less time away and worked more at home. He was earning quite a lot of money from the two contracts and much of the service backup on the original system could be handled by telephone as Eleanor had become very competent correcting small faults or blips in the system. They were usually the result of incorrect entries which Gerald could explain how to correct. He continually proved to be a genius who had developed an ability to impart technical facts in easy-to-understand terms and she found her knowledge increasing continuously. When she suggested attending evening classes, Gerald modestly countered by claiming it was highly unlikely she would meet any tutor with his background so used some of their weekend time together to enable him to continue teaching her at home.

Discovering a very willing pupil, he filled her head with information about mainframe computers, microprocessors, time-sharing systems, microcomputers and personal computers and how they would all revolutionise the future of business. His enthusiasm for the topic was contagious and he really was very good at explaining things in a simplistic way which enabled her to follow and absorb the information.

By joining the Chamber of Commerce, Gerald made contact with many business people and picked up two extra clients but realised software systems required computers to run them and that most businesses required a complete

package. At a Chamber business meeting, he met up with an office equipment salesman, Jack Hollingsworth, who had become frustrated at his company's reluctance to embrace the computer market, preferring to stick to photocopier machines as their main line. Jack possessed the confidence and empathy which Gerald admitted he lacked but recognised the potential of the pair working together and invited him home to meet Eleanor. The handsome six-footer with slightly greying hair and the build of an athlete exuded confidence and his ready smile conveyed warmth and sincerity. Whilst his demeanour and immaculate dress screamed professionalism, he possessed a charming manner and quickly persuaded people to talk about themselves. Jack would condemn the common description of good salesmen and women having the gift of the gab and emphasised the skill of listening to be far more important.

Having collected business cards and made detailed notes in respect of all contacts made, Gerald suggested Jack might take a few days' holiday from his job and arrange appointments with a few potential clients, with the two men making joint presentations. From five such appointments, they produced three formal quotations and received two orders with Jack negotiating deposits on the equipment. Needing to purchase the hardware, both Jack and Eleanor called in sick to their respective employers as the trio met up with a supplier, arranged terms, inclusive of service agreements and used the deposits which they had already collected to place the order.

By the time the equipment was delivered to the flat, Gerald had written the appropriate software. Jack used another 'sickie' to help deliver and install the hardware and it was he who signed up the clients for maintenance contracts

for both the hardware and the software, sub-contracting the hardware side to the original supplier.

In his mid-thirties, married with two young sons, Jack invited the young couple to Sunday lunch at his house in Hendon during which he made a proposal to the pair. Confident in the rapid development of the computer industry, he suggested they open a retail shop in addition to developing the commercial side. His wife, a very pleasant, tall, slim lady called Christina, having remained at home since the birth of the boys, could work part time. As a shorthand typist, she had experience operating electronic typewriters, including word processors so understood much of the basics. Jack could be available on Saturdays until such time as they could afford him to leave his current job and if they got the right premises, Gerald could carry out his programming work there so be available to talk to customers in the shop if required.

It took a return Sunday lunch at Holland Park and dinner in a Hungarian restaurant in the West End to finalise the details followed by discussions with Ebenezer regarding premises. He had a retail shop in Golder's Green with the current tenant wanting to retire, so they signed a lease covering the ground floor shop, upstairs storage plus a small office for Gerald, including a toilet and a tiny kitchen. Furthermore, recognising the ability and enthusiasm of the group, the property owner took advantage of an opportunity to acquire a share of the business instead of taking rent for the premises.

In addition to computers, they introduced a photocopying service to generate regular cash flow and a small selection of word processors to run alongside computers.

Within six months, they had signed up five more highly profitable commercial deals and sold several word processors

and small computers enabling Jack to hand in his notice. Appointing an accountant and a solicitor, they set up a limited company with the two couples having equal shares. Each of the four had twenty-two percent with Ebenezer receiving the remaining twelve as he registered them for VAT and secured a small overdraft facility.

Using the shop to invite prospective business clients proved ideal and they picked up several more customers. Jack made a point of calling on every other retailer in the area, being rewarded with several lucrative sales. Christina employed an eighteen-year-old shop assistant and although they considered the possibility of Eleanor, who helped out at weekends and evenings, leaving her job to assist further, the consensus of opinion decided the contracts with her company were a vital part of their business and it would be better if she remained where she was so she could keep an eye on them.

Gerald still saw her superior, Vincent Montgomery, on a regular basis, but when quizzed about his progress, the young man remained a little guarded, advising he was doing all right but avoided offering further details. Montgomery had recognised the developing relationship between the computer whizz kid and Eleanor and his calculated opinion was that the company benefitted as Eleanor was easily the most proficient of the girls using the computer systems and if she was receiving private tuition, then the general manager had no issue with this. He also decided there was a possibility he could use an excuse to travel north to check on progress and take the girl with him. Having her inside the company certainly helped Gerald manage the contract as his girlfriend, with first-hand knowledge of any blips, would spend her time in the office checking through things before

contacting Gerald for guidance on the necessary remedial action. In addition to saving him time, she was also building up her own knowledge of troubleshooting.

Collectively, working extremely long hours was exhausting but rewarding although spending their gains on long holidays was out of the question. It was Jack who insisted both couples did enjoy an occasional weekend break from the business and almost bullied the younger pair to share time away enabling mini breaks in Brighton, Hastings and Stratford-upon-Avon. Jack suggested they maximise the benefits of having their own business, investing in a combination of increasing knowledge by visiting exhibitions alongside enjoyment by attending those in attractive areas to visit, with the couples taking turns to visit Amsterdam, Cologne, Geneva and Paris.

It was also Jack who had the foresight to warn his colleagues that their expansion would become an explosion and was proved correct with the launching of the world wide web, internet and increase of demand for personal computers rapidly expanding the market.

The business went from strength to strength, requiring them to recruit staff with an ex-colleague of Jack's, a service engineer from the photocopier company, being the first to join and assist with service contracts with the hardware. Gerald interviewed several IT graduates, taking two of them on and training them in both software program writing and sorting out the increasing number of occasional problems with customers.

A new client recommending system was introduced, with customers rewarded with either additional free callouts or discounted prices on contracts. Gerald learned the importance of good customer service from his senior partner

and the inexpensive and highly beneficial way in which Jack used this to obtain new business. He was aware he would never have the courage to ask for recommendations in the way the other man did, or the skill used to calm customers down when problems did occur. Whilst Gerald would have reacted to a problem by dashing over to see the client immediately, Jack would initially try to solve the issue on the telephone but then schedule in a visit at a convenient time if required.

Christina accepted responsibility for collecting money from rare late payers whilst, having started as a silent partner, Ebenezer became involved with financial negotiations, particularly with the bank manager. Through his efforts, extended overdraft arrangements were made and it was he who fought off a suggestion of Jack's house being used as security using a 'floating charge' on the business instead.

With additional staff in place, holidays could be taken for a longer period and Eleanor and Gerald managed a week in the Costa Brava together. Jack and Gerald took to visiting exhibitions further afield, travelling to Hong Kong and the United States with the salesman's negotiating skills coming to the fore. Despite them being small and still new, he persuaded a US software developer and Chinese computer manufacturer to trust them with exclusive sales agency agreements for the UK market. This time Ebenezer could not help with suitable property so they rented a small 'lock up' underneath a railway arch to store the hardware goods.

Under Jack and Christina's guidance and advice, the younger couple got themselves on the property ladder with a small semi-detached house in a Hertfordshire village with easy access to public transport to the city. With three bedrooms

and a garage, there was more than enough room and Gerald commandeered the smallest bedroom for an office. By investing in the right equipment, he could provide out-of-hours backup services for software and the ever innovative ex-copier salesman came up with the idea of selling seven days a week, twenty-four-hour service packages, recruiting an additional service engineer. He argued that, realistically, most businesses operated Monday to Friday nine to five, but that the new innovation would provide comfort to the clients. He used the opportunity to upgrade existing arrangements on the basis that the customer signed a new twelve-month deal and almost all new clients chose the option of the increased coverage which became an important feature in their sales pitch to new clients.

Believing the business required all of their attention, Eleanor and Gerald agreed there was not yet time for a family and by the time Eleanor reached her thirty-first birthday, the three-bedroom semi had become a four-bedroom detached with a double garage housing two cars.

In her opinion, it was a late night following their entertaining Jack and Christina for dinner, which brought about an unplanned life-changing event. She recalled they had made love afterwards and both fallen asleep with Gerald's rubber-covered penis still inside her. A missed period and two bouts of sickness sent her scurrying to the doctor for confirmation that a new being would be entering their lives.

Shopping entailed not just maternity clothes but also a wedding dress as a Registry Office wedding was quickly arranged and Eleanor had to own up to her relationship with the IT consultant. The heart palpitations were calmed when she realised the general manager had made the correct

assumption of the liaison and even accepted an invitation to the small gathering to celebrate the marriage. It took place mid-week which was the most convenient time for the shop, allowing Jack to act as best man and Christina matron of honour. Her parents travelled south to attend and the rest of the small staff team and a few of Eleanor's colleagues from the paper company were able to join for the celebration dinner which took place in a French restaurant in the West End.

Spending the first two nights at home, the couple flew to Paris for a short honeymoon before both returning to their respective places of employment. A combination of light work and very healthy state throughout enabled Eleanor to work late into the gestation period before commencing her maternity leave. The birth was uncomplicated but painful as a comparative heavyweight seven- and three-quarter pound Alexander McLoughlin stretched the organs of his petite mother as he made his entry into the world. Eleanor had gritted her teeth, squeezed the hand of her husband and gulped in a combination of gas and air as she had been encouraged to push hard by a midwife of West Indian origin until the head of the baby popped out. The welcome sound of the cry came without any required smack and she was soon cuddling her first born.

After just two days in hospital, she was allowed to return home with her son to introduce him to the tastefully decorated blue nursery. The ability to breast feed reduced the inconvenience of night time feeds and Alexander thankfully slept for most of the day and night. His passive nature continued, presenting to his parents as a perfectly contented child allowing them mostly uninterrupted sleep patterns.

The Volkswagen Golf, which had replaced the famous Beetle, boasted a 1.6 litre engine capable of doing 110 miles

an hour, not that Eleanor had any ambitions to do that but she was really delighted with the car. She was also pleased she taken the trouble to have driving lessons earlier so she could use the licence which she had held for some time.

The Porsche 959 was totally outside their financial capabilities and drastically exceeded the requirements which Gerald needed, but it was his toy and he felt he had earned it.

Apart from computers, cars were his only other real interest and he followed all types of racing, including Formula One and rallying, and attended the various car shows, even travelling to Geneva in order to do so.

CHAPTER 3

As soon as she could, Eleanor abandoned the pram for outings, selecting one of the latest McLaren buggies which enabled her to take Alexander to the city, proudly showing him off to work friends on one such trip and the staff of the business on another. Deciding against attending 'baby' classes and not yet having made friends in the area, she used the local park to occasionally meet up with others with small tots.

As weeks and months passed, she noticed her son was slower to master the skill or ability to sit upright in a swing and remained more passive than his peers when placed on the lower part of a slide. Mentioning her concerns to Gerald, he suggested she take their son to see their doctor but she then became defensive, arguing that children develop at a different rate and brushing aside her own concerns. Often quickly changing the subject to business, in her opinion, he did not show sufficient interest in his son causing her motherly instinct to care for, protect and nurture her offspring. Again, expressing concern when she was unable to return to work as Alexander was not sufficiently advanced to join a nursery, Gerald's response emphasised that they did not depend or even require the income from her job and again suggested a visit to the doctor. As forecast by Jack, the business was really booming, producing a generous income

for all concerned although taking up more and more time and dedication from the senior staff.

When the youngster could neither walk properly and hardly talked at all well past his second birthday, Gerald insisted he accompany Eleanor to take the boy to see the local GP who arranged an appointment to see a specialist.

Doctor Alistair McGregor smiled kindly at the couple and their child. 'How can I help?'

A grey-haired, portly man with half glasses over which he surveyed the trio, he looked to be at an age when he should be taking retirement. Dressed in a checked jacket over which he had a three-quarter length white coat, the stethoscope around his neck made him look the part. Several framed certificates decorated the walls of his office confirming his various qualifications and, on his desk, a gold-coloured frame held a photograph of a smiling girl in mortar board and gown holding a rolled-up parchment.

Gerald cleared his throat. 'It's our son Alexander. He is over two years old and I believe he should be making more progress than he is. He seems behind most children his age, although my wife just thinks he's a bit slow.'

'Children are all different, aren't they?' the wife in question interrupted.

'In what way?' the doctor ignored her, concentrating on her husband.

'Well, he doesn't speak, can't walk or even stand on his own without support. He doesn't crawl but rolls along the floor sideways to try to get to where he wants to be.'

'How about eating?' A ballpoint pen was extracted from the top pocket of the white coat which McGregor used to scribble notes on a pad.

'He eats well,' Eleanor chipped in.

Gerald glared at her, then turned back to the doctor. 'He's still on baby food or mashed up food.'

'Well, he has difficulty swallowing anything else. I have tried.' Eleanor, feeling threatened, flew to the defence of her offspring.

Her lips trembled with tears in her eyes as the two men, Gerald coaxing, the physician practical, persuaded her that the youngster should be further forward than he appeared to be and it would be in the interests of all, especially the baby, if some tests were carried out. They would be referred to a paediatrician at the nearby hospital and would be notified regarding an appointment.

It took six weeks for the date to come through and a further ten days to the date of the visit and it was the most miserable time of their marriage. Eleanor stubbornly refused to believe her offspring was anything but perfect and doted on the boy, often to the exclusion of her husband. She tried to prove her point by trying to help the little one to do things beyond his capabilities, such as helping him to stand and talking to him incessantly in an attempt to get a response. Gerald left her to it, throwing himself into the business in which she took less interest. He started coming home late, staying at the office to work before calling at a pub for a drink on the way home, something which he had never done before.

There were few arguments, just a sullen silence between the pair but by the time of the visit, Eleanor had begun to accept that whatever she did, or tried to do, made no difference. As she sat beside her husband listening to a Sri Lankan doctor named Rajapaskse, she paid full attention, trying to listen with an open mind but the ordeal devastated her.

Doctor Rajapaskse went to great lengths to inform the pair about cerebral palsy, explaining it was a general term for a number of neurological conditions which affected movement and coordination.

She put her hands between her knees to stop them shaking as she heard about neurological conditions caused by problems in the brain and nervous system responsible for controlling muscles. The Sri Lankan explained the condition could occur if the brain developed abnormally or was damaged before, during or shortly after childbirth. On cross examination, she had to admit Alexander displayed some of the main symptoms including muscle stiffness or floppiness, weakness, balance and coordination difficulty and occasional uncontrolled body movements.

Her brain numbed as the man went on to say that some people with the condition have communication and learning difficulties, although intelligence is often unaffected.

The tears began when she learned there was no cure for cerebral palsy and for several minutes, she was inconsolable and in the first physical contact for weeks, she nestled against Gerald until the sobs subsided into sniffles and she apologised for her actions.

It was no consolation to hear the condition only affected one in four hundred, or that it was not progressive as the original problem with the brain did not become worse with age and life expectancy rarely influenced. Nor was it any comfort when the pair received warnings of the physical and emotional strains of living with a long-term condition such as cerebral palsy, causing stress on the body and producing further problems in later life.

Over the following weeks during which further tests were carried out, Eleanor did her best in attempting to become an expert on the condition. Having been provided with lots of leaflets by the hospital, she went to the library and poured through books, making notes in a hard-backed book which she had purchased for the purpose. She read about the numerous treatments available, which could treat many of the symptoms and help those with the condition to live life as independently as possible.

She read about a wide range of equipment and techniques, which had an umbrella term of augmentative and alternative communication which could support or replace speech, including signing, perhaps using a system such as Makaton, symbols, word boards and electronic voice output communication aids. A speech and language therapist could assess children and help parents decide the most appropriate aids.

A health visitor was appointed to assist as was a physiotherapist whose task was to prevent the weakening of muscles not normally used, preventing them shortening. Speech therapy failed whilst an occupational therapist tried very hard to train the infant to undertake small tasks with limited success.

Eleanor became withdrawn in her single-minded dedication to making the life of her son as comfortable as possible. Changed habits, paying less attention to her own appearance, unlike normal practice, not changing her clothes for days on end, and snacking resulting in Gerald coming home to no meal ready put a strain on the relationship.

It was only when, very late one evening, Gerald made up a bed in the spare room that things came to a head when she asked him why.

'Because I'm fed up living in a shit hole and sleeping next to a miserable, dirty woman who smells like a tramp.'

'But I'm busy looking after my son. Don't you care that I'm doing my best for him?'

'He's not *your* son.'

She stood shocked as his voice raised to a shout.

'Alexander is *our* son, Eleanor. Don't you think I want the best for him too. It's just that you're ignoring everything and everyone else including yourself. Look at you. Your hair hasn't been washed for days and I can't remember when you last had a shower. Anyway, I need an early night because I have an early appointment and will be late and will be having dinner out.'

As he stormed off, she remained standing in the lounge in shock at his words, feeling betrayed and deserted at his attitude.

Jolted into action, she responded by showering, washing her hair and changing her clothes but the relationship remained strained and he refrained from moving back into the shared bedroom.

Having ceased visiting Jack and Christina, she only learned about the progress of the business on the rare occasions when Gerald offered information, usually about new contracts. She assumed things were continuing to progress successfully and received no argument when asking if she could take on a cleaner so she could continue to concentrate on Alexander.

The boy had reached his fifth birthday when Gerald insisted a small party should be held to celebrate the event and invited the Hollingsworths. Initially reluctant, Eleanor shopped for cold meats, salad, cakes and other nibbles

and even balloons. Jack and family arrived with presents in attractive packaging and Gerald had to accompany the older man to carry in two unexpected treats. The first was a small specially adapted electric wheelchair which required a few slight alterations until Alexander fitted into it perfectly and Gerald ran through the control systems with the little boy. With a tremendous amount of patience, the two men worked with the birthday boy and within an hour, he could use the movement of his fingers to navigate his way around the ground floor.

At this time, the second present was retrieved from the boot of Jack's car and fitted to the front of the new wheelchair using a special attachment: an extremely powerful computer. The contraption came complete with small keyboard, screen and sockets to house tapes which enabled sound and visual recording. Alexander looked in amazement as Gerald typed a few words on the keyboard which were shown on the screen then spoken in a mechanical voice when the boy's father pressed a key.

Jubilation showed on the face of the two men when, some time later, Alexander made the machine speak his first announcement. Over the next weeks and months, the boy was then shown how to generate standard sayings which were already programmed in to the unit, providing information about the owner including his name and very brief description of his condition and how he could communicate using the equipment. In respect of where he lived, the information provided details of the village but not the actual address.

Eleanor was speechless, both at the brilliant technology and the ability of her son to operate it. Whilst Eleanor was always convinced, Alexander confirmed his intelligence.

He had really struggled in his efforts to speak which she identified as lack of control of his vocal cords as opposed to lack of knowledge.

A few days after the birthday party, Eleanor had another surprise as Gerald came home with what looked to be a brand-new Volkswagen Golf but with differences. It was a little higher than normal, the rear seats had been removed and there was a metal-plated base with securing rings above which an electrically controlled hoist was in place. Taking Alexander's new chair outside, Gerald demonstrated how easy it was to load the chair into the car and secure it, reversing the process to take it back to ground level. He then brought his son out to allow Eleanor to practise taking Alexander out of the chair and placing him in the passenger seat then loading the chair into the rear of the car. With guidance and after two attempts, she was happy she could manage the task without assistance.

There were extras as Gerald produced an unusual folding table which fitted over the lap of the boy and to which the mini computer could be clipped, allowing him to use it whilst in the car. Alexander had practised since his birthday, becoming more competent at operating the keyboard, thus speeding up his ability to create short answers to questions. It was still a little laborious but a tremendous opportunity to allow the youngster to communicate.

CHAPTER 4

As Alexander grew over the years, not being a sporting activist himself, Gerald did not miss the common habit of fathers and sons kicking a ball around in the park but now taking more interest in the boy and his development, bombarded him with information about computers, taking advantage of their new method of communication to do so. A larger electric wheelchair chair was acquired, this time with the facility to be enlarged later and he upgraded the computer equipment and made two more specialist tables: one to enable the boy to operate his computer in the passenger seat of Gerald's Porsche 959 and the second fitting over the steering wheel to allow himself to use his own laptop. A 'double-headed' connector to fit the cigar lighter socket enabled both machines to be powered by the car battery.

Realising his son was exceptionally intelligent, during evenings and weekends they would occasionally go out, park up and communicate via the machines. Using connections through mobile phones, Gerald showed how easy it was to sit close to the building of an office or home and 'hack in' to the computers of unsuspecting businesses or individuals. He explained to the boy the various security systems available, but few computer owners took threats seriously and also how it was not difficult to overcome the majority of those on the market.

Private tutors were hired to deal with some school subjects, but Eleanor undertook responsibility for most subjects herself. The tutors found their pupil ahead of the vast majority of his age group in most subjects, appreciating that he had developed a phenomenal memory for detail and was very good at problem solving.

When possible, borrowing Eleanor's car to transport the chair, Gerald took the boy to exhibitions on computers and office equipment for specific knowledge and the Ideal Home Exhibition for general interest. The boy and his equipment would attract the attention of exhibiters and visitors alike with the vast majority, even on technical equipment stands, appreciating the capabilities, design and clever construction.

Without even thinking about it, Eleanor continued assisting in the personal ablutions of her son, including his toilet requirements and bathing. Still not having mastered any words without the aid of the computer, the majority of his communication was by a series of grunts and eye movements. A combination of these two created a problem for his mother, forcing her to make a crucial decision.

Using sponges and flannels to soap and wash him had never caused problems in the past, but on this particular evening they did. Gerald was at a late meeting and Alexander was enjoying his pre-bedtime bath when it happened. As she washed between his legs, his penis unexpectedly sprung to attention, remaining in the rigid state even when she quickly moved her hands away. Excited grunts and a pleading look in his eyes left no doubt what he wished her to do and as she hesitated, unsure how to react, the grunts became more urgent and demanding. Perched on the small stool which she used to make her task easier, she sat stock still for several long

seconds but the pleading grunts did not cease. Embarrassed but an absolute slave to her son's requirements, she soaped her hands, took a deep breath and reached for him.

Later, Eleanor lay in bed, reliving her earlier experience with her son in the bath, feeling a strange stirring in her loins as she did so. She had tried to avoid eye contact, gaze fixed between his legs, as her fingers stroked him, slowly at first but then a little quicker; the up and down movement seeming to make him harder. It was only a matter of three or four minutes when a really loud groan caused her to look at his face, saw his eyes closed and returned to look at his penis dispensing white slimy liquid spurting out elongating itself in the water. His pleading had made it crystal clear what he required her to undertake, with the hesitation very brief. She told herself that, if necessary, she would kill for her boy so whilst embarrassing, what she had done was a small price to pay for his relief and presumable pleasure. She wondered if he had learned about sex from his science teacher or if he had searched for information on the internet. It may have been neither, she decided, and just that his body had reacted automatically.

Whilst not happening every bath time, she appeased him by carrying out the ritual regularly, initially in complete silence but on occasions when his taking longer started to make her hand and arm ache she found herself encouraging him, urging, 'Come on, Alexander. Cum for Mummy,' as her fingers moved faster and faster, to be rewarded by even louder groans as he responded.

His increase in size and weight meant Eleanor found it almost impossible to carry him and it was difficult to get him to help her to move him around. By working out a technique with the electric chair, she could manage the loading and

unloading in the car. Up and down stairs was not at all easy so an investment was made to build an extension at the rear of the house which accommodated two additional bedrooms and a bathroom. An open door between one bedroom and the bathroom enabled an electrically operated hoist to be connected to a steel rail attached to an open beam, which allowed her to lift him out of bed, transfer him over the bath and lower him into waiting warm suds.

Gerald purchased an overbed table which he adapted to house the computer, attached a bracket to a wall on which to fix a television and modified an intercom system between Alexander's room and the couple's bedroom which Gerald once again shared with his wife.

It was he who suggested they should investigate the possibility of using the services of a nurse occasionally, so they could go out in an evening. Obtaining contacts through the social worker, they met two prospects and chose a kind, middle-aged lady with a considerable amount of nursing experience. Neither she nor her subsequent replacement, a slightly younger lady, lasted long, Alexander sulkily advised his parents that he did not like either of them. Thinking that a male might be more suitable, they engaged the services of a young Asian trainee male nurse. Ahmed was a totally different matter with their son, not only singing his praises but even suggesting that his parents go out more often as he was happy to be left with Ahmed. The slim, swarthy, handsome young man looked no more than fifteen and had to produce identity to prove his nineteen years. He was eager to please and both Gerald and Eleanor were captivated by his work ethic and attitude. There were occasions when the couple took the chance to go to the city and see a show when the nurse would sleep in the spare downstairs bedroom so they need not hurry back.

CHAPTER 5

Jack Hollingsworth was worried.

Whilst understanding Gerald's wanting to make the life of his son as fulfilling as possible, Jack had become concerned at the amount of money which his partner was taking out of the business in order to achieve his goal. Considerable expenses had been occurred financing trips to the US, Europe and even China as Gerald searched for the most advanced equipment, passing the trips off as business, linking the technology to the computer industry. Jack had no worries about that, it was just that they had agreed that any 'perks' would be kept record of and adjustments made when they declared the director's bonus scheme.

Boom time in the industry was beginning to wane due to the development of off-the-shelf software systems and whilst they were still doing well, they had to work harder for it than in the past and Gerald's excursions put more responsibility on the team which they had built up, although none of them could match his undoubted skills with software. When discussing the matter with Christina, she had actually sided with their friends, having taken Eleanor under her wing and fallen in love with Alexander, prepared even to sacrifice some of her own bonus payment, if necessary, to help make his life more comfortable.

The seriousness of the matter crystalised at the next quarterly meeting when they would agree the bonus payments and Jack dropped the bombshell that Gerald would not be due any. Personal costs had been incurred in excess of the considerable amount which would have been due. During the first ever heated exchange between the group, Gerald argued that the money had been spent helping his son, a fact with which Jack did not dispute but made a proposal that any money released to Gerald, instead of being shown as a bonus, should be converted to a director's loan.

Gerald McLoughlin sat in his Porsche with his fingers busy on the keyboard of his laptop. His recent confrontation with his partners over the financial arrangements had infuriated him. He was the brains behind the operation and he felt he deserved more than anyone and the extra money which he had taken was for the benefit of his son. They needed him, but he did not need them and he would prove it.

Parked in the city, he was outside a medium-sized office block which contained the offices of a very large accounting company, a firm of legal partners and the headquarters of a small chain of hardware stores. His company had installed software systems in the accounts firm and both hardware and software to the hardware company.

Connecting his laptop to his mobile phone, he typed in a series of figures and numbers, pressed a further button and after a slight pause was rewarded when the screen filled with details of lots of file references. Clicking on a folder entitled 'clients' following another slight pause, he was able to view the names of every single customer of the accounts company. Scrolling down, he recognised several household names. Ignoring these and selecting the name of a company

unknown to him, he opened the appropriate computer files, searching through until he found one headed 'payroll'.

Fifteen minutes later, the company Streatham and Croydon Ironmonger Merchants, unknown to themselves, had an additional employee by the name of George Wilson on a salary of £4,500 a year. George's details showed bank account information and his national insurance number so the Inland Revenue would receive their share of his modest salary. Within the next hour, 'Alison Smith' had joined the ranks of those employed by a small restaurant chain and 'Will Jones' could look forward to collecting a salary from an East End clothes manufacturer. Satisfied with his evening's work, Gerald closed the programs on the laptop, stowed it away in the Porsche and the engine roared into life as he started his journey home.

The task had been very elaborate and equally painstaking, involving visiting graveyards, selecting the most common surnames from headstones of those who, within the past two years, had tragically passed away before having passed their fifteenth birthday. Having 'borrowed' the name of a genuine solicitor, he opened a fictitious branch at an address which contained a vacant derelict piece of land between two retail shops, filled in a redirection form to a PO box and collected mail from a newsagent and tobacconist in Edgware Road. Creating an authentic-looking letterhead on his computer, he printed letters requesting, on behalf of his clients, copies of birth certificates which he used to acquire national insurance numbers which, in turn, alongside the birth certificates and forged personal references, were used to open bank accounts. It took a considerable amount of time to secretly manage the operation and he used the offshore trust to divert the

money back into his own bank account. Deciding against enlightening his business partners about it, the trust still ticked over with agency fees being received and paid from the dealings with Montgomery and the Iranian. The trail was long, complicated and difficult to follow, passing through companies in Guernsey, Isle of Man and Malta.

Compiling his information and generating income through clients of the accountants proved lucrative but by using names of people who would have only been school leaving age, he had to limit the salary accordingly. By using a group who had died young but several years earlier enabled him to increase the stakes. Using the same solicitor's letterhead, he used the ploy that his clients had spent time abroad so had not required details of their national insurance number earlier. The workforce of a very large frozen food supplier would have hardly noticed an additional six salaries being paid each month and a huge construction company acquired ten extra staff spread around various sites.

Considering himself a computer genius, Gerald dared not disclose his secretive and illegal activities to anyone but wanted to impress his son by showing his talent. Parking after work time in an industrial estate, he showed Alexander how easy it was to break through flimsy computer security systems and learn secrets of the businesses, illustrating his prowess by opening confidential files and correspondence. On another occasion, they parked in a housing estate and watched three different individuals surfing the net and were even able to read emails being sent in and out. Father and son enjoyed hilarious conversations, following a prank played by Gerald. Forty yards from where they parked was a sign-written van displaying the name and logo of an electrical company. Gerald sent an email to a person whose computer they were

observing, warning him that he was being monitored by the occupants of the van. Within minutes, a middle-aged man walked swiftly passed them and hammered on the door of the empty van, ignoring the Porsche as it carried the real culprits past him to disappear into the night.

CHAPTER 6

Alexander was becoming excited as his parents busied themselves, getting ready to go up to the city to see a show, followed by dinner which meant Ahmed would be staying overnight. The services of the two female nurses had been dispensed with as, unlike his mother, they had ignored his grunting pleas for sexual relief with the first one accusing him of being disgusting. Ahmed, the kind, considerate young man from Bangladesh, was totally different and on the first two occasions used his fingers to ease the boy's frustration. The third time had been heaven. Fondling Alexander's penis, he teased the youngster for a while then advised him to be patient. He finished washing him before lifting him onto his bed and placing him on a fluffy towel to dry him. As he slowly and carefully patted the boy dry, he again teased him by running has hands up and down his body, initially staying clear of his genitals but, reacting to a pleading grunting, began playing with his hardening phallus then caused his patient's heart to beat fiercely as he kissed the end of it before taking it into his mouth. Releasing it, he used his tongue and lips to lick and kiss the shaft and fingers to circle the base of it then took it into his mouth once more. Slowly, he moved his lips up and down, occasionally pausing to look at the boy's face, eyes closed, teeth clenched, before sucking again. After several minutes repeating the routine, he sensed an urgency

Alexander. With little control over his own movements, the boy could only open his lips to allow limited entry of the dark invader of his mouth but was able to use his tongue to make contact with it, even if a little clumsily. Trying to concentrate on both sensations, he felt stirrings in his own manliness as blood vessels filled it, whilst feeling proud to be pleasing his lover. Although he himself could not move much, Ahmed took control, hands and mouth working to please Alexander, hips rocking back and forth to drive his own rod into the welcoming mouth. Having already ejaculated once, Alexander could enjoy the built-up sensations much longer whilst the Asian fought to delay his own release as long as possible before Alexander felt the warm sweet liquid pour into his throat. It took a little longer to join his partner in ejaculating after which the pair lay exhausted for some time.

Dressing himself first, Ahmed got the youngster into pyjamas and this time they used the computer-aided system to discuss their actions. Alexander confessed to having watched things on the internet and grilled his seducer about his own experiences, wanting to know about anal sex and the other's sexuality. Ahmed admitted to having full homosexual experiences and also making love with girls when in a threesome at college but under laborious cross examination expressed a preference for sex with males.

Motivated by wishing to be more active and contribute more to the sexual encounters, Alexander asked Ahmed to assist in teaching him how to get more control of his own body. In the past, his attitude had varied between nonchalance and utter despair as more than one physiotherapist had unsuccessfully tried to improve things. Now he had an incentive and showed more determination.

It took a few days and many attempts for him to stand upright, albeit totally supported by his tutor and he was able to exert a little pressure with his arms around Ahmed's neck. In addition to his condition, there was the added complication of muscles never having been used and not, therefore, developing as he had grown. Often, relatively small activity would make his muscles ache, causing Ahmed to carry out massage to smooth the pain away. This, in turn, caused other issues as the pressing, squeezing and other manipulations would trigger something in the brain of the youngster and he would feel himself becoming aroused, penis standing to attention, requiring attention. Prior to the arrival of Ahmed, Alexander would, at irregular intervals, become aroused, requiring relief to ease his discomfort. Things had changed and the close presence of the body of the other would create feelings of desire, heightened by the memories of recent experiences. Limited ability to manage his body movements did not curtail the hormones taking more control of his feelings and Alexander found himself thinking about sex almost constantly.

Sometimes Ahmed would pretend to be strict and make the youngster curb his needs to a more appropriate time, but would more often than not use his fingers or mouth to bring relief, unselfishly leaving his own satisfaction out of things.

In between, Alexander became more proficient in mastering small movements under the patient guidance of Ahmed. They would work on his fingers, training him to curl and straighten them and Ahmed bought two small rubber balls to squeeze. At times, the mind of Alexander made him imagine that he was squeezing the penis of his lover and when they concentrated on his trying to control individual fingers, he envisaged using them to penetrate the anus of the

man from Bangladesh. Alexander was becoming obsessed with sex and often wondered if 'normal' boys his age went through similar emotions.

'Alexander is below the legal age to have sex.' Eleanor stared at Ahmed as she delivered the words.

'I know,' he replied, meeting her gaze.

'I really should ask you not to come here again.'

'I know.' The two words were delivered matter-of-factly, belying the heavy beating of his heart. He needed the money to help to pay for his studies but had also developed a very strong feeling for the boy. If it was not love, it was certainly a close comradeship, not just about sex but all of the other things which they shared and he really believed he had brought something into the boy's very limited life.

Although feeling defensive and far from confident, he decided to go on the offensive and justify his actions.

'Mrs McLoughlin, you invited me here to assist in the caring of your son. We must all admit he has a very limited ability to obtain much pleasure from life, despite being extremely intelligent, gregarious and loving and living life to the best of his pretty secluded existence. Whilst, through no fault of his own, his brilliant brain is prevented from controlling his developing body, it also cannot control the urges which he experiences and which cry out for relief. The law would allow him to achieve this by masturbation, but his body struggles with that process. His fingers are capable of holding himself, but he cannot make his arms strong enough to do what is necessary. He told me that, although he made his requirements clear to the two lady nurses, they refused to help him.' He paused.

Eleanor felt she was being accused, wondering if Alexander had confessed to his mother pandering to his desires.

'I suppose that my simply masturbating him to relief is technically a criminal offence of which I am guilty, but do not suppose that I would be the first person ever to commit that particular crime.'

He knew what she had done for her son, she decided, as the handsome man continued.

'We progressed to do other things at the request of Alexander and if you called in the police, I'm sure he would verify that in my defence, unless you persuaded him to lie, which would be cruel.'

The eyes of the pair locked during an extended silence during which he could not remember breathing.

'What do you think I should do?' she eventually asked.

Breathing again, the young man suddenly felt he was in control of the situation, that he did not face prison, the police, disgrace or even losing his part-time job. Still holding eye contact, it was an endless thirty seconds before he replied, having already decided on his preferred outcome.

'If you really love your son and care about his wellbeing, I would suggest the best thing is nothing and allow us to carry on. Making me go away will not remove his urges, you know that,' he said, pointedly reminding her of how much he knew as he carried on. 'If I do not help him, then who will? Or are you prepared for him to be frustrated and miserable?'

The boy's mother knew she had lost, but also examined her own motives and wondered if this was the outcome which she desired anyway, wondering if she had been mistaken in bringing the meeting about in the first place.

'You will be careful,' she weakly offered.

'In what way?'

Eleanor herself had no idea what she meant; her own mind muddled, cluttered with thoughts of her son's safety, wellbeing, happiness and protection from pain. All she could think of was, 'Don't hurt him.'

CHAPTER 7

In an attempt to obtain business locally, Gerald had applied for and been accepted as a member of the Conservative Club in town and had also joined a business networking group who had a system of providing sales leads for each other. Limiting themselves to usually only one of each trade or profession, he attended early morning meetings to share knowledge and information with a solicitor, accountant, estate agent, builder, hotelier, printer, restaurant owner, dress shop owner, bank manager, business trainer, office furniture supplier, journalist, plumber, graphic designer, mobile phone provider, travel agent and electrician, amongst others.

The group collected a number of each other's cards and the theory was that whenever talking to their own clients, they would mention they were part of a business group and could recommend other professionals if services were required. Initially concerned about being recommended by people who did not know his work, his fears were quickly dispersed as he obtained business from quite a few of the group. He also found himself being invited to offices or, more rarely, houses of others as they conducted a 'one-to-one getting to know more about one another' session. On occasions when he was the host for such sessions, he provided the option of his guest travelling to Golder's Green or meeting him at home.

As some of the group were also members of the same Conservative Club, they would occasionally join others in attending functions held there. Invited to events run by the Round Table, Lions and other charities, the social life of Eleanor and himself changed quite markedly. The lady dress shop owner benefitted when Eleanor decided she had nothing suitable to wear on more than one occasion and he also arrived home one day to be advised she had put their name on a puppy. One of a litter of standard poodles owned by the wife of one of the groups to which they now belonged. Having initially resisted the idea, he also fell in love with the white fluffy bundle of joy when his wife persuaded him and their son to accompany her to see it. Alexander was rapturous when the puppy was gently placed on his lap and he was allowed to stroke the soft curly fur and his mother had to take him back twice more before the new family addition was eventually old enough to return home with them.

Arguing over names, they eventually decided on Marilyn after the late American sex symbol Marilyn Monroe when someone had referred to the dog as a blonde bombshell. A trip to the local pet store was costly as dog food, treats, toilet mats, food bowl, water bowl, training whistle, collar, harness, lead, name tag and several toys were loaded into the shopping trolley. Whilst impatient to take her out, they had to wait until it was time to visit the vet for completion of the vaccination course. In the meantime, training was required before Marilyn learned how to ask to be let out to complete her ablutions.

Some of their new friends, who also had dogs, advised Eleanor where the various walks were to be found and there were two large adjoining fields within a short walk of the house and these were chosen for the first excursion.

The poodle pulled eagerly on her lead as they neared the entrance to the field, but Eleanor decided to wait until they were further in before releasing her. There was a wooden gate securely closed to which was attached a notice advising people that the field was private property and trespassers would be prosecuted. Immediately to the right of the gate stood the first of two silver birch trees, about eight feet apart, between which was a well-worn path entering the field. To the right, a long wooden rail fence provided a barrier between the field and adjoining woodland, mostly consisting of conifers. As she entered, she looked to the left where, after some hundred yards or so, the field dipped down out of sight but with a tall row of distant trees indicating where it finished. Down both sides were rows of very high mature hedges which included blackberry and elderberry bushes alongside hawthorn and various other combinations with nettles safeguarding all of these.

The field was about sixty to seventy yards wide, after which she passed through a gap of about ten feet to move into the second field, slightly larger than the first but this time with houses beyond the fence. As she let the dog off the lead, they were the only occupants and the poodle bounded ahead of her, intent on exploration and she panicked a little as it hurtled towards the fence near the houses, relieved when using her training whistle resulted in Marilyn galloping back to her owner.

It was a beautiful morning as Eleanor welcomed the freedom, examining her surroundings and as she progressed further down the field, she was able to see the part that fell away to the edge of it. The view also opened up a combination of farm fields, countryside and in the distance, she could see the spire of the church standing proudly above

the many trees in the area. Soon she was walking downhill towards the bottom border of the field, but was able to view through gaps in the hedge leading to further areas which she did not bother to investigate, instead following the path turning left and taking them back towards the first field. The bottom border was a combination of hedges and trees and she recognised ash, sycamore and birch at the base of which brambles completed the barrier between the field and whatever lay beyond.

As she approached an obvious gap in the far corner, which led back to the first field, she was able to peer through and observe a path running alongside the field, separating it from one beyond which contained cattle. Making her way through the gap, she appreciated the steepness of the slope as she made her way back uphill, enjoying the early morning sun and the short freedom from responsibility. Marilyn kept running away, exploring her new surroundings but regularly coming back to check on her mistress and seemed to be thoroughly enjoying her own newfound freedom. At last, they had company as she reached halfway back up the field to meet a man coming the other way, accompanied by a black labrador and, on seeing Marilyn bounding towards her, had her tail wagging obviously eager to play. Eleanor learned the labrador was a two-year-old bitch and quite sturdy but not as tall as the poodle.

Although not exchanging names, the pair discussed the dogs and the man advised her that the field was private property but dog walkers had been using it for four or five years and although other fields owned by the same farmer were used to grow crops, these two were left fallow apart from the hay being harvested.

Alone with her own dog again, Eleanor checked her watch and decided she had time to complete a second circuit before returning to relieve Ahmed of his duties of caring for Alexander.

Gerald liked showing off his skills to Alexander and coached his son to obtain understanding and develop abilities of his own. In order not to attract attention to the Porsche, he would occasionally use Eleanor's car as he and Alexander would take delight in learning secrets about computer operators without their knowledge, tormenting and teasing them. Gleaning information, they would send provocative emails to see what reaction followed. Balking at tempting people outside too often in case they became observed, they avoided pretending that they could see their culprits.

Following trails of emails sent and received was laborious and slow, so Gerald devised software which he could attach to an email and, if people were trustworthy enough to open them, could enable watching from afar. In order to encourage people to read his attachment, he constructed a small program which would tempt the computer user to produce information about themselves which would create a personality profile. He had copied information from astrology details, so whilst they inserted several items of information, such as date of birth, interests, marital status and other personal details, it was only the date of birth which he required in order to compose the profile. During the time they were completing the questionnaire, Gerald's other software would install itself on the hard drive of the computer and then the owner was invited to click on another link. This would enable them, without charge, to download

the information on the profile. It would also enable Gerald to access all files held on their machine. The downside was they would be observed if they tried to enter and carry out any activity on behalf of the owner whilst the machine was being used. They could, however, watch and see all activities taking place including web browsing and details of emails being sent and received.

In order to have fun at the expense of their victims, Gerald showed his son how to use his computer to snare one user whilst he contacted another. By creating email addresses for imaginary people, they caused confusion by replying to emails sent to a different person.

Emails could be sent from anywhere so, without the knowledge of his father, Alexander memorised addresses and sent a few emails from two new addresses which he set up. He started regular communication with two people, one male and the other female, pretending to be the opposite sex. Following initial questions or statements, he then used his victims' responses, simply passing messages on to continue the interchanges, often through the night when his parents thought he was fast asleep.

Marilyn seemed to love all dogs and all people and quickly learned to join in the playful games with other animals and would eagerly search for company, showing disappointment on occasions when they did not meet either canine or human company on a walk. The combination of a summons from the whistle and reward of a treat when responding made her quickly learn how to behave although if with other dogs, would often ignore the call.

Whilst she adored her son, Eleanor really enjoyed the relative freedom of her walks and made an arrangement

with Ahmed for him to call in for an hour to care for Alexander whenever he could do so before going to college. Nervous of the dog at first, Ahmed warmed to her friendly attitude, happily shaking her offered paw and would often help in getting food and water ready for her return from the morning walk.

In early times, Alexander was thrilled when Marilyn, as she often did, curled up on his lap and the pair would often drop off to sleep in harmonious peace. As Marilyn quickly grew, she became too big to continue this indulgence but on occasions when allowed in his room, she would patiently sit very close to the boy so he could ruffle her fur. Eleanor wondered if she had erred in choosing such a large dog but the poodle was so bright, intelligent and lovable.

An excursion to the vet resulted in creating havoc in the household although solving one problem. Entering the large waiting room, they saw a small white mongrel with black ears housed in a large dog cage with a notice asking if anyone could urgently provide a home for the animal. The two puppies went berserk. Marilyn surprised her owner by breaking free from her grasp as she bounded towards the cage in excitement as the other stood on its hind legs to enable the pair to kiss through the bars of the cage. As Eleanor retrieved the lead and tried to coax her dog away, both started wailing pitifully and Alexander guided his chair so the small one could lick his hand. Thirty minutes later, the family had expanded. Another visit to the pet shop was required for essentials for the new addition.

Naming the newcomer was not easy but eventually they compromised on Ragamuffin which all thought suited her looks and personality, but was quickly shortened to Rags.

The two dogs adored each other and the small one enchanted Alexander. No doubt due to having some part of a spaniel in her genes, she appeared spring heeled and could easily jump onto the young boy's lap and would do so immediately on return from the morning walks. The nature of the walks changed as, although Marilyn still searched for other dogs, she would happily play with her new sister whose much shorter legs worked like pistons as she galloped to keep pace with the long loping relaxed canter of the poodle.

Despite being provided with separate dishes for food and drink, they often swapped or shared, eating or drinking from the same bowl and they slept as close as possible together unless allowed in Alexander's room when Rags would lie on his lap with Marilyn at his feet.

Infatuated by computers and obsessed with sex, Alexander's life had changed dramatically and even more so when he used his knowledge of one to satisfy his curiosity of the other. The internet enabled him to watch all sorts of eye-opening sexual activities. His gradually strengthening hands allowed him to fondle himself whilst watching until reaching the relief of ejaculation. Always in the habit of short napping through the night and curious of the habits of others, he invaded the privacy of some of the victims of his father's hacking, observing others also watching porn sites. Aware his own nocturnal habits were not shared by the majority of occupants in the UK, he searched their email address details to locate contacts abroad.

Over a period of time, he built up a collection of individuals so that no matter what time of day or night he could experience the weird pleasure of watching what others were using to satisfy their own needs.

CHAPTER 8

Eleanor watched the two dogs bounding around the field chasing one another in turn; the poodle teasing the mongrel before galloping away in long strides. Rags' little legs worked at breakneck speed as she struggled to keep up with the larger dog. They covered a hundred yards before turning around and galloping back to their mistress. This time the smaller one in the lead as they continued their game.

Eleanor espied a man in the distance who she had not seen before and who was accompanied by two black labradors. The two sets of dogs started running towards each other but a sharp call from the man caused the labradors to about turn and run back. Marilyn and Rags were not so well trained and followed the others, fussing around the now dutifully seated pair, tails excitedly wagging but obtaining no response. Suddenly feeling embarrassed, Eleanor hurried towards the group, calling the names of her own dogs who totally ignored her as they tried to persuade their new friends to play.

'I am so sorry,' she apologised as soon as she got close enough, adding, 'They're still very young and I'm afraid they're not as well behaved as yours.'

Looking every bit the country gentleman dressed in a tweed jacket, corduroy trousers tucked into expensive-looking gun boots and a checked shirt with a cravat at his

throat, the man raised a tweed trilby, one of many in his collection, and greeted her friendly enough.

'Good morning, dear lady. These are working animals so it's important that they respect discipline and control.'

His tone was understanding and kind enough, although it was clear he had control over his own dogs and even Eleanor's duo had sat down obediently.

Surprising her, the man addressed all four dogs asking, 'Do you want to play?'

In response, Marilyn and Rags leaped to their feet excitedly, whilst the others simply wagged their tales until the man gave the order.

'Off you go then.'

All four dogs leaped into action, galloping off, playing chase and catch and Eleanor felt a little proud as she realised the poodle could easily outrun the others and even the little one could keep up.

Formally holding out his hand, the man introduced himself as Colonel Cedric Foster-Clarkson.

Studying him as she advised her own name, she saw a lean, still handsome man despite his mature years which she ascertained could be anywhere between sixty and seventy. Before he replaced his hat, she had glimpsed a full head of hair, albeit silver grey, and behind gold-rimmed glasses, steely blue eyes suggested strength of character. The twinkling also suggested charm as she imagined his firm grip held her hand just a little longer than necessary. His complexion was a healthy ruddy colour, posture straight and bearing exuded confidence.

As they watched the dogs, she confessed to being a novice in ownership, although volunteered information on being a walker for two labradors when living in London and

also confided to being a relative newcomer to the village. Finding him a good listener, she told him a little about the business which Gerald had set up and how they had operated from their home initially. He, in turn, told her about his introduction to labradors as 'sniffer' dogs and how he had used lots of Alsatians in a security business in which he still had an interest.

Walking slowly as they talked, dogs happy in each other's company, time passed quickly, until Eleanor realised she was late to relieve Ahmed and, apologising, gathered up the dogs and hurried away.

Returning home from his encounter with Eleanor, and after struggling to get his boots off, Foster-Clarkson decided he would have a coffee. Not bothering to put on fresh coffee from the machine, he helped himself to one of his wife's packets of instant cappuccino, not ideal but quick to prepare.

The dogs watched him as he headed towards the cupboard which contained the biscuit barrel then paused and winced with pain as his hips protested, so changed direction. He headed for the medication drawer and took out two paracetamol tablets, which he washed down with water. Automatically checking the clock, he saw he had been up and about for three hours and these were the first tablets he'd taken since awakening. Despite the discomfort caused by osteoarthritis, he was loathe to take the four recommended doses every day and was prepared to put up with this situation, rather than keep feeding drugs into his body without any idea of the long-term effect. He did religiously use the gel with which he had been provided, massaging it into his knees morning and evening in an effort to reduce the pain caused by his condition.

The dogs sat patiently waiting as he removed the biscuit barrel and took out four of the biscuits which were reserved for the animals, not dog biscuits, but cheap digestive ones which he understood would not do much harm. In any event, he believed the exercise which the dogs were glad to participate in, burned up anything that might turn to fat in their bodies or sugar for that matter, so did not feel too guilty about giving them biscuits designed for humans.

He could not imagine why, but meeting the woman had reminded him of his past and challenging but happy times when he started his business in the capital. Following a short career in the British Army, he had then served as a mercenary soldier in Africa and used his military experience and knowledge to persuade clients to utilise his services as a bodyguard.

Using small discreet advertisements in *The Times* and *Financial Times*, he received more enquiries than he ever anticipated, all prepared to pay well. Deciding to recruit additional help rather than turning work away, he submitted small advertisements in two of the popular tabloid newspapers. He also invested a proportion of the generous amount of money which he had earned in the past to rent two upper floors in Soho which he used as an office, ensuring discreetness.

Providing personal protection had been his initial idea, but he was amazed at the number of people who required security for buildings as the country enjoyed a time of expansion. Quickly becoming an expert in alarm systems and building a team of dog handlers, bouncers, couriers and bodyguards, over a few short years he had a thriving, much sort after business. His team were looking after office blocks, warehouses, factories, escorting children of

foreign ambassadors to and from school and accompanying businessmen on trips to countries where safety was not as secure as that as home.

Personally taking care of some of the major clients himself created a problem coping with the administrative side of things, which was remedied by using an agency to engage a secretary. After interviewing several, he decided on a lady who had been forced back to work following the death of her husband, leaving her to cope with an unruly son. Going by the name of Agnes O'Flanagan, she turned out to be a gem, grateful she was allowed to occasionally bring her boy, Michael, to work with her and put in far more hours than contracted for. She managed the accounts, paid the wages, chased up invoices, organised the shifts for the staff, placated customers on the occasions when things went wrong, dealt with the moans of the men and made her boss a perfect cup of coffee when required.

Cedric noticed the change in her over the weeks as she used some of her wages to improve her wardrobe, applied more make-up and changed her hairstyle, transforming her original frumpy image. As Michael was only allowed to accompany her when school was closed, it was some time before Cedric met the boy and the first thing he noticed was he had a cleft lip. At fourteen years of age, he was sullen and quiet in the company of his mother's boss and Agnes tried to ensure her son did not bother him. She had advised her employer that Michael had been named after his Irish father and when Cedric raised the subject of the lip, she said he had been operated on which had improved the situation.

Cedric happened to be in the office on the day Agnes received a phone call from Michael's school, asking her to collect the youngster as he had been in a fight with other boys.

She tearfully related the story to Cedric who despatched her on her way to navigate the various tube journeys to collect her boy, suggesting she take him home afterwards.

The following morning, Michael accompanied her as she came into the office and Cedric saw the bruises on the boy's face and invited him to explain what happened. He learned that the boys had been taunting him about his literary speech, told him he was a freak and three of them kept pushing him until eventually he retaliated and attacked the ringleader. In the ensuing short but violent exchange, which was quickly surrounded by a baying group of onlookers, the other boy had suffered a bloody nose and a split lip although Michael had a black eye in return. Michael explained he was ribbed and bullied constantly about his deformity.

Without further ado, Cedric insisted the three of them go to see the headmaster at the school, collecting his car. Along with several other company vehicles, it was housed in an underground car park. Cedric had an agreement with the owner as partial return for him providing security systems and ongoing physical protection of the vehicles parked there.

On arrival at the school, using his title of colonel when demanding an immediate interview with the headmaster, the trio were escorted to the office of the school leader. Whilst admitting he had been made aware of the bullying of Michael, he shrugged, said that boys would be boys and that he was powerless to do anything about it.

An embarrassed and almost shocked Agnes sat speechless as Cedric asked the headmaster in what circumstances the boy could be assigned to Cedric's company for some form of training scheme.

'Let's face it,' he angrily told the head, 'You're not doing him any good and he's not feeling very happy being here.

I can get him some private tuition or get him in some college somewhere where they have a different attitude to bullying.'

It was somewhat a relieved headmaster who agreed to the colonel's suggestion, calling in his secretary to type up a letter of agreement which would be followed by a more formal contractual arrangement.

The journey back to the office was accompanied by a detailed discussion during which Cedric assured Michael that, as long as he worked, Cedric would ensure he would not be bullied by anyone anywhere. He also reeled off details of useful training Michael could undertake, instructing Agnes to find out details as a matter of urgency.

Michael became a changed person, soaked up all the knowledge and experience on offer and immersed himself fully in learning about the business. Reluctantly, after three years, he was packed off to university to undertake a degree in business studies, which he completed with flying colours and following which he was quickly established as Cedric's right-hand man.

Cedric found himself taking his dog walk at the same time each day, expecting to meet up with Eleanor whose company he really began to enjoy and believed the feeling was reciprocal. As often when strangers meet, they told each other things about themselves which they had not discussed for some time, even with close friends or relatives. She told him much about the business of her husband, although did not mention details of her intimate relationship with their landlord in London or experience with her general manager. He, in turn, related several experiences during his time in the Army, experience as a mercenary soldier and also the development of his own business, but kept to himself the secrets of certain events which had taken place in Africa years earlier.

The overnight rain had cleared and whilst the day was dull and damp it was dry overhead and underfoot was not too bad, so either the rain had been fairly light or thirsty plants had soaked it up. As she entered the field, Eleanor noticed several branches of the bushes had been snapped off and large tyre tracks, similar to those of a tractor, suggested it had done so mechanically, leaving branches strewn all over the path.

As the dogs raced off into the distance, for a change it was Marilyn who led the foraging into the bushes with her small sister in hot pursuit. The poodle had obviously picked up the scent of something and was running up and down either side of the bushes which separated the fields, trying to locate the animal. Their antics carried on for several minutes before it was Rags who disappeared into the bushes, presumably having found something to attract her attention. Unusually, she did not respond to Eleanor's whistle although appeared briefly just to check the whereabouts of her owner before scurrying back into the bushes.

As she walked around, Eleanor noticed some of the usual early companions entering the area, recognising the majority of them. There was a lady who Eleanor knew to be a hairdresser accompanied by a spaniel, and an elderly lady with two small dogs who always panicked a little when the poodle approached them. She had once explained that one of her dogs was frightened by larger animals, making Eleanor wonder why she brought her dogs to the field in the first place as her own dogs were shooed away by the woman.

A loud-mouthed American oil rig man, who she only saw rarely as his work took him away on a regular basis, bid her good morning as he passed by with his Staffordshire bull terriers. She had already met the man's other half, the dress

shop owner, who was assigned the responsibility of walking the dogs when he was away. Eleanor had her own experience in the past of having to survive whilst her husband was away on business, so she sympathised with the woman of eastern origin.

Eleanor picked her way carefully between branches and roots as she progressed through one of the gaps between the two fields, having to duck to avoid overhanging hawthorn and also watch her footing on the muddy area. She saw the woman with the small dogs in the distance, so set off in the opposite direction in order to avoid further confrontation.

Eleanor categorised dog owners like most people with the vast majority being pleasant and just a very small proportion being unsociable. She often thought the same statistics applied to dogs but believed this reflected the attitude of the owners. She had encountered soft Alsatians, playful Rottweilers, lazy labradors and vicious little terriers. Having discussed dog behaviour with many of her walking colleagues, she was of the opinion that it was the way in which the dog had been brought up which shaped their personalities.

Occasionally, Gerald would take Alexander into middle-range housing estates, where tradesmen could afford the houses, outside which they would often park their small vans, sign-written in order to advertise their services. This would enable the pair to actually know where their victims lived when the person in question used the name of their company as part of their email address and certainly their websites. They also learned that many of these hard-working people would carry out computer work in an evening and it amused them to be able to send emails to their unsuspecting victims and await a reaction. They would advise the victims that

their activities were being monitored and describe vehicles parked near to the sign-written vans from where the spies were operating. Very angry people, mostly men, would hurry outside of their house, approach the appropriate vehicle and try to obtain entry but be thwarted as they would be locked. On two occasions, the suspect cars were rocked, causing even more mirth as shrieking alarms brought owners running out.

To confirm and show off his skills even further, Gerald hacked in to some of the home computers of their neighbours and showed his son how easy it was to discover their interests, observing the local estate agent's fixation with tennis and the bank manager and accountant with golf. He became extremely embarrassed one evening as he heard excited groans from the passenger seat and discovered Alexander had clicked on a link on the computer of the estate agent, taking him to a porn site featuring homosexual activity.

Unaware of his son's own experiences and not knowing how to react, he simply suggested, 'I don't think we should pry too much on things like that, son. Your mother and I know some of these people.'

Reluctantly, Alexander closed the link but not before he had surreptitiously saved it to his own machine.

Noticing the disappointment and sullen look on the boy's face, Gerald suggested they 'go phishing' and try to get the email details of someone close and have a bit of fun. Alexander cheered up as they started searching for unsuspecting victims who were either too lazy or too ignorant to protect the information on their machines.

When heating engineer Patrick Doherty did his friend and fairly near neighbour, Jonathan Robertson, a favour he could not have imagined the disastrous consequences. Jonathan

and his wife were off to a short holiday abroad, driving to the airport and leaving his house unattended. Over a beer, Patrick had volunteered to park his van outside Jonathan's house, just fifty yards away from his own detached building, in order to deter possible thieves. Thus, when Gerald sent an email to Patrick, he was unaware he was parked outside Patrick's house and not fifty yards away.

After sending the email suggesting that Patrick was being watched by a car outside his house, he and Alexander looked fifty yards down the road to await events. Instead, the burly Irishman rushed out of his house, crossed the road to the Porsche, started hammering on the roof with his fist and kicking the door, terrifying the occupants as the man shouted and screamed at them. In a panic, Gerald started the car and pulled away, knocking the man sideways as he pulled out to overtake some of the other parked vehicles. He then looked in his rear-view mirror to see the man was all right and standing up, completely oblivious to the car coming the other way and was therefore unable to avoid an almost direct head-on collision.

Already concerned when her husband and son were unusually late in returning, Eleanor was horrified when the doorbell rang and she opened the door to be greeted by the sight of a police constable and policewoman who, upon ascertaining her identity, asked if they could come in. Eleanor sat in shock as they explained there had been an accident and both her son and husband were in hospital and could they take her there to see them. They explained they did not have many details as the information had been relayed to them from the police station and they had simply been asked to call round and advise her of the situation.

Concerned about the welfare of the dogs, she asked if they could wait a few minutes while she telephoned Ahmed to ask if he could come around and keep an eye on them.

Forty minutes later, she was sat by the bed of Gerald, terrified as she saw the various pipes and wires connected to the still form and the bank of machinery bleeping around him. Her brain didn't register all of the details she was provided with, but vaguely remembered being told about him not wearing a seatbelt and how he had been smashed against the windscreen with broken ribs and a punctured lung amongst the long list of injuries, many of which she could not recall. She was advised to prepare for the worst but was too numb to show any emotion as she asked about the welfare of her son.

Escorted to a separate room, she found Alexander in a similar state to his father, although there did not appear to be quite so many tubes and wires around.

There was a policeman stationed outside each of the rooms and she was advised they were waiting to take statements, whenever that was possible, as the person in the oncoming car had died instantly.

Thankfully, Ahmed was on holiday from college, so was able to look after the dogs and the house as she spent most of her time at the hospital whilst her husband and son fought for their lives. Gerald's fight only lasted for six days after which he succumbed to his injuries and expired without ever having regained consciousness. Alexander's battle lasted four weeks but, unlike his father, he won his fight and was able to return home having provided the police with as much information as he could recall, although he had blanks in his memory. Whilst the police insisted on keeping Gerald's laptop as possible evidence, they were persuaded to

let Alexander retain his in view of the fact it was his main means of communication with the outside world.

Eleanor remained in an almost zombie state for several days, then mentally girded her loins as she contemplated her future and tackled the question of how she could support her son and their current lifestyle. She realised how little she knew about their financial affairs, which had been left to her husband who had provided her with two bank cards: one for general housekeeping and one for her own and Alexander's fairly modest spending money.

Gerald's business partner, Jack Hollingsworth, and his wife Christina came out to see her in order to express their sympathies and to ascertain if they could assist in any way. She was shocked to learn Gerald had borrowed a considerable amount of money from the business. So, due to the repayments, he had only been paid a fairly low amount each month. When Jack disclosed how little that amount was, Eleanor knew sufficient about finance to realise that would have not have covered the mortgage and living expenses.

With Jack's aid, she looked through Gerald's home office and discovered bank statements showing the monies received from the business plus a considerable, although variable, deposit received towards the end of each and every month from an overseas bank. When quizzed by Jack, she could cast no light on details of this but they checked back to confirm the transfer had commenced some time ago and occurred without fail. A quick calculation showed it covered the majority of their outgoings, arriving on the twentieth of each month in time to meet direct debits for gas, electricity, water, mortgage, insurances and enough to cover Eleanor's bank card expenses.

Further searching of Gerald's desk revealed little help, although there was a business card of a representative of a

Swiss bank and one of a Guernsey-based accountant. With Eleanor's agreement, Jack telephoned the telephone numbers shown on each card. In respect of the Swiss bank, he received a recorded message and was requested to insert a password before his call could be transferred to the correct department, but was unable to do so. The Guernsey number enabled him to get through to a switchboard and he was able to speak to the man whose name appeared on the card and who claimed never to have heard of Gerald McLoughlin.

CHAPTER 9

The next few weeks became a nightmare as insurance companies refused to pay out, citing the failure to use a seatbelt as an excuse. The monthly deposit to cover the outgoings did not materialise and payment demands gradually started coming in. When the mortgage company threatened to take action to evict her, Eleanor decided she required professional help and went to see solicitor Richard Fothergill, one of their Conservative Club group of friends. As she explained everything to him, Eleanor's emotions eventually overwhelmed her and she sobbed her heart out. Richard summoned his secretary, who quickly called Richard's wife, Peggy, who arrived within minutes. She sat with Eleanor, listening to her tales of woe until the sobs subsided to sniffles, although not before she had used half a box of Kleenex.

Accountant Hugh Barker was also invited to join them. He was able to do so after a short delay and Eleanor listened numbly as the trio took over. She agreed to let Richard have all of the letters, statements and other papers in respect of her financial affairs which, with her full agreement, he would share with Hugh. Between them they would make contact with all of her pursuers. Peggy would arrange to accompany her to the bank where she held cards and also take her to the Citizens Advice Bureau where she could receive further help and advice. When Eleanor started to explain she had

very little money so could not pay them, her protests were brushed aside.

Peggy insisted on accompanying Eleanor back home, assisted her to make out a list of food and household requirements for at least two weeks then accompanied her on the drive into town to purchase the items from a major supermarket. Eleanor felt very guilty as the other woman used her own bank card to pay the bill but was admonished by Peggy as her words of gratitude were swept aside.

Gradually, Eleanor regained her physical and mental strength and resilience, so was in a much better state to deal with the next setback. Jack advised her he needed to bring in a new partner to replace Gerald, had to agree to a shareholding, and advised her that, due to loans taken out by her husband, there were problems. The loans outweighed the value of the shares so, not only would she receive no financial gain, the debts would go against Gerald's estate and her monthly payments would cease.

Richard Fothergill used his influence to set up a meeting for her with the manager of the local branch of her bank, Geoffrey Wilkinson. Smartly dressed in a grey three-piece suit, moustache providing a military look of efficiency and authority, he was charm personified as he sympathised with her recent loss, the situation in which she found herself and told her there was absolutely nothing he could do to help.

Despite the assistance of Citizens Advice and Peggy helping to obtain certain benefits and relief such as council tax reduction, it dawned on Eleanor that she was in serious trouble financially but had developed a fighting spirit as she decided what she could do personally in order to improve things. There were very few shops in the village, but the local convenience store had advertisements on a board, one of

which required someone to walk a dog twice a day. She noted the number, saw a different advert for someone requiring a cleaner and noted that also. She ignored one for call centre work in town but made a note of the one requiring delivering leaflets door to door.

The following week found her cleaning the house of the Filipino lady who owned the dress shop in the village and also vacuuming the shop on three evenings a week. Her first dog walking position commenced a week later by which time she had placed her own advertisement in the shop and spent a little of the money she had left to have a hundred business cards printed offering her dog walking services.

Her first dog customer was a Chihuahua, whose owner gave her instructions that he was not allowed to be let off the lead during his lunchtime walk which was really an excuse to let him out to complete his ablutions. Working in town, the owner had tired of driving home each lunchtime for this purpose and trusted Eleanor with a key. Whilst she asked for references, Eleanor had to advise that she was new to the situation, explaining she had very recently become a widow. A Yorkshire terrier and a Scottie completed a trio of small dogs who were never allowed to stray, so an active Dalmatian was very welcome as she could allow him to join her own dogs when they all went to the fields later in the afternoon. This saved her time in the morning when she did her cleaning work and also left her free to clean the shop in the evenings.

Home and much stronger, Alexander had a long conversation with his mother during which he advised her of the things he and Gerald had got up to, telling her about the spying via computer and how it was possible to extract money from people with secrets. Horrified at the thought, Eleanor took a considerable amount of persuading but

eventually allowed her son to show her how he could see things on other people's computers without their knowledge.

He showed her they could only watch the same files as the operator if the computer was in use, but during the night, when they were likely to be asleep, could examine all of the documents and links held on the machine. She sat very still, silently watching the screen as her son laboriously worked his fingers on the keyboard, then was suddenly viewing pictures of houses as Alexander told her they were watching the personal computer of the local estate agent. He was working at home and the pair watched enthralled as they saw him expertly collate script and pictures to create a sales brochure for a house which he had presumably been engaged to put on the market. Eleanor was filled with admiration at the skill of the operator as the creation came to life resulting in a ten-page brochure. Each page was flicked through until the agent must have been satisfied with his homework.

When Eleanor suggested it was interesting but hardly a dark secret, Alexander urged her to carry on watching, rewarded as the screen went blank for a brief second then came back to light with a different set of pictures. There were lots of coloured stills, mostly of either scantily clad or naked people, some clearly taking part in sexual activities. Another change as the still from one of the pictures filled the screen and then became live as two men and a woman engaged in a series of sexual activities, causing Eleanor to become extremely embarrassed as she viewed them with her son. Her embarrassment increased as she watched the men kiss and caress the woman all over, causing Eleanor to feel both envious and aroused at the sight, eyes now transfixed to the screen eagerly anticipating what would happen next. She felt herself squirm as, for the next twenty minutes, all of the

woman's orifices were invaded by the men, individually then together until the film ended with both men ejaculating on the woman's face, white sperm clearly visible as she opened her mouth to receive as much as she could.

Aroused and also ashamed, she wanted to leave the room to gather herself but again Alexander insisted she stay. The screen went completely blank, then black, remaining so for two long minutes before Alexander indicated he was now going to take over the operating of the estate agent's computer. Again, Eleanor watched as the Windows programs appeared, waited patiently at the time it took for her son's slow fingers to navigate the various files until the screen was filled with the naked bodies of three men, two white and one black.

For the next thirty minutes, she sat in complete shock at the events occurring before her eyes and, recognising one of the men, was totally convinced Alexander was correct in his earlier revelations.

CHAPTER 10

Estate agent Theodore Farquharson embraced the bright morning with just a fairly gentle but cold breeze as he followed the white husky into the field. The grass was wet underfoot from very early slight frost, but the day was bright and the ground green as he cast his mind back to the previous year when the husky had been difficult to locate against the snow which covered the ground at that time.

Theodore was in a good mood, thoughts filled with the potential sale which had engaged some of his previous Saturday evening at home, preparing the various sales blurb to get the house on the market. A week earlier, he had received the contractual agreement to sell the property. Being a five-bedroom detached it should make a princely sum on which, of course, he could earn a substantial amount of commission, although not quite as much as the good old days before the marketing of properties changed. Old-fashioned estate agents were no longer able to get rich quick on single sales but thankfully, he had two or three clients with portfolios of buy to let properties, which at least kept turnover ticking over on a regular basis albeit on a lower percentage.

The internet had certainly changed his way of life and like others in his industry he had to work much harder in order to make the same kind of money as in the past. He had dabbled in overseas property sales but the previous

very high commissions had also been affected as the market had contracted in the period of austerity at home. In his forties, he felt comfortable with his way of life, position in the community and financial security. Still playing tennis and a reasonable golfer, if he was a little overweight, he wore sensible clothing which disguised the fact.

In the distance coming towards him, he saw a person with a white standard poodle together with a little mongrel, also white but with black ears. The dogs appeared to recognise one another, scurrying to meet and, accompanied by much tail wagging, fussed around one another, taking turns to chase. As the owner of the other dogs got nearer, he realised it was a woman who initially seemed friendly enough as she explained the dogs had met on several earlier occasions when accompanied by a woman, presumably his wife.

He introduced himself, explaining he was a local estate agent, causing Eleanor to look at him closely, heart missing a beat as she recognised him but had never before observed him dressed. Suddenly embarrassed and uncomfortable in his presence, she did manage to advise him she was a dog walker although explained the pair with her at the moment were her own. The woman who she had met a few times with the husky had never mentioned her husband's profession and for a moment she experienced a tremendous feeling of guilt, aware that Alexander's plan had gone into operation the previous night.

Deciding the woman had little to offer in terms of being a potential customer, he was not rude but a little abrupt as he called his dog to heel and took his leave, much to the relief of Eleanor.

She was aware that Alexander had researched Farquharson, using the man's own computer and the internet,

learning about his successful business but also that he was a committee member of the local tennis club where his name was on the honours board in both singles and doubles. Also, he was an active member of the local golf club and interested in many other sports and depending on the time of year he would often check cricket scores on the teletext first thing in the morning and throughout the day in his own back office at the estate agent business.

In his private room, Theodore Farquharson stared at the images on the screen and felt himself harden. He watched his fingers grasp the large rigid penis and steer the red end towards his face, his lips widening as he took the throbbing muscle into his mouth, feeling himself tremble as he waited for what he knew was to follow.

His mind flitted back to the hotel room near Heathrow where the fateful event had occurred and as he watched himself on the screen, his fingers unfastened the zip of his trousers. Reaching inside, feeling for his own rigid penis, his eyes were transfixed on the huge black hand probing his creamy white buttocks. He half closed his eyes as the onscreen hand smeared oil down the crack between the globes then opened them wide, hearing his own voice react, almost whimpering a combination of expectation and slight fear. Watching intently as the camera picked out the tip of the cock about to ravish him, his distant voice whimpered, 'Oh my God,' as he saw the hand stroking the tool up and down pause at the wrinkled entrance to his anus then ease its way inside. As he watched the slow invasion, he recalled he had released the white phallus from his mouth, only for strong hands to place themselves at the back of his head and force him down to continue his swallowing of the monster.

The screen separated into two images. On the left, he watched the invasion of his arse, gradually opening up, taking more of the black cock whilst the right showed his face being pushed against the white penetrator of his mouth. His choking groans on the soundtrack were muffled as he tried to breathe, mouth held almost to the man's stomach causing Theodore to gag before managing to break away and gasp for air. His fingers caressed himself as his mouth was forced back onto the upright helmet, glistening with his saliva.

The left screen showed the long black tool, filmed from above, withdraw, then plunge forward to possess him once more. The camera held at the side of his face showed his cheek bulge as the thrust from behind forced the head of the cock deeper inside his mouth, hand at the back of his head preventing any retreat. His imagination brought back the memory of total submission as the left picture confirmed the big black dick was buried into his arse, right up to the hilt. He watched himself free his mouth to gulp in air but this time voluntarily went back to his sucking task with gusto. The molesters, almost as if by arrangement, developed a similar rhythm as they fucked his face and anus simultaneously.

He remembered the black man reaching underneath his body to grasp his penis, fingers stroking at a similar rate. Theodore's own fingers matched the pace as he wanked himself as he watched the violation of his own body. He had seen lots of porn but knew this was different. There would be no withdrawal and spurting of white semen. He could not say he could feel the liquid which pumped into his rear end but he tasted the sweetness of the stream which hit the back of his throat to be swallowed greedily. A lesser amount shot out of the end of his own rigid tool, a carefully placed white handkerchief collecting it. His own onscreen body prevented

him from seeing him spurt but he knew he had cum at the same time as the others.

As the image faded, he used the cordless mouse of the computer to hover over the 'delete' icon, ready to erase the memory forever.

It was a teenage boy who brought the envelope to Theodore, having knocked at his door before handing it to the estate agent.

'I had to sign for this,' he advised his boss, for whom he had been working for as an apprentice for some months, enjoying the work considerably.

Theodore examined the envelope which was quite stiff, marked private and confidential and with no postmark stamped cross the front of it, but a white label which showed it had been sent recorded delivery.

Waiting until the boy had left his office, he used an ornately carved wooden letter opener to slit one end of the envelope and extracted a letter and two A4 size colour photographs.

He looked at the first photograph and froze. Whilst the image was far from perfect, it was clearly a photograph of his face, mouth wide open as his lips engulfed the enormous penis. Quickly slipping the offending picture back into the envelope, he sat back in his chair, trembling in fear, forehead suddenly clammy and fingers shaking uncontrollably.

It was probably no more than two minutes but seemed longer as his heart beat frantically inside his chest and he controlled his nerves sufficiently to allow him to help himself to a plastic cup full of water from the cooling machine, situated in the corner of his office.

Returning to his desk, he stared at the envelope for several seconds before opening the flap and removing the additional contents. The second photograph, although side on, clearly showed it was him, naked on his knees being penetrated from behind.

Trembling fingers struggled to remove the accompanying letter, which was extremely formal although there was no name or address of the sender. It was addressed to him personally, headed private and confidential and dated two days earlier.

Dear sir

We are really sorry that you are unable to support our fund which, as you have been previously made aware, is for the benefit of a very needy cause. We find this regrettable but are returning to you the photographs which you kindly provided, although we are keeping copies for our records, as you would expect.

We will also be taking the liberty of sending copies to your dear wife, Lydia, who will no doubt be very interested and later this week intend further copies to be sent to the captain of your golf club and secretary of the tennis club which we are sure will be appreciated by your fellow committee members.

With kindest regards

The very simple school style signature was impossible to interpret.

Deciding to examine the label, he ascertained it had been despatched from West London. Although possibly not appropriate, he carefully removed the white postal sticker before returning the letter and photographs to the envelope which he locked in a drawer in his desk.

Theodore was hardly paying attention as the husky entered the field, nose to the ground tracking unknown creatures, possibly rabbits although he had not seen too much evidence of those, but in the past the husky had startled and chased a small deer before he called it back.

A man with a young labrador, whom Theodore recognised, was about fifty yards away and the two dogs raced towards each other and quickly united in a playful gamble. Totally engrossed in his own thoughts, Theodore moved in the opposite direction and was relieved when the other man did the same, thus avoiding the necessity to make small talk at a time when his head was spinning. Tiring of the game, his dog re-joined him as he continued his walk.

Either the postman hadn't been or there was no mail but he was aware that very often their first delivery didn't arrive until after three in the afternoon. Explaining to Fay, one of his part-time sales staff, that he felt a little bit queasy, he had slipped the envelope into his briefcase and left for home, comfortable in the knowledge he had no appointments for the rest of the day.

As he wandered around the field, he had no idea what he should do. Whilst clearly being blackmailed, the evidence cleverly referred to charity donations and although obvious as threats, the promise to send copies to his wife and the golf club did not specifically refer to the conditions of his failing to make contributions.

Eventually, he used his mobile to telephone the office and Fay answered.

'Hi, it's Theodore. Can you stay behind a little this evening please? There's something we need to discuss. I'll be back to the office just after normal closing time, so can you wait until then?'

She hesitated only briefly, nothing to rush home for but was concerned at what the problem was.

'Are you all right, Theo? You sound very stressed. Can you tell me what this is about?'

'Can't talk on the phone, Fay, but I'll explain everything this evening. Don't worry, it's nothing too serious but something that I'd like to chat about face to face. If it's okay, I'll see you later.'

As she replaced the telephone, it was her turn to be worried. She had worked for him since an acrimonious divorce three years earlier, did quite well on a commission scheme and could not afford to lose her job.

Fay heard Theodore unlock the door and let himself in, just as she was returning from the small kitchen with a cup of tea which she had made for herself.

'Coffee or tea?' she asked, then noticing his pale serious face asked, 'Are you sure you're all right, Theo? You look quite pale.'

'Coffee please, strong,' was his reply adding, 'Then let's go into my office.'

Using his key, he entered the inner sanctum, always locked when he was out of the building with him being the only keyholder. Apart from his personal confidential items, the filing cabinet also disclosed information on clients in addition to his financial affairs and the recent change in the

law regarding information about customers meant the details that were available on paper had to be locked securely away. He flopped in his chair as his assistant brought in the drinks and made herself comfortable opposite him.

'What's this all about? You really got me worried. Is it the business? Have we got financial problems? Please. I'm really worried, can you explain things to me?'

Extracting a bottle of scotch and two glasses from a drawer in his filing cabinet, she shook her head as he showed them to her.

Pouring himself a generous tot, he sighed audibly.

'I'm being blackmailed.'

She looked at him incredulously before replying. 'Blackmailed? How, why? What about?'

He paused, took a sip of his whiskey, then looked her in the eye.

'I hate to admit it, but I had a one night stand some time ago and someone is now threatening to tell Lydia about it. It was only once, Fay, and I've been ashamed ever since. Believe me, this is the only time in my life I've been unfaithful to Lydia and now it looks like I'm being made to pay for it.'

Fay felt almost relieved, thankful he was not going to ask her to leave, as she studied him carefully.

'Theo, if it was only one occasion, I'm sure Lydia would understand. You must not succumb to blackmail threats over something such as this. Come on, it's not as though infidelity is uncommon these days. You have so much going for you, the pair of you, so I'm sure Lydia will be understanding and forgive a one-off occasion. Anyway, who's trying to blackmail you? Is it the woman involved?'

'That's the problem, Fay.' He hesitated, trembled inwardly, took another deep breath and then blurted out,

'I spent a night with two men in a hotel near Heathrow and now someone sent pictures to me and demanded money.'

'Shit' was the only word she could think of to describe the current situation and looking at the bottle of scotch announced quietly, 'I think I'll take that drink now.'

There were tears in his eyes as he related the full story to her, explaining about the requirement to fulfil a fantasy, that as far as he knew he was not gay, but admitted to really enjoying the experience. Listening without a word of interruption, feeling more and more amazed as he related the information, she waited until it finished and then quietly advised him.

'You must not give in to them, Theo. Blackmailers never give up from what I hear and they'll just come back for more. I know Lydia. You're obviously not proud of what you've done but I'm sure she will understand and your marriage is much too strong to let a single thing like this destroy it. You must be strong, Theo.'

Tears stung his eyes as he returned her gaze.

'You don't understand, Fay. They're threatening to send copies of the photographs to the golf club.'

'Fuck,' she exclaimed then held her hand up to her mouth, embarrassed at using the word before continuing. 'Who are they, Theo? Is it the men you were with? How did they know where you were? I think you need to contact the police immediately. You must not let yourself get into the grips of these people, whoever they are.'

He placed his head in his hands, said nothing and they remained silent as the pair contemplated the situation in their different ways.

Theodore stared at the computer and was transfixed by the attachment which he had downloaded and which was a

copy of the letter addressed to the captain of the golf club. It mentioned him by name and, like his own letter, was very formerly addressed although again with no name or address of the sender.

Dear Captain

If your tradition is that someone achieving a hole in one pay for a round of drinks, then I'm sure that one of your members is owing a round. As you can see from the enclosed, he could really perhaps be qualified as getting two holes in one. I am sure that if you show him the photographs he will be delighted to pay up.

Kindest regards

The accompanying email simply read:

Sorry we missed the post with the attached today, but will be sending it tomorrow if we have not heard from you by then.

Just in case you had misplaced the original contribution form, we have attached a further copy should you wish to enter your details.

Regards

Theodore stared at the computer for two more minutes then, with a deep sigh, downloaded the document and started filling in his bank details.

CHAPTER 11

Glenda Wilkinson returned to her seat on the train, following her excursion to the toilet where she had removed her knickers. Slowly and carefully, she crossed her legs as she met the gaze of the man occupying the seat opposite, then picked up the magazine from the seat alongside her. The wife of bank manager Geoffrey Wilkinson was on her way to London on a shopping expedition, which she did regularly, but today was going to be different. Glenda was on a mission to acquire something special, having contemplated doing so for some time.

She had never considered herself pretty, believing she had a mouth which was too big, nose that flared too wide at the nostrils and hair which she struggled to manage, mostly controlling it by having it cut short. Not very tall at five feet five inches, she had always believed, along with many others, that her bottom, hips and legs were her best features alongside her still quite slim waist. In earlier years, she had been embarrassed by a small bust but was relieved that, having expanded during her first pregnancy, it never went back to its original size. She had worked hard at retaining her slimness, being careful what she ate and drank, learning to make a glass of wine last a long time on occasions when having to attend formal functions with her husband.

The couple's two children were now adults and had moved out, her son having married and now working in the

Far East, and daughter not married but living with a partner in Brighton where they ran a small restaurant. Glenda had become bored at home following their departure, being prevented from working by her husband, but volunteered in a charity shop once a week. Older than the paid staff, she found herself enjoying listening to their gossip which centred around reality TV shows, which she never watched, and their sex lives, which differed dramatically from her own. Not only was hers limited in variation, it had dwindled over the years, becoming extremely spasmodic with sometimes a gap of three or four weeks between bouts.

Initially embarrassed at some of the things which they described, especially when detailing ways of making love which she had never experienced, she noted websites which they recommended. Glenda purchased a laptop, on the pretext of wishing to write her memoirs, and would spend many an afternoon looking at the sexual activities on the sites, becoming aroused and masturbating as she watched. Her selection was varied and she watched girl-on-girl, threesomes, group sex and self-satisfaction with the aid of a range of sex toys. The main purpose of her trip today was to acquire at least one of these. The daring removal of her briefs made her feel sexy and a tease.

Having made a few purchases in Oxford Street, she made her way to Soho, but passed three sex shops twice, before plucking up the courage to enter one of them. Accustoming her eyes to the dull interior, she noticed a large black man at the till then looked around and made her way to an area which displayed a range of sexy lingerie, mostly red, black or a mixture of both. Glancing around, she saw an illuminated glass display case which housed a selection of vibrators and sidled across to the display, a wide choice of differing colours,

shapes and sizes. She was amazed at the options available as she looked through the glass top of the closed unit then jumped, startled, as a male voice spoke from behind her.

'Can I help? Would you like me to show you anything?'

Sat by the till, the man had looked large but standing behind her he was huge, towering above her, very muscular if a little overweight. Without waiting for a reply, he proceeded to unlock the display case, lifted the top, reached inside and, selecting a huge black dildo, offered it to her.

'Do you fancy something like this?'

Paralysed with embarrassment, she remained perfectly still but the man was not going to let her escape, pushing the monster towards her. She could smell his powerful aftershave or cologne.

'See how it feels, just like the real thing.' He stared at her, willing her to take the phallus from him.

Tentatively, she touched it but did not take hold of it.

Replacing the item, he selected a pink-coloured vibrator which was called a Rampant Rabbit and he showed the item to her, explaining that the penis-shaped part was for insertion in the vagina with the other piece designed to tickle the clit.

'Hold it,' he ordered.

Then, as she took it from him, he caused her to jump by twisting the end, making the contraption come alive, vibrating powerfully in her hand.

'Just imagine that inside you,' the man said quietly, taking it from her and stilling the vibration by twisting the end again. 'We have a room at the back if you would like to try it? All part of our personal service.'

Suddenly realising there were no other customers or staff in the place, she was frightened, yet excited at the same time, turned on by the array of toys, some of which she had seen

used during her internet browsing but also by the sheer size, strength and masculinity of the man. Her head told her to leave, her body told her to stay and in utter turmoil she stood rooted to the spot as she watched him walk to the door. He turned the key, switched the notice on the door from open to closed, then slowly walked back towards her, holding out his hand.

Fay Atkinson sat with a glass of wine, mulling over the traumatic events of the day. She was still in shock regarding the revelations from Theo, not least of which had been his admission of his homosexual activities, and she could not think of any other logical reason the men with whom he had shared the experience were not the ones attempting to blackmail him. She had seen the state of mind Theo was in and in her opinion, he was very close to the edge, extremely concerned about the possible danger to his business and social life he had built up through the network of contacts in his profession. Should word about any of this get out, inadvertently or deliberately, she shared his fear at the repercussions and how they would also affect her own livelihood as she was very dependent upon her earnings from the estate agency.

One of life's survivors, Fay had overcome the trauma of an unfaithful husband, the subsequent separation and quite nasty divorce. Concentrating on bringing up three children who had now left the family nest, she had no idea of his infidelity, believed their relationship and sex life had been fine and was amazed when he left for someone totally different. Fairly short and possessing what she admitted to be a full figure, Fay was an extreme contrast to the five-foot-ten skinny person to whom her ex-husband was now

married. A divorcee herself, the woman worked in the same insurance office in the city and apparently the relationship developed following after-work drinks prior to him catching his commuter train home.

A dab hand at sewing and the owner of an electric sewing machine, Fay's first part-time job had been in town, carrying out minor repairs and alterations to clothing in addition to dry cleaning being carried out on the premises. She had also replied to an advert for a part-time assistant at the local dress shop and, in addition to dealing with customers, was able to provide a service of carrying out alterations to purchases made. She still did this on occasions although it contributed very little to the budget, unlike her work at the estate agent. Very gregarious, without being high pressure, she had developed a technique of enthusiastically portraying the features of properties which she showed to clients and had by far the best record of the three of them who were involved in selling. Respecting her abilities, Theo had made her the senior salesperson, financed her attendance at two short-term training courses and provided her with a small saloon car, bearing the logo and details of the agency. The others were 'pool' cars which had to remain at the agency when not in use, but Fay was allowed to take hers home and use it privately. In her fifties, she was aware of the still biased attitude to older people and feared her way of life could rapidly deteriorate if, for whatever reason, she lost her job.

Not quite remaining celibate since the divorce, Fay had met a total of four men through dating sites, never inviting any of them home, but had shared a couple of hotel rooms and risked spending the night at the homes of two of them, but avoided any kind of long-term commitment. She had occasionally attended a few functions with Theo, sometimes

so she could drive and allow him to have a few drinks, but their relationship had always been platonic throughout, progressing no further than a peck on the cheek from either side. They had enjoyed an occasional celebrating bottle of champagne when a particularly lucrative deal had been completed, and in the main enjoyed a really pleasant relationship, both business and personal.

With a sense of irony, whilst hoping he wasn't a closet homosexual, she wondered if it explained why he had never ever made a pass at her.

Mentally shrugging, she deliberately crossed her fingers before draining the glass and commenced her routine for retiring for the night.

CHAPTER 12

Having been sorely tempted as the big black man offered to demonstrate the vibrator, Glenda Wilkinson managed to control her feelings and resist the offer. She had agreed to purchase some items and left the shop with a plain carrier bag which contained the pink Rampant Rabbit, a two-pronged contraption which she understood would penetrate and vibrate in her vagina and bottom at the same time, and a huge black vibrating dildo.

She could not wait to try them and the second she heard her husband's car drive away, she got out of bed, went down to the kitchen and made herself her morning cup of coffee which she carried back to the bedroom, silk dressing gown over her long silk nightdress which flatteringly accentuated her curves.

Retrieving her laptop from the bedroom, which she used as a study, together with her bag of goodies, she brought everything to the main bedroom, connected the computer to the large screen wall-mounted TV and emptied the contents of the carrier bag onto the bed. Selecting the big black item, she inserted the four required batteries, tested the phallus vibrated when she twisted the end then, turning it off, placed it by her pillow.

Finding the porn channel, she searched the contents until she found a full length offering of a threesome in which the desires of a white woman were attended to by two black men.

Propping herself up on her pillows, she patiently watched the story develop as the men kissed and caressed the woman before slowly undressing her and themselves. They lifted her onto a bed and as one used his fingers and mouth to squeeze and lick her breasts, the other kneeled at the foot of the bed, lifted her thighs, buried his head between them and started licking between her legs. Abandoning her breasts, the man at the woman's head offered his generous penis to her mouth which she welcomed, taking in the head and holding the shaft with her fingers.

Glenda reached for her own black phallus and licked then sucked the end, mimicking the action on the screen. She watched as the man between the legs of the woman changed position and, holding his own penis, stroked the head of it where he had been licking. Glenda removed her black monster from her mouth and copied the actions on the screen, thighs trembling as she slid the monster up and down her labia, already wet with her own juices. Eyes still firmly fixed on the screen actions, she teased herself by nudging the large rubber head between the dark hair of her pubis to the entrance of her vagina. After a few tries she managed to insert almost half of the beast, feeling it stretch the walls of her welcoming cave.

Returning her gaze to the screen, she watched the man begin a thrusting movement as he invaded the body of the woman. Unable to control her own emotions, Glenda twisted the end of the cock inside her then bit her bottom lip as the vibrations commenced, producing a feeling which she had never experienced in her life. Gasping with pleasure, she used her right hand to insert the massive dick further inside her and fingers of her left had to press her clitoris in order to allow the vibrations to stimulate it. No longer watching the

screen, she closed her eyes as she desperately tried to delay the inevitable as long as she could, panting uncontrollably, hips pushing upwards, inner walls of her centre gripping the pulsating rod. It was only a matter of minutes before she felt herself soaring to heights never reached before, thighs and buttocks clenching of their own violation and she could not prevent a loud wail escaping her lips.

Having achieved an unbelievable climax and unable to stand any more pleasure, she twisted the end of the black monster responsible for her intense feeling then almost passed out as more powerful vibrations made her realise she had twisted it the wrong way. In panic, she quickly withdrew the culprit, managing to make the throbbing cease. She could not resist moving her tormentor to her mouth so she could taste herself but then returned the rod to her vagina, suddenly deprived of the luscious invasion.

She lay still for a while, but her insides were prevented from contracting as, unlike the few pricks which she had welcomed, there was no softening; the rubber-covered plastic version keeping her walls stretched.

Looking back to the screen, she saw the woman still being pleasured by the men and noticed they had all changed places and that, on her knees, she was being penetrated from behind by one whilst she tried to swallow the cock of his friend. Intently watching the action, Glenda amazingly felt her own desire returning, thoughts going back to her encounter with the huge black man the previous day. With trembling fingers, she twisted the end of the intruder nestled between her legs, visualising the muscular physique of the sex toy salesman. It took a full fifteen minutes for her to climax, during which time she had to increase the strength of the pulsations as she imagined it was the black man penetrating her.

Checking her meagre bank balance, Eleanor discovered her account had received a deposit of five hundred pounds from the charity account which Alexander had set up and which, in turn, had been received from the business account of the estate agent and she hurried through to inform Alexander. The man had arranged a direct debit, so she could look forward to receiving the same amount each month, although realised this was a long way short of their requirements.

Her son could access several other computers, thanks to hacking carried out with his father, but so far had been unable to discover any secrets worthy of demanding money. He did come across one careless person who used the same password for everything and used the information to authorise the man's bank to set up a monthly payment of twenty pounds to the fictitious charity.

Still feeling very uncomfortable, Eleanor justified her fierce love, protection and care for her son to still her conscience.

Her accountant Hugh Barker and solicitor Richard Fothergill were trying to stave off her creditors as best they could, but deep down, she knew she was going to have to move to somewhere smaller and reluctantly decided to put the house on the market. Correctly believing it would be strange if she did not use the services of Theo who was a friend of both of her current helpers, she was relieved it was Fay who came to take all of the details. She had met the woman occasionally when carrying out her cleaning duties at the dress shop and quite liked her.

Fay was very understanding and patient, listening sympathetically to Eleanor's explanation regarding her financial crisis as she took photographs and measurements of the various rooms, having quickly made friends with the dogs.

She went away to prepare the brochure and website details, arranging to return to discuss these and the price which she felt the property could command. Eleanor was warned that the alterations had made the property special which had benefits and drawbacks, the latter being it would not match requirements of the vast majority of clients but was ideally suited for someone with a dependent with special needs, reliant on the additional installations which the house possessed.

'Don't worry. There are plenty of those about, not everyone wants their elderly parents stuck in a care home.'

'But Alexander will need them,' Eleanor protested.

Fay suggested coffee and patiently explained it would not be easy to find the ideal client and if they did, it was essential that the facilities were already in place and they would not have to replace them if they had been removed. Fay said she was very confident that wherever Eleanor moved to she would qualify for financial assistance to convert the new property.

Glenda Wilkinson's knees were still weak and shaky as she entered the field with the schnauzer. She was shortly followed by the woman with the white standard poodle and the mongrel, both of which bounded after them and started playing with her dog.

Feeling she would prefer to be alone with her thoughts enabling her to rerun the morning's experiences, some of which she planned to repeat before her husband came home, she felt it impossible to ignore the other woman without seeming very rude and waited for the other to catch up. She had only seen her from a distance in the past but the dogs appeared to be getting on very well and this was, after all, one of the reasons why she brought her own pet to the field.

The pair greeted one another. Eleanor described herself as a dog walker, although explained these two were her own, and the bank manager's wife felt unable to refuse as Eleanor asked her who and what she was. As they watched the dogs happily playing together, Eleanor asked the other woman if she would mind if she took a video of the dogs using her mobile phone. As she did so, the woman was reminded of videos which she watched recently and the pair stood still as Eleanor recorded the activities of the three very happy animals for several minutes. She showed the result to Glenda and asked her if she would like to receive a copy, explaining that if she provided her with an email address, she could quickly send it to her later that day, handing the woman one of her cards to safeguard against the email going into her junk box. Glenda actually quite liked the video and had no hesitation in providing her email details when the other woman produced a little book in which to enter them.

She had no idea what effect this interlude would have on her life.

There was not a cloud in the clear blue sky as Amalia walked along with the two Staffordshire bull terriers, evidence of the early frost still sprinkled around the field. She mentally chastised herself for forgetting to put on gloves and her fingers were quickly very cold; the bulky leads preventing her from putting her hands in her jacket pockets.

They met a man who she'd never seen before, who had a spaniel type looking hound which immediately took to her dogs and they spent the next few minutes chasing around and playing quite energetically. Enquiring what type of dog hers were enjoying the company of, she was advised it was some kind of Italian hound, the name being unfamiliar to

her. She quickly learned it was an ex-rescue dog, was two years old and that the owner had spent six months trying to train it since he first acquired the dog when the previous owner, an elderly lady, had passed away. As always, she was still surprised at how much information dog owners were prepared to give about themselves on first meeting, almost as though dogs were a conduit to pass on this information. Within five minutes of making the man's acquaintance, she knew which village he was born in, that he was retired, and that he'd worked as an odd job person on farms and other places during all of his life.

As the sun was still low, she was pleased at having thought to put on a peak hat which kept it from shining directly into her eyes although sensibly she had put on her sunglasses. Bidding farewell to the man as they went their separate ways, she continued watching the dogs run around, exploring the bushes and generally happy with life. Her thoughts, however, went back to her recent discussions with the dog walker who had offered her services in addition to her cleaning duties. As she contemplated it, she decided it was a good idea as she had to leave the shop to return home and let the dogs out which was sometimes quite inconvenient. It also invariably took more than the half an hour or so she allowed herself to complete the task, sometimes due to her feeling guilty at spending such a short time with the dogs, occasionally having to answer telephone calls offering to sell her double glazing or other commodities not required. She could certainly see the advantage of having the dog walker and decided she would talk further with her husband that evening.

They had met in the Philippines where she was born and where he had been visiting on business, which had something to do with the oil industry. She was working in a bar, waiting

on tables, occasionally behind the bar and sometimes helping in the kitchen. American, despite telling her he lived in England, he appeared to be very wealthy, flirted with her as he entertained two of her countrymen and a Chinese man who she learned was based in Singapore. He left a very large tip and, much to her surprise, returned alone early the following evening to enjoy a drink prior to entertaining different guests and asked what she was doing afterwards. Advising him she finished late, he persisted and made her agree to have a drink with him later. She allowed him to take her back to the bar at his hotel which served drinks to residents and guests all night if required. Not used to alcohol, she shamed herself when she became very drunk, finished up in his bed, vaguely recalling them making love, and awoke naked and alone at 11 a.m. Seeking her clothes, she hurriedly dressed, aware she was due back at the bar in less than an hour. She sulked and nursed a hangover throughout the afternoon. Then in the early evening, she was amazed when her American returned to eat alone. Embarrassed to have to serve him, she scurried away as fast as she could after delivering each course until he took hold of her wrist, preventing her from leaving his side.

'Can we meet later?'

He refused to take no for an answer and she found herself agreeing to meet up afterwards. Off duty, just before midnight, she was taken by taxi to his hotel where he ignored her protestations and refused to let her not partake in alcohol. Enquiring about her life she told him she had moved to the city some two years earlier having worked in a clothes factory as a designer, and now shared a small apartment with two other girls. She admitted to having no further ambition, having accepted her lot, pleased to escape the clothes factory

and the village where she had been brought up by her parents, along with five other siblings.

In turn, he provided few details about himself: a Texan who had been born and bred around the oil industry, travelling the world seeking new fields and potential. He let her know he was quite wealthy, a divorcee with no children from the marriage and lived most of his life in the United Kingdom although had an apartment in Singapore City. Amalia found him fascinating but also fearsome, sensing a selfish person used to getting his own way. He advised her he would be flying to Singapore but would be returning in just over a week, suggesting she accompany him. When she said she didn't have a passport, he informed her he had contacts in high places and would try to pull some strings to organise it.

Drink had obliterated memory of the first love-making but although he insisted on her drinking, she sipped slowly as they sat in the bar, then he rose to his feet, held out his hand which she meekly took and accompanied him to his room. The sex was very physical but not hurried as, well endowed, he pummelled her body but she felt herself respond, surrendering herself to him as he tore into her, fan cooling their perspiring bodies until he eventually groaned in satisfaction before collapsing onto her body. Within minutes, gentle snoring warned her he had fallen asleep and it took her some time to extricate herself from beneath him. The out-of-town hotel was too far from home for her to consider walking so she dressed, shyly went to the Filipino night porter manning the front desk and asked him to call a taxi.

Again, the Texan surprised her by returning to the bar nine days later with a photographer in tow and within a week, complete with passport, she made the first flight of her life,

in addition to leaving her home country for the first time. Six months later, having signed something called a pre-nuptial agreement, she was Mrs Chamberlain, wife of Warren Chamberlain, living in a large modern house in Hertfordshire and owner of a boutique dress shop and two dogs.

CHAPTER 13

It was Peggy Fothergill who introduced the colonel to the Conservative Association, the Conservative Club, several of the local business people and eventually his future wife. Short and dumpy with a head of massive professionally dyed silver curls, Peggy was the wife of the solicitor Richard Fothergill who did the conveyancing when he purchased his house in the village. It was also she who persuaded him to stand in the local elections and become a councillor.

Peggy was a lovely busybody, interfering in everyone's business, full of good intentions and although slightly overbearing, a kindly soul who wanted the best for everybody. Her very different husband was a large cigar smoking jovial character and an excellent solicitor with a good reputation in the area.

Thanks to his generosity with donations for raffle prizes, buying lots of tickets and attending jumble sales, fund-raising events and expensive black-tie dinners, the colonel proved a popular member of his new inner circle of friends. When the recently separated wife of a member of parliament, Penelope, returned to the village to stay with her elderly mother whilst searching for accommodation, Peggy could not resist pairing them up at a dinner held at the Conservative Club where a retired England cricketer was the guest speaker.

Neither of them interested in the sport, unlike the majority around the tables, they chatted amicably with Penelope providing details of her accommodation requirements, which needed to be not too far away from livery stables on the edge of the village to where she intended to move her two hunters. The colonel guessed Peggy must have advised the woman where he lived, but found himself inviting her for coffee the following day, explaining where he lived, in case he had done Peggy an injustice.

After the speech and whilst the majority crowded around the celebrity eager to learn even more about his exploits, the pair adjourned to a different bar. Penelope accepted his offer of a lift home and pausing just long enough to advise Peggy and her husband with whom she had arrived, she joined him in the car park, belted herself up in the passenger seat and off they went. With an offer of coffee at the house a little earlier than originally planned accepted, Cedric proved to be an exceptional listener as she poured out the story of her torturous marriage to, if half of her story was true, the most self-centred egotistical moron on earth. Although the marriage broke down because of his affair with his secretary, Penelope agreed to a divorce on the grounds she had been having an affair with a stable boy where her horses were kept. She had actually entered into an affair in order to prove the matter on the promise of a substantial financial settlement from her ex-husband, including a share of the sale proceeds of a house, bought jointly, with him submitting his share from the sale of a terraced house in London.

The tale was accompanied by several glasses of port and brandy after which Cedric gallantly walked her the short distance to her mother's house, noting the modern two-seater Mercedes parked on the short drive.

The following morning, she turned up at the time suggested for the original coffee invitation which was followed by a tour of the house and grounds, lunch at the local pub and an offer of temporary accommodation from him when she complained about the overbearing attention of her mother.

Before he could change his mind, Penelope went to her mother's house to collect her things. A week later, she disappeared for a day to collect even more possessions from the large London flat which had been the family home.

Her search for a more permanent abode lessened in intensity, for which he blamed himself, assuring her he had plenty of room so there was no hurry. She turned out to be an excellent cook, introducing him to new dishes, some classic, some improvised, and they enjoyed the odd lunch out. It was she who set the pace for further intimacy when, following a nice meal at home accompanied by two bottles of Bordeaux, she sat close to him on one of the chesterfields and kissed him to thank him for his kindness. Blatantly, she asked him if he would like to spend the night in her bed for a change. On reaching her room, he was more hesitant than she as, without any signs of embarrassment, she removed all of her clothes then slid between the sheets to wait for him to join her. The copulation was unhurried, gentle and eventually satisfying as she told him and showed him what she did and didn't like.

On one of the sites Glenda Wilkinson watched, there were different categories and she was able to observe women using a variety of sex toys for their masturbation, sometimes alone, often in pairs. One used a banana, another a cucumber and a third a carrot in addition to all the professional variety of sex aids which she knew to be available. Some of the things

which women stuck up their front and back entrances absolutely amazed her and had she not viewed it, would not have believed the sizes some of them managed to get inside themselves.

Some of the things were quite grotesque, although she could not resist continuing to watch as the women on screen stretched both their vagina and anus to absolute extremes.

She did enjoy seeing women being masturbated by men using various aids, getting quite turned on watching those who were tied up during the operation. She also realised how many of these sex videos showed the face and features of the woman but omitted to do so for their male counterparts, assuming that, although willing, women had been persuaded to participate; it was often for the benefit and gratification of their partners.

Although sometimes the filming was less clear, she liked the 'amateur' sites and eventually could no longer resist the temptation to use her mobile phone to film herself. At different times, she filmed herself using all of her toys intruding or stroking various parts of her anatomy, transferred the images to her laptop for use to stimulate her masturbation on later occasions. After making several of these, she eventually changed the procedure and whilst using the double vibrator with a prong filling each of her holes, moved the camera to record her face as it contorted in orgasmic pleasure.

After observing her activities for several weeks, this was the video which Alexander McLoughlin captured on his own machine.

The fashion show had been booked to take place in the premises of the local cricket club and Amalia was organising her team: Fay in charge of dress fitting, Chloe on make-up, a

twenty-something girl called Sophia with pink hair to assist with hairstyles, and amateur models Lydia Farquharson, wife of the estate agent, Henrietta Barker, head of year at the local academy in addition to being the wife of accountant Hugh, Nichola Blanchard. wife of a salesmen, and bank manager's wife, Glenda Wilkinson. Eleanor McLoughlin had been roped in to assist with fetching and carrying, making drinks during the afternoon preparation and then helping with having garments ready in the evening. Everyone but Glenda had turned up to help out in the afternoon, suitably dressed in jeans and other casual clothing but had brought changes of clothes for later having been offered the use of the showers to freshen up. Fay was on hand to carry out any required last-minute alterations to any garment.

There was an air of excitement as they busied themselves, converting men's changing rooms into an area suitable for swift changing of costumes, arranging mirrors on a large rectangular table which dominated the centre of the room. They brought chairs from the bar area as the bench seats were not suitable in addition to being difficult to move. Spasmodic music blared out as a young man tested sound levels, whilst a strip of red carpet was laid down the centre of the large bar area.

There was a short tea break and then Amalia and Fay supervised the placing of the evening dresses on mobile racks, which had been brought in for the job.

Eleanor did not think she was the only one who became embarrassed when it came to freshening up time as the showers were communal and they were all in full view of each other. She was relieved she trimmed the fur between her legs regularly, but noticed at least two bare pubes amongst her colleagues. She was thankful she had selected her best

bra and pants to change into and a three-quarter length dress with medium heel shoes.

Fifty minutes from opening time, Amalia was furious when her mobile rang. The call was from Glenda Wilkinson to advise her the train bringing her back from a shopping trip to London had been cancelled. As part of the show, aimed at the more mature market, she had been designated to model a business suit, but more importantly the final item, which was a showpiece evening dress.

'We had picked the size to suit her,' Amalia raged. 'Bloody woman. We'll just have to leave it out as it won't fit anyone else and you'll be wearing your own finale frocks.'

'Eleanor could do it,' Fay piped up.

There was a hush as Eleanor blushed, all eyes on her.

'She's right,' Lydia Farquharson chipped in smiling at Eleanor. 'Could not help noticing in the shower, you have a similar figure to Glenda, with maybe a little more up top.'

This caused Eleanor to colour up even more as everyone stared at her breasts.

'Right.' Amalia was back in charge. 'Fay, check the dress to see if any changes need to be made. Chloe and Sophia, hair and make-up. We'll skip the business suit.'

Sitting dutifully in her chair, nerves reduced, although not eliminated, by a large glass of wine, Eleanor allowed Sophia and Chloe to set to work on her hair and face. Without access to the mirror, she was unable to see the results and was amazed when eventually one of the girls produced a hand mirror to allow Eleanor to see her reflection. The transformation was incredible, the result extremely glamorous.

Fay took over and asked Eleanor to remove her bra, so they could put the dress on her. Despite her protests, it was clear the style of the dress would make it impossible for her

to wear her existing brassier. The very plunging neckline featured a criss-cross effect designed to show a substantial amount of her breasts. Removing her bra, she allowed Fay to slide the figure-hugging dress over her head and was delighted with the vision she was shown, until Fay then shocked her further.

'Sorry, Eleanor, the pants will have to go.'

With the dress fitting her hips like a second skin, Eleanor could not disagree that the pantie line spoiled the effect. Quickly removing the dress, Sophia and Fay looked expectantly at Eleanor whose heart was thumping rapidly, and felt she really had no choice so, inserting both thumbs in the waistband, moved the offending garment down to her ankles, stepped out of them and placed her best knickers alongside her bra on the chair. She felt herself flush with embarrassment, unable to remember when she had last been naked in front of anyone, prior to the earlier showering, and here she was exposing her body to the really close examination of two women.

She had to admit that when the dress was once again rolled down her body, the effect was much improved, emphasising every contour of her figure.

Fay asked her to remove stud earrings, replacing them with elaborate dangling pear-shaped earrings with white stones, from which hung ruby-coloured round stones, closely matching the colour of the dress. A matching necklace was placed around her neck, then Fay asked her to wear a ring to complete the image. It would only fit on the middle finger of her right hand, but this was agreed to be acceptable.

The matching shoes, sporting six-inch heels, thankfully in her size, were provided by the Filipino. Whilst they fitted her perfectly, she struggled while getting used to walking

in them, encouraged by Fay to take only short steps. She walked up and down the room a little, until she became more confident, feeling like the proverbial million dollars.

The increasing noise from the main bar area signalled customers arriving as the place filled up quickly, and it was time to get the show started.

As Eleanor waited for her turn, the other girls came and went, carrying out quick changes until eventually Lydia returned and advised it was Eleanor's time to close the show.

Still feeling nervous, heart rate only having reduced slightly, she walked through the door and paused as she had been instructed to, then slowly walked along the designated path. Feeling scores of pairs of eyes feasting on her, she experienced a strange cocktail of feelings, a combination of nerves, embarrassment, pride and above all sexiness She flushed as a generous round of applause accompanied her as she made her way towards the mark where she again stopped. Turning first left and then right, she then slowly made the return journey, with one final look back before gaining the sanctuary of the changing room, but not before hearing the whisper of the Filipino.

'You were fantastic. Well done.'

The respite was short lived as the girls had to troop out in order once again to receive the enthusiastic applause of the crowd, with Eleanor the last in line. Completely in time, they turned left then about turned in order to let the audience have a last look at the creations.

As Eleanor led them all off, Amalia told them all to keep on their current outfits and return to mingle with the crowd who were now being offered nibbles following the conclusion of the show. This was a change in plan as they had all expected to change into their own clothes, but the dress

shop owner, seeing the reaction of the crowd, decided to give them a further opportunity to appreciate the collection of evening outfits.

Lydia approached her, smiling broadly. 'Eleanor, you were fantastic and you look absolutely incredible.'

As they congregated at a table where a magnum of champagne sat in an ice bucket, Eleanor felt very self-conscious about her nudity under the dress, but after a couple of drinks, began to feel quite sexy.

Ordered to circulate, she carried her drink around the room and was approached by an Indian man who congratulated her on her performance. Even in her high heels, she had to look up to the incredibly handsome hunk with jet black wavy hair on the top of his head matched by an equally jet black bristling moustache completely covering his upper lip, and eyes, deep brown pools, which seemed to stare into her soul, in addition to feasting themselves on her breasts.

Introducing himself as the captain of the cricket team whose hospitality they were enjoying, he was admiring the dress and obviously her cleavage and, nodding towards a much younger blonde woman, asked Eleanor, 'Do you think my wife would look good in it?'

Containing her surprise and concealing the disappointment at the mention of a wife, she observed a gorgeous and very young blonde girl as she followed his gaze, but she had no hesitation in advising him.

'Your wife is quite beautiful and would look good in anything.'

Finding herself surrounded, mostly by men, her glass was regularly replenished as free champagne flowed, included in the entrance fee charged for the event, much of which was to be donated to charitable causes.

Her accountant Hugh Barker, another man with the unusual first name of Jackson who she vaguely remembered being some kind of salesman, and bank manager Geoffrey Wilkinson, whose wife never did put in an appearance, all congregated around her. As the effects of the drink made her more daring, she flirted with them as they appraised her very exposed bosom and, totally out of character, at one stage she whispered in the ear of the banker who had refused to help her out of her financial difficulties.

'You men are all the same and you just want to get into my knickers.' With alcohol-fuelled confidence, she giggled as she added, 'Well, you can't, because I haven't got any on.'

Busybody Peggy Fothergill had been watching events, approached the group and, on the pretence of wanting Eleanor to meet somebody, she steered her away from the attentions of the men. Suggesting it would be a really good idea for Eleanor not to drive, she offered her a lift home and waited whilst she changed out of the glamourous gown and into her more modest outfit. Realising she was feeling tipsy, Eleanor did not protest and sat quietly in the back of the car as Peggy took the wheel, husband Richard also believing himself to be over the legal limit.

Only a little more sober, and still feeling very sexy, Eleanor went straight to her bedroom, stripped, did not bother to remove her unusually large amount of make-up, climbed into bed naked and masturbated for the first time in weeks, with visions of the attractive Indian man in her mind. Although already excited, the effect of the alcohol made her take longer to achieve orgasm.

Afterwards, she could not stop herself from crying, which eventually became quiet sobs as she cried for her son, the lost love of her husband, but mostly for herself.

Banker Geoffrey Wilkinson was also influenced by alcohol and the events of the evening as he returned home after the fashion show. Expecting a reprimand at failing to show up, his wife Glenda was pleasantly surprised at the attentions of her husband, who could not wait to get her upstairs to the master bedroom and get naked. With a minimum amount of foreplay, he penetrated her. With more energy and enthusiasm than he had shown for months, she responded equally enthusiastically as she urged him on. She did not know or care that his thoughts were on the dog walker as, in her mind, the pulsating tool inside her was black and connected to a very muscular Afro-Caribbean from Soho.

Sunday morning brought a dramatic change in the weather, which was now calm but very cool as bank manager Geoffrey Wilkinson and accountant Hugh Barker would not have been recognised by their clients without their smart suits as they followed the springer spaniel and miniature schnauzer along the well-worn path across the field.

Wilkinson was slightly the taller of the two with thinning grey hair and equally grey moustache, producing quite an elegant look. The overly long hair hiding the tops of his ears and trilby, which he wore at a slight angle today, created an almost roguish look. Fiftieth birthday having been and gone, whilst not considered one of the superstars at his bank, he was a respected senior manager, receiving a salary enabling him to enjoy a pretty comfortable life.

The accountant had a face which he believed had made him look middle-aged in his twenties, but thankfully had not aged too much since. He could do nothing about the protruding ears, for which he had been ribbed constantly as a youngster, and even now he tended to grow his hair a

little longer in an effort to camouflage them slightly. He still sported a reasonable head of hair, although this was now tinted with a considerable amount of grey, and while still quite active at golf and walking, he would admit his liking of food and wine had contributed to his adding on the pounds over the years.

They were following a Sunday morning ritual, taking responsibility for the dogs' early morning walk prior to meeting up to play golf.

Both keen golfers, they would play in the medal competition through the summer, but during the winter months met up with two other friends on occasions to play a four-ball or sometimes just played between the two of them.

It was the accountant who broached the subject, which had been in both of their minds since Friday evening.

'So, what did you think about the dog walker on the catwalk then?'

'Gorgeous,' was the reply.

'I've seen her before, but usually dressed up against the weather or quite dowdily and didn't realise just how much she was hiding from us,' the other replied.

'By Jove, yes. She wasn't hiding much at all,' retorted the bank manager, with a knowing smile. 'Have to admit I couldn't take my eyes off her tits and at one time thought those strings were going to break and give us an eyeful.'

Looking around to check there was no one else within earshot, he leaned closer to his friend as he advised him, 'She actually told me she didn't have any knickers on. I must admit she certainly is a looker for her age. I wouldn't mind playing around with her and I'm not on about golf, old boy.'

'I wonder how much she charges?' suggested the accountant.

'What? Do you think she sells it then?'

'No, silly. I was thinking about dog walking. One of the problems with dog ownership is having to come back and let the dog out every lunchtime which, frankly, is sometimes bloody inconvenient, so it would be nice not to have that responsibility.'

'Can't help you there. My wife has her hands full with this little blighter, so couldn't take yours as well.'

'No, no,' the accountant quickly replied, 'I was very aware of that and don't mind paying. I guess the only problem is letting a stranger have the key to your house, as she would obviously have to get in to take the dogs. I'll have to have a word with Henrietta.'

They walked towards the red-coloured sky, changing the conversation from their previous topic to the weather and then dogs as the white husky entered the field, followed by its owner, estate agent Theodore Farquharson.

CHAPTER 14

Deputy Head Henrietta Barker felt herself lubricating between her legs as she walked back to her own small office, having left the much more spacious one of the headmaster. When summoned to his study at short notice, initially she had been curious, then terrified as he asked her how she got on with the sports master, Eugene Williamson. Relief and excitement followed as she was asked if she would like to accompany him to a conference in Manchester. Just a month earlier, she had enjoyed an incredible full hour of sex with the six-foot-four West Indian, who had not only reminded her what she had been missing for some time, but had carried her, mentally and physically, to heights which she had never achieved before. Ironically, it had been a cruel remark by her accountant husband, Hugh, which had triggered the unplanned assignation. They had been getting ready to attend a fund-raising event organised by the local mayor and she had sought her husband's opinion on which outfit to wear.

He had preferred a long red skirt as the green cocktail dress exaggerated her 'expanding tummy'. She had turned away to hide the tears and her anger at the cutting comment. Whilst her tennis playing days were over, she believed two sessions of badminton each week had helped to preserve her slimness and was careful of her diet, which was more than

she could say about her critic. His waistline had expanded from thirty-two to thirty-eight inches, whilst her size ten was only one size up from her wedding dress, last worn twenty-five years earlier.

A natural self-critic, Henrietta was aware her bust was not quite as firm as in the past and her waistline did indicate a little bit of flab but at fifty years of age, she felt this was not unreasonable. Always making a point of retaining her posture with an upright walk, many of her friends had commented how glamorous she still was, hair kept fairly short with the suggestion of a fringe over her forehead. The cheekbones were still high, eyes still very blue and her job ensured she should always look presentable. She had made this comment to Eugene when she had gone to see him for advice on toning up her tummy muscles, which caused the disagreement. Not only had he prepared a programme for her, but he agreed to her request that he would allow her to train after school, fitting the sessions in before the schedule of evening sporting events for which the gymnasium was regularly utilised, including her own badminton club sessions.

Offering to help until she got used to the programme, not only did she not take offence of what she thought was occasional lingering contact as he assisted in her limbering up and positioning her limbs, she welcomed it. Afterwards, when she told him her muscles were screaming in protest, he gently massaged the offending parts and she found herself looking forward to this part of her activities more than the strenuous efforts to tone her body up.

She found herself paying more attention to her appearance, taking the trouble to have her hair attended to by visiting the hairdresser instead of relying on her own habit of taking care of it personally. If her husband noticed

the difference, he did not mention it, although did notice when she changed her glasses for a lighter pair, explaining her optician had recommended that her lenses required updating.

It was on the fourth occasion when he stroked her thighs that, almost involuntarily, she parted them wide, causing him to look into her eyes. Sensing her wanting and keeping eye contact, he ran his fingers over her pubis.

Having just masturbated her on that occasion, when he repeated the exercise the following week, he took her hand and guided it to the front of his tracksuit trousers, where she encountered his huge erection and gasped in surprise and desire as she released it.

They were both aware there were no late sports sessions scheduled. Struggling just to get the head of his monster in her mouth, she did not think there was any chance of it fitting in her vagina, but amazed herself by engulfing the whole length and breadth of it. Powerful hands lifted her naked body and held her so she straddled him, placing the end of his giant rod to the entrance of her tunnel, glistening with lubrication from his saliva as he had licked her for an age. Gently easing her down his shaft until totally buried inside her, he had carried her around the hall until backing her against a vaulting horse and fucking her like she had never been fucked before. Using his powerful knees and thighs to ram himself inside her, she almost passed out under the onslaught, clinging to him as she wailed to signal her climax. There was no let up as he lowered her down onto an exercise mat and, still not having reached orgasm himself, recommenced the piston-like action until he emptied his seed deep inside her.

She had practised at home on some of her phallic-shaped make-up bottles, so she could take more of him inside her mouth the following week, followed by another stretching of her insides. Now she could contemplate spending two whole nights with him and she could not wait.

CHAPTER 15

Eleanor had heard Rags bark at ten minutes past six but refused to get up. In the past she had been fooled into believing the dogs wished to go outside for their ablutions and, fearful of the consequences, had made herself go down and let them out. She soon realised this was mostly not the case. So, like today, resisted the temptation to haul herself out of bed.

She must have dozed off as the next time she checked her mobile it was twenty-eight minutes past six and stubbornly decided not to get up until the alarm went at half past. Initially thinking the extra two minutes would be a welcome benefit, it was not long before the jingle of the alarm forced her into activity. Silencing the intrusive machine, she pulled back the covers, swung her legs out and got out of bed. As was her custom, she stripped off her nightie, letting it fall to the floor, before making her way naked to the bathroom. After a quick brushing of teeth and an even quicker splashing of water on her face, she returned to the bedroom to get dressed for the morning walk. With the mornings becoming progressively lighter, she would not even stop for a cup of tea before venturing out.

They reached the field without seeing either people or dogs on the way and, as soon as they were released, Marilyn and Rags sprinted off, burning up the built-up energy accumulated during their night's sleep.

Clouds were grey but high; the meadow damp underfoot but not soggy, though she had decided to wear her wellingtons as opposed to walking boots.

Crossing between the two fields, she could not resist a childish urge to walk through a puddle she should normally have circumnavigated, deliberately stirring the water with her feet as she did so.

'Eleanor, you really need to get a life,' she muttered to herself, then was a little surprised on entering the second field to see her solicitor in the distance with his white West Highland terrier and black Scottie. They were both quite happy dogs who she had occasionally met with Peggy, and Rags bounded over to them followed by the loping poodle. Usually, Eleanor encountered the solicitor's wife later in the day and had not seen the man himself in the field for some considerable time. She had not, of course, even considered him as a client, not least of all because she liked him very much and he had helped her considerably in the move and with other legal matters. He was quite a big man, slightly portly, still rather old-fashioned and, for work, always wore a waistcoat with the chain of a gold watch dangling from it, and was never without a tie. There was no tie this morning as he tramped around in an anorak whilst they chatted about the weather, unusually mild for the time of the year, and watched the red sun rising in the east.

Eleanor enquired about the man's wife and was advised she was on a family trip to London, hence his being designated to carry out the morning walk.

As they fell in line behind the dogs, happily trotting along together, he asked if she could be on standby to let his dogs out at lunchtime, if need be, as he had a meeting which may drag on. Obviously prepared for the encounter, he fished into his pocket and produced a key which he handed over.

When they reached the incline, he had to ask her to slow down. Never a physically active person, he was aware of the fact he led a very unhealthy lifestyle, smoking too much, drinking too much red wine and overindulging with his diet. Despite all warnings by his doctor, the media and nagging by his wife, he refused to change and accepted how he was, but always maintained a jovial manner. In the past he had allowed his wife to persuade him to try a friendly rollup at bowls, at which she herself was proficient, but did not take to that either although would sometimes go along to the social events.

Outside of work, his only passion was poker and he enjoyed a weekly session at the Conservative Club, where a regular game took place between five or six usually business people who played for fairly high stakes. He considered himself a better than average player at the Texas hold 'em version of poker, the format chosen by majority decision, and would usually win quite a few pounds on each session.

By the time they finished their walk, the possible had turned into a definite and she had acquired a new client for the nicer part of her business.

CHAPTER 16

Jackson Blanchard saw Eleanor and the accountant Hugh Barker ahead of him and immediately quickened his pace so he could catch the pair up. He and the accountant were friendly associates and had been for some time, both enjoying membership of the local golf club and the Conservative Club. Being a self-employed sales agent covering a wide area of the country, Blanchard had not embraced the local fraternities as much as the others, staying away made it more difficult for him to develop the regular day-to-day relationships, as did his profession. He had avoided being sucked into the active politics scene, rightly believing his nomadic business style would not suit or allow him the time. Blanchard considered himself more of an order taker than a salesman as the vast majority of his time was spent collecting repeat orders from existing customers.

As he approached the couple, he could not help but think of how different the dog walker looked in her outdoor clothes, which hid the figure which had been on view so openly at the recent dress show. Jeans, anorak and wellington boots were no comparison to the magnificent dress which she had worn the other evening.

His dog bounded ahead to join the others, drawing attention to the fact he was approaching them, so the pair paused, allowing him to catch up. Jackson was still slightly

annoyed with himself for allowing his feelings to get carried away as he had, like some of the others, blatantly flirted with the woman on the evening of the fashion show and he reminded himself of his policy of not crapping on his own doorstep. Whilst the challenge was a tempting one, he would leave that to the others and continue his own policy of keeping his playing as far away from home as possible.

His overnight stays included Norwich, Cambridge, Brighton, Reading, Lincoln and other university towns, having selected these when younger in order to mix with the student population, some of who might be attracted to an older man with money to spend.

There were also more mid-week activities in these areas and whilst the dance halls of his younger days had disappeared, there were plenty of large pubs where groups of young people would get together. He had long since given up attending the late-night clubs, preferring to make sure he got plenty of sleep for the following day's business.

Only occasionally had he kept in touch with his conquests, but had paid the price when they became too clingy or too questioning. In any event, he enjoyed the chase of new conquests, although often missed the old-fashioned way when he could do his chatting up in the ballroom, instead of having to make himself heard in noisy atmospheres.

The trio greeted one another as he caught them up and, as they chatted away about recent national and local news, Jackson realised Eleanor was not just a pretty face, albeit a mature one, but a very intelligent woman. She had strong views on the European situation and had no hesitation in saying that, whilst the country, in her opinion, had been wrong to vote to leave, their wishes must be fulfilled.

Clearly a 'Remainer' and expressing concern at what would happen following the exit, she did put forward an opinion that the Europeans had every right to stand firm.

'After all,' she advised them, 'It was we who decided to leave the club because we didn't want to abide by the rules. What gives us the right to feel we can still pick and choose and use the benefits we want to, without having to pay the admission prices. Would you pair be expected to use the bar and all the facilities of the golf club, but not abide by the rule regarding dress code, women membership and other little laws? Not that women membership is a little law.' She smiled. 'I remember years ago Maggie Thatcher only being allowed in a certain room in the Conservative Club in Peterborough, despite being the prime minister of England and leader of the Conservative party.'

'You're not a descendant of Emily Pankhurst, are you?' laughingly enquired Jackson.

'No,' she replied, 'But you have to be honest. It's only fairly recently we've not been pigeon-holed and categorised as only suitable to do jobs which men decide we're best qualified for.'

The conversation continued in a similar vein, light heartedly but with serious issues at the same time. Both the accountant and salesman realised they had met their match in debating, but reverted to earlier male attitudes as she took a different route whilst they admired her shapely backside.

When the two men eventually parted and the salesman left the field, Hugh Barker could see Eleanor in the distance, making her way up the hill. On an impulse, he retraced his steps and started walking towards the gap between the fields so their paths would inevitably join.

'We meet again,' she said.

'You are very attractive,' the accountant blurted out.

Eleanor felt herself blushing at his words, not feeling particularly attractive at the moment in her outdoor dog walking attire. Although her face was bare of make-up, she did support a reasonable complexion thanks to spending so much time in the open air.

Being chatted up at an event during which copious amounts of alcohol were being consumed and wearing next to nothing was one thing, but in the cold light of day on an open field, it was something else. The only response which she could possibly think of was 'thank you'.

Then he surprised her totally by asking, 'Will you have dinner with me?'

Shocked, she stopped strolling and stood stock still, mind racing for a suitable response eventually deciding on, 'What would your wife say to that?'

'Come on, Eleanor. This is the twenty-first century and in addition to you being a client, I also thought we might be friends. Surely people are allowed to do that in this day and age. I'm only suggesting dinner or did you have something else in mind?'

Again, she felt herself blush, almost feeling as if she was a guilty party as he continued.

'Anyway, I'll tell my wife the truth which is that I'm having dinner with a client, something I do on a regular basis and sometimes our clients are women.' He then added with a twinkle in his eye, 'Although not as attractive as you.'

She hesitated. Dinner would be nice, the company of a male being would be nice, and what harm could come. Just to safeguard herself from possible embarrassment about being alone in a car with him, when they agreed the date and venue, in town, she suggested they meet there.

The television was showing highlights of the previous day's football, not a sport Eleanor was particularly fond of, but it did precede a morning political programme which she usually watched although, as the scene turned from sport to ministers being interviewed, her mind was not taking in the words as she was thinking of her encounter with the accountant.

He had made it blatantly obvious he was interested in her and, if she was honest to herself, she was enjoying being pursued. On the evening of the fashion show, he had lewdly asked her if she provided services other than dog walking, which under normal circumstances would have annoyed her, even that he would consider she would pass on favours in return for money, but at the time, her buoyancy, resulting from her wine drinking, allowed her to ignore the barbed comment.

Today, there was no doubt that the perfectly sober accountant had made it blatantly obvious he was interested in other things and so was a perfectly sober dog walker.

CHAPTER 17

Glenda Wilkinson's heart was working overtime as she entered the dress shop. She had received an email with two photographs attached to it: one showing her lying on her back with the double pronged vibrator clearly inside her bottom and her vagina and the second one her ecstatic face as she reached orgasm. The email also requested a donation of five hundred pounds to a charity and provided bank details to which she could make the deposit.

Whilst her husband was generous with her spending allowance, he also expected her to use debit and credit cards, and systematically checked every transaction on the pretence of ensuring she was never overcharged. In emergencies she was allowed to draw fifty pounds in cash, but had to provide details of why it was required.

She could never have got away with explaining five hundred pounds, so was returning a recent purchase in order to obtain a refund. Earlier she had tried the same ploy at a large chain store in town, but was advised the amount could only be credited to the same card with which she had made the purchase. Hoping the small shop would be less strict, she was very disappointed when Fay, on duty at the time, explained they had the same policy, resulting in Glenda demanding to see the owner.

Amalia confirmed the policy, explaining they tried to keep as little cash as possible on the premises. Glenda got quite worked up, indignantly reminding the Filipino of how much she spent with her and how important it was that she had her refund in cash. Sensing desperation in the woman, Amalia asked her to wait a few minutes as she went to the safe in the back office where she had an emergency float of a thousand pounds, taking half back to the shop and, obtaining a signature, acceded to Glenda's wishes.

Having forgotten to top up her reserve, when Amalia was approached on the second occasion, she had to ask the woman to come back later in the day in order to allow time to drive to the bank in town and withdraw cash.

When she was approached for the third time, Glenda seemed even more uptight than previously. Fortunately, Amalia was alone in the shop and, feeling both sorry for the woman and extremely curious, she made a decision to try to discover the problem.

'Glenda, this may be none of my business, but what is happening? You've never done this before. Don't you like my dresses? Won't Geoffrey give you money?'

As she posed the questions, Amalia considered secret drinking, gambling and even a boyfriend, but was totally unprepared when the older woman burst into tears then blurted out the complete details, omitting nothing. She confessed to her trips to Soho, obsession with sex toys, the black man, self-videos and the blackmail threats. Clearly, she was terrified of her husband finding out, more than anything else, although when questioned she admitted he had never hit her or even threatened to do so throughout their marriage. Not knowing him too well, Amalia thought him pompous

and old-fashioned, and had observed him peering down the cleavage of Eleanor on the evening of the fashion show.

Adamant she could not tell him what was happening, Glenda took a considerable amount of persuading to agree to let Amalia accompany her to the police station in town. Concerned any delay would give Glenda time to change her mind, as soon as Fay returned from a brief lunch break, she made an excuse about having to go to the bank and drove the still distraught woman to the station. They were made to wait fifteen minutes before being escorted to an interview room, where a man who introduced himself as Detective Chief Inspector Smith and a policewoman in uniform listened to the story, delivered between sobs and accompanied by much wringing of hands. Details were noted down and the detective was evasive when asked for advice although emphasised the police did not normally encourage victims of blackmail to pay up. In this particular instance, there was no threat of any violence or danger to any property.

Joseph Smith had only ever had one career, unless a paper round and serving behind the bar during his university time qualified as careers.

The eldest of three sons of a man who also had a long career working in a car factory, but did not want his sons to follow in the same industry, Joseph delighted his father with his decision to join the police force. Working hard at training college and in his early career as a uniformed constable, he welcomed the opportunity to join CID and used a combination of common sense and hard work in order to further his career. Guided by his father, he learned the importance of keeping his superiors happy and relying on logic, rather than flair, to progress steadily through the ranks.

At fifty years of age, he was still conscientious although his dedication had cost him a marriage, mainly due to irregular hours and a limited life outside of work.

Never over keen on playing sport, he had welcomed the opportunity to attend football matches early in his career whilst, a few years earlier, a spreading midriff persuaded him to join a gymnasium which he used spasmodically. Not particularly tall at five feet ten inches, the detective was aware he ate too much junk food, but always blamed lack of time for his dependence on takeaways or quick snacks, hastily consumed at inexpensive eating houses. Television and reading made up the rest of his pastimes but Joe admitted to being a workaholic.

He was also sympathetic and had felt really sorry for the distraught Glenda. He utilised the services of one of the junior staff to investigate the details of the charity to which her payments had been made, from which they learned nothing. Whilst opening a file on the case, he realised that, sadly, it would have to take a very low priority in the ever-extending list of matters requiring his attention.

CHAPTER 18

Eleanor's first choice of skirt and buttoned-up blouse, totally concealing any cleavage, was discarded as was a smart trouser suit and eventually she settled on a cocktail dress.

It was red in colour with a rounded neck, clearly showing the start of her cleavage but not too low. The arms were full length, but the outer material was see-through, the waist accentuated her figure and she wore a short chunky type necklace with matching earrings. Rummaging through her collection, she found red shoes and a small matching red handbag.

She was already regretting insisting on driving herself into town, particularly having to drive back at whatever time it was. Ahmed had agreed to spend the night at the house in order to look after Alexander and the dogs.

It would also mean she had to watch the alcohol content, but then decided that so would the accountant who would not, therefore, presumably be under the influence of alcohol if he gave her a lift home. She was aware that very often it was alcohol which removed the inhibitions of the male species, providing them with confidence to try to impose themselves on the fair sex.

On impulse, she decided to utilise public transport, trusting she could request a lift home.

In order not to draw uninvited attention to herself, she donned a light rain coat over her dress and walked to the bus stop with only two minutes to spare, before the twice an hour single decker bus service arrived. As she boarded, she moved to the back of the bus, thankful as, glancing round, she saw no one who she recognised although mentally chastised herself for the cloak and dagger thoughts running through her mind.

The short walk to the restaurant was not too comfortable in her high heels and she was relieved to eventually enter the hotel foyer in which the restaurant was located. She looked for and found an area where she could leave her coat, then made her way to the sign indicating the whereabouts of the bar.

He was already there, quickly vacating his bar stool and hurrying towards her. He took her hand and kissed her lightly on the cheek, before leading her to a table by the window.

'I changed my mind about driving,' she advised him, 'So I hope that it's all right to have a lift home afterwards.'

He assured her it was, delighted he would be able to enjoy the journey back to the village with her. He asked what she would like to drink and called the waiter to order the pink gin which she required. Never having had the pleasure of consuming one before, she had read in one of her magazines that it was popular and accepted the waiter's suggestion that she have tonic water and ice with the drink.

Admitting to her host that she had never had the type of drink before, she took a tentative sip, assured him it was nice and settled down to observe her surroundings.

The back of the bar had a floor-to-ceiling cabinet in mahogany-coloured wood, on which were inserted several glass shelves to accommodate the large selection of drinks, reflected by the mirrors behind. At each side were two short

rows of books, with red matching spines, and obviously from a collection although, from her observation point, she was not able to read the titles. The rectangular-shaped serving area had a brown laminated surface, below which mirrors ran along the length of each side and with a traditional foot rail at the base.

After two rows of attractive tiles, the rest of the floor area was wooden, highly polished and light-coloured to match the surrounding tables and chairs, the padding of which she could only think of describing as a mustard colour, with the round tables a light natural wood.

At the top of the bar display, four lantern type lights hung from quite large ornamental angle brackets, and chandeliers were dotted around the ceiling of the whole area. The walls were a collection of mirrors and pictures and the whole combination produced a warm, welcoming and cosy effect.

There were two restaurants, one situated in a conservatory extension with tables of either four, six or eight whilst the cosier smaller one, chosen by her host, carried on a similar theme to the bar area.

Accepting the offer of one of the two menus the waiter had delivered alongside the drinks, Eleanor studied the comprehensive selection before choosing what was described as an Asian noodle soup and then as a main course settled on grilled fillets of Loch Duart salmon, marinated in garden herbs, lemon and olive oil.

Their early conversation, whilst still in the bar, was restricted to safe topics such as the weather, the latest news headlines which described floods in some parts of the world and fires in others, avoiding topics of war and fighting.

After the starter, she found herself relaxing more, after two or three sips of the Cote du Rhône, which he had

suggested to accompany the meal, more suitable for his rib eye steak then her fish, they started talking more about themselves. He outlined information about his progress to university, qualifying as an accountant and moving from a large organisation to set up his own practice locally. Aware that he knew of Gerald and his recent demise, she told him a little bit about how they had worked together to build up his business, but also reminded him about her situation with Alexander and having to care for him.

Over the main course, they discussed musical tastes and she was surprised to learn he was a heavy metal fan, an interest which she did not share, but when discussing books, they did identify two authors of which they were both fans.

Already concerned that he had consumed two thirds of the bottle of red, she became even more so as, without consulting her, he ordered brandies with coffee but, before she had time to remind him he was driving, he suggested they could get a cab back to the village, sensibly explaining that his licence was too important to risk driving, but charmingly pointing out to her he had enjoyed a lovely evening.

As they settled in the back seat of the taxi, he initially put his arm across the back of the seat, and they had not travelled very far when she felt his hand against her upper arm. After tensing up initially, she relaxed and actually snuggled against the warmth of his body, making physical contact with a male for the first time in longer than she could remember. Sensing her resistance subsiding, he turned his head towards her to gently kiss her mouth and she found herself responding. For several minutes, mouths hungrily sought one another and she welcomed his tongue in her mouth. Feeling his hand on her breast brought her back to reality and she pulled herself away from him.

'I'm sorry,' she said, 'This isn't right.'

He moved away from her immediately. 'Sorry,' he apologised, 'It's been such a lovely evening and I'm so sorry if I spoiled it.'

'No, you haven't,' she said. 'It has been really nice and I just don't want to do anything which I may regret tomorrow.'

The remaining few minutes of the short journey was carried out in silence, but as the taxi came to a halt outside her house, she surprised him by leaning over and giving him a short kiss on the lips.

'Thank you for a wonderful evening,' she murmured, let herself out of the car and hurried up the path.

As she closed the door behind her, Eleanor leaned against it, kicked off her shoes and gave a big sigh.

She admitted to herself that she had thoroughly enjoyed the evening, enjoyed the getting to know him, the flirtatious comments and the physical contact in the taxi, thankful it had not been in his car, which might have made it more difficult for her to bring an end to the situation. She had to admit she found him an attractive and interesting person, but also reminded herself he was married and they both lived in the same small village.

She stayed at the door for two full minutes before going to the kitchen to greet the excited dogs who welcomed her with wagging tails.

CHAPTER 19

Picking up dog poo was not one of the nicer parts of dog ownership, and today it was worse as Eleanor had run out of the little black bags which she normally used. Consequently, she had put several clear plastic freezer bags in her pocket and it was one of these that she used to collect the deposit made by the poodle. Marylin was eagerly straining at the lead, nose to the ground, obviously having picked up the scent of some animal and couldn't wait to follow. As soon as she was released, she galloped off in pursuit of whatever it was, lost the scent after fifty yards or so, and returned to her mistress. They were still only some seventy yards into the field when it was entered by a newcomer, a young lady with a white husky dog. Eleanor's dogs were already friendly with one of these and, perhaps mistaking the newcomer for their existing friend, bounded up to greet the dog. The lady bent down, realised the dogs approaching were friendly, and let her own dog off the lead as they instantly started playing happily together.

Eleanor learned the newcomer was just nine months old, liked to play with other dogs and, following the morning's walk, was going to training lessons so she could sometimes learn she was not allowed to mix with other dogs until given permission to do so. Whilst Eleanor found this attitude commendable, she had never bothered to go for training

lessons with her dogs which, for the vast majority of the time, were very well behaved and would return to her when called. All three dogs played happily together and then converged on yet another walker who entered the field with two small dogs, one sheltie but Eleanor was not sure of the pedigree of the second, even smaller dog. There was no panic as the three playfully surrounded the two small dogs, the owner looking slightly nervous, but soon realised the animals were friendly enough. All three owners watched the group carry on the greetings for a few minutes then separated, but Eleanor was still with the husky owner.

As they played and, after asking permission, Eleanor made a short video of all of them together, presented the woman with her card and said that if she would like to email her, she would send copies of the video.

Eleanor had no idea if the woman would respond as she also had no idea what the situation was, but all this took was time, and time was something which Alexander had plenty of. They finally parted company as the lady with the husky had to get to her dog training lesson and, as the morning was so beautiful, Eleanor decided to make a second circuit. There was no objection from the dogs who, now having lost their new friends, galloped off in the distance, hunting amongst the bushes together, tails wagging confirming they were just happy to be alive.

Left alone with her own dogs, Eleanor's thoughts turned towards possible victims.

Despite sending copies of videos to about twenty-five people in total, Alexander was only able to find information to coerce a few people to hand over relatively modest sums. One man coughed up fifty pounds but quickly removed all

traces of the pornographic sites which he had previously been visiting regularly. Another who wore dresses in secret from his wife made three contributions of fifty pounds each so far. Larger sums were received from a priest, enjoying a relationship with a woman from his congregation, and a female psychiatrist, who had enjoyed a weekend away with an eighteen-year-old boy without the knowledge of her husband or the medical profession.

There was one occasion when an indignant Alexander, having discussed it with his mother, traced one man who was using his computer to view pornographic material of young children. Instead of trying to extort money from him, and with agreement by the pair of them, they advised the police and, by searching through the files on the computer, were able to divulge information about his name and address. Rather than risk sending this by email and making their own contact details known, they typed the information out on paper and placed it in a plain envelope which was posted to the police station in town, ensuring the letter was also untraceable by posting it at the main post office there instead of in the village.

Alexander quickly learned the most common sins committed centred around sex or illicit relationships.

Eleanor's thoughts were interrupted when a man entered the field wearing jeans and a red top, and the dogs raced up to him, puzzled that he was not accompanied by an animal, but happy to be petted by the newcomer.

Eleanor was sometimes suspicious of people, particularly men, who ventured into the field alone. She had actually got into a conversation with one such person, who explained he had lost his dog but could not get out of the habit of walking

the area, pleased to see other dogs. He did explain that he sometimes felt quite awkward and received a few quite suspicious looks and at one stage he admitted he would carry a newspaper, pretending to have taken a shortcut through to the village shop.

CHAPTER 20

Hugh Barker took a sip of coffee as he stared at his computer screen, his thoughts very much on Eleanor McLoughlin. The screen showed a demand for a donation to a charity of which he had never heard, but who certainly seemed to know quite a lot about him.

Initially thinking he had blown his opportunity when perhaps trying to go too far on their very first date, he had been pleasantly surprised when Eleanor accepted an invitation for lunch a few days afterwards. She had brushed aside his apology for his behaviour on the first night and, following an excellent lunch, agreed to meet up again for dinner.

It was on the third such dinner date that she accepted his suggestion of staying overnight, welcomed his advances, culminating in, what for him had been, an incredible session of love-making. Perhaps it was the lack of recent activity between the sheets or the wine that removed inhibitions but she had consented to things which his wife had not partaken in for years and he found himself totally infatuated with her, almost feeling like a lovestruck teenager.

On his weekend dog walking duties, he tried to make sure his timing coincided with hers. On one Saturday morning occasion, when they were, in the eyes of any onlookers, innocently walking their dogs together, they cut through the gap between the bushes to move from one field

to the other. He could not resist reaching for her, delighted as she responded and they kissed passionately. Hearing approaching voices, they quickly broke off the embrace and continued their walk, reluctant to join others, so they could at least carry on a private conversation.

The buzzing of his telephone startled him, bringing him out of his reverie, and one of the office clerks advised him Eleanor was on the line.

'Hugh, oh, Hugh,' she started. 'I've had a terrible email asking me for money, by someone who claims to have seen us in the bushes and also talked about hotels. Oh, Hugh, please help me. I don't know what to do. I think I'll have to send the money. I wouldn't be able to keep my head up in the village if this came out. Please, Hugh, what shall I do?'

'Eleanor, calm down, darling, calm down. Listen, I have an engagement at lunch, but why don't we meet in town at, say, three o'clock? Usual place okay?'

'I think I'm going to have to pay them,' she blurted out. 'We shouldn't have done this.'

'Eleanor, please calm down and let it wait until we talk about it this afternoon.'

There was a pause before she answered.

'Yes, yes, all right. I'll see you later.'

She still sounded very frantic as, breaking the connection, he pondered what to do.

Admitting to himself he had considered it was her who had instigated the email addressed to himself, he now dismissed that idea in view of her terrified attitude.

Throughout his whole career, this was the first time he had come across a situation anything remotely like this and, if he was honest with himself, he had not got a clue how to deal with it. While she was concerned about her reputation in

the village, that was nothing compared to the damage which it could do to his life, as it would or could have an effect on his business, in addition to devastating his private life. Several times during his dalliances with Eleanor, he had admitted to himself that the life which Henrietta and he shared embraced a very good social life, in addition to enabling them to live in a nice house, have regular holidays and want for very little and he hoped he had not endangered this. If their sex life was not what it had been in earlier years, they still had one, albeit much less frequent than in the past. Eleanor had rekindled things, bringing back more than a little excitement into his life.

Sitting at her computer, Eleanor pressed reply to the email from the fictitious charity and typed in her message.

Dear sirs

Thank you for your email and I am pleased to be able to inform you that I will happily make the donation which you request, and will arrange to transfer the money into your account within the next few days.

Regards

She then carefully, in the 'silent' column in which to copy recipients, entered details of the accountant's business email address and, with an audible sigh, pressed the send button.

'Why didn't you wait until we met before paying?' Hugh snapped, looking at her angrily.

Her lips trembled.

'I was frightened to. They were going to tell Henrietta and I couldn't put her through that. Oh dear, I'm terribly

sorry. I know I should have listened to you and waited until we talked, but it really got to me and I didn't know what to do. Perhaps we should go to the police. Shall we go around there now? The station is not far away.'

'No,' he snapped quickly. 'Not the police, not yet anyway.'

Only too familiar with leaks that came out of the high office in London, let alone local police station, he knew there was a high risk of the information getting out. At the same time, he was reluctant to give into blackmailing, and although the donation required was fairly modest, he had the sense to believe that this would only be the start.

Unsure of his exact feelings towards Eleanor, whilst he did not believe it was love, he had become very fond of her and also a little protective in view of her personal situation so felt responsible. Opening his wallet, he took out a sheaf of twenty-pound notes, which he had withdrawn from the cash machine earlier, passing them across to her.

'Look, there's your money back but, make no mistake, by paying it this time I'm sure you'll have opened the door to further requests. If they carry out their threats, then they would not be in a position to demand further money which would stop a source of income.'

His own brain back in business mode, he realised that if he did not pay his demand to whoever they were, they would also realise that, should they divulge information to his wife, it would mean no more money from Eleanor. He had not told her they had demanded a much larger sum from him.

CHAPTER 21

Javendra Bhattacharya tried to think of a way to contact the woman who he had met at the fashion show held at his club. A past professional top-class cricketer, who had represented his home country, India, on a few occasions in the past, had played the limited version for one of the home counties, still played well and was the club's residential professional as well as captain of the first eleven. He occasionally thought himself unlucky, to be past his best, when big money came into the game but had enjoyed his experiences.

With the money he had made, he invested in a small hotel in Luton and employed a friend and his wife to run it. Realising the advantage of being close to the airport and the M1, he advertised special discreet adult parties for couples, and when spreading the word around to his sporting contacts, also learned there would be a good market if he could provide female partners for unaccompanied men, but occasions like that would need to be separate from the 'swingers' events.

Opening the bar to the public, with special very low prices for unaccompanied ladies, attracted quite a few young girls who may not have been served in other bars. They were encouraged to bring their girl friends, and Javendra invited some of his cricketing colleagues to balance the mixture of the sexes. The girls were a mixture of white and Asian and,

as they paired up, the hotel manager would quietly let it be known that rooms could be rented by the hour.

Javendra did not hesitate to use his natural good looks, turn on the charm, and use alcohol to persuade some of the girls to accompany strangers, rewarding them with a small fee for doing so. It was his friend, the manager, who introduced drugs, which would be sold to the paying clients and given to the girls to 'get them in the mood' to entertain men. It was also his idea to advertise in newsagents near the main London stations for trainee 'adult models' who were prepared to travel to Luton, resulting in at least one girl a week turning up for an interview. One such young lady was Carolyn Droy who had come from Gloucestershire to the city, hoping to become an actress. She had succumbed to the temptation to model and turned up at the hotel with a portfolio of nude photographs of herself.

Carolyn believed she possessed good looks, but was perhaps unaware of how beautiful and attractive she really was, oozing sex appeal from the top of her dyed blonde elongated locks, cascading to her gorgeous shoulders, to the tip of her well-managed nails of her size five dainty feet. Her perfectly shaped oval face, straight nose and high cheekbones, sensuous mouth, flawless complexion and wide hazel-coloured eyes were an incredible combination of youthful innocence and sexual promise. Her graceful shoulders led to slender arms, jutting proud breasts providing self-support, smooth flat stomach down to incredible thighs, the commencement of long legs which were surely designed for someone taller than her modest five feet five inches.

Unable to find work in London, Carolyn was desperate to earn money, and although disappointed and felt she had been conned by the advertisement, Javendra plied her with

alcohol, charmed her and paid her over the normal rate to spend a couple of hours with a visiting cricketer from the West Indies. Having a drink with Javendra afterwards, she was advised she could stay the night at the hotel, provided she shared a bed with him. Although beautiful with an unbelievable body, it was soon apparent her enthusiasm for sex on this occasion was somewhat limited, either due to excessive alcohol or feeling she had been coerced into it. Whilst copulation took place and he achieved his orgasm, there was not much response from his partner.

A second night's stay proved totally different, thanks to his friend, the hotel manager, providing a small pill which Carolyn was persuaded to swallow before they went to the room. She was insatiable, the extremely fit and athletic Indian struggling to keep up with her demands as she refused to let him sleep, demanding more and more of his highly toned body and it was almost daylight before he was allowed any respite. An exhausted Javendra slept until noon, leaving the still sleeping girl as he dressed and went downstairs to be greeted by his friend, grinning broadly as he asked him about his night to be answered by a sheepish thumbs up sign.

When Carolyn eventually surfaced, he advised her he had to go out on business, but asked her if she would stay another night, waving aside her objections about no clean underwear by handing money to his friend's wife, who was asked to take the girl to the shops in town to purchase the required garments.

Three days later, he drove her to London to collect her meagre belongings and moved her permanently into one of the hotel bedrooms. He persuaded her to entertain other men which, with the assistance of the little pills, proved not difficult to do and reports from highly satisfied customers

were very favourable. Her looks were absolutely stunning and the wife of his friend was entrusted to take the girl shopping for sexy clothes designed to enhance her beauty.

Two other girls from the growing collection, one white and one Asian, were also offered permanent accommodation and money, in respect of providing services as and when required. Other girls congregated in the bar and were allowed access to the rooms if they wished to entertain a client, paying by the hour and charging whatever fee they could extract from the men. Creating a small collection of photographs on his phone, Javendra would readily show them to anyone he met. He would visit the larger hotels in the town, search the bar for unaccompanied males and engage them in conversation, quickly getting to the point of what he was offering. He learned how to accept the rejection but brought in many clients. Taking the operation a stage further, he bribed the hotel concierges and provided glossy pictures of the girls and contact details of the hotel. Encouraging the concierges to enlist the assistance of waiters and bar staff by sharing their payments, he introduced a bonus system, carefully recording where the clients were sent from, and providing an envelope filled with cash to his main contact at each hotel.

Still having his own share of the favours of Carolyn, he took care of his own physical needs. Under the effects of the pills, she became a wanton, hungry, demanding sex object who could not get enough of what, with the help of the drugs, became her favourite pastime. As the effects wore off, she would retire into her shell, quiet and a little sullen with few signs of contentment or satisfaction with her lot. Javendra struggled to have any kind of meaningful conversation with

her, finding her reluctant to enlighten anyone with details of her past. The situation changed one afternoon when, unusually, she had no clients, but had a few drinks although without the pills. Slightly drunk and off guard, she told the Indian he had no idea of life in the real world and confessed to him she had been sexually abused by her father, pimped out by her mother and had a baby girl who was taken away from her, all before she reached the age of fifteen.

Javendra changed his attitude and pressed her for more information over the days, weeks and months. He became fascinated and fond of her and occasionally took her out for the afternoon. He found that, after a couple of drinks, she would loosen up, could become quite pleasant but emotional, and would clam up if she continued drinking.

Receiving invitations to sporting events, he risked taking her along, but watched her carefully in respect of her alcohol consumption.

On the way home from one such event, she surprised him by bluntly asking, 'Am I your trophy girlfriend like some men have trophy wives? Same as Julia Roberts and Richard Gere?'

Familiar with the film *Pretty Woman*, he was surprised at her reference to it, although had often seen it advertised amongst other favourites on bank holiday weekends.

Having long since lost time of the date when his legitimate stay in the UK was scheduled to end, his memory was rudely awakened when he received a letter inviting him to an interview to discuss the situation. It took much rummaging through his desk to find the documentation confirming he had only a short time left on his visa. He used the time to persuade Carolyn to become his wife in order to

guarantee his continued stay. The low-key event took place at the local registry office, followed by a buffet at the hotel and as a honeymoon treat, the girl was relived of her entertaining duties for two nights, but back on duty on the third.

Accumulating a large amount of cash had tremendous benefits, but was not easy to invest without attracting the attention of Her Majesty's Customs and Inland Revenue. Having met him at the cricket club, he had talked to accountant Hugh Barker, providing a brief and guarded description of his business, and decided he was not the person to ask how he could retain the profits made.

Using cash which he made from the seedy side of the hotel and the girls, he invested in several small catering and convenience stores, mostly run by Asians, for whom he provided part of the funding in return for interest rates which were higher than banks. The attraction to the client was that he was far more informal than banks, whilst he relied on them to work hard in order to make the operation pay, enabling them to repay him. Only twice had he encountered difficulties when clients fell into arrears and, on each occasion, he visited the property with two friends who were equally fit and athletic, and whose appearances persuaded the clients it made sense to pay up.

Also using his cash and the income from his present operation, he invested in buy to let properties and had built up a substantial portfolio in the UK and abroad. Although still owning the hotel, he reduced his day-to-day involvement in the running of it, but occasionally his wife and he participated in the pleasures of the intermittent, but money-spinning meetings, of like-minded swingers.

As his standing in the community developed, Javendra was invited to, and expected to attend, more events which

were dominated by couples. Frightened his wife's upbringing and attitude may cause embarrassment, in Eleanor he had seen someone who was very attractive for her age and also seemed to possess charm. He wanted to find out if she was prepared to help him train his own wife in how to behave.

CHAPTER 22

The day was incredibly calm following howling gales, which had ripped through the area during the night, rattling windows and doors and, according to the television, resulted in trees falling down in some parts. The storm had now passed as the sun was rising behind him as the colonel entered the field.

His thoughts were on the previous day's visit to London when his partner, who by now should be his ex-partner, had made his proposal.

The purpose of the visit was to collect the final instalment in the pay out, so the business now became the property of Michael O'Flanagan who, having shown tremendous ability, loyalty, dedication and provided unbelievable hard work, Cedric looked no further than when thinking of finding a buyer for the business. Not requiring an initial deposit, Cedric came up with a payment proposal plan, which would allow the younger man to pay in instalments over a period of three years. Cedric was confident that, provided the business kept running properly and did not take too much for himself, Michael would have no problem finding the payments for this. He had built in a clause which would have enabled them to take back the business at any time should the payments not be made, but he was confident Michael would ensure that would not happen. The colonel had been proved right and,

apart from just a few late payments due to very short-term cash flow problems, Michael had kept his part of the bargain

Over their traditional lunch, the young man had surprised his senior partner by asking him to undertake the responsibilities of staying on in the business as chairman, but with a smaller shareholding than before. He had been offered a retainer figure for his continued participation. Cedric did not need the money and certainly did not need to work, not that it involved much: bi-monthly trips to London and occasional meetings when he would be rolled out as the head of the organisation, very useful when dealing with major clients, occasionally bank managers.

Cedric had been surprised to see Glenda Wilkinson, the bank manager's wife, in Soho and was not totally convinced of her explanation as to why she was there. He always thought on her as being a little pompous and stand-offish, very like her husband and had been quite amused at the encounter.

'Good morning, dear lady.'

Glenda stopped in shock, recognising Colonel Cedric Foster-Clarkson. She immediately flushed up in embarrassment, having been caught in the seedy part of Soho, but quickly regaining her composure, responded to the greeting.

'Good morning, Colonel. How nice to see you. This area is like a maze, isn't it? I've been booking theatre tickets, but also a friend told me about some herbal remedy shop which is in this area. I'm afraid I've left the exact address at home and have wasted some time having to look for it. What brings you to Soho?'

He smiled. 'Sadly, not the high life, madam. Those days are long gone. I have an interest in a business that needs an inexpensive office and many of these are to be found in

this area. The overheads are low and, in this case, it's not important to have a flash glass-fronted office to attract the customers. Enjoy the rest of your search and I hope you find what you're looking for.'

Judging character and reactions had played a major role in his success and, occasionally, even survival in life, and he believed he'd been lied to by the woman, but also decided it was nothing to do with him and she could be assured his lips were sealed.

She thought she detected some sarcasm and disbelief in her story, hoping he wouldn't refer to the visit to anyone, but made a mental note to stick to the story of the herbal shop, having seen one along her walk.

CHAPTER 23

It was a little misty and when Eleanor thought she was going to have the whole walk to herself, she and her dogs met up with an elderly couple with a beagle who were stood talking to a much younger couple whose dog, she learned, was a cross between a cocker and springer spaniel. The four dogs had a whale of a time, jumping, running, chasing or playing extremely happily as the five adults stood chatting. Within ten minutes Eleanor learned the elderly couple had lost their daughter and son-in-law in the 2004 tsunami when they had gone to Thailand on honeymoon following a decision to get married, although already having a son and daughter. The devastated couple had been left to bring up the two grandchildren, who by now were grown up and had provided the couple with great grandchildren who they occasionally had to look after.

The younger couple admitted to living in the town, but occasionally drove out to the fields in order to allow their dog to enjoy the company of others. They parted, the young couple going in the opposite direction whilst Eleanor continued talking to the elderly couple who she quickly found to be an absolute hive of information, listing many of the dogs Eleanor had already met and providing information about the owners. The beagle, poodle and mongrel continued playing happily with one another, all extremely fleet of foot,

full of energy and eager to play as they ran around in circles, then took turns in chasing one another, happy to have the freedom to do as they pleased.

The owners conversed about the weather, the political situation in the country and the cricket test match score somewhere abroad, in which she had not the slightest interest. With the conversation moving on to race abuse, ethnic minorities and the enforcement being put in by law in order to try to make sure these were integrated, the man talked about some volunteer work which he did. He emphasised that even there they had to have a strict policy on equal opportunities which, if not followed, could limit their ability to raise funds for the particular charity for which he worked.

They also advised her it was their great grandson's birthday, that he would be five years old and that his sister was now seven.

As they eventually parted, prompted by the reference to ethnicity, Eleanor's thoughts strayed to Javendra Bhattacharya, her day's outing with the Indian man and restless night which followed, sleep interrupted with thoughts of whether or not she should take up his offer and could she actually achieve what he wanted. She was also disturbed that she had felt excited and comfortable at the same time in his company and being pampered by the waiters in his employ. The meal at the restaurant, in which he had an investment, had been absolutely fantastic, and there was a magnetism about her host who showed nothing but politeness and charm, both to herself and his staff.

She interrupted her thoughts to look round for the dogs. She thought she could see their shapes in the distance, decided against whistling for them, but scolded herself as

she realised the animals were getting quite wet. Then she returned her mind to the Indian.

She had only met his wife briefly at the fashion show, finding her quiet and subdued, but now understanding the reason behind the behaviour. As for coaching the young lady in airs and graces, Eleanor did not see this as too much of a problem, provided the girl wished to learn. She also had to consider the Indian as a possible client for her project on improving the life of Alexander, and she was already beginning to feel awkward about her relationship with the man, although he had already given her plenty of ammunition to use against him.

She also felt a little frightened of him and shuddered at the thought of his reaction if he found out it was part of her plan to extract money from him. Her thoughts were interrupted as she realised that, whilst Marilyn was close by, the little mongrel was nowhere to be seen. She used her whistle to no effect so, with the poodle alongside her, she retraced her steps towards where she had last seen the little one and was rewarded to see the white body and black ears galloping towards her. Reunited, the dogs ran off together, quickly disappearing into the mist again, which seemed to have got denser since she set out although she had now moved out to the hollow, where it undoubtedly sat heavier and more concentrated.

As far as she could see, the rest of the field was deserted, then her thoughts were interrupted by the ringing of her mobile phone, reminding her she had set off early but had also forgotten to change the alarm time from the previous day.

Brain still racing, she decided to carry out the second half circuit of her usual course, thoughts once again returning to the possible task of educating the young woman.

'Of course, I will pay you,' the Indian had explained, 'Think about it and how much you would want to charge which I suggest we discus later. Perhaps I can call you in a few days, and you can meet my wife in order to see how you feel.'

Again, she realised Rags had disappeared and decided she needed to concentrate fully, this time becoming a little concerned when there was no response to the whistle. So, she stood with the poodle and gave four more long blasts. Eventually, Rags returned, face decidedly black with mud. Pausing just long enough to reassure her mistress she was okay, Rags bounded back from whence she came causing Eleanor to go back to find out what the attraction was and persuade the little one to join them again.

Mentally reprimanding herself for not giving the dogs her full concentration, Eleanor gave a huge sigh, then set off with the poodle to look for the smaller one.

CHAPTER 24

Henrietta Barker breathed through her nose and tried to stop herself gagging as she felt the head of the huge black penis at the back of her throat push urgently, opening her throat as she swallowed as much as she possibly could. She raised her eyes to try to look at the face of the owner of the giant phallus, but could only see his hand, holding the phone with which he was videoing the scene. She moved her head back, released her mouth from the rod, gulped in as much air as she could and returned to her task. Henrietta had used her laptop to watch women swallow similar sized weapons until their noses rubbed against the pubic hair of their partners, and she was stubbornly determined to achieve the same result.

She slowly took a fraction more of the invading monster, lubricated by her own saliva. Each time, she bobbed her head down and had almost captured all of it, when she felt his powerful hand push her head closer, holding her in position as he pushed himself forwards until her nose touched his abdomen. The deprivation of oxygen produced a cocktail of fear, dizziness and incredible excitement until she had to force her head back, gasping for air. Giving her partner a triumphant gaze, she opened her mouth again and used her lips to masturbate the glans until, accompanied by his

loud groans, she felt the sweet tasting liquid spill into her welcoming mouth.

Returning from the conference room at the Manchester hotel, they had hurried to his room on the fifth floor, taking advantage of the lunch break to spend as much time as possible enjoying their sexual pleasures. Arriving in time for dinner the previous evening, they had used her room shortly after devouring a hurried meal, and spent most of the night making love, until he returned to his own room at 5 a.m. Excitement and anticipation had reduced the feeling of fatigue and they had managed to concentrate on the first morning, struggled to keep a reasonable distance between them, and could not resist the lunchtime opportunity. Apart from kicking off her shoes, she was still fully dressed, whilst he had discarded shoes, trousers and boxer shorts to facilitate her fellatio.

Sadly, there was insufficient time for him to reciprocate as they quickly tidied themselves up before joining colleagues for the buffet lunch.

Henrietta struggled to concentrate during the afternoon session, but made the effort as she appreciated the importance of the topic. The speaker talked a great deal about resilience, how the reduction in competitive sport had an effect on this and which, in turn, was also partially responsible for the increase in mental health issues amongst the young. The seating arrangements had been deliberately designed to split up colleagues who worked together, so Eugene was a few tables away from where she sat, and also had his back to her so eye contact was difficult without being obvious. Thinking she was behaving like some besotted teenager, she felt smug and at the same time almost proud of her

lunchtime achievement as her thoughts regularly strayed to the experience.

When he had pressed her head in the successful effort to force all of his gross tool in her throat, the prevention of oxygen, whilst frightening, had stimulated her senses and she had almost orgasmed herself. She had read about accidental asphyxiation when sex games had gone wrong and, carrying out her own research on porn sites, had observed men hold their hands around partners' throats, wondering if that induced the same effect. Staring at the back of her lover, her mind filled with anticipation at the coming night's adventures, and wondered how soon they could leave the dining room without attracting too much attention. Perhaps sensing her stare, he turned, smiled and winked at her, leaving her hoping that no one had noticed but unable to prevent herself blushing.

The vast majority of the group made for the bar in the short interval between the end of the day's activities and the time when dinner was available. Tables had been allocated as part of the special rate for the lunch, but at least she was able to sit next to Eugene during the three-course menu. When most returned to the bar, Henrietta claimed to have brought work with her and went straight to her room with Eugene excusing himself after just one drink.

Depositing his papers in his room, avoiding the lift, he went down one flight of stairs, where the light tap on her door brought an instant response. Removal of the light robe exposed the freshly showered naked body, which he scooped up into his arms and carried to the large bed, placing her across the width of it.

Following a lengthy passionate tongue twisting kiss, he pulled his mouth away and whispered, 'Your turn.'

Pulling her hips to the edge of the bed and placing his huge biceps under her thighs which opened to allow access, he buried his face between them.

For more than half an hour, she luxuriated in the manipulations of his tongue, lips and fingers, climaxing twice, clutching the crinkly hair as she did so.

As they lay together afterwards, she related her earlier feelings and thoughts about lack of oxygen as she fondled his hardening penis. When she swallowed it again, this time with her lower lips as he powered into her with long, slow, vigorous thrusts and at her request, when his own climax approached, he grasped her throat until she called out 'enough' feeling herself soaring into a mass of coloured lights.

CHAPTER 25

Colonel Cedric Foster-Clarkson was only half-heartedly paying attention to the dogs as they played with one another when he noticed the old dear in the distance with her small dogs who, on seeing the labradors, put her own on the lead. As always, on the rare occasions when he saw her, he wondered why she bothered bringing small dogs to an open field where there were always other dogs around if she did not want them to take part in the regular activities. He made a slight detour to avoid going close to her; his mind racing over the events of the previous evening.

Much to his surprise and delight, he had been asked to stand for the position of local mayor in the forthcoming elections in May. There was no question of him having to be elected onto the council as his seat was not due for renewal. As usual, amongst the Conservatives who had dominated the council for years, it was standard practice that the deputy mayor would step up and take over from his or her predecessor. Unfortunately, the current holder of the position had advised his fellow councillors on the previous evening that, due to illness, he had decided not to put himself forward, immediately standing down as deputy to pave the way for whoever they decided on. Several of the party members had already served a term as mayor, so the colonel had been the choice of his fellow councillors and had agreed

to undertake the position. His mind now wandered, seeing photographs of himself in the local newspaper opening shops, talking to school children, attending garden fetes and so on. He had been advised he would have a generous expenses pot in order to enable him to fulfil his engagement and access to a chauffeur-driven car. After the meeting, half a dozen of them had adjourned to the local pub, so by the time he got home, his wife was already in bed asleep and still slumbered on as he had hastily dressed to bring the dogs out for their morning constitution.

Engrossed in his thoughts, he suddenly realised one of the labradors was missing but a quick blast on his high-pitched whistle brought it running from somewhere in the bushes to join him. Whilst there were a few clouds around, the sky was fairly clear, the wind still, and the sun already showing its redness towards the east. He much preferred the summer when he could bring the dogs out at six as, unlike a couple of his fellow walkers, he refused to wander around locating dog poo by torchlight and didn't really see the point of it. Whilst sympathising with those who had to go to work, after ensuring the dogs had received sufficient exercise, he was thankful he did not suffer the same problem. He was jolted out of his reverie by a cheerful greeting.

'Good morning, Colonel.'

He saw Eleanor following along behind her dogs, who started mingling with the labradors. Bursting to tell someone about the recent events, he decided to take the woman into his confidence and explained he would become the local mayor in the coming May. She was really enthusiastic and genuine in her congratulations, assured him he must have deserved it, and he obviously had the confidence of his fellow members of the local council.

'I'm sure you will do really well,' she said as they stood and watched the animals play together. 'Don't forget, if your duties make it difficult for you to walk the dogs, I'm always available.'

She smiled and, not for the first time, he noticed what an attractive woman she was, but then quickly reprimanded himself. As mayor, he was expected to be clean living and free from any scandal. They exchanged a few more pleasantries, before going off in different directions with their dogs.

CHAPTER 26

Eleanor sat at the kitchen table, a calculator by her side, a four lined pad, one red pen, one black, the third one blue and also a pencil, complete with eraser at the end.

She had decided to create a budget of known expenditure and possible and probable income in order for her to plan her finances. She viewed the care of Alexander as a project, almost a business proposition, and the people, present and future, supplying the funding as her clients.

Pausing for a sip of the coffee steaming in a mug beside her, she started listing, in red ink, the items against which she would put costs. These included the major items of care for Alexander, but also her own living costs including food, tax and insurance on her small car, petrol, electricity and gas, for which she had a dual arrangement, water, dog expenses including vet bills and food, and her own food and clothing.

As for council tax, she had no need to worry about that as her circumstances allowed her to claim exemption. That in itself represented quite a saving, and even if they had known about it, the small amount which she received for dog walking would not affect this. Her other income, of course, was totally hidden away.

Meticulously, she listed the various allowances which she received, in blue ink, including the contribution from cleaning the dress shop.

Her biggest problem was the huge mortgage, although with Richard Fothergill's assistance, she had an arrangement whereby she only paid a nominal amount at present, but that would not continue for much longer. She was also sensible enough to realise the 'other money' which she was bringing in would not be easy to use.

One of her reasons for the budget was to help her calculate how much she should charge the Indian for coaching his wife, having decided that may play a major part in sorting out her financial dilemma.

Having scoured the internet to see what kind of money various consultants and life coaches charged, Eleanor came up with a figure which she felt was extortionate but decided to make a pitch for it, prepared to be cut back if necessary. When she telephoned him, they agreed to meet at the village pub for lunch.

The eighteenth-century building was run by Terence Smart and Trevor Fletcher, and had built up an excellent reputation in the area. Trevor, in his mid-forties, was an airline pilot, flying mostly package tours from Luton airport. He had encountered Terence, twenty years his junior, working in a bar in Malaga whilst on a stopover. Quite camp, the younger man was obvious about his sexuality, offering no objection when Trevor invited him back to his hotel. The experience had been repeated twice more before Trevor, who had not been in a serious relationship for over two years, asked the younger man if he fancied moving back to England.

A keen amateur cook, Trevor suggested the possibility of them finding a country pub or restaurant. Free of any ties, Terry agreed to consider the idea and, using an agent who specialised in the business, Trevor brought Terence over to view three possible sites, of which the one in the village

became their selected choice, and free spirit Terence packed his bags and they took over the business. The freehold was in Trevor's name only, but both names appeared above the door of the pub as joint holders of the licence. As Trevor continued flying in order to subsidise the operation, they took on a part-time cook to fill in during his absence. Referred to by some of the locals occasionally as Tweedledum and Tweedledee, the pair were very popular, putting on occasional quizzes and other entertainment, although it was their catering which was the biggest money spinner, with people travelling from the town and surrounding villages to enjoy both lunchtime and evening delicacies.

The pair were quite contrasting in looks. Trevor, at about five-foot-ten, was stocky with very dark thinning hair. Terence must have been six-foot-two, lean and lithe, with a slim waist many women would give their right arm for, with his already blonde hair dyed even lighter. Whilst he wore his homosexuality with overt pride, Trevor came across as being very masculine.

Their sexuality being no secret, despite getting access to their computer, Alexander could find nothing suitable as blackmail material and when he tried to set up a direct debit it was quickly spotted by whoever operated the computer, cancelled and passwords changed instantly.

Having ordered the dish of the day, a minted lamb shank, from Terence who could not keep his eyes off her companion, Eleanor made her presentation, having produced detailed notes of her financial situation to which she constantly referred. She emphasised she had to care for a son with disabilities and, under pressure to be open about her true situation, she allowed the businessman to look at the account details which she had prepared. After he studied them, she,

perhaps recklessly, agreed that Javendra could come to her house after lunch and meet Alexander, but not before being tempted by Terence into trying a speciality cheesecake.

'Are you my mother's boyfriend?' Alexander asked on his voice machine.

Although taken off guard at the immediate directness, Javendra smiled at the boy as he tried to figure out his reply to the very unexpected question.

'Well, Alexander, I like to think that I am a friend. As for boy, I think I long ago ceased to qualify for that particular adjective to describe me, don't you?'

There was a pause as Alexander worked on his machine to compose the next question.

'Why are you here?'

'That is easy,' the Indian replied. 'Your mother told me about the wonderful son which she has, and I have to confess I asked if there was any possibility of meeting the impressive young man about whom I had heard so much. Do you have a problem with that, Alexander?'

Again, there was hesitation to allow the youngster to transfer his thoughts into words and the machine spoke.

'Why are you interested in my mother?'

Eleanor intervened. 'I told you, darling. Javendra has asked me to do some work for him and, of course, I talked about you and he said he would be interested in meeting you. It's very helpful for people to know one another when they're working together and he just wanted to know more about my family and you are my family.'

'What kind of work?'

The question could have been addressed to either of them, but the man chose to answer.

'I have someone very close to me who has a few problems. Your mother has very kindly agreed to help and I'm really grateful for this.'

More hesitation before the machine replied. 'My mother is not a doctor.'

The Indian smiled at Alexander.

'You are right, of course, she's not a doctor. However, I'm sure you don't need me to tell you this is an extremely caring, considerate, passionate lady, who is totally unselfish and, in my opinion, very highly qualified to help me with my problem. You see, the young lady in question is my wife. She is very young, much younger than myself but is experiencing all sorts of issues. I have tried my best but failed to solve the problems, some of which are minor, others more serious. It's true I have only met your mother fairly recently but she has, of course, met my wife who is happy for your mother to help us. Whilst it is a kind of business relationship, it is also based on personal interaction.'

Alexander did not appear to be either convinced or happy, suddenly feeling he would have to share the affection of his devoted mother.

'Will you have the time, Mother? What about me?'

CHAPTER 27

The sun was rising in the east and a pale half moon was still high in the sky in the west as Colonel Foster-Clarkson entered the field, grass covered with a light dusting of white frost and a mist blocking the view down in the hollow. Ahead of him, he espied a woman with a golden retriever and a brown and white spaniel, both on their leads. As he caught them up, the pair paused to discuss the weather for a few seconds and both continued on their journeys in opposite directions.

Feeling an ache in his thighs, he put it down to the previous day's golf, but he had awoken three times during the night with painful muscles, blaming a combination of his tablets, the golf and alcohol after the game for the bouts of cramp which had caused considerable discomfort. Two trips to the bathroom had eased the situation as he had stood on the cold tiles in an effort to reduce the pain.

By the time he reached the bottom of the field, the mist lifted completely. He could see, through the trees, the bright red sun making its way into the now clear blue sky, punctuated by a vapour trail from a distant aircraft, no doubt destined for foreign soil with a combination of holidaymakers and business people on board.

He had remembered to put on his scarf, but regretted not having included gloves as his hand holding the leads became very cold, the other one deep into his pocket for warmth.

He was looking forward to a busy day, very much out of his normal routine and whilst not as exciting as many people's daily lives, he looked forward to the change, not least of which was to dress more formally than usual.

Owning two types of white shirts, the colour of which he preferred for the majority of the time, he owned two batches with two differences. The newer ones, whilst a fraction whiter than the others, had smaller buttons and buttonholes which he struggled with on occasion due to his arthritic fingers.

Today, which he considered important, he selected one of the more pristine items of clothing, regretting it almost instantly as he struggled to fasten the second button down. His fingers located the button without problem, but the numbness in the index and first finger of his hand made him struggle with locating the buttonhole in which to insert it. It took him several seconds, which seemed even longer, until he eventually succeeded, then had no problem with the next few buttons. The bottom one he couldn't master and changed to concentrate on the buttonholes in the cuffs where he had a selection of two different buttons on each and managed to fasten the outer one in each case without too much difficulty. Returning to the bottom button of the shirt, his frustration eased this time, locating button and hole immediately, and carefully threaded one through the other.

Having already donned light grey trousers, he selected a multi-coloured tie, staring at himself in the full length mirror as he struggled to fasten the top button having knotted the tie with the Windsor knot, still his preference.

Eventually, satisfied with the result, he selected a lightweight dark blue pinstripe jacket, whose matching

trousers long since ceased to fit, but he was reluctant to throw away the jacket, still in pretty good condition.

He realised this was an important day with the fitting of hearing aids for which he had already been tested, followed by a meeting at the Town Hall to check the robes of deputy mayor.

Collected from the waiting room by a young woman wearing a very colourful bright striped dress, which showed her more than generous curves indicating excessive weight, he actually complimented her on the attire, advising he just been looking at a magazine article, which referred to decorating, but encouraged people to be bold.

'Your dress is certainly bold, my dear,' he told her.

Smiling gratefully, whilst inwardly feeling she was in the company of a lecherous old man, she swept her long hair back, invited him to take a seat and carried out the checking of the hearing aids.

Placing each one carefully in his ears, she played some recording of noises, different sounds, varying from high, middle and low pitch, advising him he needed to do nothing. She then removed the aids, placed some apparatus around his shoulders and played some more sound, this time through a speaker. These included a lady speaking different languages and he could not understand what was being said, despite recognising Spanish and German.

This particular exercise finalised, she then replaced his own new hearing aids in his ears and commenced to make various adjustments. At the end of this, she explained the controls to him, telling him how he could switch off the rear of the two microphones if he was in a really noisy area,

showed him how to insert the batteries in the correct position and also how to turn the units off and clean them.

Leaving the hospital with hearing aids in place, he first noticed the sounds of his own footsteps echoing in the long corridor, certainly something he had not heard on the way in. Outside, his feet crunched on salt that had been used to safeguard against the recent late frost and again he would not have heard the sound earlier.

Crossing the road, he made his way back to his car, got inside and jumped when he turned on the ignition, the loudness of the radio seeming much higher than it had been previously, due to his now assisted hearing.

The young lady had warned him he would need to get used to the hearing aids and they would adjust themselves the longer he persevered.

Hearing the car engine louder than ever before, he drove to the Town Hall and parked the car in a reserved space. He entered the impressive building, introduced himself to the lady receptionist and was escorted to the mayor's parlour. The mayor was already there as was Fay, part-time estate agent and part-time seamstress. Accepting the offer of coffee and a digestive biscuit, he allowed the mayor to help him on with the robes of the deputy mayor, panicking as they were clearly much too short for him.

Helping to remove them, Fay quickly allayed his fears as, turning them inside out, she indicated the very large hems inside, smiling at him as she announced, 'I can make these fit anyone from four-foot-nine to six-foot-six and you look to fit into that category to me.'

Busily unpicking cotton with a small pair of sharp scissors, she helped him put the robes back on and kneeled by his side with a mouthful of pins. She adjusted the length

to make it the right height from the floor then turned her attention to the sleeves.

Gathering up the garments, she announced she would return within the hour, leaving the two men to enjoy more coffee. During the hour, the colonel was invited by the mayor to stand in for him on a local event, but the second was a little more demanding. Cedric's first official engagement on the following day was attending the opening of a local charity shop, but the second, due in a few days' time, was a much more complicated event. Concerned with recent scandals of harassment by people in power, the council had joined many others in agreeing to allow its senior people to attend a two-day training course on how to behave in public office. Wives or partners were encouraged to attend and the Home Secretary would be guest speaker, alongside the contracted training organisation. Leeds had been selected as the venue for the forthcoming course and all expenses for the necessary overnight stay would be met.

His head was still spinning a little with the pace at which things were moving, when Fay returned with the robes which now fit perfectly.

After carrying out his duties the following day, he returned to the Town Hall to discard his robes, then drove home to an enthusiastic greeting by the dogs, his wife having gone to London to purchase the appropriate clothing for the forthcoming trip.

Changing into his slippers, he climbed the stairs to his office, looked through his neat collection of business cards, selected the one with details of the dog walker, picked up the telephone and made the fateful call.

CHAPTER 28

Being collected by the Indian in his car, Eleanor felt guilty as they lunched at the hotel where she usually met with the accountant, but her fears were swept away as he offered to not only meet her original terms, but to exceed them. He overcame some of her objections by telling her some of the money would be paid in cash, and advised her to use this for clothes, food purchases and any luxuries, but not those which carried guarantees. After they had agreed the financial details, he called for champagne and consuming this after wine which accompanied lunch, Eleanor found herself relax, enjoying the occasion. When they followed the champagne with an after-lunch brandy with coffee, feeling quite light headed, she did not argue at his suggestion that he needed a rest before driving, allowing herself to accompany him to a bedroom on the second floor.

Memories of getting out of their clothes were vague. Eleanor squirmed as the Indian held her two wrists in one powerful hand, kissing her gently at first and then with more urgency. His lips nibbled at her throat and slowly and agonisingly moved down to her nipples, which had become erect and felt on fire. His moustache tickled her skin as his tongue licked against first one nipple and then the other before, shielding his teeth, he gently nibbled at them, drawing them into his mouth, enlarging them even

further. She thought they were going to burst as he toyed with them, but felt disappointment as his lips abandoned the nipples. Her legs trembled as she felt his tongue travelling south and involuntarily her thighs parted in anticipation. She experienced a moment of frustration as the lips bypassed her nether regions, moving down her left leg, kissing and licking her thigh down to the knee.

There was a further pause as he changed position, moved down the bed and continued working on her leg, licking and kissing down to the ankle, swapping to the other one, and retracing his journey back up her body. Again, shifting position, his tongue licked the inside of both thighs, then he used it to part her lower lips and seek out the already throbbing clitoris, beginning to slowly manipulate it with his tongue, flicking his muscle from side to side and then up and down. He placed an arm under each of her knees as he dived deeper into her being with his tongue, now penetrating the already soaking wet tunnel guarding the entrance to her body. For the first time in her life, she felt a moustache tickling and tantalising the erect clitoris and lifted her head slightly so she could look down at him. He must have sensed this as, simultaneously, he looked up at her and, as the pair locked eyes together, she pushed her body up to meet him.

Eleanor was flying, floating on a cloud of ecstasy never experienced before in her life, not even when she masturbated herself, and certainly for the first time ever with a companion. She felt the change as one of his thumbs stroked the wetness of her labia and then inched its way inside her vagina, and she felt her lower lips clutching at the invasive digit.

Her senses floated between the facial hair teasing the nerve ends of her bud and the thumb, now joined by two fingers, stretching her lubricating insides. A fleeting thought

flashed through her brain, wondering if this was to become a regular part of what was expected from her to earn her money, half hoping it was, as she clamped her thighs against the double invasion of her being. Desperately trying to extend the sensation, she eventually surrendered, a kaleidoscope of colour flashing before her eyes as she reached orgasm, her complete body shaking uncontrollably.

He moved up to lay alongside her, arm around her as she snuggled in his embrace. Kissing her gently but firmly, the dark eyes stared into her soul as he pulled his mouth away to quietly advise her.

'I hope you're not in a hurry to leave as 'm going to suck and fuck you until you cannot walk.'

Without further hesitation, he placed his penis between her legs, forced it inside her, meeting little resistance as she was already wet, and immediately commenced his pounding. Again, her brain recycled the multitude of thoughts, but she pushed these to one side as her body opened up to welcome the intruder. All she could do was put her arms around his neck and clutch him as she endured the vigorous thrusting in and out. She wrapped her legs around him, making her body even more open as the violation continued, thrusting, piercing, poking. It was vicious, it was violent, but she welcomed every millisecond of it, giving her body up, adjusting to and enjoying the rhythm of the invading tool, experiencing feelings which she had never felt before, exhilaration in being possessed. Her nails raked his back as she recognised the voice which was her own, urging him on to greater effort.

Her body surrendered itself to him as the onslaught continued for she knew not how long until she felt a rapid acceleration in his movement and heard a deep groan,

surrendered her mouth and tongue to his, and his sperm emptied deep inside her as she pulled the perspiration covered, muscled, sleek body to her bosom.

Alexander realised Ahmed had changed his life and attitude dramatically. Always aware his parents and everyone else constantly failed to give him credit for his intelligence and mental ability and whilst his father had recognised his skills with computers, he did not appreciate the other things in which his son had taken an interest. The majority of people also just seemed to recognise the teenager in a wheelchair, probably not even considering what type of brain lay behind the inquisitive eyes. As a result, in the main, Alexander retired to his shell, and even though he was now playing a major part in the survival of the family, he believed even his mother saw him as being one-dimensional.

The Asian had done much to change the situation and Alexander's own feelings about himself. Triggered by Alexander's exclamation of 'fuck' during their love-making, Ahmed worked with him patiently and painstakingly until gradually his vocabulary increased and, although very slowly, the youngster managed to string a few words together. He himself wondered if it had been some kind of mental block that had prevented him from using this method of communication, but now became a willing pupil as his carer patiently helped him to pronounce new words, starting with very basic three and four letter ones, feeling rewarded when Alexander was sufficiently able to make it clear what he was trying to say. As for the boy himself, the increased ability to express himself, both verbally and sexually, provided him with a new purpose in life and a determination to widen his own horizons.

Whilst in the past, he had shied away from public appearances, when Ahmed was available to accompany them, he would occasionally go into town with his mother on a food shopping trip and, accompanied by his friend, would dutifully follow her around the supermarket in his chair. On the rare occasions when fellow shoppers would take the trouble to address him, his initial response would be via his computer which contained an introductory message saying he could speak, but it was slow and would require the patience of the listener. Both his mother and Ahmed had learned not to interfere and talk on his behalf, and although it didn't happen very often, he did occasionally enjoy a two-way conversation. One such occasion happened when they met a girl, also in an electric wheelchair, and whose speech was not much quicker or clearer than Alexander's. She told him she lived in the town and, just before Eleanor and the girl's father reached the checkout, the man suggested they meet for a coffee in the supermarket café, so the youngsters could continue their conversation. Somewhat reluctantly, Eleanor agreed, but then was very pleased she had done so. Never before having seen her son engage in such a meaningful conversation with someone in a similar situation to himself, she really enjoyed the experience.

The girl told him how she had, with considerable help, scaled a climbing wall, learned how to cook, went to the specialist college where she was learning sport and led quite a busy life.

As the adults drank their coffee, the young pair chatted away, including Ahmed as the girl, whose name they discovered to be Daisy, told the others about a day centre which she attended and where she was learning to complete puzzles and carry out small tasks such as basket weaving. The

girl's father, Brian, suggested he could arrange a free visit if Eleanor wanted to take Alexander to the centre. He persuaded her to exchange telephone numbers and email addresses, so they could retain contact and he could make the arrangements should she decide Alexander wanted to visit.

CHAPTER 29

After filming her swallowing his huge tool, Eugene had emailed the video to Henrietta's email address, so she could enjoy watching her accomplishment on her laptop. Whilst realising she should have deleted it immediately, she retained it on the machine and would often watch it, occasionally masturbating as she did so, the memory of the occasion accelerating the speed of her climax. They still managed to enjoy the trysts in the gym, but Manchester would remain indelibly on her memory forever.

On being advised she had received a recorded delivery large envelope, Henrietta hurried to the school office, believing it would contain documents following up the conference.

Taking the package from the school secretary, she explained this as she eagerly opened the envelope and extracted the contents, then froze in shock as she saw what they were.

'Are you all right, Henrietta?' the secretary asked.

Taking a little time to reply, she pushed the contents back inside and said, 'Yes. Yes, I'm fine,' then turned and fled the room.

Eugene looked at the photographs then stared at Henrietta Barker in amazement as she asked, 'Did you send these?'

'Are you crazy? Why would I do that? Anyway, why didn't you delete the video?'

He was angry. Angry at her stupidity but livid at her suggestion it could be he who would try to blackmail her, thinking they had something together, although aware it had no long-term commitment. Meanwhile, he had to admit she was a willing and very accommodating partner and, if they had to keep the relationship secret, that was okay with him. With no permanent attachment, he occasionally travelled up to London for the weekend where he rarely failed to locate a willing partner closer to his own age in one of the clubs. Whilst many were very attractive, none worked as hard as Henrietta at satisfying his desires, and he also hoped she benefitted in a similar way.

Hurriedly, she looked at her watch. 'I have to go.'

'What will you do?' he asked as she headed towards the door of the library where they had met.

'God knows.' And she was gone.

Following her out, he quietly mumbled, 'Shit.'

Alexander had developed a clever technique of producing letterheads and his task was made simpler by organisations that published all of their details on the internet.

He had created one from a hotel in Norfolk, which showed a picture of the building and included details of facilities, including being close to a golf course, catering for weddings and meetings, and with some bedrooms possessing a sea view. He copied onto the letterhead a draft letter addressed to Nicola Blanchard, the wife of professional sales agent, Jackson Blanchard.

Dear Mrs Blanchford

We hope that both you and your husband enjoyed your recent visit when you stayed at our hotel, and it was certainly our pleasure to entertain you.

When the maid was cleaning out your bedroom the following morning, she came across a pair of knickers, which we can only assume are yours as we clean our rooms meticulously every day. They are bright red with a black band going around the waist and a little black bow in the middle of the back. If you can confirm that these are yours then we will happily post them on to you.

Regards

Manager

To Jackson Blanchard, he had drafted an email which read:

Dear Mr Blanchard

We are so glad that you're considering making a donation to our charity, which is a very worthwhile cause, operating on a worldwide basis.

The following are details of our bank account to which you should send your donation, and you are no doubt aware that you are able to claim full tax relief on donations of this kind. We have completed your details as much as possible, including the amount of your donation and you can remit by card or direct debit, whichever is most convenient for you.

Your support is most welcome to a worthy cause and we really appreciate your generosity.

In anticipation of the receipt of your donation, the attached letter will not be posted for a period of twenty-four hours.

Regards

Completing the email and attachments, Alexander pressed the 'send' icon and the message winged its way through cyber space to the unsuspecting recipient.

Jackson Blanchard generally tried to limit the times when he was at the beck and call of his regular stream of emails and text messages, allocating certain times when he attended to them, the vast majority of which were concerned with his job. Coincidentally, he was nursing his laptop whilst watching TV with his wife, not paying too much attention to the programmes as he looked at possible accommodation for the following week.

Frightened of missing orders, he had a good screening system on his electronic communication, but he still received some junk messages which he glanced at prior to deleting. The current one almost received the usual treatment, but the message heading which referred to his wife's knickers stopped him in his tracks.

As he read everything through, he wondered how the hell they had got to know he was in the hotel, considering the possibility that someone working there had provided the information. What he did know was that the description of the knickers was totally wrong as the lady who stayed in the hotel with him that night had worn a white thong and matching white bra.

'Jesus,' he muttered.

'Something wrong, darling?' his wife inquired.

Quickly recovering his composure, he assured her it was just a minor problem to do with an order and, taking the laptop, scurried to the spare bedroom which he used as an office.

A search of the internet indicated the charity was registered offshore, but had a very impressive, genuine-looking website, created by Alexander, plundering images and even videos from other websites throughout the world.

Not a man to panic, and deciding he needed time to think, he sent a reply to the email, advising he was away from his office for a few days and gave the date of his return.

Aware that his mother had seen the man's car earlier, Alexander resisted the temptation to challenge the lie in order not to draw suspicion to their closeness, so he simply acknowledged the reply and recorded a day and time when he should follow up.

CHAPTER 30

An unexpected visit from Jack brought bad news in respect of Eleanor's finances. In view of the passing of Gerald, Jack had decided he needed to take in an equity partner in order to share the responsibility of the finances of the business, but also to provide the necessary IT background which Jack was aware he was missing.

Having looked through the accounting details, the newcomer raised the question of the outstanding loan which had been made to Gerald, and insisted that some agreement was made for the repayment of this, even if it was on an instalment basis. Jack had brought an agreement for Eleanor to sign, but didn't insist on it being done immediately, happy for her to talk it over with her solicitor, which she advised him she would.

Having already decided to sell the house, she made a list of the more valuable contents, deciding she should try to sell some of them, in some instances replacing them with smaller and much cheaper versions. With the assistance of Alexander, she placed the items for sale on the internet, consequently replacing an eight-seater dining table and large Welsh dresser with a cheap folding table and four chairs. Two chesterfield sofas were replaced by a bed settee, her pride and joy four-poster bed superseded by a three-quarter size divan, and solid wood wardrobes, chests of drawers and vanity table

changed for cheap modern replacements. Shedding a few tears at their loss, they only yielded a few hundred pounds, making only a slight dent in her financial commitments. She did acquire a second-hand reproduction desk and chair cheaply, but realising she really had to do something more fruitful, Eleanor considered how she could extract more from some of her clients.

Alexander had assured her he was nearly there in respect of being able to commence the exercise against the colonel, and Eleanor wondered if they should risk losing the money from the bank manager's wife by providing her husband with the evidence of her activities in an effort to squeeze him for considerably more money than she had been paying. Theodore, the estate agent, was also someone else to whom she could look for increased contributions and she would love to find out something against the very wealthy American owner of the dress shop and his Filipino wife.

Reduction of her regular outgoings would be more difficult to tackle but she made an effort by turning down the thermostat in all of the rooms apart from Alexander's, and skimped on food for herself although ensured the dogs were well fed.

A telephone call from an organisation offering will writing services prompted Eleanor to realise she needed to update her own will, not having changed it since the death of Gerald.

At the time of the original will, the provision in respect of Alexander was that any money left should be allocated to him being looked after in a care home, as neither she nor Gerald could see any alternative. Her parents certainly would not be able to cope, even if they wanted to. The situation had been changed with the arrival on the scene of Ahmed and Eleanor was not quite sure what would be for the best. She

certainly did not want to create a situation where her son would be separated from his lover, but was also aware Ahmed had a limited time during which he would be allowed to stay in the country legally. She decided she should discuss the matter with both Ahmed and Alexander in order to decide what to do and the reaction when the matter was raised absolutely stunned her.

'Married?'

'Yes, Mother,' Alexander repeated very slowly and continued, 'So Ahmed can stay in England.'

Eleanor sat silently, thoughts racing through her mind at the implications of what her son had just announced. Generally conservative in her tastes, Eleanor would not entertain going on any protest marches in favour of gays and lesbians, adopting an attitude of live and let live, but not feeling strong enough to stand up for anyone's particular rights. She had accepted her own son's homosexual relationship, but mostly because it took care of his physical needs, which she had experienced personally and, although the relationship had clearly escalated, she had not allowed herself to think of very long-term arrangements. Now the matter looked like it had to be tackled. She thought of the attitude of the people in the village who were not aware of her son's sexuality, indeed probably most thought he had none, and Eleanor had certainly not shared her secret with anyone. She could not help thinking it was also an opportunity for Ahmed to stay in England, wondering if he was prepared to undertake the marriage to her son in order to avoid having to go back to his own background, but quickly tried to put the thought to the back of her mind, feeling she was being unfaithful to the pair who obviously were very devoted to one another.

'So, what do you think, Mother?'

Her thoughts were interrupted by Alexander pushing her for a response.

'Well,' she said, 'I can see the advantage, and it would be nice to make sure Ahmed could stay in this country for as long as he wanted. Are you sure that's what you want, Ahmed?' She turned to the Bangladeshi.

His response was to reach out and take the hand of Alexander as he looked Eleanor straight in the eye.

'I love your son, Mrs McLoughlin, and I know that he loves me, and I want to take care of him forever. Yes, of course, I want to stay in this country, but I want to do so because of Alexander. He has brought meaning and purpose into my life, such as I have never experienced before.'

Eleanor could not think of any logical argument. The possibility of Ahmed's eventual necessity to return home was something that could not be overcome in any other way, and all three were very aware of this.

With this, she announced, 'Well, we would need to go to the council offices in town to see what arrangements need to be made.'

'Can we go tomorrow?' Alexander enquired.

The wedding was a quiet affair in the registry office in the town, and probably would have remained so had it not been for a young rookie reporter who had been hanging around the registry office in search of some story. She had latched on to the marriage between two males, used her mobile to take a photograph of the pair and, having obtained their details from the list on the wall, asked them if they would like to be interviewed.

Eleanor fought back from trying to dissuade them from talking to the reporter, fearful she would be indicating either embarrassment, shame or both if she did so. She also tried to ignore the fact the pretty young journalist talked mostly to Ahmed, looking extremely handsome in his new suit. Sensing the girl was trying to flirt with him, she desperately tried to believe the Bangladeshi was sincere in his intentions and her son was not being used. She brought the discussion to an end by reminding the newlyweds they had booked a table for lunch at an expensive Asian restaurant.

There was a telephone call from Peggy Fothergill a few days later who called to congratulate her son and asked Eleanor if she had seen the coverage in the local paper. She hadn't but, going out to buy a copy later, saw the reporter had managed to get coverage of almost a full page of the event, including two photographs, which would ensure everyone in the village would soon be aware of the situation.

Two major adjustments which Eleanor had to make in her own life were the fact she now had a son-in-law and, whether she liked it or not, Alexander not only had a husband, but a new next-of-kin, meaning Eleanor no longer had control or even responsibility for his life. As for the couple, the relationship was now permanent, and she could not help but notice the happiness which this had brought to both of them, making her feel guilty about her own reservations regarding their feelings for each other.

CHAPTER 31

Although the fields were not vast, the undulating surface occasionally meant walkers could be in the fields at the same time and never set eyes on each other. This had been the case as Eleanor had re-entered the first field only just in time to catch a distant site of the colonel and his labradors.

The information about the colonel becoming mayor made Eleanor's thoughts turn to the research which Alexander was still carrying out in an effort to trace anything of the present or past of the man. As mayor, he would certainly have to be in a position where any kind of character deficiency would count against him, and no doubt place his position in a precarious situation.

Their recent spying escapade had taken a mere ten nervous minutes parked in the dark near the colonel's house for Alexander to discover they had three computers in the house, all of which had ultra safe systems. This made hacking from outside almost impossible, and certainly not within the realms of Alexander's expertise.

'The only way is to actually put the memory stick inside the computers,' her son advised her. 'I thought you were going to dog sit for him? You will need to get inside his house.'

As she removed her walking boots, Eleanor noticed there was a brown patch on the side of both her socks. Further investigation showed the underneath to be really quite damp. Inspection of the first boot showed an extremely thin slit along the side of it, with the viewing of the second one indicating a similar situation.

This could only be either a recent happening or the fact the ground had been unusually wet today as she had never noticed it before. Scraping the mud away, she examined the boots further, decided they were in too good condition to throw away, but that she would have to revert to wellingtons if the ground was wet.

Turning her attention to the dogs, she sighed at the state of Rags, face still very dark from whatever she had found in the undergrowth. She went to get one of the older towels, reserved for use by the dogs,

Eleanor was a little concerned of the youngster's stubbornness and rebellious attitude of recent times, although had always attributed this to the equivalent of reaching teenage years in children. Not that Alexander had been able to experience much of the fun of those years. Her thoughts were interrupted as she noticed the light on the telephone, advising she had a message and her heart lifted when she played it. The deputy mayor wanted to know if she could look after his dogs as he and his wife had to go away for an overnight stay.

CHAPTER 32

It was a lovely clear morning as Eleanor approached the field with the colonel's dogs on their leads. Obedient though she knew them to be, she was frightened to let them off the lead and terrified of the possible consequences. They had the field to themselves but her thoughts were filled, not with the dogs, but the exercise which she had to undertake on her return to the house. She was acutely aware of the vitally important memory stick nestling in her pocket, which Alexander had provided, together with explicit instructions on what to do when attaching it to the computers, of which she knew could be as many as three.

She had carefully followed the instructions provided by her client to nullify the alarm system, nerves jangling just in case she got it wrong and heard bells ringing, sirens blaring or whatever happened when the system was triggered. The dogs barked throughout the two minutes it took her to enter the various passcodes and gain entry then, recognising her, excitedly scrambled for attention, both trying to receive their pats on the head first.

The sun shone even more brightly as she completed her circuit of the first field before entering the gap into the second one, the extending leads enabling the labradors to enter the longer grass in order to carry out their ablutions as they continued their walk.

The bleep on his iPhone warned Foster-Clarkson that someone had entered his house as he was sitting having breakfast at the hotel in Yorkshire. Punching in the link, he glanced at the screen, which showed Eleanor fussing over the dogs whose energetic wagging of their tails made it clear they were pleased to see her. Satisfied that all was well and that at least on her first stint the dog walker was doing the required job, he flicked off the link and slid the phone into his pocket.

The security system was top of the range, allowing him to know what was happening from anywhere in the world where he could locate an internet or mobile phone signal. It warned him of house entry and allowed him to view every room in the house, including, and unknown to his wife, the en suites and bathrooms.

The next bleep came almost exactly one hour later, confirming she had, as agreed, given the dogs an hour's walk, but having entered the meeting room, he and colleagues were requested to turn their appliances off, or to silent, as the training was about to start. After doing so, he watched for a few minutes as Eleanor, as instructed, put out the food for the dogs in their respective dishes but, receiving a dig in the ribs from his wife, disconnected and slipped the phone into his pocket. This meant he was not observing when Eleanor took off her boots and made her way upstairs.

Having had a hearty breakfast and happy his dogs would be well looked after, the day started well but nosedived quite quickly as the training session began. The invigilator announced a change of speaker for the afternoon session which, instead of the expected Home Secretary, would now be undertaken by one of his junior ministers, the Right Honourable Justin Harrison, who just happened to be the ex-husband of Penelope Foster-Clarkson.

He arrived during the mid-morning coffee break and, looking around for familiar faces, spotted Penelope. He came across, gave her a peck on the cheek, held out his hand and introduced himself to her new husband, mistakenly, or possibly deliberately, addressing him as Colin, to be quickly corrected by Penelope.

Cedric took an instant dislike to the man, deciding he was a supercilious egomaniac, confirming Penelope's description of him during their own early relationship, and similar to some of the officers who he had met in the Army.

Although not speaking until the afternoon, the MP sat at the top table along with the other speakers, ready to deal with questions at the end of the session.

Lunchtime was an ordeal with him latching onto them and dominating the conversation, reminiscing about times when the pair were married, much to the disgust and annoyance of her present husband.

Dinner was equally disastrous. There were only thirty people attending the convention and the hotel had set out four large circular tables with guest place names. Foster-Clarkson was livid when, instead of sharing the table with the Home Secretary, he had to listen to Harrison holding court as he talked incessantly about the government and the party, but mostly about himself. Penelope feigned a headache to save him from further misery as the rest of the group returned to the bar.

'Sorry, darling,' she apologised as she raided the mini bar for gin, tonic and whiskey, pouring drinks for both of them. 'You see why I was glad to see the back of him.'

She looked over the top of her glass at him as she added, 'What can I do to make the end of your day better than the rest of it, and which bed would you like me to do it in?' She

was referring to the twin beds, of which they had occupied one each the previous night.

They chose the one furthest away from the window as she took the lead and made the colonel appreciate what an incredible body she still possessed, and how she knew exactly how to use it to please her current husband.

An hour and a half later, he drifted off to a satiated slumber as she gently removed the recently refilled whiskey tumbler from his fingers.

CHAPTER 33

Just when he thought he had heard the last of the potential extortionist, Jackson Blanchard heard the bleep on his laptop advising he had a message. It was not the expected order which he awaited, but a repeat of the earlier threat to write to his wife. The salesman had earlier decided it was highly unlikely the people responsible would take matters further. The knicker description was wrong, and he believed that whoever had sent the email was bluffing, so decided to do nothing.

Three days later, the package arrived, thankfully when he was at home, addressed to Mr Blanchford, although the letter inside, typed on the hotel letterhead, was addressed to Mrs Blanchford. The knickers enclosed matched the description of the original threat, and scrawled across the bottom of the letter were the words, 'We have another pair and will address the letter correctly tomorrow.'

Blanchford reached into his back pocket for his wallet and took out his debit card.

Cedric Foster-Clarkson carefully scraped the mud from the soles of his green wellington boots on the brush side of his latest aid, before using the opposite side to assist the removal of the footwear. He used a long-handled shoe horn to ease his stockinged feet into brown brogues, then cursed aloud as his arthritic fingers struggled with fastening the laces. On good

days he felt grateful his only ailment was osteoarthritis, but at times the frustration of the numbness of his fingers and the pain in his hips and knees caused more than a little irritation.

This morning had not been the best start to the day and his walk with the labradors had not been comfortable, each step causing him to grit his teeth against the constant discomfort. Discomfort had turned to anger when a search through the pockets of his waxed coat yielded an empty plastic strip, which had previously housed paracetamol tablets. Although his plentiful supplies were free on prescription, Foster-Clarkson rarely took even half of the recommended dose, not being in favour of the imagined or real side effects of painkillers. Occasionally he succumbed, when his body reminded him his condition would never improve and the feeling in the joints turned from niggling discomfort to actual hurt. That had been the case as he followed the dogs up the hill halfway through the walk. Unusually, he had not met any fellow walkers to allow a pause in his trek as he strode out without slackening his pace, although the dogs had forged ahead. Eventually, barking from over the brow of the hill alerted him that his charges had encountered company and he breathed a sigh of relief when his dogs came into sight, frolicking with a German shepherd and a Staffordshire bull terrier.

He should have been in a better mood as the previous day he had been officially sworn in as mayor and formally donned the robes for the first time. The reliable Fay had already made the required alterations to ensure a good fit as they were draped around him by his predecessor, who added the heavy chain of office. Penelope had been attired with the clothes and chain of the mayoress, and the pair had posed for an age to cater for the group of photographers, professional

and amateur, looking to save the occasion forever. Some were posted on social media instantly, whilst others would appear when the local newspapers printed their daily or weekly publications, although many also produced websites for those impatient for news and gossip.

He partly blamed the celebratory drinks for his present condition, but was aware he could not rest as his car was collecting him for a visit to a local school. Having already left for her morning gallop, Penelope was expected to accompany him and would be rushing home to shower and change before the pair were taken to the Town Hall to be suitably robed.

CHAPTER 34

Eleanor realised she had not undertaken an easy task. Carolyn would be quite sullen and difficult to engage in conversation with different lifestyles, upbringing, age and differing interests. The only common denominator being the Indian. Both were guarded with the younger woman unaware Eleanor knew anything about her past. She did not raise the subject and her new mentor, having been provided the information in confidence, was reluctant to pry.

One of the more pleasant parts of the task was taking Carolyn to lunch at expensive restaurants in order to work on her table manners. After two glasses of wine, she would relax and talk more. The difficulty then was being strict in not allowing her to have more wine or any kind of alcohol. This was not easy and caused friction between the pair and, occasionally, Eleanor found herself giving in to the pressure of the girl, allowing an additional half glass of wine. It was on one such occasion that Carolyn opened up somewhat and told Eleanor she had given birth, with the baby being taken away. Feigning surprise, Eleanor was still moved as she listened to the narration, and when the girl burst into tears, moved around the table to the bench where she was sitting and put her arm round her, allowing the youngster to put her head on Eleanor's shoulder and sob her heart out.

As a waiter came across to see what the problem was, Eleanor just shook her head and he diplomatically moved away. Thankfully, the venue chosen was a small country pub, so there were only a few other diners witnessing the scene.

When the Indian collected her later, in front of Carolyn, Eleanor told him his wife had provided her with information about the baby, but played down the amount of distress which it had caused.

This seemed to open the floodgates for Carolyn and, at their next assignation, sharing coffee and biscuits in an upmarket hotel in town, Carolyn provided more information about her background, including her move to London in search of work and replying to the advert in Luton and her drug dependency.

Shortly afterwards, over afternoon tea and cakes in a small quaint teashop, Carolyn asked Eleanor if she would help her to get off the dependency on drugs.

A subsequent lengthy telephone conversation between Eleanor and the Indian, during which therapy and rehabilitation were discussed in addition to other options, the Indian came up with the idea of Eleanor taking his wife to a remote holiday camp in an effort to allow Carolyn to go 'cold turkey'. He overcame her objections about transport, dogs, her own work and, most importantly, Alexander, so Eleanor found herself in a large three-bedroom static caravan on a campsite in a small village on the Lincolnshire coast. She had brought Alexander and the dogs in the Golf, whilst the Indian borrowed a friend's saloon car to transport Carolyn and Ahmed and the bulky luggage.

The accommodation was ideal with a ramp enabling Alexander easy access. Eleanor allowed the two lovers to

share the master bedroom, with her and Carolyn having compact twin-bedded rooms each.

As soon as they had unpacked, Javendra, accompanied by Ahmed, set off to the nearest supermarket armed with a list of requirements provided by Eleanor.

The kitchen section of the caravan had a gas cooker, microwave oven and fridge freezer combination, and was fully fitted out with crockery, cutlery and cooking utensils including pots and pans. The large lounge area incorporated a dining table and an L-shaped settee type bench with stools under the table on the opposite side. It really was a home from home, and included double glazing and central heating, the heating certainly unlikely to be required at this time. There was a large television, plenty of storage for clothes in the bedrooms and Wi-Fi, so Alexander could connect to the outside world. The camp itself was quite compact, with easy access to the wide sandy beach, visible both ways as far as the eye could see.

The first morning was beautiful, sun shining brightly as Eleanor got up and put a light dressing gown around her relaxing short pyjamas. She let the dogs out onto the veranda in order to carry out their ablutions, scooping up the poos and using a bucket of water to disperse the other half of their excretions.

After making a cup of tea for herself, she lazily leafed through one of the women's magazines the Indian had brought from the supermarket trip.

Ahmed was the first to join her, clad in boxer shorts and T-shirt reminding Eleanor what a handsome boy he was. She had grown more and more fond of the Asian, grateful for his love and dedication to her son.

Carolyn seemed in a happy mood when she surfaced and came into the lounge area, seeking a cup of tea, unconcerned at her short nightie showing all of her bare legs and the contours of her nipples protruding against the material, not unnoticed by Ahmed. Eleanor managed to refrain from making any comment, aware of the background of the girl, and not wanting to appear old-fashioned in the company of the youngsters, although became a little worried, remembering Ahmed had confessed to being bisexual and not totally gay.

By eleven o'clock, they were passing through the gate which led to the seafront and which had a zigzag style ramp, allowing Alexander to propel his wheelchair onto the concrete walkway making the promenade, which ran alongside the beach.

After some thirty yards, Eleanor, Carolyn and the dogs were able to use steps to descend to the beach, allowing the dogs to scamper towards the water's edge, whilst the two women kept pace with Alexander and Ahmed some six feet above their heads. In the distance, as they headed north, they could see the big wheel, helter-skelter and big dipper on the amusement park of the nearby tourist town. The North Sea was fairly calm; a gentle breeze and an almost cloudless sky creating a perfect setting.

They stopped and had drinks. Alexander's wheelchair parked alongside a large bench on which the trio sat. In the case of Carolyn and Eleanor, they sipped coffee from paper cups provided by the vendors, whilst Ahmed had his own bottle of cold green tea and assisted Alexander to have his drink.

Although having already put some cream on her son's face and arms, Eleanor reinforced it with an additional coat, handing a separate tube to Carolyn, to be shared by Ahmed.

Drinks finished, they carried on towards the town and, seeing flashing lights of amusement arcades on the opposite side of the road, Eleanor allowed Carolyn to persuade them to go over and experience the attraction which was dog friendly with bowls of water at the entrance.

Using a note to get change from the assistant and then changing pound coins into small denominations, Eleanor watched as Carolyn and Ahmed fed the coins into the machines, attempting to win the pile of two pence pieces sliding backwards and forwards with tantalising closeness to the edge. Alexander was totally enthralled, grunting in excitement every time a few coins dropped into the reciprocal, only to be retrieved and fed back into the machine by the eager gamblers.

Sensing the boredom of the dogs, Eleanor dragged the group out of the arcade and they walked along the pavement, listening to bingo callers and music. They looked at the shop windows and their merchandising displays, sometimes with mobile stalls at the front of the shops, offering everything from shoes, fancy T-shirts, buckets and spades, tents, even garden tools, amongst hundreds of tempting items.

Eleanor did succumb to the request to acquire T-shirts for the three younger people, promoting the attractions of the town, resisting Carolyn's suggestion that she got one for herself.

Back on the promenade, the smell of food was too tempting and, moving a chair to accommodate Alexander's wheelchair, they sat in an open-air café which sold a wide variety of fast food. Eleanor and Carolyn chose traditional fish and chips, Ahmed shared a pasta dish with Alexander, and the dogs were given treats from Eleanor's rucksack.

The return journey was taken at a more leisurely pace, this time Eleanor staying on the promenade with Alexander

to allow Ahmed to take off his socks and shoes and feel the sand between his toes as he and Carolyn walked along the beach with the dogs.

In the sanctuary of the caravan, Alexander dozed off whilst Carolyn and Ahmed looked through the various brochures that had been left for them, advertising things to do in the area, which reminded Eleanor of the real reason for their visit, from which the eventful day had distracted her.

It reached a pleasant conclusion when Ahmed and Carolyn both assisted to prepare the evening meal and then, with lack of a hoist, Carolyn helped Ahmed to get Alexander ready for bed. Showing no signs of embarrassment, she helped him in the shower cubicle and supported him on a plastic stool whilst Ahmed used the portable shower to wash him thoroughly before drying the majority of the water off. She helped the Asian to carry him into the bedroom. Unfazed, the girl's reaction to Alexander's erection was playfully tapping it and advising Alexander she had no doubt Ahmed would take care of his problem later, being rewarded by excited grunts from the boy.

Everyone having retired fairly early, blaming the walking and the sea air for causing the tiredness, the second day started much earlier and they were greeted by more sunshine.

This time Eleanor insisted they take a packed lunch with them, so Carolyn helped her to produce the necessary collection of sandwiches, crisps, biscuits and drinks, which they loaded into rucksacks including one fixed onto the back of Alexander's wheelchair.

On arriving at the promenade, they turned south, away from the direction of the town, with Eleanor walking alongside Alexander, allowing the two younger ones to walk

along the beach with Marilyn and Rags. As the tide was a little further out, they wandered away from the promenade and, parking Alexander's wheelchair, Eleanor sat on a bench and watched from a distance as Ahmed, Carolyn and the animals ran in and out of the sea, dogs barking in unbridled excitement. She noticed Carolyn scooping water and splashing Ahmed, who retaliated by kicking sea water onto the girl in a happy everyday scene, although Eleanor found herself disturbingly aware of the growing friendship between the pair. She recommenced her slow journey along the promenade as the incoming tide brought the couple and the dogs back closer to them.

It was Carolyn who spotted the slope from the promenade down to the sand, and persuaded everyone to help as they negotiated the descent with Alexander's chair, all three helping to manoeuvre him some ten yards from the wall, so he could sit with his wheelchair on the sand and enjoy watching the approaching water.

Thoughtfully remembering to bring towels, Eleanor spread these on the sand to enable the snacks to be laid out on them as the group happily enjoyed their packed lunch.

The late evening brought Eleanor back to reality as, having helped Ahmed get Alexander ready for bed and the two males having retired for the night, Carolyn told Eleanor she needed something and, despite Eleanor's protests, would not believe the Indian had failed to provide Eleanor with some emergency supply of drugs just in case.

Feeling disloyal and guilty, she lied to the girl, assuring her he had not done so. She reminded her that the purpose of this break was to try to eliminate her dependency on drugs and told her she had to be strong. She tried to distract

Carolyn, reminding her of the two days they had enjoyed, pointing out she had not required the support of drugs during these happy times. Before the end of the talk, Carolyn had visibly started shaking and over the next two hours, Eleanor had to withstand a barrage of begging, pleading, bullying, threatening and sheer desperation, so as not to give in to the girl's request.

Eventually, she persuaded Carolyn to go to bed, but she would only do so on the promise of Eleanor staying with her. Whilst Carolyn got ready, Eleanor slipped into her own room to don pyjamas, then re-joined Carolyn, whose shaking hands had made it impossible for her to unfasten her bra. An embarrassed Eleanor unclipped the garment, embarrassment increasing as Carolyn turned around and, wiggling her breasts at Eleanor, asked her to confirm they were nice.

Eleanor felt even more uncomfortable when the younger girl insisted they share a single bed, but was aware of the girl's discomfort, still shaking, so they lay on their sides spoon style and Eleanor, putting her arm round the girl's waist, held her as the lithe body shook uncontrollably, despite constant soothing reassurances from the older woman.

Gradually, the shaking subsided to a tremble, eventually ceasing as the even breathing of the youngster let her carer know she had, at last, found sleep. Frightened to move unless she disturbed the girl, Eleanor remained in the same position until she eventually drifted off to sleep herself.

It was pitch dark outside when she woke up. She realised Carolyn's short nightie had hitched up and her bare buttocks were moulded against Eleanor's pyjama-covered groin with bare legs pressing against her own, but horrified to discover

her left hand was cupping the shapely left breast of the young girl. Furthermore, her own hand was covered with Carolyn's, suggesting it was she who had guided Eleanor's into position.

Tentatively, she removed the hand, extricated herself, then transferred to the other bed but spent the rest of the night cat napping.

It was still dark when she awakened with a start, then panicked as she realised the other bed was empty. She started breathing again as she heard the flush of the toilet and sensed Carolyn returning.

Carolyn climbed into bed, relieved Eleanor had not woken earlier as she slipped the bank note under her pillow. She desperately needed something and believed it would be possible to satisfy her needs if she could persuade the others to go back to the amusement arcade. On their previous visit, she was certain she had espied a pusher, eyeing up the younger clientele, and had actually made eye contact with him.

In her mind, she was not sure she could ever give up the habit and the lovely freedom which it gave her from the realities of life, even if for a short period of time. She was also missing sex. Confident the young Indian, or whatever he was, had certainly shown an interest, he had already played a part in her fantasies whilst masturbating. During the night she had woken up with a tremendous urge for satisfaction, fingers groping down between her thighs, and she had even moved Eleanor's hand up to her breast, considering then quickly resisting the temptation to awaken her to see if she could persuade her to take part in a girly session, something which Carolyn had enjoyed many times, although she feared she may be rejected on this occasion. Pity because, despite her age, Eleanor had a super body, which the short pyjamas did little to disguise.

At the sessions at the hotel, particularly swingers' weekends, Carolyn had been subject to sexual advances by all shapes and sizes and, with the help of the little magic pill, had once been taken on a rollercoaster ride by a middle-aged, quite flabby woman who really knew how to use her lips, tongue and fingers to carry a girl to paradise. She had responded enthusiastically, burying her face in the abundance of hair between the woman's legs, licking her vagina and clitoris energetically, to be rewarded by a loud groan of, what she thought at the time, was equal enjoyment by her tormentor.

She wondered how she could possibly tempt Ahmed as he very rarely left the side of the disabled boy, of whom he was clearly extremely fond and loyal.

The thoughts of sex aroused her again, and she was tempted to go across to the other bed for the closeness of the female body but, instead, relied on her fingers to stimulate herself until sleep came at last.

For the second time in five minutes, Eleanor checked every room in the caravan, just to confirm there was no sign of Carolyn. The cover of her bed had been turned down, and her bright coloured trainers were missing, so it would be a reasonable assumption that she had left to go somewhere, and that it was her craving which had been the driving force. Quickly discarding her pyjamas, Eleanor put on pants, shorts, bra and T-shirt, donned her own trainers and was about to set off for a frantic search for the girl when an inspirational thought occurred to her.

Locating Carolyn's short nightie, she presented it to the dogs in turn as she kept saying the word Carolyn, pushing the garment to the noses of each of the animals. She silently prayed the idea would work. She had never used any of the

dogs to track anything, but was aware they would often pick up the scent of some animal whilst on the field back home, and could go along at a fair rate following the trail.

Letting them out of the door, they waited patiently as she opened the gate of the veranda and then, risking the wrath of the park owner by leaving them off the leads within the park area, she followed as they immediately bounded towards the gate leading to the seafront. At the gate, caution prevailed and she decided to put them on their extending leads, worried lest they should pick up the scent and gallop ahead, confident in the fact that neither had tremendous road sense. Once through the gate, they immediately climbed onto the promenade, turned left towards the town and, with her nose to the ground, Marilyn pulled strongly on her lead, hotly pursued by her smaller sister. Eleanor had to almost jog to keep up with the animals as they carried on relentlessly, and she only hoped it was the scent of Carolyn attracting them as they neared, then passed, the amusement park and the, as yet, unopened outdoor café where they had lunched two days earlier.

Shortly after this, both dogs turned immediately left and she had to hold them up at the pavement as they strained to cross the road. Waiting for a pause in the traffic, Eleanor trailed behind them as they reached the safety of the far side footpath and turned right. It was Rags who started barking excitely as she observed Carolyn, sitting outside a café with a hot drink and toast in front of her. Eleanor's first thought was to wonder where she had obtained the money to pay for the items, knowing that, as part of the agreement, she had no cash whatsoever on her, then also realised she had left her own purse back in the caravan.

'What happened? We were worried,' Eleanor said, desperately trying to control her emotions as she approached the girl.

'Sorry, I couldn't sleep. Decided I needed a walk, then got hungry and didn't want to wake you, so decided to try to find somewhere open.'

'How did you pay?' Eleanor enquired.

'Sorry, I borrowed money from your purse. Hope you don't mind but I didn't want to disturb you. You were fast asleep.'

Deliberately looking closely at the girl's eyes, Eleanor challenged her. 'You've had something, haven't you?'

'I'm sorry, Eleanor. I really tried. Honestly, I did. You simply can't understand what it's like when your body is absolutely craving it.'

'Where did you get it?'

'The arcade wasn't open, but there were a couple of guys hanging around outside and they were carrying. I'm not sure if they were pushers, but one of them sold some to me.'

Aware she had not even had a cup of tea and thirsty herself, Eleanor said, 'Well, I forgot my purse so you'll have to buy me some tea and toast as well.'

As she seated herself, Eleanor suddenly noticed the girl's wrist and contrast of thin white band of skin against the healthy tan of the rest of her arm.

'Where's your watch?' she asked the girl, then gasped. 'Oh no, Carolyn, you didn't?'

She saw the guilty look on the face of the other.

Whilst the day was not quite as bright and warm as earlier ones, they still spent quite a bit of time on the beach, lunching on the sand with Eleanor accompanying Alexander

whilst Ahmed and Carolyn splashed in the sea. Ahmed came jogging back and advised he would take over and that Eleanor really should go and get her feet wet. He ignored the protestations, pulling her to her feet and gently pushing her towards the incoming tide where Carolyn was happily paddling.

Passing through very shallow breakwaters where the sea was warm, Eleanor was startled by how cool it was when she actually arrived at the lapping waves that ventured as far as her mid-calves before retreating, only to be splashed on the back by a playful Carolyn, presumably settled by her fix and back in a happy mood.

The evening passed pleasantly enough with television viewing and, with not too much argument from Carolyn, Eleanor decided to use the second bed in Carolyn's room just in case.

Following an uneventful night, the quartet and dogs enjoyed a similar day, avoiding going to the town. Eleanor was not prepared to take any risks, although Carolyn did not seem so desperate. An evening of television was followed by another early night, but this time, after they had been in bed about an hour, Carolyn gently woke Eleanor, told her she wasn't feeling well and asked Eleanor to join her in her own small bed. The shaking of two nights earlier had returned and, following gentle reassuring words from the older woman, the trembling slowly subsided and then, much to Eleanor's horror, Carolyn took Eleanor's hand which was around her waist, steered it down to between her thighs to her shaved pubis, lower lips already parted and extremely moist.

Turning her head, she whispered, 'Please, Eleanor, please.'

A tight grip ensured Eleanor was unable to withdraw her hand which, for the first time ever in her life, was touching

female genitals other than her own, having resisted a couple of approaches in her teen years at school.

'Please, please.' Carolyn turned back again, reminding Eleanor of the desperation of her own son the first time she had brought him relief.

Taking a deep breath, she started stroking the wetness as Carolyn lessened her grip, allowing Eleanor the freedom of movement to stimulate her. It took about ten minutes before her efforts were rewarded by a sharp cry of exultation, and she felt the trembling of the girl's thighs as they clamped tightly, preventing any more movement as the climax arrived. It was a few minutes before the thighs relaxed sufficiently for her to remove her hand. Carolyn struggled in the confined area, but managed to turn around to face Eleanor and, before the older woman knew what was happening, put her hand behind her head and kissed her quite passionately. At the same time, she felt the other hand creeping inside the top of her pyjama shorts.

Eleanor quickly pulled her mouth away and said, 'No, Carolyn, no.' She grabbed hold of the girl's wrist to prevent further invasion.

Carolyn then pleaded, 'Can I just hold you then please? I'm so lonely, Eleanor. Please just turn over and let me cuddle you.'

Reluctantly, Eleanor did as she was asked, upon which Carolyn snuggled her thighs into Eleanor's bottom, thankfully protected by the shorts. Carolyn's arm went around her waist, then up to cup her breast and before Eleanor could do anything about it or even comment, the girl gently kissed her bare shoulder and whispered, 'Thank you, Eleanor. You really are kind and good to me and I want you to sleep. Good night.'

It was not long before steady breathing signalled the girl was asleep whilst Eleanor, no longer sleepy, as her body, moulded against the beautiful curves of the younger woman, screamed out for relief, her own nipple erect under the hand of the girl. For what seemed like an age, she resisted the temptation to use her fingers to relieve herself,. She gradually drifted off into sleep, interrupted by dreams of being ravaged by a very handsome Indian man and his beautiful English wife.

Somehow, they managed to get through until the Saturday without further incident, with all developing healthy-looking sun tans, under the watchful eye of Eleanor who ensured the use of lots of sun cream. One evening, when Ahmed and Alexander had gone to bed before the others, Carolyn was chatting about sex and told Eleanor about being encouraged to entertain visitors. She explained about the pill she would be given, admitting it not only removed all inhibitions, but made her actually want to enthusiastically participate. She explained how it made her nipples burn and made her heart pound, and described the psychedelic effects as she reached not just one, but multiple orgasms.

Eleanor listened without comment, but her own heart started beating quickly as she became suspicious this was what happened to her on her first evening with Javendra. She had blamed alcohol for her sudden yearning to participate in the sex session with him, but now became terrified at the description which Carolyn had given and which matched her own on the occasions which she had indulged with the Indian. She suddenly knew why she had experienced things which had never before happened in her life. The revelation really frightened her and made her decide she had been right in deciding to break off the intimate relationship, but was

now really angry at the way which she now believed she had been used and abused by the Asian. She had to admit to herself she had incredibly enjoyed what she now suspected to be a drug-fuelled experience, but was terrified of damage done to her body and was now very concerned at what had been happening to Carolyn, and maybe other young girls exploited by Javendra and his friends.

Javendra arrived early in the afternoon.

'Have you kept clean?' he demanded before he had even sat down.

Eleanor advised she hadn't been and explained the situation about Carolyn stealing the money to go and get some substance. Carolyn confessed about using the watch for currency. The change was as sudden as it was unexpected.

'You stupid fucking cow,' he shouted at his wife. 'After all the money I spent on the watch, and this trip, and this is how you repay me.'

He lashed out with his powerful arm, catching Carolyn on the side of her face and knocking her to the ground. A fraction of a second later, he joined her there as the poodle Marilyn launched herself at him, supported by Ahmed bundling the man to the floor. He let out a scream as the dog sunk her powerful jaws into his wrist. Rags joined in biting at his ankles as Eleanor deliberately paused for a short space of time before calling the dogs off, but the pair stood over him whilst Ahmed clambered back to his feet. The Indian, still on the floor, cradled his wrist from which a sliver of bright red blood trickled. He started to lever himself to his feet, but ceased when the dogs immediately started barking at him with Marilyn baring her teeth. Eleanor had never seen her dogs in this mood and, whilst she would always have expected them

to defend her, they obviously looked upon Carolyn as a friend who was being attacked. Ahmed, meanwhile, helped Carolyn to her feet, settled her into a chair and examined the rapidly developing bruise on her cheek, gently checking with his fingers to ensure there was no serious damage to the girl's face.

Holding the dogs by their collars, Eleanor eventually allowed the Indian to get up.

'How is your wrist?' she asked quietly.

Silently, he offered the wrist to show her. The wound was fairly short, but deep enough to show concern.

'Would you like me to take you to hospital?' Eleanor enquired. 'It looks quite deep.'

On his refusal, she asked Ahmed to go to the first aid box which she had brought with them and found some wadding, iodine and plasters. Gritting his teeth, Javendra managed to remain silent whilst Eleanor dabbed on the solution, covered the wound with a small piece of cotton wool, also soaked in the liquid, and then put a long plaster across it.

'They were only defending Carolyn,' Eleanor explained unnecessarily. 'I've never seen them attack anyone before, but they've enjoyed walking on the beach with her this week.'

She watched his face, eyes clearly conveying the inner turmoil going on in his mind then, taking a very deep breath, he said, 'I'm sorry, but that watch cost a bloody fortune.'

She waved her hand towards Carolyn. 'It's her you should be apologising to. It can't be easy for her, and for most of the week she's been absolutely brilliant and allowed me to keep an eye on her, even letting me share her bedroom.' She decided against providing too much detailed information.

'You can see how well she looks,' continued Eleanor, waving to the girl's tanned arms, legs and face. 'Did you really expect miracles in one week?'

'I'm sorry, darling,' he blurted out, turning towards his wife, who instantly recoiled from him.

Rage contorted his face as he again lost control, shouting, 'Right, get your stuff. I'm taking you home.'

'No,' was the sullen reply. 'I want to stay with Eleanor and the others.'

'You're my wife and you will do as you're told, you bitch.' He lurched towards her, but was immediately stopped in his tracks by the frantic barking of both dogs and the appearance of a knife in Ahmed's hand.

The Indian glared at all of them, turned around and left the caravan, slamming the door loudly and, seconds later, they heard his car pull away.

CHAPTER 35

A distraught Eleanor sat on the settee in the lounge area, sipping at a cup of coffee and asked, 'What will we do now?'

Javendra had returned after an hour with a pleading charming attitude. He had apologised to everyone and brought a small box containing a replacement gold watch, which he promised Carolyn she could have if she accompanied him home. He reminded Eleanor and the others that the accommodation had been paid in full for a further week, and they could keep the food and cash which he had already provided. A reluctant Carolyn had been persuaded to pack her things and been driven away by her husband.

Ever practical, Eleanor's thoughts, which she spoke aloud, centred around how they would get back in her small car, with the addition of Ahmed and the luggage. Ahmed's solution was that he travelled by train, but Alexander went on the internet, and found the journey torturous and very long having to make several changes on the way. They also decided that with everything already paid for, including a generous supply of food, it would be folly not to stay for at least a few days longer.

Spirits were lifted for the trio as the usually unreliable English climate produced continuous sunshine and they continued their routine of walking on the beach, eating their packed lunch on the sand, with early evenings chatting

about their day and problems before all-round tiredness encouraged early retirement. Eleanor helped Ahmed to a certain extent preparing her son for bed but, embarrassed at his seemingly uncontrollable erection, left Ahmed to dry him off when he returned to the bedroom.

During one of the discussions, Eleanor expressed the opinion that by discarding the suitcases and not bothering to take any leftover food, with careful packing and squeezing, they could all get into her car. They would use the dirty clothing to spread out around the floor, allowing the dogs to utilise them as a bed on the journey. Ahmed could sit in the passenger seat, with Alexander having to travel in his chair, safely bolted in the back of the car.

Having discussed it with Alexander, Eleanor decided they should bring Ahmed into their confidence regarding the method of generating income in order to support Alexander's upkeep and wellbeing. No stranger to corruption, the young man understood perfectly, and not only agreed with their actions but asked if they were obtaining money from the Indian by this method. On being advised that this was not the case, but he had paid Eleanor for trying to help his wife, Ahmed suggested they should include him in their list of victims. Eleanor was already convinced she had enough information with which to frighten him.

During discussions on the blackmail of the Indian, they all sat round putting forward various ideas. Ahmed was particularly helpful in explaining details about the culture and pride and the importance of not losing face.

Alexander looked to the man's details on Facebook and LinkedIn, of which there were plenty, deciding that whilst the threat of the Inland Revenue would have very serious

consequences for Javendra, for him to be exposed to his cricketing colleagues would be disastrous.

It was Alexander who suggested they send an email to the Indian, attaching photographs of them during their holiday and attaching the computer virus so Alexander could obtain access to the man's computer. They had taken many pictures on mobiles, including several of his wife, and just hoped he would be curious enough to want to have a look at them, knowing that once the files were opened, the software would get to work.

Eleanor warned they had to be very guarded in respect of the information which was used in order not to indicate to the victim she was the blackmailer.

Not normally a big drinker, preferring to use alcohol to gain an advantage over others, Javendra had overstepped the mark last night, sharing a bottle of red wine with his wife. She had sulked throughout the long journey home, and it had taken two glasses of wine, one of which contained the powered contents of a little pill, which changed her feelings quite dramatically. They had enjoyed a marathon sex session, leaving her fast asleep, with him totally exhausted but unable to sleep. Wondering if he'd made a mistake in the way he had reacted at the coast, he was convinced he had totally destroyed the relationship between himself and Eleanor. He really believed she had been doing a terrific job on helping his wife with her etiquette, and that to get involved in kicking the drug habit had probably put an end to all of that.

Not normally easily cowed, the combination of the dog and seeing a knife in the hand of the Bangladeshi had really frightened him. He was annoyed Carolyn had not reacted to his bullying, concerned she had developed too close a relationship

with Eleanor and her family, and he hoped she had not done too much talking about herself, but more importantly about him. He also hoped Eleanor had not provided details of his relationship with her, but felt that unlikely.

The naked form of his wife turned over in her sleep and feeling restless, despite it being early on a Sunday morning, he climbed out of bed, put on his boxer shorts, removed earlier for their energetic activities, went to the bedroom used as an office, and switched on his computer.

Opening his email index, he saw an email from Eleanor, heart pumping as he quickly opened it, thinking that perhaps he'd been forgiven. The brief note simply advised she was attaching some photographs and a short video of the holiday. He opened the attachments, watched his wife and Ahmed painstakingly help Alexander to get his wheelchair back across the sand, and help Eleanor's struggle to get Alexander in his wheelchair back to the slope leading to the promenade. He saw Carolyn and the Bangladeshi paddling in the sea, the scene changing to Carolyn walking along the promenade alongside Alexander's wheelchair. Throughout, everyone looked happy, and he guiltily admitted to himself he had never seen his wife look, and act, so relaxed. As he watched the sunny scenes, there was a warning bleep on a computer, located a hundred and thirty miles away in Lincolnshire, to signify the software had completed the task of loading itself onto his computer.

CHAPTER 36

The internet was a blessing and a curse, and could provide information useful for many positive things, but also for negative things.

Alexander had used it to dig up all sorts of information for him and his mother to use against their victims, and undoubtedly his most resourceful, which included painstaking time and effort, was to be in a position to expose the colonel. Facebook was used to contact all friends, colleagues and even family who had dispersed throughout the world. It was also a valuable source of information for the kind of work which Alexander and his mother were doing. He had looked into the past of the man describing himself as a colonel, opened a Facebook account on his behalf, and put feelers out to try to locate anyone who knew him. It took several weeks, but Alexander had plenty of time on his hands and eventually his luck turned when he received a message from a man the same age as Foster-Clarkson, and who had spent time with him in a Barnardo's home when the pair were youngsters.

With Alexander masquerading as Foster-Clarkson, they quickly built up sufficient confidence in each other to exchange private email addresses, going over the good times of their youth. As the colonel, he told the person that his experience in battle had affected his memory somewhat, and

used this as a reason to ask about their times together. The other obliged, with descriptions of the home, the names of the carers looking after them, and the activities which they got up to, including playing snooker and table tennis.

It was table tennis that produced the lightbulb moment as the colonel's friend mentioned that Cedric and his friend Peter Ellis made a good pair playing doubles together. He mentioned this had been helped by the fact the colonel was left-handed and as his mother had quickly established this was not the case this raised the first chink of some possibility that things weren't as they appeared to be.

Digging again into the past, the boy found evidence, under the Freedom of Information Act, which actually named the colonel and all of his colleagues at the time when, in battle on an expedition, everyone had died apart from the colonel. He then meticulously checked out the background of everyone involved in the expedition. There were not many, and he quickly found all but three had existing relatives still living. His imagination ran riot and he wondered if Peter Ellis was one of those three, and looked at the possibility of how he could prove this.

Setting up Facebook accounts for all three, he conducted searches to see if anyone from the past knew any of them, using his excuse that he was carrying out research for a book on people in the forces at that particular time. After a few weeks, during which he had sent out numerous emails, he thought he'd narrowed his search down to Sergeant Ellis. From all accounts, Ellis had been the colonel's second-in-command and the two had quite a close relationship. Sergeant Ellis was also right-handed.

Peggy Fothergill was in her element. It was her first year as chairperson of the village fete, and she was determined

to make it the biggest and best ever, pushing everyone she knew to have a stand or participate in some other way. Even Eleanor was persuaded to take a small space in order to promote her dog walking services. Peggy generously allowed her to pay just ten pounds, instead of the normal twenty, for the smallest display area.

Eleanor quickly realised that wasn't the end of it as she had to pay for some promotional flyers and provide shelter for herself and assistants against the elements of either the sun or possible rain. Peggy solved the latter by loaning her an inexpensive folding gazebo, two folding chairs and a table.

Eleanor used photographs of her two dogs for the brochure, which Alexander designed and printed off on his computer.

Taking place in a field situated at the edge of the village, generously loaned by a local landowner, the fete was opened by the mayor, Colonel Cedric Foster-Clarkson. Weather conditions were ideal, nice and sunny, but with a slight breeze making walking around the area a pleasant experience.

Eleanor felt like a poor relation as she looked around at some of the other exhibitors. The accountant, her friend Hugh, and Peggy's husband Richard had professionally printed gazebos with all of their details on, whilst estate agent Theodore Farquharson really went to town with a hospitality tent providing drinks, in which Fay served tea, coffee or alcoholic drinks for potential clients.

Two car dealers from the town used huge areas to display shiny new Peugeot and Ford cars, a company's outdoor clothing stand occupied a large area, whilst another had a huge variety of items for dogs, including food, leads, collars and everything else any dog owner would require. A nearby garden centre stand displayed furniture and

barbecues and a display of wrought iron gates, whilst an amateur vendor promoted second-hand books, bric-a-brac, children's toys and a selection of antiques. Double glazing windows, conservatories, hot tubs, kitchen utensils, used bicycles, plants and flowers, sports goods, an Air Ambulance helicopter on display... and Eleanor couldn't resist buying a new pair of walking boots from the clothing stall. The Round Table ran a tombola stall, and the bowls club displayed sets of bowls and had a rolled-out mat, albeit very uneven, for people to have a go. The cricket, tennis and football clubs had all been persuaded to participate, with the football club offering an opportunity to score penalties against their goalkeeper for a chance to win a cuddly toy. The local Scouts, Guides and Army Cadet Force were involved, with the British Army turning up with several Land Rovers and other vehicles. The fire brigade demonstrated a fire engine, St John's Ambulance was in attendance in case of emergencies, with the Women's Institute showing a range of knitted toys and potted jams.

There were two fast food catering vans, an ice cream van and an outside bar: the most popular stand at the show. Throughout the day, music was provided by the local town band, supported by a quintet of pimply faced youths who had drums, keyboard and three guitars.

Eleanor, Ahmed and Alexander shared responsibilities. Eleanor or the other two would man the stand, allowing the others to wander around the rest of the displays, with Marilyn and Rags having a fantastic time, able to meet and greet the huge number of other dogs accompanying their owners.

Many of the exhibiters thoughtfully put down bowls of water for the visiting animals, additional supplies available from a large water bowser near the entrance to the site.

Wearing his chain of office, the mayor, accompanied by his wife, visited all of the stalls, posing for photographs with the stall owners, and the newspaper from the town sent a reporter and photographer, who spent the day interviewing and taking pictures of the exhibitors.

Small children enjoyed the bouncy castle, an inflatable slide, a chance to throw soft tomatoes at teachers, who the Round Table had persuaded to put their heads through old-fashioned stocks.

Eleanor thoroughly enjoyed herself, good mood made even better when Fay and Theodore's wife Lydia called her to the estate agent stand and forced two glasses of wine on her. It was the first time she had seen Lydia since the fashion show and was delighted to renew the acquaintance. She pushed any guilty feelings about extracting money from her husband to the back of her mind as she looked around at his lavish stand. She was less comfortable to find Henrietta Barker helping her husband on the accountant's smaller stand. Apart from taking money from both of them, she was also sleeping with the woman's husband, although tried to justify this by reminding herself what Henrietta got up to with the very fit PE teacher.

Alexander was ecstatic when three hefty firemen lifted him out of his wheelchair and placed him behind the steering wheel of the fire engine, the event recorded by Ahmed. Tears appeared in his mother's eyes as she was shown the evidence, the look of happiness on his face absolutely priceless.

At the end of the day, a tired but elated Peggy found she had achieved her objective, the show being the biggest ever, producing record profits, blissfully unaware that some of her fellow committee people had got together during the day, complaining the event had become much too commercialised.

Pulling her lower lips apart with her fingers, Henrietta Barker slowly lowered herself onto the penis of Eugene as he lay on his back on the exercise mat in the gymnasium. Already lubricated following twenty gorgeous minutes of licking by his tongue, she had no problem impaling herself right to the hilt of the huge phallus, pausing before commencing her up and down movement to stimulate both herself and the man beneath her.

For three agonising weeks, she had avoided their regular sessions, but had eventually succumbed to temptation and made the necessary arrangements to pay the amount demanded by the charity, hearing nothing further from them. Her mind, and her body, yearned for the recommencement of her exercises with the willing PE teacher.

Having overcome the initial terror and fear that the affair would be exposed, she now believed this would not happen. Whoever the people were, they were happy to receive her payment. She had, grudgingly, wiped the earlier footage from the laptop, so there was no longer any evidence, although she was aware that whoever had contacted her in the first place would no doubt have copies. Since Eugene had reawakened her interest in sex, she had read items in magazines, even checked the internet about women paying for services, and decided she was getting far better value than she would with a paid gigolo, with much less risk.

Ironically, her husband Hugh had recently seemed to regain some of his sexual appetite, so Henrietta was feeling quite content, happy in both her private and professional life. There was an added bonus as her teaching role now included the task of working closely with Eugene, following their visit to the convention together.

Her partner in crime was also content with trips to London much less common as Henrietta was more than eager to satisfy his own needs, as she was doing now. He lay back, allowing the woman to do all the work, raising and lowering herself slowly at first, leaving just the head of his penis remaining inside her body then plunging back to engulf him completely. This had become a regular routine, and she carried on for some fifteen minutes before increasing her tempo, prompted by him taking hold of her hips in his giant hands, pressing on the downward movement, then easily raising her again. She lowered and raised herself more rapidly until suddenly, under his control, she found her body being bounced up and down until she felt the seed pouring out of him, carried by the warm fluid deep into her womb.

CHAPTER 37

Alexander could not control his excitement as he browsed through the contents of the Indian's computer. He had been able to copy several long columns of email addresses listed under different spreadsheets, including the few legitimate users of the hotel, a separate list of people that took advantage of the swinging weekends, his cricketing contacts, and the local businesses to whom he had loaned money. The list had been carefully compiled under the different headings. The information contained email details, telephone numbers, postal addresses and details of the clients. In the case of married couples or partners, the information was vital to the operation of the Indian, but a pathway to riches as far as Alexander was concerned. He discovered photographs, sent by satisfied customers, which he and Ahmed had giggled over, and which were now located on the Indian's personal file on Alexander's computer server.

Although having agreed with his mother that he would not start using the information as yet, he decided to undertake research on some of the people who had attended the swingers' weekends. He was amazed to find out how many of the participants were open about their sexual preferences and activities, and were members of two or three groups of like-minded people. The more discreet ones turned out to include a circuit judge from Shropshire, two barristers

from London, a head teacher from Swindon, a clerk to the council in Norfolk, the chief executive of a large charity, the chairman of a pretty large public company and, the biggest prize of all, a member of the House of Lords. There were three members of overseas ambassador staff, including two from Africa and one from Asia.

Most of the information would be used later but, in the meantime, he would use tax evasion to fire the first salvo in the direction of the Indian entrepreneur.

Eleanor McLoughlin kneeled at the toilet in the en suite adjacent to her bedroom and clutched her stomach as she vomited into the bowl. As far as she could remember, she had not eaten anything that was at all likely to give her food poisoning and had not felt weak or ill in any way. The attack of nausea had been very unexpected.

The last foreign food she had tried had been prepared by Ahmed during their Lincolnshire coast trip but it was memory of that which suddenly, in addition to nausea, brought fear to Eleanor's stomach. When packing things into her little car, unable to bring back the suitcases, she remembered being embarrassed, putting sanitary pads into a little bag to be laid amongst the dirty washing on the floor of the car. The recollection caused her to realise she had now missed two periods, which was the reason for the fear now consuming her.

She had not taken precautions with either Javendra or Hugh, believing she was going through the menopause as, for months, her discharge had been very light or not at all and she had quite frequently missed a full month. Wiping her mouth with a tissue, she flushed the toilet, returned to the bedroom where she located her address book and, using the bedside phone, dialled the number of the local medical practice.

CHAPTER 38

Javendra Bhattacharya stared at the screen, body shaking with rage. He was being threatened with exposure to Her Majesty's Revenue Collection department, and whoever sent the email seemed to know quite a lot about his activities.

The email sarcastically stated that the sender was not concerned about the immoral way in which he accumulated his income, but pointed out that even people who obtained their wealth from such methods still had a duty to pay tax to the UK government.

It went on to describe itself as a charity, trying to help poor children in the African continent, and was sure he would be more than willing to help and, due to avoiding what probably mounted to a very large amount of tax, was in a financial position to do so.

Javendra's immediate reaction was extreme anger, not fear, as he wondered who could be behind the threatening document.

He did not doubt there were plenty of people with motives, including many of those who he had helped financially who were appreciative of how he had enabled them to be in business, but begrudged paying him the interest rates on their loans, and also envied his own lifestyle, not having to work the exorbitant number of hours they did in order to make a living.

Having rejected the idea of Hugh Barker looking after his accounts, he had appointed an Indian qualified accountant based in Luton to look after his interests, including submissions to the revenue, and as far as he knew, his VAT returns and tax payments were up to date, although he was fully aware that a certain amount of creative accounting had been utilised.

Without checking the time, he speed dialled the number of the accountant, left a message on the voicemail summoning him to a meeting at the hotel at lunchtime, turned off the computer and went back to the bedroom to shower and dress.

The sleeping form of his wife reminded him of Eleanor McLoughlin and he wondered, for a moment, if she could possibly be his tormentor, certain his wife, Carolyn, had taken her into her confidence with some things about his operation, but then decided she had joined him in conspiring to avoid paying taxes by agreeing to take part of her rewards in cash.

Minutes later, under the hot shower, he started making a mental list of possible suspects, also analysing the information in the email which, on reflection, provided quite a lot of innuendos and not actual facts about his activities.

His anger built as he soaped himself under the steaming water, spun round to rinse the foam away, stepped out of the shower, put a large towel round his naked frame and padded back through to his office to restart the computer.

Retrieving the email, he pressed the reply button, and simply typed in the words: You can go and fuck yourself. He pressed the send button then returned to the bedroom to get dried and dressed.

Using a piece of nan bread to scoop the curried meat swimming in a spicy sauce, Javendra placed it into his mouth, but interrupted his chewing to ask, 'So, what do you think?'

Arati Patel, memorising the contents of the email which had been forwarded on to him following a hasty conversation between the pair, explained, 'I couldn't find any official record of the charity, and came up against a blank wall when trying to find out who owned it. Whoever it is, they're certainly no fools and have created a competent and complicated system of making it difficult, if not impossible, to trace and the bank account is held in Switzerland, so no chance there. There are some brilliant scammers about. Have you received any strange emails lately and downloaded any attachments?'

Javendra scooped up another mouthful of curry and chewed it slowly before finally answering.

'I never open attachments from people I don't know or who have not been contacted before. Occasionally satisfied customers send photographs of them enjoying themselves at the hotel, if you know what I mean. We do get quite a few of those thanking us for our service. You should try it yourself some time.' He smiled as he added, 'It might brighten up your boring accountancy life.'

One man had sent a picture of his wife kneeling in some stocks, white penis up her backside with a black one in her mouth, the small black mask providing a minimum disguise. Another woman had a picture of her husband being pegged by a lady with a strap on, his head buried between the thighs of a different woman, and another satisfied customer sent a picture of his wife being penetrated by three men at the same time.

Typical of the attitude of some of his clients, he could not envisage any of them being the blackmailer, although he was in no doubt that their activities were not known to their friends and neighbours back wherever they lived.

'My wife would kill me,' the accountant told him.

'Bring her with you. She might enjoy it. Mine does.'

Patel didn't think so. His wife was very much a Hindu traditionalist, and while she did not complain too much about the lifestyle of her husband, she was a non-drinking, fairly religious person with a large family in the area, including four children of their own. The combination of this and her religion took up most of her time, grateful her husband provided enough income to enable her to do so. He also allowed his imagination to run riot, as he remembered the beautiful young white girl to whom Javendra was wed.

'Would any of your satisfied customers try to blackmail you?' he enquired of the hotel owner.

'I don't know but why should they? We really don't know much about them, other than their interest in taking part in the activities which we provide.'

'What about some of the girls?' Patel enquired.

'God no. Most of them are pretty hooked on some kind of drug, and I'm sure they would not have contacts in Switzerland.'

'What about some of your cricketer friends? India is really clued up on computer technology these days. Some of the youngsters out there are really switched on. In fact, I work with a couple of outsourcing companies who do a lot of the donkey work on my accounting. I scan in all of the documents, send it over to them and they do all the hard work then I just present the accounts with my bill.'

'You haven't sent any of my stuff over there, have you?'

He realised his mistake in divulging this information as his client was clearly angry at the thought of what he had just heard, that he had provided too much information.

He quickly replied. 'No, no, no. Don't be silly. We have a special arrangement which nobody on earth knows about.'

Javendra paused to wipe curry from the corners of his mouth. He put his plate away and sat back, certain he had just been lied to.

'So, what should we do?'

'Just wait and see what happens,' the accountant replied. 'You have made it pretty clear you're not going to play ball at the moment. If this is a scam, people like that tend to try things once, then don't waste time pursuing the ones who will not cooperate, operating on the basis of there being plenty more stupid fish in the sea who will.'

'Don't you fucking dare call me stupid,' the enraged client replied.

'Sorry, sorry.' The accountant realised he had underestimated the seething anger boiling beneath the surface of his client.

The two men decided there was nothing they could do at present, but Javendra was not totally convinced by the accountant's explanation that the information submitted to the revenue was watertight and would stand up to any investigation. He also felt certain the man had lied about sending information about his activities over to India.

The drive from the hotel to home had done nothing to temper his anger, which increased when he found Carolyn still in bed.

'How about getting up, you lazy slut,' he shouted angrily as he headed back towards his office and then suddenly stopped dead in his tracks remembering he had opened and downloaded the video sent to him by Eleanor following the time spent on the Lincolnshire coast.

Her late husband had been a whizz kid on computers, and he knew the son to be very bright. He had certainly

admitted a little bit about his operation, but remembered his wife had been with the woman for a week. Retracing his steps, he stormed back to the bedroom and pulled the sheet covering her naked body.

'Wake up, you bitch. How much did you tell that bloody dog walker woman about us?'

She reached for the sheet to cover her naked form. 'Nothing.'

The stinging blow knocked her to the other side of the bed.

'Liar,' he screamed as she pulled herself back into a sitting position, hand rubbing her already reddening cheek.

'Tell me,' he repeated. 'How much did you tell her?'

'Well, I might have mentioned the tablets.'

This time it was the back of his hand on the other cheek which again sent her flying across the bed, only to find herself being grabbed, bent over his knee and backside pummelled by the huge hand as she wailed in protest. The punishment continued until he eventually flung her limp form across the bed, returned to the computer to retrieve the threatening email and remind himself exactly how much information it contained.

CHAPTER 39

'Well, I think I can confirm that you are pregnant.' Doctor McIntyre looked at her and then continued, 'Is this good news or unwelcome?'

She slouched in the chair opposite him, shoulders drooped, feeling tears welling up in her eyes.

'No, not good news I'm afraid, doctor,' she said unsuccessfully trying to force a smile. 'I will have to get rid of it. Can you make the arrangements?'

'What about the father?' he asked. 'Who is he? Does he know and shouldn't he have a say in this?'

'It has nothing to do with him,' she curtly advised.

Smiling himself, the doctor said, 'Well, I would have thought it has quite a lot to do with him, unless you're claiming to be competing with the Virgin Mary. Would you like to tell me who it is?'

'It doesn't matter,' she said, adding sharply, 'Look, if you don't want to help me just say so, and I will sort matters out myself.'

In truth, she was not sure who the father was. Having missed a couple of periods, she thought she was going through the change, thus making it unnecessary to take precautions, and had slept with both the Indian and the accountant within a week, so either could be the father, but she was not prepared to divulge all this information to the friendly Scot.

'Of course, I can help you,' he replied, 'But I have to make a reference, so you can get the necessary abortion on the

NHS. We will need to site your situation with your son as a reason why you do not wish to proceed with this pregnancy. Eleanor,' he added kindly as she burst into tears. 'Don't be upset. I can get this done very quickly and no one will know anything about it.'

'He told us to go and fuck ourselves.' The slow pronunciation by her son brought a faint smile to her face as he answered her query about the reaction of the Indian.

Alexander had been delighted with his findings when foraging into the memory of the Indian's computer, obtaining email addresses of his swinging party clients, together with some of the photographs, which they had sent to the Indian afterwards.

He had yet to use the information against them personally, believing the use of the photographs would immediately put the Indian down as the blackmailer, but confident the information represented a very convenient lever, which could be used later in the event of non-cooperation by their latest victim.

CHAPTER 40

It was a young lady in a smart bank uniform who brought in the private and confidential envelope addressed to the bank manager, and for which she had advised she had signed a receipt to confirm delivery.

Geoffrey Wilkinson occasionally received documents in such a way, usually confidential items, which often included things like wills to be lodged with the bank for safety.

He waited until she left before using the letter opener from his desk tidy to carefully open the letter and slide out the contents.

The letter was on the letterhead of the official-looking charity with the post office box number, asking for a donation to support their worthy cause of helping children in Africa. The list was quite lengthy, outlining benefits for the children and emphasising that they relied on donations from generous people such as himself.

Putting the letter to one side, the next document was a photograph of a woman's thighs, between which a double-headed dildo occupied the back and front entrance of her nether parts. Picking it up to turn it over, his eyes were immediately attracted to the second photograph with a wider picture showing the face of his wife, whose vagina and anus were accommodating the intruding object.

He stared at it incredulously for more than a minute then picked it up to expose the final document, which was on plain paper, in the middle of which capital letters spelled out the name of the chairman of the bank, followed by the head office address.

Also, in capital letters were the words: 'We hope you can make a donation, otherwise we feel we would need to ask your chairman to do so on your behalf.'

Geoffrey racked his brain all morning, which was only briefly interrupted by telephone calls as he pondered the situation.

Looking at the photographs again, there was sufficient background information to confirm they had been taken in the bedroom, which he shared with his wife, but he wondered who had taken them and how it had come about. Furthermore, the ecstatic look on his wife's face disturbed him, and he wondered how she allowed herself to get into that situation. He quickly considered, then rapidly dismissed, the notion it really was someone else onto which his wife's face had somehow been superimposed, but evidence of the surroundings quickly eliminated that idea.

He next considered their sex life, which he admitted had deteriorated over the years, but was amazed Glenda had felt she had to resort to what he could see had been happening.

Obviously, he was going to have to raise the question of the whole situation with her and, thankfully, they had no social event organised for this evening, so he would have an opportunity to discuss the matter, deciding perhaps they would dine first.

All good intentions went out of the window, however. Closing the door behind him, he put his briefcase on the

floor, removed his jacket, which he hung up, picked up the briefcase again and announced, 'We need to talk,' leading the way into the lounge.

Removing the envelope from the briefcase, he extracted the two photographs and thrust them into her hands.

'Can you please explain to me what this is all about?'

Glenda's knees went weak and she reached for the arm of the large chair to help herself ease into a seated position. 'Where did you get these from?' she asked.

'Never mind where I got them from. What's it all about?'

'Well, you no longer seemed interested in sex,' she blurted, 'So I had to do something as I felt so frustrated. I went to Soho and got some sex toys which I've seen advertised and, frankly, they've given me much more satisfaction than you have for years. I'm afraid I couldn't resist taking a video of myself, which I copied onto my laptop. Somehow, someone has managed to get a copy of it and started to blackmail me. I paid up at first, but the Filipino lady from the dress shop persuaded me to go to the police, so now I've stopped paying. Where did you get them?' she asked him again.

'Jesus' was his only comment as he rose to his feet, crossed to the drinks cabinet and poured himself a very large single malt.

'Do you want to drink?' he asked.

She nodded and waited whilst he took his time preparing a gin and tonic, even going to the fridge to get ice cubes and a slice of lemon, definitely biding time to think what to say next, totally shocked by the sequence of events. Carrying a drink to her and then re-seating himself, he took a small sip before asking, 'So, who else knows about these?'

'Only Amalia. I had to take her into my confidence as I needed cash as a refund, plus the detective at the police

station in town. I had to show him to see why I was being blackmailed.'

'What have the police done?' he asked.

'I'm not sure. I've heard nothing from the blackmailer since, and the detective did say they often give up easily if you don't pay.'

'So, what did they threaten?'

She took a sip of her own drink before replying. 'They said they would send copies of the pictures to you.' She took another sip before adding, 'And to the secretary of the golf club.'

Sounding much calmer than the rage going on inside, he simply stated, 'Well, it doesn't look like they've bloody well given up, does it?'

The accusations and counterclaims carried on in a heated way for some time before she ran upstairs in tears, slamming the bedroom door, at which point, he retrieved his jacket and, with an equally loud banging of the front door, stormed off to the pub.

'So,' said Chief Inspector Joe Smith as he looked at the Wilkinsons, 'It looks like the blackmailers were prepared to carry out the initial threat, so presumably they'll be prepared to carry out this one. Although, frankly, apart from embarrassment, it's hardly likely to change your life, is it?'

'What is also unlikely is that it'll encourage the chairman of the bank to recommend me for promotion. Isn't that right, Chief Inspector?'

'I'm sure your chairman is aware that sex aids are in common use, so in discovering that the wife of an employee is using them is surely no reason to curb the chances of anyone's career.' He saw Glenda blush at his words.

'You're possibly right, Chief Inspector, but being open to blackmail certainly is. Surely you should know that many bank officials have been put in danger, or rather their families have, when people are used as a tool to try to force the opening of safes. Apart from the chairman, the next threat might be to distribute copies amongst our friends and neighbours. We could be a laughing stock. Bank managers are supposed to be highly respected members of society, you know.'

Joe Smith looked at the man, clearly more worried about his personal reputation and the effect this would have on it than the feelings of his wife.

Whilst the file on the blackmailing had not been closed, he was still in the middle of a murder enquiry, so did not have the time himself to spend on a much less important matter, particularly if it was just to protect the reputation of the supercilious twit sitting across the table.

'Can't you do anything?' Wilkinson asked.

'Very difficult,' was the immediate reply. 'We tried before when your wife first came in but could not trace this supposed charity, although they do have an impressive website, of which the ownership is some obscure trust fund which we, so far, have been unable to trace. We don't think it is in this country, but that doesn't mean to say it is not controlled by somebody over here.

'So far, the one or two instances which I've come across are only based locally, although that doesn't mean they're not taking place elsewhere. It does not yet appear to be a big enough case for me to start contacting police forces in other parts of the country, just on the off chance. Until today, the amounts were relatively small, so it hardly seems to be

the crime of the century, does it?' Joe struggled to control his emotions, although liking Glenda, he had taken an early dislike to the pompous attitude of the manager of the bank, thankful he used a different one himself.

'What do you think I should do?' the man asked.

'Well, you could suggest that you do not want to risk tracing anything, so would like to pay in cash and ask them who you could meet and where. This would give us an opportunity to at least identify the people if they went for it, although I think it highly unlikely. They have gone to great lengths to disguise their identity and, from their point of view, it would be too risky.'

'What would you do if you were me?'

Joe glanced at Glenda, not for the first time noticing that, whilst pretty would not be an apt description, she was very attractive, had obviously taken care of herself and had an incredible figure. His immediate response would have been that Wilkinson should have paid more attention to his wife and catered for her needs and, presumably if he had done so, the situation would never have arisen.

Instead, he said, 'I'm afraid I couldn't possibly give you advice, sir. In the main, we do not encourage people to give in to blackmailers. Our experience shows the majority don't carry out their threats, although in this particular instance, it would appear they have done so, and they're pressurising on moral issues as opposed to anything illegal. Only you can value your standing in the bank and in the community, but I do know that once blackmailers start getting paid, they keep coming back for more and obviously this is the case here. When your wife stopped paying, they looked for the next possible donor.'

Looking at his watch, the chief inspector addressed the couple. 'If there's nothing else, I'm afraid I've got a meeting shortly. It appears there is very little we can undertake at the moment, but please don't hesitate to get back to us if anything else develops.'

CHAPTER 41

The overnight rain had obviously not lasted very long as underfoot was still relatively dry when Colonel Foster-Clarkson entered the field with his dogs. He was unusually early, having been awakened with aches and pains in his knees and hips, caused by the incessant arthritis, and also woken up twice in the night with cramp, on which he blamed a combination of his condition and too much alcohol.

He realised he had been stupid the previous evening, drinking four pints of beer before driving, and although he persuaded himself that, as it had been done over a few hours, his blood count would still be legal. It was more the self-chastisement for him breaking his own rule of two pints only when driving.

His regular haunt, the Conservative Club, had put on a musical memory evening and, for once, he had persuaded his wife to join him. He saw the retired couple with the beagle coming towards him and, although not in a talkative mood, he could not have avoided them without appearing extremely rude, so had to hear the latest instalment about the exploits of the couple looking after their great grandchildren.

They were really nice people and he sometimes felt guilty at his attitude to people who were retired and seemed to do very little apart from walking their dogs.

Returning from his walk, he spent several minutes wiping the paws of the dogs, which was a routine prior to them being

allowed to accompany him upstairs to his study. His wife was all right with the animals being allowed around most parts of the house, and as her car was missing from the drive, he assumed she had gone off riding, so decided to allow the dogs upstairs with him so he could check his emails.

He scanned the list to see if there were any important ones before beginning his routine of systematically deleting the junk ones, but one suddenly caught his eye which had been send by someone called Peter Ellis, with the subject announcing: 'Good morning, Captain. Nice to catch up'.

Immediately opening the message, he looked at it open mouthed.

Hello Captain

Really nice to have found you after all of these years. I understand you've done very well for yourself.

I'm doing work for a charity based in Africa, and I'm sure you would want to share your success, and a little of your wealth, to help children there. For your convenience, I have attached a donation form with all of the bank details and suggested amount on it and look forward to receiving your remittance.

Sorry to have missed your mayor making, but I'm sure your fellow councillors will wish to share information about your heroics as a soldier.

Regards

Peter Ellis, Sergeant

As he looked at the screen, Cedric suddenly felt sharp stabbing pains across his chest, perspiration formed on his brow, and he started to feel very weak; his legs would not respond as he tried to stand. Aware something was terribly wrong, he reached for the telephone and punched in the number of his wife's mobile. Penelope answered immediately, listened to his description about his condition and told him she would be home within a few minutes, advising him to keep calm and dial 999. She disconnected the call and drove home as quickly as she could.

The door slammed behind her as, breaking their own house rule, she ran upstairs to his office without removing her riding boots to find him still talking to the emergency services. Although looking extremely pale, he managed a wan smile at her as he advised the person on the other end of the telephone his wife had arrived and handed it across to her. The call centre operator immediately reassured her an ambulance was on the way, asked if there was aspirin in the house and, if so, to make him crunch and swallow at least two immediately. She was also told to make sure he remained still, ensure any pets in the house were out of the way, that the entrance was clear and the front door unlocked.

'Just a minute, darling,' she said as she dashed to the bathroom, returning with a pack of aspirin from which she extracted two tablets.

She placed them between his lips and asked him to crunch and swallow them as soon as possible. Leaving him again just briefly, she went to a bedside cabinet in the master bedroom and retrieved a handkerchief, which she used to mop his glistening brow when she returned to the study. Taking the dogs downstairs, she shut them in the kitchen.

For fifteen tense and frightening minutes, she waited, trying to keep calm. She eventually let the arriving paramedics into the house, escorted them upstairs then watched, trying not to panic or interfere, as they attached various things to his chest, arms and ankles. She listened to the bleeps of the machine to which they were connected, feeling helpless as she saw the pain on the face of her husband.

The female paramedic, who appeared to be the most senior, kept talking to him, calling him Cedric all the time, reassuring him as the process continued. She gave him an injection, Penelope not knowing what it contained, but just assumed it would help.

Then she heard the woman ask her husband, 'Cedric, sweetheart, if we help, do you think you could walk downstairs? We need to take you to the hospital for some more checks.'

'Will he be all right?' Penelope asked.

'We just need to get him to the hospital,' the woman advised, adding, 'So we can get some blood tests done before we can give you an accurate diagnosis.'

For the first time in an age, Cedric spoke hoarsely to his wife.

'Dog walker, address book, leave key,' he said, almost in a whisper.

As the paramedics packed up their equipment and assisted him downstairs, she quickly went to the kitchen, let the dogs out briefly and brought them back in. The address book she had located on his desk and popped it into a handbag. She took the spare back door key from the hook and put it under the mat outside as she locked the door and squeezed her own key into the tight pocket of her jodhpurs. Penelope walked up the ramp into the rear of the ambulance where

her husband was already connected to various machinery. As the tailgate was lifted and the door closed, the woman stayed with them in the back, whilst the man went to the front, started the engine and put on the sirens.

For five frustrating hours, Penelope watched helplessly as people came and went and Cedric was subjected to injections, removal of blood, further heart tests and had all sorts of checks carried out including temperature, blood pressure and swabs from his nose, the nostrils of which were then made to accommodate two ends of a tube, which she learned was connected to an oxygen supply. They were asked endless questions about the history of his health and lifestyle, often having to repeat them to different members of staff who explained this to be for his wellbeing, ensuring that information provided was consistent and recorded accurately.

She left the room briefly to call the number against the words 'dog walker' in his address book, explained the situation and asked if the woman would be kind enough to see to the dogs, explaining where she had left the key.

Eventually, she was told her husband would have to wait several hours before a second blood test could be taken, but they suspected he had suffered a heart attack, the severity of which could not be confirmed until the later blood results were known.

Penelope could do no more than sit and hold her husband's hand as he drifted in and out of sleep before it was formally confirmed. A young doctor advised Cedric had suffered, what hopefully was, a fairly minor heart attack and further tests would be carried out the following morning.

As arrangements were made to move Cedric to a main ward, Penelope was advised he would probably be required

to stay in for five days. Still drowsy, she was pleased to see a little colour back in his cheeks as, using a notebook from her handbag, she listed things to bring in and telephone calls which she needed to make.

On being advised there was no available transport, she telephoned for a taxi, kissed him goodnight as his evening meal arrived, and went to the main entrance to await her ride home.

Letting herself in the front door, Penelope discarded her riding boots and without even bothering to put on slippers, hurried upstairs and into her husband's study.

The computer screen was blank, but a blue light showed on the hard drive so, hitting the space bar, she brought the screen to life, only to see the screensaver picture featuring some exotic waterfall somewhere. In the middle was the white space asking for a password, which Penelope did not know. She made a mental note to take that matter up with her husband, suddenly realising that should anything happen to him, she would not have access to the vast amount of information retained on his computer. It also reminded her that, as far as she could remember, she had not advised him of the password on her laptop either.

Earlier in the day, she had only glanced at what was on the screen during his illness. She remembered it was an email signed by Sergeant Ellery or Ellis, or some similar name, and wondered if that had played any part in his sudden attack.

Knowing he kept a bottle of single malt whiskey and glasses in the bottom drawer of his desk, she extracted the half full bottle and poured a generous measure into a small crystal tumbler.

Staring at the waterfall on the screen, she realised neither of them had paid sufficient attention to cope with the event of either one of them dying without warning.

They had made wills, which contained details of their respective independent and joint bank accounts and which, basically, left everything to the surviving partner in the event of the death of one of them. He had no family and she had only one distant sister, living in some part of America, married to a quite wealthy businessman. In the event of them both dying at the same time, then the instructions in their respective wills was to sell the assets and, with the proceeds of that and the existing bank account, three charities would benefit, including one which looked after retired racehorses, another caring for service veterans and a cancer charity.

Whilst happy not to have access to her husband's computer, she felt this should be secreted somewhere with details in his will, and she should do likewise with her own, although was quite happy to allow him access even now, believing she had no secrets from him, nor planned to have any in future.

Although the fear had subsided, she had been terrified at the thought of losing him. Old-fashioned and very conservative in many of his ways, he had been nothing but kindness itself during their relationship, and whilst the courtship and marriage had not been perhaps as physically active or passionate as younger people, they had developed a comfortable way of life, with freedom on both sides and without the intense observation, which she had had to endure in her previous marriage. There had been very few arguments over the relatively short years of their togetherness, she being allowed to enjoy as much time as she liked with her horses, him with his political interests and golf and, whenever possible, she had gone along to the various events to which they had been invited. The only stipulation was she refused to be seen too often wearing the same outfit, receiving no

complaints from her husband at this excuse to create a substantial wardrobe.

Thwarted in her ability to satisfy her curiosity regarding what triggered the attack, she suddenly felt in need of a shower, having been in her riding gear all day, so returned to the bedroom, stripped off her clothes and entered the en suite.

CHAPTER 42

Eleanor McLoughlin was terrified. Unlike Penelope, she did know the password to Cedric's computer, so was aware he had been looking at the email despatched by Alexander when, what she now knew to be, a heart attack had struck him. Penelope had related the information when calling to ask her to feed and let the dogs out and to care for them the following day, which she planned to spend at the hospital.

Her mind was absolutely filled with guilt, believing it was the email which had triggered the attack. She refused to console herself with the knowledge that he must have already had some kind of heart condition and found it difficult not to imagine herself as an attempted murderer, although she also reminded herself that, in the past, she had been prepared to kill in order to make the life of her son better. Unable to shake off her depression, she looked in to make sure Alexander was sleeping peacefully and then, unusually, had a very large brandy with her bedtime drink, both of which she took upstairs for what was to turn out to be a very restless night.

CHAPTER 43

Eleanor was not the only person who did not sleep well. Cedric Foster-Clarkson, quite heavily sedated, drifted in and out of consciousness all night, a night which brought back visions of a time in Africa. Flashbacks incorporated the patrol led by Captain Foster-Clarkson with Sergeant Ellis as second-in-command. The party of twelve had been ambushed by a group of twenty rebels with eight of the group mowed down before having time to take any cover, and a further two suffered serious injuries as the captain and sergeant lay down, pretending to be dead or wounded, which resulted in eighteen of the rebels coming into the clearing, guns at the ready.

At the whispered command of 'Now' given by the captain, he and the sergeant quickly rose to their feet and machine-gunned the approaching group, not ceasing their fire until every one of them collapsed. Sergeant Ellis checked them all and, finding one still alive, immediately emptied more bullets into his chest. Feeling pain in his left arm, he realised he had also sustained injury and, turning around, was shocked to see the captain lying on the floor, writhing in agony, clutching his stomach, hands covered from the blood pouring from the wound. Quickly covering the few yards back to his leader, he found the captain in a terrible state as he pleaded with him.

'There will be more of them. I'm going to die eventually. You must put me out of my misery. Don't let me be found in this state and tortured, please.'

'No, I can get us out of here.'

The sergeant sat cradling his leader's head on his lap as he watched the life slipping away from him, but was then jolted back into reality as, although very distant, he heard voices shouting. His commander seemed to pass out as he released himself from beneath his head. Ellis searched around the rebels and took a gun which lay beside one of them. Walking back to the captain, he unfastened the shirt and removed his identity tags before putting a single bullet through his heart, resulting in no further pain or fear.

Sergeant Ellis suddenly saw an opportunity, which had never entered his head prior to this particular second. He carefully removed the captain's blood-stained shirt and searched his pockets, removing an identity card and wallet. Next, he removed the man's belt, together with its holster, although he had to scout around for a few yards to find the revolver which fitted in it. The contents of the trousers included a few coins and a handkerchief, all of which he left, but then removed his own wallet from his pocket, took most of the cash out, then put the wallet in the pocket of the trousers of his captain, identical to his own fatigues. Carefully, he removed his own identity tags, putting them round the captain's neck, double checked everything and, using the same machine gun, this time let off several blasts right up to the face of his friend who instantly became no longer recognisable.

He removed the captain's rucksack, together with its contents, and painstakingly pulled the body forward, so he could replace it with his own. Finding another revolver

from one of the rebels, he picked up two light machine guns, checked they had ammunition and set off into the jungle, wincing as he did. Valuable time was wasted retracing his steps to the body of the medic, searching for medical supplies and discovering packets of painkillers in one of his pockets. He then went into the dense lush greenery.

In his heart of hearts, at the time, he did not rate his chances of survival very high, but after three weary days, during which he had not travelled very far, weakened with fatigue and also malnutrition as all he'd be able to find were berries and nuts, he came across a small mud hut in a clearing.

Staying out of sight, he watched it for three hours, after which time he was satisfied the only occupants were a man and a woman, with no sign of anyone else. Checking the revolver was loaded, he gingerly approached the hut and rapped on the wooden door, which was opened by a totally shocked native.

Suddenly, his legs gave way and everything went dark.

The next thing he knew when he woke up, he was lying naked beneath clean white sheets.

'Good morning, Captain,' a friendly female voice greeted his return to the living. 'I'll go and get the doctor.'

Initially, the greeting confused him, then gradually things started to fall into place as memories of the recent horrific events flooded back into his mind, realising they must have searched his pockets for identity details.

On his arrival, the doctor pieced together what proved to be a week's events. He learned that, following his collapse, the man in the hut had gone for help to the nearby village, resulting in his being stretchered for two miles, then ambulanced to a hospital in a town a few miles away. A raging fever had

possessed him, accompanied by nightmares, during which he rambled incoherently as his temperature soared during the twenty-four-hour watch on his progress.

Having been brought up in the same Doctor Bernardo's home, orphans Peter Ellis and Cedric Foster-Clarkson were sufficiently alike to be mistaken for brothers on more than one occasion. Together from the age of seven, they developed a close bond and were inseparable, would play together, fight together and join forces to fight alongside each other if any of the other children threatened them. Full of energy and adventure, they had been allowed to join the Cub Scouts and then the Army Cadets, becoming enthusiastic participants in both groups.

They had similar haircuts, dressed alike, talked about everything together, including sex, resulting in the sharing of masturbation activities, although avoiding the temptation of touching each other. Being allowed to go camping with the Cadets, they developed a yearning to join the Army, worked hard at schoolwork to gain the required qualifications and, as soon as they were old enough, both were accepted as officer cadets at Sandhurst, passing out with flying colours.

As young lieutenants on their first posting abroad together, they befriended two Wrens, broke service rules by associating with them and risked their still fledgling careers by allowing themselves to be smuggled into the barracks of the young ladies. It was the third such occasion when they heard the approach of the duty officer and escaped through a first floor window. Peter, lying in agony with a twisted ankle due to the fall, urged his friend to escape as he shouted out to attract the approaching servicemen, diverting attention from his friend. Refusing to name his accomplice, Peter was court martialled and reduced to the rank of lance corporal. By the

time he had been promoted to sergeant, Cedric was a captain but it was the latter who suggested they quit the service. He had learned how much more they could earn as mercenaries and, after taking a few months to secure their freedom, soon found themselves in Africa. Given the ranks shown on their discharge papers, Cedric was still commissioned, but protocol was less strict than in the British Army, so the pair could renew their close friendship. Peter sensed a change in Cedric on their first patrol, when they lost comrades. He machine-gunned a group of eight rebels, ensuring none were left alive, ignoring Peter's advice that they may be able to provide information.

'Information won't bring my men back,' he retorted; the expression on his face made his second-in-command not argue.

A few more patrols made Peter wonder if his friend had actually started to enjoy the killing as they very rarely took prisoners. That was all over now.

Thankfully, the pair had spent almost all of their time out in the bush, so were hardly known by anyone, allowing Ellis to carry out his deception.

Opening a new bank account was not too difficult, which he did on his return to his unit, thus able to draw a considerable amount of back pay. He had resisted the temptation to empty the savings account in the name of Sergeant Ellis, knowing that, in time and under his new name, he would be the beneficiary when the will came to light.

On leave back in England, claiming to have lost everything in the conflicts in the jungle, he wrote to the various authorities to obtain copies of his friend's birth certificate and driving licence, and took out a new passport.

Moving around over the years, he served in both the Far East and Middle East as well as Africa and South America, progressing through major, lieutenant colonel and finally colonel before deciding he had had enough fighting and, thanks to his higher rank, had accumulated a small fortune.

To date, he had not shared his secret with anyone, but now it looked like someone knew and he could not possibly think who that someone could be.

CHAPTER 44

Javendra Bhattacharya and his accountant sat silently in the restaurant at the hotel with three large ring binders occupying the table as the men awaited the arrival of an expected visitor from Her Majesty's Inland Revenue and Customs.

The letter had arrived a week earlier stating that two representatives would be visiting them in order to carry out preliminary investigations into their accounting procedures.

Despite assurances from Patel, Javendra was still very nervous, having convinced himself the visit was too much of a coincidence not to be related to the blackmailing threats, but without realising just how closely related they were and how accurate his assessment was.

The letter, including the very authentic letterhead, had been constructed carefully by Alexander, name of the signatory obtained by Ahmed, who had telephoned the department to obtain a legitimate contact name. Now seen as an important member of the team, Ahmed was only too willing to assist in anything to harm Bhattacharya, for whom he had developed strong feelings of much more than just dislike. Whilst he used his witnessing of Javendra striking his wife as his reason, Eleanor wondered if there were deeper feelings, linked to matters thousands of miles away, but did not press for details.

For the third time, Javendra checked his expensive watch, and it was now some twenty minutes past the time at which the appointment had been arranged for.

Patel was very confident, having done accounts for many organisations, the owners of which resented paying tax in any form. He used his knowledge of the system to ensure the amount payable was as low as possible. Whilst not averse to using creative accounting like many of his accountant colleagues, he believed a fairer system would reduce the necessity for this. He was aware an army of accountants devised methods to close loopholes on behalf of the government, and an equally large army on the other side sought to open additional ones instead.

He had many clients who were looked after by just a small number of staff in the UK, but had back office support from two different companies in India. One of the companies was quite a large organisation based in New Delhi, with the other one a much smaller, recently started up company in Mumbai. The system enabled him to be competitive, when he needed to be, in order to attract larger clients, and to make more profit on the smaller ones, by not passing on the savings of utilising a lower pay rate in the subcontinent.

After a further ten minutes, it was he who looked at his watch.

'Shall we eat?' he suggested. 'I've never known them be this late before without phoning, and I somehow think they're not coming.'

Returning home later, Javendra learned his wife had taken a call, some forty-five minutes after the scheduled meeting time, to apologise. She received a slap across the cheek for not relaying the message. An email in his inbox confirmed the apology and stipulated an alternative date.

The next letter to arrive at the hotel, and marked for his private and confidential attention, was from the social services department of the county council, advising that, following a complaint, they wished to interview him regarding underage drinking by vulnerable people on the premises. Without giving an option, they specified the day and time when the meeting would take place at the hotel. Having friendly acquaintances who worked in the council offices, he was able to confirm that the lady who had signed the letter did work in the social services department, in a senior position, but his contact, being unable to obtain sight of any files or reports on the matter, explained they would be highly confidential and locked away.

Again, the meeting never took place and again there was an apologetic email follow up advising it would be rearranged as soon as possible.

The third and most disturbing event took the form of a telephone call from a very angry Yorkshireman. The man's anger had been increased by having to phone four times before being able to talk to the hotel owner and screamed down the phone when he, at last, got through. He wanted to know what the fuck was going on and was it Javendra trying to blackmail him.

Visions of the person, who he remembered as six feet six inches tall, a giant of a man, who played Rugby League, and who he would certainly prefer not to tangle with. It was his wife who had subjected herself to be shagged up the arse, whilst swallowing a big black penis, and had sent the photograph to Javendra as a memento.

The Indian was now getting really worried at the information his tormentors apparently had access to and was

now prepared to believe that, somehow, someone had gained access to his computer.

Whilst not the slightest bit interested in the morals or ethics of his clients, he was aware that, if word got out, the very lucrative swinging weekends would be boycotted by those in the know. He was still not sure whether the visits from the tax people and social services were genuine or otherwise as, although the people concerned actually worked in the correct departments, this information could be obtained quite easily, although the letterheads had certainly appeared very genuine.

Aware his computer contained a mountain of information, much of which he would not like anyone else to see, he was reluctant to take it to a speciality shop to check for viruses or anything else which it may contain. Several of his countrymen in the area had small computer servicing businesses, so perhaps it might be an idea to try to locate one who could be discreet. The risk was they would also have access to all of his files, possibly leaving him at the mercy of yet another extortionist.

Cedric Foster-Clarkson felt a little nervous as he lay on the trolley, listening to the words of the surgeon as he explained the procedure for an angiogram, which basically was that his bloodstream would be injected with a coloured dye by which they would be able to examine his arteries to see if there was any furring up or blockage.

Tests carried out at the hospital, following his attack, confirmed he had suffered a minor heart attack, causing some damage to his heart, but now they wanted to try to ensure they could safeguard against further attacks. He had been told about the possible alternatives, the simplest one being

the insertion of a stent which would widen the narrower parts of the artery, but had also been warned about a possible bypass operation if there was too much blockage. Although the surgeon had already been through the procedure on a pre-operation meeting, he asked again if Cedric was happy for them to insert stents today, if required, in order to save a further invasion of his bloodstream, to which he had consented. He was warned that, at times, it would feel like he wanted to urinate during the process.

Drowsy but awake throughout the procedure, he learned that two of his arteries were narrow at one point, so they were going to insert stents in order to improve the flow of blood, the reduction of which had caused his earlier attack.

The procedure did not take very long and he soon found himself in the recovery area where his wife was allowed to join him. Penelope had accompanied him to all meetings with doctors and the surgeon. Eager to give her full support, she was still very concerned that she could have lost him. She felt guilty at taking their marriage for granted and was determined to make amends.

They were later joined by the surgeon who assured the pair everything had gone well. The stents were in position and Cedric should be back to normal in a very short time. The damage to the heart had been minimal, and even if it did not repair itself, it should not present any serious problems. The surgeon explained he had prescribed medication, which would include aspirin to keep his blood thinner, a statin to help reduce his cholesterol level, although he was assured this is not too high, and a tablet to keep blood pressure at an acceptable level. The surgeon told Cedric his current routine of dog walking and golf should help his cause, produced a letter and asked the patient to use the information to

telephone and make an appointment to discuss dietary requirements. He advised that his wife could take him home later, with instructions to take things easy for a few days.

On arriving home, they fussed over the dogs, let them out to do whatever was necessary and Penelope made a pot of coffee, before they moved to the lounge and settled down.

Penelope asked if he was all right and comfortable before firing the unexpected salvo.

'Who is Sergeant Ellis?'

Taking a sip of coffee in order to give himself time to think, he could only assume his wife had seen the email on the screen, otherwise how could she possibly know the name. Neither could he remember how much was in the body of the message or the attachment, so was unaware if she knew about the demand for money.

'He's dead.'

'All right, who *was* Sergeant Ellis?' she persisted.

He sighed then replied softly, 'He was the best friend I ever had. We grew up together in a boys' home, joined the Army together, fought battles together and then, sadly, he died and I survived. But I'll never forget him as long as I live. I'm feeling a little tired, darling, so do you mind if we continue this conversation some other time?'

Frightened she was putting him under undue stress, she quickly agreed and changed the subject to organising the trip to talk about diet, exercise, medication and the other things he needed to attend to following his illness.

It was after their next trip to the hospital when the subject was raised again. They had seen plastic replicas of lettuce, carrots, potatoes, cucumbers, tomatoes, fried eggs and bacon, sausages, cake, trifle, brown bread, white bread and

many others as the 'nutrition' sister in her starched uniform went through the nutrition and cholesterol levels of each and every one. She talked about sensible diet, the fact he didn't need to live like a monk, but should learn to balance his diet, regulate intake of alcohol, stick to an exercise routine, and generally take care of himself.

The physiotherapist confirmed the exercise routine which he already had would be fine, although suggested that when out with the dogs, if only for a few minutes, he increase the speed at which he walked in order to step up the blood flow through his veins.

The pharmacist discussed the various medications which he had been prescribed, checking he had no allergies to any of them, and emphasised the need to take them at the same time each day whenever possible, and in the prescribed manner.

All three assured him he could carry on a normal life without many adjustments and that, if so, there would be no reason why he should not enjoy continued healthy living.

When they returned to the house, it was he who raised the question of Sergeant Ellis, telling his wife the story of their growing up together, joining the Army, leaving to become mercenaries and moving to Africa, explaining the ambush in great detail, with just a few amendments in the tale. They had already briefly discussed his career after the services, so he did not feel he needed to go over that particular part of his life again. She knew he was still involved with the business, which required occasional trips to the capital. He did not tell her about the request for fifty thousand pounds, still unsure if she knew about it.

'If he's dead, then who sent the email?'

'I don't know. I get all sorts of cranky emails, even more since I became mayor, but this is the first for anything like this.'

'Should we go to the police?'

'Why should we involve the police?' Now, not certain how much she had seen, he was fishing.

'Well, if someone is pretending to be another person, that's wrong, isn't it?'

'No,' he replied, too quickly, then tried to make amends for his hastiness. 'There's nothing they could do, and they have enough on their plate without dealing with cranks.'

'Are you sure it's a crank?'

They spent another few minutes discussing the topic, failing to come up with any sensible answers, before she changed the subject to express her fears when he was ill to see if they could provide solutions to how they would access information if anything happened to either of them. She felt a little concerned when she offered to divulge her passwords and he did not concur but counter proposed they would be kept in a sealed envelope alongside their wills, which were stored in a safe in solicitor Richard Fothergill's office.

The threat from the Yorkshireman to come down and punch his lights out, and telephone calls from two further clients, persuaded Javendra he needed to do something about his computer. With the name of a discreet contact, provided by the hotel manager, he went to see a specialist at the man's shop in Luton and negotiated a price for him to come and look at his computer and check for any viruses or any other way in which access could be made available.

The man took three hours, during which he advised the Indian he had cleared thirty-five different pieces of software, much of which was spyware, others linking to advertising which, the man assured him, would stop lots of unwanted promotional material.

The man also told him he had contracted all the information on the computer, thus saving space, which would improve the speed at which the unit operated. He also agreed to reduce his original quotation for payment in cash with no paperwork.

Neither man knew that the software, cleverly devised by Gerald McLoughlin and now used by his son, was completely undetectable from such examination and that, whenever he needed, Alexander could visit the computer. In fact, during one of his throughout the night browsing sessions, Alexander was aware of the work which had been carried out.

Javendra also realised the potential blackmailer already had much of the information.

It was beginning to dawn on the Indian he was somewhat out of his depth and required further help if he was going to take away the threat of his mystery tormenter.

Searching through the internet, he obtained the details of several investigation and security companies from which he made a shortlist of three and telephoned them in order to make an appointment. The most promising turned out to be run by Michael O'Flanagan, partner of Colonel Foster-Clarkson, although the latter fact was not known to Javendra at the time.

Noting the office was in Soho, and that one of the others was in the Victoria area, he decided to allocate a day to visit London and meet up with both of them. He made an appointment to see Michael in the morning, with the second

alternative in the early afternoon. He decided to go by train, leaving his car parked at Luton station.

Michael was really impressive without being pushy and Javendra took an immediate liking to him. Having heard the Indian's story and looking through the threatening letters, he agreed the ones from HM Revenue and social services were excellent, but fakes, and that the blackmailer had been toying with his emotions by making appointments and then not turning up. Michael's relaxed and easy manner encouraged the Indian to open up to him, providing almost accurate information about his own operations, but increasing girls' ages by two or three years in order not to admit to being operating against the law.

Michael also advised him that, whilst he personally was not an expert on computers, they employed, on a part-time ad hoc basis, a highly qualified and trained computer expert who was a lecturer at the university, but was always eager to earn extra money. He did explain it would be helpful if the man could look at Javendra's computer, but this might need to take place on a Saturday, or even a Sunday, if that was not inconvenient.

Having declined an offer of coffee on arrival, Javendra accepted the second offer, which was served by a young Polish girl and when Michael suggested lunch, he decided he had made up his mind that this was a man with whom he could work and trust, so decided not to turn up for the afternoon appointment.

A pleasant lunch in a local Chinese restaurant convinced him even more so as Michael showed a keen interest in following cricket, although admitting he had not personally taken part since his early school days. Michael was, however, very knowledgeable about the international scene and became

very impressed when he realised he was in the company of a former Indian international.

When they returned to the office, Javendra agreed to allow Michael to make copies of everything which he had already shown him, providing the Indian with the copies and Michael retaining the originals in case they provided any additional clues.

As it turned out, it was a weekend visit which was agreed, with the university professor volunteering to drive himself and Michael to the home of the Indian in order to enable the professor to inspect the computer system.

With neither Michael or Javendra understanding how he knew, the computer expert ascertained the email address which was used by the bogus charity had actually been set up in the UK. Like the man from Luton before him, he did not locate the presence of the software which was the cause of the Indian's difficulties, but confirmed that, as far as he knew, the computer was now virus free, with security systems intact and working perfectly well. In order to prove the point, the professor used his own laptop to try to send an email message, which was corrupted and which was rejected immediately.

Regarding further investigation, Michael advised the Indian that, if he really wanted to trace the source, then Michael may need to visit the Channel Islands, the Isle of Man and possibly even countries further afield, trying to identify the true owner of the Swiss bank account. Baulking at the thought of possible cost implications, the Indian suggested they wait and see if the threats continued.

As they were within seven miles of the home of Michael's partner, he had telephoned the colonel the previous day and arranged to call with the professor in order to introduce

him but also to pay a social visit. Over a cup of tea, Michael happened to mention he was working on a blackmailing case without revealing the name of his client, but did provide a little information as to how the blackmailer had gone about things. Cedric's ears pricked up as he listened to the story, but stopped himself from providing information about his own experience in front of the man from the university. He made a mental note to discuss things with Michael later. It could be that Cedric could benefit from the investigation already being financed by someone else, which may shed some light on his own situation.

CHAPTER 45

Feeling a little restless, the colonel decided to carry out a second circuit of the usual double field journey, aware that by now his wife would have gone for her first horse ride of the morning. She had certainly seemed to enjoy the previous evening and he had commented they should do that kind of thing more often, although aware she preferred the company of horses to humans. She could turn on the charm, however, and was quite sparkling the previous evening, chatting to the wives of a couple of fellow councillors who had been at their table. In fact, since his heart scare, she had appeared more sociable, although she had never been stand-offish. The event had seemed to bring them closer together, with her appearing more supportive of his activities and had even made cakes for a fund-raising sale.

Back in the house, after struggling to get his boots off, he decided he needed a coffee and, not bothering to put on fresh coffee from the machine, helped himself to one of his wife's packets of instant cappuccino, not ideal for his diet but quick to prepare.

Hunger pangs suddenly struck him and he was not sure why but recently this would come upon him quite quickly. He could be fine for a while and then suddenly feel tired or, as now, feel all right and then suddenly feel very hungry. Occasionally, this would happen when he was out shopping

with his wife, and he admitted to himself, and to her, that being hungry did not help his temper.

Not quite sure what to do to remedy the current situation, on impulse, he decided to have a simple fried egg sandwich. He took just the one egg from the fridge, searched for and found a small frying pan, located the vegetable oil and set about his task. He was very fussy about his eggs, no matter what method they were cooked, and stood over the pan until he felt it had achieved the right perfection, quickly scooped it out and placed it on one of the two slices of bread, which he had already spread with low-fat margarine.

As he carried the plate to the kitchen table, he reminded himself he would have to get rid of the evidence by washing the frying pan independently as opposed to putting it into the dishwasher. He would also have to dispense with the tell-tale eggshell in order to avoid being nagged by his wife about his cholesterol level and dangers of too much fried food. Normally he was very good and, since his heart attack, had stuck to a pretty sensible diet for most of the time but occasionally did treat himself by having what he called sins. During his military career he had scoffed at what was now looked upon as unhealthy food, confident his extremely physically active life burned up any excessive fat or sugar.

He resisted the temptation to add salt on the egg and wolfed his sandwich down quickly before rinsing the residue of egg from the plate, which he placed in the dishwasher. He cleaned the frying pan and put it back in the cupboard from whence it came. The kitchen was certainly the domain of his wife, although she would occasionally allow him to cook something special for them, and he considered himself quite good at using leftovers to rustle up a tasty dish, many of which contained spices, although his wife's tastes differed

from his own and he had to cut down the intensity of the spice.

Still a little bit peckish, he helped himself to a banana from the fruit bowl before retiring to his study to open up the computer and check what emails had arrived that day.

There had been no follow up to the email from Sergeant Ellis and Cedric Foster-Clarkson had racked his brain about who might be behind the email from him. Not sure why, he believed it was someone local, part of the logic based on the pause between the first email and the follow up, which he believed was due to his hospital admission. He needed time, so drafted an email pointing out much of his wealth was tied up in long-term investments, which would take time to be released and was sure the charity would appreciate this. Meanwhile, as a gesture of goodwill, he was forwarding to their account the sum of two thousand pounds, which he trusted they would accept as a payment on account. He re-emphasised it would take time for him to have funds available and he would be in touch in the fairly near future.

Having done that, he contemplated things for a full two-hour period before pressing the send button. During the two hours, he had listed every single person he currently knew and was in touch with including all the people in the village.

The morning was beautiful, the field already bathed in sunshine, as Eleanor followed the dogs past the defunct gate and let them off the leads. Eleanor's thoughts were on the forthcoming visit to the clinic in London where they would take the necessary action to rid her of the unborn and unwanted child in her body. Thankfully, she was showing no signs of increased weight, but had recently taken to wearing loose fitting clothing just in case. It had been a little time

since her most recent assignation with the accountant, so no one had seen her naked.

She had not progressed far when, from the opposite direction, she saw the couple with the beagle accompanied by two small children who were introduced as their great grandchildren. The dogs made a fuss of both. The little girl, who must have been seven or eight, was interested in both dogs, but the younger boy was slightly reticent, keeping his distance from the animals. Eleanor picked up Rags to take her to the boy so he could see how friendly she was, but it was still a quite reluctant hand which reached out to stroke her.

The elderly couple explained they were childminding for the day, allowing their granddaughter and her husband to go on an outing somewhere, but did not explain exactly where.

They said their goodbyes and the temperature dropped slightly as Eleanor passed into the area shaded by the long line of bushes and trees that separated the fields, so she made her way through one of the gaps into the adjoining field which was still fully bathed in the sun's rays. The dogs ran ahead, so by the time she picked herself carefully along the path, the mongrel had disappeared but returned from somewhere in the bushes at Eleanor's first blast on her whistle.

She thought about the couple as she walked. They had a computer which, thanks to downloading a photograph accompanied by the software, Alexander had obtained control of but had only spent a brief time examining the machine, which showed not much usage. There was evidence that one or other of the pair had briefly visited porn sites on a few occasions, but nothing which could be described as an obsession. They had also done a bit of online shopping and their bank details revealed they were not particularly wealthy, although appeared to have some reserves, presumably set

aside for their even older age. Alexander and his mother decided against trying to extract any money from the pair and had left them in peace.

Eleanor occasionally had to work hard to blank out any feeling of guilt over what she and her son were doing, convincing herself they were only taking money from people who could easily afford it. Her obsession with the wellbeing of her son overcame any other feeling. She had sometimes wondered if she could kill for him, decided she could if it was necessary and, occasionally, during dark moods, wondered if she would die for him, with those same dark moods deciding she would if it could make him whole again. These thoughts, and seeing the children, reminded her she was planning to end a life herself as she struggled with her mixed emotions.

CHAPTER 46

Cedric Foster-Clarkson was already in the bar of the country pub, where he had arranged to meet Javendra, when the Indian arrived. The colonel immediately rose from his seat to walk across and greet him.

'Good afternoon, Mr Bhattacharya. So kind of you to meet me. What would you like to drink? Then we'll go into the small dining room where there's a quiet table.'

'Just tonic water with ice please,' the younger man replied, fidgety, impatiently showing signs he wished to know what the meeting was all about.

Javendra managed to contain himself during the time he was ushered into a separate room, carrying his drink, whilst his host retrieved his own soft drink from the table at which he had previously been seated.

'First of all, I should inform you I'm a director and partner of the security company run by my colleague Michael O'Flanagan, so there's no breach in confidentiality as the documents which you signed enable Michael to discuss your situation with people inside the company and appropriate ones outside.'

Javendra's immediate reaction was very guarded, realising he had gone all the way to London to find a discreet organisation, only to discover one of the people involved was on his doorstep.

'I'm sure Michael is the best person around to help you,' Cedric continued, 'But there is another issue which he did not know at the time, and which I have advised him since. You see, I am also being blackmailed, and it's possible it's by the same person or persons.'

The Indian hesitated, taking a sip of the tonic water before replying, relaxing and deciding to trust the man to a certain extent, who would no doubt have all the information about him anyway.

'Mine is supposedly an African-based charity pretending to help people over there. I have many business interests, and I'm sure I'm one of the vast majority who feel the tax system in this country is not as fair as it might be. I also have a hotel, which sometimes caters for broad-minded people wanting to have a good time, if you know what I mean, Colonel. There's nothing wrong or even illegal about this, but the people are trying to discredit me amongst friends, some of them in positions where they will want to avoid embarrassment. What about yourself?'

The old man sighed. 'Something that happened many years ago, which could also be a little embarrassing.' He smiled. 'I guess people like us, with high profiles, are always targets of envious people wanting to bring us down, don't you think?'

Javendra was already beginning to like the man as Cedric went on.

'The reason I asked you to meet me today was to see if there is a common interest, and if you would like to work together on this. Even prior to letting Michael know the situation, I have been compiling information about people I know, and my instinct tells me that either the people behind it, or certainly working with them, are based locally.

Unfortunately, I had a heart attack some time ago when the first blackmail threats arrived and they seemed to back off a little during my short convalescence, which may indicate someone who knew what was happening.'

'Have you contacted the police?' Javendra asked.

'No. Sadly, our police force is very busy on other matters and don't have enough staff to deal with serious issues. I'm sure our little difficulties would not be high on their priority list. You're no doubt aware I'm also the local mayor, and having spent many years in the security business, I'm not sure even our police force is able to keep the lid on everything. I take it that the fact you've approached Michael means you've also taken the same attitude?'

Javendra nodded before asking, 'Do you have any suspects?'

'Mr Bhattacharya, one thing I learned in the security business is patience and not to jump to conclusions. We can assume the motive for these crimes is greed and it would appear to be some kind of information, which is somehow being obtained by the use of computers, although at this stage I'm not sure what.

'In my village, we used to have a young man who was a computer whizz kid, but sadly, he got killed in a car crash leaving a widow and disabled child to take care of. I actually know the lady quite well as she has done some dog minding for myself and my wife when we've had to go away on political business.'

Javendra had been in the process of raising his glass to his lips but stopped as the words sunk in.

'Do you mean Eleanor McLoughlin?' he asked.

'Well, yes, as a matter of fact I do. Do you know her?'

'Yes, I do.' His brain was roaring through the gears, wondering just how much to confide in the man opposite,

shocked to think she would stoop to such tactics, but also aware it was fairly soon after their differences the threats began.

He was spared making the decision as a waiter came into the room and asked them what they would like to order, neither of them having inspected the menu, but broke off their conversation in order to do so. The lunchtime special was homemade shepherd's pie, with Javendra confessing he was not strictly religious regarding diet and Cedric deciding it would suit him also.

'Have you met her son?' he asked the colonel.

'No. Have you?'

'Yes, and he knows a lot about computers. Apparently, his father taught him and I've heard he was an absolute genius.'

As Cedric drove home following the lunch with Javendra, Eleanor McLoughlin was very much at the centre of the local mayor's thoughts. She was clearly a common link between the pair of them, and they had shared ideas with each another during the remainder of their lunch. Cedric remembered, somewhere in the back of his mind, Eleanor offering to send him, or email him, a photograph of his dogs, but which he had refused. This information was offered when the Indian had volunteered the information he had downloaded a video of his wife when she was on a short break with Eleanor and her family.

Aware the woman had been in his house whilst he was away, whilst Foster-Clarkson was convinced his security system was fine, he had to admit to the unlikely possibility she would have taken advantage of having access to his computers. Trying to keep calm and not to hurry, he was trying to remember how long the CCTV system retained

information which it viewed. He knew that after a period of time it automatically wiped itself clean of earlier recordings, but was not sure how long that period was. He had seen Eleanor in his house with the dogs when he was attending the conference, but had been interrupted and had not continued watching events later.

On arriving home, Cedric went straight to his computer, disappointed to discover the CCTV footage for the time when he was away had already been deleted. It was such a time since the system had been installed he wasn't sure if it was saved for a longer period by the people who had provided the software, so made a note in his diary to check with them the following day. Meanwhile, he telephoned Michael O'Flanagan to advise him of his conversation with Javendra Bhattacharya, including what may possibly be a common thread, providing Michael with details of Eleanor McLoughlin and her son. In his own mind, he did not see the woman as a blackmailer, but was also aware of her financial situation, emphasised by the fact she had to take on mundane work in order to make ends meet. Javendra had described some of the technological equipment he had seen Alexander use, so was not prepared to dismiss anything at this stage.

Michael O'Flanagan sat in a waiting room for fifty-three minutes before eventually getting a chance to talk to Chief Inspector Joseph Smith, but left the police station convinced the wait had been very worthwhile. Whilst not prepared to divulge his clients, Michael advised the detective he was representing two people who were being blackmailed and he wondered if the chief inspector had received complaints from anyone else in the area. Both men were guarded regarding the information which each one was prepared to divulge,

but the mention of the charity based in Africa persuaded Joe to admit he had been approached by someone local. Furthermore, he was prepared to believe the incidents were linked.

As Michael left the police station on his way to see the colonel and advise him of his news, Joe Smith sat at his desk beginning to be convinced the tip of the possible iceberg was getting bigger, the mystery deepening, and he really needed to pay more attention to the case, although had been unable to persuade the security man to provide him with much information regarding his own clients.

Having been advised of the conversation between his client and his business partner, Michael had hinted at the possibility of a dog owner being involved and suggested the name of a village which may be worth checking.

CHAPTER 47

Detective Chief Inspector Joseph Smith felt very conspicuous as he and the young dog handler entered the field. The presence of the two German shepherd police dogs, which they had brought in an effort to blend in with the locals, did not make him feel any less obvious. He had believed this kind of approach might be less frightening than to simply walk into the field on his own and start asking questions of dog lovers.

So far, he had drawn a blank on the bank details the blackmailer used, with the trail leading to a maze of complicated overseas trusts and eventually a blank wall. The trouble the blackmailer had gone to, and the meeting with Michael, had convinced the detective that Glenda Wilkinson was not an isolated case.

Questioning the woman, he had not been able to find any kind of motive against herself and her pompous husband and tried to dismiss the idea that many bank managers were disliked. Being familiar with the huge increase in cyber-crime, when he had questioned Glenda about any strange emails, he had been advised about her receiving the photograph of her dog from the dog walker. Discreet questioning revealed the dog walker was a widow, but her late husband had been a computer whizz kid. The link was very faint, but he managed to persuade his superior to allow him to investigate to see if any other dog owners had suffered the same fate.

Whilst not expecting to see a pack of dogs and owners, he was disappointed that himself and the dog handler were the only occupants of the field upon their arrival. In his pocket, the chief inspector had a list of descriptions, some with names alongside, of people who were known to regularly walk their dogs in the two fields which they now occupied. It was a bright sunny morning, and the dog handler and himself were dressed casually in jeans and T-shirts in an effort to blend in with the local community. They were on the second circuit of the first field when they met their first dog owners: a couple with a beagle who had been described on his list, but for whom they did not have names. Very aware of the fact the collection of evidence had to be carried out in a transparent way, whilst the suspicious beagle lay down some distance from the police dogs, the detective produced his ID to the couple. He advised them he was carrying out enquiries regarding incidents, which may or may not have connections with people using the field and invited them to assist him in his enquiries.

Sometimes interrupting one another, the couple provided information about people who they regularly saw, occasionally providing names, always giving information on the types of dogs and sometimes with names of the pets. Within twenty minutes, his own list had been extended considerably, the couple making three walks a day, meeting up with more other walkers than the ones whose details he already possessed.

Thanking them for their cooperation, they went their separate ways and the inspector did not believe he had met either the blackmailers or victims, although had taken full details of how they could be contacted.

They talked to people with Border collies, spaniels, retrievers, Jack Russells, cockapoos and labradoodles, before encountering the colonel with his labradors.

The detective inspector's many years of interrogating people had developed additional sensors and he detected a feeling of fear in the elderly man, who was extremely guarded in many of his replies to their questions, but was extremely happy when asked to provide contact details.

An elderly lady with two small dogs was very chatty and gossiped about everybody and anybody and was able to provide very detailed information about some of the field users.

The man with a white husky, who owned up to being an accountant, was also very guarded. Joe was convinced he had things to hide, although there was no response when Joe enquired if any of the man's clients had confided in him.

The pair returned to the police vehicle mid-morning to allow the dogs food and drink, and for them to enjoy their own flask of coffee, before returning to the task. They broke off again at lunchtime before continuing once more in the afternoon. They did meet one lady who admitted to having received a copy of a photograph of her dog from the dog walker, but she had received no demand for money.

It was the following morning before they met the woman with the poodle and the mongrel.

Seeing the Alsatians, the white poodle bounded towards the newcomers, hotly pursued by the galloping mongrel. Under the control of the dog handler, the shepherds allowed themselves to be greeted in a friendly manner by the newcomers and, after checking the field to see no other dogs were around, he allowed his charges off their leads to

enter into a game of chase with the other two, enabling the detective to open the conversation with Eleanor, asking if she could help with his enquiries.

'Oh, Chief Inspector, I'm so sorry,' she blurted after he had formally introduced himself. 'Is it about the blackmailer. I know I should have come to see you, but I really was so ashamed, and after a few payments, I stopped paying. Have you caught them? Have they been blackmailing others? Oh dear, how can I possibly help?'

Joseph Smith looked at her, taken totally by surprise at the outburst, and recognised the strange cocktail of emotions ranging from terror, through fear to relief. Shocked into silence for a fraction of a second, he realised the woman had almost seemed prepared for this confrontation and was not sure if it had been recent or something she expected to happen in due course.

Determined to identify which of those situations to be the most accurate, he asked, 'How did you know about this enquiry, madam?'

'This is a small village, Chief Inspector, and people gossip.' Then she noticed a man entering the field with his dog and added, 'I can come to the station when it would be more convenient for you. It's difficult out here with people coming and going and I would really like to help.'

He suggested a date and, taking out her smartphone, Eleanor entered the details as they arranged the time. She called her dogs to heel, which took a full minute, and then went on her way, leaving the policeman to interrogate the newcomer.

At the police station, Eleanor produced the copies of the blackmailing emails and the transactions making the first payments.

'I was really frightened,' she explained, 'I don't know who it was that saw me do this terrible thing.'

She related her concocted story about stealing the dress, before continuing. 'And you can imagine what kind of shock it was when I received the first email. Whilst I knew I had not been apprehended, I had only recently made some very good friends in the village and did not want to jeopardise the position with them, even being suspected of theft. You can understand why I could not discuss it with anybody.

'I know we're supposed to be innocent until proven guilty in this country, but very often people are tainted with being suspected of crimes, as opposed to actually committing them, and the amateur judges and juries sentence without trial. I'm sorry, Chief Inspector. I know I really should have come to see you, but was terribly afraid of losing my friends. Can you understand that?'

Her lips trembled and she wiped away at the corner of her eye to prevent the tear falling onto her cheek.

The detective's heart went out to this woman as he shared her pain. His enquiries had unearthed the fact she was a widow, who looked after a very disabled son, and had taken on dog walking duties in order to try to make ends meet. Everyone spoke highly of her and her courage at fighting to provide her son with some kind of life. Whilst being trained never to assume, the inspector believed there was no way in the world this woman could be his blackmailer.

Back in her car, Eleanor slumped in her seat and let out an extremely audible sigh of relief.

Thankfully, she had been tipped off by the couple with the beagle about the inspector asking questions. Considering abandoning her walk in order to avert a possible meeting,

she discussed the matter with Alexander and they agreed that would be folly and she should face up to the meeting, introducing herself as a victim who was prepared to cooperate in any way. She had been thankful for the warning, which gave her time to gather her wits and prepare her presentation to the inspector.

She felt quite happy with her performance and felt it highly unlikely she was on his list of suspects.

Arriving home, she discussed matters with Alexander and suggested that perhaps they should ask their victims for a final lump sum and then cease the operation in case the police enquiries uncovered the real culprits. As ever logical, her son suggested this would only risk more people going to the police, which could only help to increase enquiries, whilst assuring her it was virtually impossible for their operation to be traced.

Eleanor panicked as the police car pulled up outside but, realising Alexander was in his room, decided he was in no danger, but always worried lest some of their secrets had somehow been uncovered. Minutes later, she was relaxed as she thanked the policeman, who had been full of apologies, having been despatched to deliver Gerald's laptop, which had been taken away as evidence at the time of the crash. Eleanor had completely forgotten about it and, apparently, so had the police as it had only been discovered when an archive was being moved into a brand-new building at police headquarters.

She was asked to sign for the machine, the mains connector and the remote mouse as the policeman explained no incriminating evidence had been found on the machine and human error had been the reason why it had not been returned much earlier. Thanking her for her understanding,

the young constable, refusing a cup of coffee, went back to his car, mission accomplished.

If Eleanor had not shown any excitement or even interest on the event, the situation was very different when she explained to Alexander his father's laptop been returned by the police, passing on the excuses made by the constable as to why it had taken so long.

Alexander couldn't wait to examine the computer and, after his mother at last placed it on his desk, laboriously plugged it in and switched it on, happy it would work off the mains but doubted that, after so long, the batteries would still be effective. The situation would also be the case with the remote mouse as he searched the drawers of his specially adapted desk to locate a wire connected version.

Gerald had taught Alexander a clever way of devising computer passwords, which were all extremely similar yet totally different. The middle seven digits, a combination of letters upper- and lower-case, numbers, pound signs and exclamation marks were all consistent and in exactly the same order. The first and last items varied, according to the folder in which the documents would be stored. Alexander's own password to his computer was the first letters of his first name and surname, and he was aware Gerald had used the same for his initial entry into his computer, and his son knew the password would carry a similar simple, yet highly complex, system. For example, Bloggs Bank would have a capital B at the start of the password, and lower-case b at the end of it. Smith's Insurance: large S at the front and small i at the end. Using this system, Alexander was soon into the computer, but an hour later, realised all of the activities that had taken place on their evening excursions, and other private items, were no longer visible.

Although he could not remember the actual accident, it had been explained to him later, and Alexander was certain his father would not have had time to carry out any deletion of files from the laptop before being rushed into hospital. He was aware how brilliant his father was, so would have no doubt there would be some device built into the machine, which would immediately hide any documents Gerald did not want to be found, and which would require a second completely different password to retrieve.

What Alexander didn't know was the name given by his father to the secret files, so until he figured that out, he could not go any further.

For the next hour Alexander tried and failed with names including charity contributions, cash receipts, money paid and many more including blackmail.

Alexander was certain the computer held the secret to a batch of money, which his father had secreted away, and it was vital he broke the code.

In the evening, he explained the situation to his mother and to Ahmed, and for the next seven evenings they came up with hundreds of ideas, none of which worked.

Alexander was determined not to give up and persuaded them to try on the Saturday morning when they were all fresh and could maybe come up with new ideas; all of the previous attempts had been meticulously recorded by Alexander on a spreadsheet, so they did not duplicate effort already made. They brainstormed, without success, for an hour, at which point Eleanor suggested a drink break, Ahmed volunteering to carry out the task. He gave Alexander his drink, which was already to hand and then went off to the kitchen to make his tea and Eleanor's coffee. On his return, he carefully put the

mug of coffee on a coaster at the side of the desk as Eleanor smiled at him and said, 'Thank you.'

Her son immediately stopped what he was doing and said in his slow pronunciation but with unbridled excitement, 'That might be it.'

'What do you mean, darling?' Eleanor replied.

Laboriously and slowly, he answered. 'Well, what do you say if someone gives you something?'

Unable to wait any longer, he went straight back to the laptop, and typed in the words in upper-case, in lower-case, T and Y, all to no avail. Eventually, he tried capital letters throughout, then with a small t at the front and capital Y at the end when, miraculously, a group of files appeared on the screen.

Clearly, Gerald had been confident no one else could have gained access to these, so there was no further password required to open the folders or files, one of which simply had the title 'banks' and which then had some details, listing the names of no less than five banks in various parts of the world. The first of these, listed in alphabetical order, was the name of a bank based in Panama and, using the password system taught to him by his father, Alexander soon obtained access. Downloading a summary of income and expenditure over the last three months, they discovered an amount of money had gone in but was then, within twenty-four hours, despatched out to a bank account number, but did not provide a name.

Further examination showed there was very little money still in the account, but the activity had been regular, and they went back and copied information from the previous two years.

The second bank, based in Malta, showed a similar pattern, and again the payments were to the same bank account number as the previous one. It was the third bank, based in Switzerland, with which they hit the jackpot. It was the account into which the other two, plus others, had been paying on a regular basis, showing constant income but, apart from quarterly bank charges, no outgoings whatsoever.

'How much is in there?' Eleanor asked.

'Over four million Swiss francs.' Alexander's fingers moved slowly over the keyboard as he accessed a site to carry out the conversion.

Out of touch with exchange rates, Eleanor had to sit down while her son converted the figure for her.

'That's over three million pounds sterling.'

The trio sat in silent shock as the information sank in and Eleanor was suddenly aware her late husband had not left her in the disastrous financial state she had been left to believe, but until now they had been unable to access the money. She also knew that to use it would not be an easy task as her experiences with Javendra had shown.

'What happens now?' Ahmed asked quietly.

Eleanor looked at the large clock on the wall above her son's desk, then turned to the Bangladeshi with a broad smile.

'What happens now is that we go for lunch. I think we can afford to eat out on this occasion, don't you, boys? Ahmed, do you want to get Alexander ready, while I get changed then we can go to that lovely Asian restaurant in town we all like. After all, it's not every day you discover you're millionaires.'

The trio had never differentiated between weekends and weekdays, so it was no surprise that, as soon as they arrived home, Alexander wanted to continue his investigation into the bank details which they had now unearthed. It appeared

there were accounts to which money had previously been paid and would, therefore, require no passwords or anything to repeat a payment. High on the list was Eleanor's housekeeping account, so just to prove a point, Alexander transferred the sum of five hundred pounds directly into this and, despite it being the weekend, within minutes they were able to check the transfer had been successfully made.

Whilst discussing the situation, they were all aware it was not going to be an easy matter using the fortune of which they had now taken possession. Eleanor knew any unusual influx of funds would be viewed with suspicion, but now with Ahmed involved, reasonable amounts could be explained from the connection in Bangladesh and, provided they did not go mad, could reasonably claim to have received financial assistance from Ahmed's family over there. It was Ahmed himself who explained that not everyone in Bangladesh was poor, and he was sure some of the wealthier ones could have an account in a Swiss bank, with no questions asked.

So far, they had only two people look around the house and Eleanor wondered if their newfound wealth should persuade them to consider remaining where they were using the offshore funds to gradually clear off the mortgage arrears. The problem was, having trawled back through the last three years, the income into the accounts had reduced and, on checking, they found payments from one company had stopped altogether. A search on the internet confirmed they had been taken over by a larger conglomerate, with their fictitious workers not being transferred to the new parent company.

Just to see how easy it was to make payments to a new account, and with Eleanor's agreement, Alexander used Gerald's password system to transfer one hundred and

twenty-two pounds directly into the account of Ahmed, which also went through without any problem. This time they had deliberately avoided a round figure, and all agreed there was probably some kind of limit above which further security checks would be necessary. Understandably, they were frightened of trying to overstep the mark, only to discover the account was then frozen.

Still buoyed by the apparent answer to their financial prayers, Eleanor was in a good mood and had to explain herself as she started giggling.

'Well, look at us,' she said laughing, 'It's hardly the picture MI5 would conjure up in their minds if they were considering trying to find a group of international operators, evading tax by transferring money from all parts of the world.'

The others also saw the funny side of things as they considered their options. For a very brief moment, Eleanor considered asking advice from Hugh Barker, but rapidly dismissed the idea of involving the accountant with whom she was still in a very loose relationship. He had actually taken over the blackmail payments from her and put them through his company. He had sensibly realised that as a gift to charity, they could be offset against tax whereas when he paid cash to Eleanor, he had to pay the full amount. She also decided there was absolutely no way in which she could talk to either her own bank manager, or the pompous ass who lived in the village, who was now making a contribution to their fund.

Eleanor also wondered if Gerald had any other accounts anywhere; the additional two were also feeding money into the main Swiss account and had obviously been set up to muddy the waters if anyone tried to locate the identity of people extracting the funds from their unknowing victims.

CHAPTER 48

Chief Inspector Joe Smith had accumulated quite a list of statistics in his investigation during his tramping round the field and information collated afterwards. One amazing piece of information, was that, for a very small village which was the centre of his investigation, there were many dog owners of which more than forty regularly trespassed in the fields to exercise their animals. Of the forty, at least four had received attempted blackmail threats, to which two had succumbed, the other two refusing to bow to the threats of the blackmailer and had not coughed up.

One person, allegedly, had three payments of fifty pounds taken from their account and paid into the same bank account used by the blackmailer. They claimed never to have authorised the money and, as soon as they recognised the transactions on their statement, cancelled the payment system set up. When visiting the bank, with the authorisation of the victim, Joe was advised the transaction had been conducted online, looked extremely legitimate and the bank had, therefore, refused to refund the hundred and fifty pounds in question. This latter incident had only come to light in the last two days and it worried Joe, particularly as the victim had embarrassingly owned up to using the same passwords for all of their confidential information.

Joe pondered for some time about this currently isolated incident of the payment to the charity, but wondered if this could be more widespread. Using the blackmail case as an excuse to carry out further enquiries, he decided to re-interview people to whom he had already talked, but had not mentioned anything about money being removed without their knowledge, restricting his questions to blackmail.

CHAPTER 49

Eleanor had decided to stay in the clinic overnight following her abortion, even though it was not thought necessary; she did not want to face Alexander and Ahmed after her ordeal.

Following her discussion with her own doctor, she had visited the clinic for an assessment to again discuss the reasons for her wanting the abortion. She confirmed her decision and used a supporting letter from the doctor explaining the reason. She rejected the offer of talking things through with a trained counsellor, but did talk to the doctor at the clinic, who advised her about possible complications. She had also been subjected to the various tests to confirm a pregnancy, clearance of any sexually transmitted disease, blood type and iron levels and had been provided with antibiotics.

Provided with various options, Eleanor had rejected the idea of the medical system, using tablets, as it would require two separate visits to the clinic. Instead, she had opted for a surgical abortion, selecting the vacuum system as preference.

This had been carefully explained to her and which could be used up to fifteen weeks of pregnancy. It involved inserting a tube through the cervix and into the womb; the pregnancy was then ended as the embryo was removed using suction.

'Your cervix will be gently widened first,' she was told, 'And a tablet may be placed inside your vagina, or taken by

mouth, a few hours beforehand to soften your cervix and make it easier to open.

'Pain relief is usually given using medicines you take by mouth and local anaesthetic, which is numbing medicine injected into the cervix. You may also be offered some sedation, which is given by injection. A general anaesthetic isn't usually needed.

'Vacuum aspiration takes about five to ten minutes and most women go home a few hours later. As with all types of abortion, it's likely you will experience some stomach cramps and vaginal bleeding too. These usually last a week or two. Sometimes light vaginal bleeding after a medical abortion can last up to a month. You can take ibuprofen to help with any pain or discomfort.

'Use sanitary towels or pads, rather than tampons, until the bleeding has stopped. Have sex as soon as you feel ready, but use contraception if you want to avoid getting pregnant again as you'll usually be fertile immediately after the abortion.

'Get advice if you experience heavy bleeding, severe pain, smelly vaginal discharge, a fever or ongoing signs of pregnancy, such as nausea and sore breasts. The clinic will give you the number of a twenty-four-hour helpline to call if you have concerns.

'You may experience a range of emotions afterwards. If you need to discuss how you're feeling, contact the abortion service or ask your GP about post-abortion counselling.'

It was all over very quickly, as she had been promised, and she was soon back in the small private room to which she had been allocated for her overnight stay. She felt a little soreness between her legs, but a tremendous feeling of guilt

and sadness in her mind as she quietly shed tears for the losing of her unborn child. So far, she had not asked anything about it, somehow feeling it may be better if she did not know which of her two lovers was the father. She also did not wish to know the condition of the embryo, having used her traumatic upbringing of her extremely disabled firstborn as her reason for having the abortion.

Glad she had decided not to face her son at this time, her feeling was she would probably never confess the situation to him.

After she had been allowed to rest for a short time, a nurse came in and carried out checks for blood pressure and temperature, before changing the pad nestled between her legs, held in place by a pair of white pants. She was advised the doctor would visit her later, just to see how she was and may need to carry out an examination.

When he arrived, shortly after the nurse, there was a look of concern on his face as he asked her how she was feeling and if she had been given a smear test recently, to which she replied in the negative.

'Is there something wrong?' she asked.

'You need to be checked out by your own doctor,' she was advised, 'And I would suggest you do this as soon as possible.'

'Then there is something wrong,' she said, suddenly frightened.

'Mrs McLoughlin, I'm not sure, but there was some unusual discharge and you just need to get it checked out, that's all. We can do certain tests here, but not that particular one.'

Her heart sank. 'You mean, cancer?'

'Mrs McLoughlin, my belief is that we all have cancer in us, sometimes it develops, often it does not. We can also

deal with many forms of cancer, but need to know what we're up against. Please do not ask me to try to guess and answer something which I cannot, but please take my advice and make an appointment with your own general practitioner as soon as you can.'

CHAPTER 50

Fay woke up to the sound of wind and rain battering her bedroom window. For a second, she had to remember why she had a hand cupping her right breast and could feel naked thighs against her equally naked bottom, then the memory came flooding back.

Theodore and herself had to travel some distance to carry out a viewing of a very highly priced house in the country, which presented an opportunity for them to earn a considerable amount of commission.

Situated in a really tranquil setting, the building was an old rectory, which had been converted to produce a stunning detached Georgian residence. It contained open fireplaces, sash windows and ceiling mouldings, typical of the time.

Set in almost two acres of grounds, the living space extended to over five thousand square feet, which took in three reception rooms, a playroom, an office, an annex with its own kitchen, five double bedrooms of which three had en suite facilities, modern gas central heating, a double garage and a double gated entrance.

Fay had fallen in love with it, the huge high rooms all sporting beautiful chandeliers, and the ground floor with hard flooring throughout, varying from wood laminates in the lounge, a real wood floor in the study and tiles in the beautifully fitted out kitchen.

The en suite adjacent to the master bedroom sported a curved copper bath, in addition to a shower unit, toilet and beautiful sink, behind which sat a full wall length mirror at the back of glass shelving, providing much storage space for necessary ablution items, but upon which the current owner had also put a few ornaments.

The house was filled with quality furniture, which looked to be either antique or very expensive and skilled reproductions.

The couple showing them around were from London and the son and daughter-in-law of the current residents who had decided to spend all of their time abroad instead of commuting between the two properties which they owned. Fay wondered how attractive their life abroad must be to be prepared to abandon the idyllic setting back home. They had instructed their son he could either have the house as his legacy now or dispose of it as he wished and take the money as a gift in the hope his parents would live long enough for him not to pay any of it back in tax.

The man, particularly, gave an impression of being in a hurry, did not want to spend time travelling from London to see various estate agents and, very surprisingly, asked their terms and conditions. He explained he would like to appoint them immediately. As the property would be around the two million mark, in addition to being a showpiece for them, it would also bring considerable earnings.

Mission completed, Theodore and Fay had stopped for an early lunch at a country pub on the way back in order to celebrate being given instructions. They had celebrated with not one, but two bottles of wine, which had loosened the pair up and she felt comfortable at raising the question of Theodore's blackmailer. He confessed he was paying, but

argued the amount was fairly nominal, that he could afford it, and could not face a scandal. She had been brave enough to tell him she believed he was not a homosexual and the alcohol-fuelled talk had got around to him volunteering to prove the fact and she, having been celibate for some time, accepted his challenge.

As she lay beside him now, she was confident that, whilst by his own admission he had enjoyed the escapade with the two men, he certainly knew how to please women and, having been deprived of that particular pleasure for some time, she had thoroughly enjoyed the experience. Somehow the grey, cloudy and damp day made it easier to go to bed in the afternoon. Now, she was very aware of the fact she had crossed the boundaries in her relationship with her boss, and was already feeling guilty about Lydia, his wife, with whom she was extremely friendly.

Over lunch, she had been unable to persuade Theodore that the blackmail payment was not a sensible idea, but he was dogmatic in convincing himself he was doing the right thing.

She felt him stirring beside her, turning to face him, thinking how much younger he looked today in a happy satisfied state.

'Would you like a cup of tea?' she asked.

'Yes please,' he replied but automatically looked on the floor to find his trousers, from which he extracted his mobile phone exclaiming, 'Shit' as he glanced at it.

'What's the matter?'

'Five missed calls from the office and two text messages.'

He checked the text messages initially, the first asking what time he was expected back at the office, the second with a more urgent message saying there was a policeman there wishing to talk to him.

The voicemail contained the tones of a nervous agent who confirmed there was a policeman there wanting to know when he would be returning, and who wished to talk to him on a private matter. A later voicemail told him the police had now left, but he needed to contact them on his return, so they could make arrangements to see him.

Whilst he was checking his mobile, Fay noticed she also had missed calls and a text message asking her if she was still with Theodore and if so, could she or he make contact with the office as a matter of urgency.

Donning a thin shawl, she hurried downstairs to make the promised tea as Theodore located the rest of his clothes and began dressing. It was too late to believe he could get back to the office in time to telephone the police. He could not possibly figure out why they wanted to see him, casting his mind back to recall if he had been speeding, decided that, to his knowledge, he had not been caught doing so, and could not possibly think of any other reason, although was concerned the conversation had referred to a private matter.

Deciding an additional few minutes would make no difference, he agreed to have the cup of tea which Fay had prepared and was thankful he had driven today, so she would not have to drive him home, guilt of the way the afternoon had been spent already creeping into his conscience. He had long found Fay very attractive, as were some of the other girls in the office, but until today had successfully managed to keep business and pleasure apart.

In the early days as an estate agent, he had twice succumbed to the temptations of grieving widows who were going to have to sell up due to the loss of their spouses, but had chastised himself for being totally unprofessional, although enjoying the experiences with the older women at the time.

Today he had felt his manhood was being challenged and been unable to resist the temptation to prove it.

'Thank you for coming in, sir,' Joe Smith addressed the estate agent. 'And I'm sorry if we caused you alarm and embarrassment by sending a police constable to your office, but I did try to telephone, and must have been given the wrong mobile number. We did talk to you some time ago, when we were carrying out enquiries in your area about people who have been blackmailed and, at that the time, you did state clearly this had not happened to you. Is that still correct, sir?' Joe stared at Theodore.

'Well, yes, Chief Inspector, nothing is any different to the last time we spoke, so may I ask what this is all about?'

'Well, sir,' Joe said, 'New evidence has come to light, both in blackmailing and other things. Apparently, there's a possibility the same culprits have been hacking into the bank account details of people. Using the information, they have been making donations to their fictitious charity, which is based overseas somewhere, so I'm going to ask you if you wouldn't mind checking your bank statements for unusual payments of which you are not aware.

'Also, back to the blackmailing, we've got some links to someone who's been walking their dog in the same field you use and possibly using emailed photographs of the dogs of their victims in order to invade their computers, thus enabling them to obtain both business and personal information about them. Does any of this ring a bell, sir?'

Theo felt a sense of fear running through him at the words, knowing that, should the police get permission to look at his bank statements, they would find the payments made to the charity and learn he had been lying to them, thus

committing the very serious crime of perverting the course of justice. Brain racing, he suddenly came up with the excuse that he could deny knowledge of the payments taken and blame the charity or blackmailers, whoever they were, taking it without his knowledge, and at this particular moment that seemed to be the best solution.

'Good gracious, Chief Inspector, that is frightening. I'll certainly go back and check my bank statements. How far back do you think I should go? We do get all our statements by the internet, but I can download them and get back to you with any unusual payments.'

'I'm not sure, sir,' the detective answered. 'Perhaps six months should be sufficient. Other victims have noticed varying amounts being taken out of their bank account on a monthly basis. Some found out quickly and cancelled the arrangement with their banks. Others, perhaps with more money than sense, have been paying for some four or five months.'

'So, how did they manage to do it, Chief Inspector?' Theodore asked.

Joe Smith sighed. 'Unfortunately, despite warnings, many computer users choose the same passwords for more than one activity, in our obsession with computers and modern technology, little realising there are people out there with more knowledge than them who are ruthless enough to take advantage of their carelessness.'

His words made Theodore feel guilty as he himself could be accused of the same thing, until the blackmailing episode when he religiously went through and changed all the passwords, but carefully kept a record of them on a spreadsheet, which was housed on his computer.

'Have you found many people being blackmailed, Chief Inspector? Are you close to finding out who did it?'

'We have a long way to go, sir.'

Theodore squirmed inwardly as the policeman added, 'Not everyone has been telling us the truth as some of the reasons for that are no doubt very sensitive. This would make our life and our job easier, but I guess that is a cross we have to bear. Anyway, once again, thank you for coming in and for your help.'

Pausing to open a drawer, he extracted a card and handed it to the estate agent. 'That contains my telephone number, so please check your bank statements as soon as possible. The sooner we get these people the better.'

Fay's mobile bleeped, as she sat at her desk in the estate agent's office, advising her she had a text message which simply read: 'Have seen the police. Meet me at your place.'

Detective Chief Inspector Joseph Smith did not believe in coincidences. A methodical organised collator, analyser and sifter of information, he would carefully investigate any links in order to try to piece together the jigsaw of a crime.

Theodore Farquharson was one of three more people who claimed to have made payments to the charity without their knowledge and the other two, following careful questioning, had admitted to receiving and downloading copies of photographs from the dog walker. He still could not believe Eleanor McLoughlin capable of these crimes, but, so far, including her, he had five victims, all of whom had connections to the woman. Eleanor was one of only two who had, so far, admitted to being blackmailed, had proved the offence had taken place some time ago, and that the payments had definitely been made. Whilst knowing as much about

cyber-crime as most of his colleagues in the force, he was not sufficiently informed to understand how clever some of the software was. A visit to county headquarters was enlightening and also confusing, leaving him none the wiser, apart from knowing he was out of his depth. Nagging at him was the undisputed fact that, if he was ignorant about computers, from all accounts, Eleanor McLoughlin's late husband was an absolute genius.

On a whim, he made another visit to headquarters to request sight of the files in respect to Gerald's death and that of the unfortunate man who had been unlucky enough to lose his life in the same accident. The only witness, heating engineer Patrick Doherty, had put the blame squarely on the shoulders of the computer man. Notes showed Gerald did not regain consciousness to provide his side of the story. The file also expressed difficulty in questioning the surviving son, due to a combination of his disability and memory loss at the time.

The reference to the condition of the boy decided Joseph he was an unlikely candidate as the blackmailer, and was not sure how adept his mother was with computers. Her own blackmailing payment was not faked, so if she was involved, she had been very clever about it, having the foresight to portray herself as a victim: a stroke of genius.

In an attempt to take her off guard, Joseph called on Eleanor on the pretext of enquiring about her habit of taking photographs of dogs and offering to email them to their owners. Fortunately, she was at home with her son as Ahmed had gone to college and, unusually, Alexander was in the lounge with his mother. When Eleanor apologised for the new but inexpensive furniture and explained she had to sell the previous quality items, he felt guilty at even considering

her as a suspect. The guilt was initially enhanced by the sight of the youngster in the wheelchair, but he gradually began to realise he was in the company of someone really clever in the computer world as Alexander explained the workings of his voice machine. There was undisguised evidence of tremendous pride as he described the creations of his late father, who he clearly admired and missed. The detective was quickly interrupted, and reprimanded, by his hostess when he asked Alexander if he could recall anything about the accident, advising Joseph of the trauma suffered by her son at the time.

Apologising, he sympathised with their ordeal leading to the resulting financial difficulties. He changed the subject to the photographs of dogs, bringing a change in her attitude.

'People dote on their pets, Chief Inspector, and the photos were a chance for me to talk to people and tell them about my dog walking services. I haven't broken the law, have I? I know we're supposed to have a good reason to ask people for details, but it has got ridiculous, don't you think?'

Accepting her explanation, he made his excuses and left. On the drive back to town, he analysed the visit, decided Eleanor McLoughlin would do anything for her son and that the late husband possessed an exceptional talent who had collated a mine of information, much of which had been passed on to his offspring. Eleanor's reaction to defend her son from his questioning was that of a parent prepared to go to any length to protect the young man.

Aware he was risking reprimand by opening up an old case, Joseph justified himself by believing the blackmail case could be much bigger than at first appeared. Deciding to question Patrick Doherty was not made easy and Joseph had to meet

the heating engineer on a building site and conduct his questioning in a cold, partially completed room of a house.

Patrick seemed wary as the event had happened so long ago and Joseph explained he was investigating a different case, which may be connected. The notes on the original case were quite sparse, and although two people had lost their lives there seemed to have been no investigation as to why the computer expert had been in the vicinity at the time. When questioned what Patrick was doing when he witnessed the event, it was recorded that it had happened close to his house. Patrick himself had been vague with his description, and explained he had been checking on his van. He did not own up to having received an email from the occupants of the Porsche and gone out to remonstrate with them. In truth, he had been scared he may have been implicated in the tragedy, which he wanted to avoid.

Joseph listened as the man repeated his story then looked him straight in the eye as he asked, 'Did you see the boy's computer?'

The hesitation was fractional, but enough to alert the interrogator.

'I just saw the car pull away and hit the other head on.'

'Did you get an email from them?' It was a complete shot in the dark, but Smith saw the look of fear in the other man's eyes before he regained his composure.

'I have never met these people, so how could I get an email from them?'

'Come on, Patrick. We get junk emails all the time, don't we? People are always trying to sell us something or other. Anyway, what were they doing outside your house at night? I take it you have a computer. Some people are clever enough

to sit close to people's homes and hack in to their computers. Has it happened to you?'

'Never.'

After his visit to the building site, Joseph made a rare lunchtime excursion to a pub, finding a welcoming one en route back to the office in which he ordered a pint of bitter and a toasted cheese sandwich, taking the drink to a corner table to await the delivery of his food.

Certain Doherty had lied to him, he wondered what he could possibly want to hide. He was not sure if he had any grounds on which to question the man further, but felt he could possibly be a victim.

As for the McLoughlins, he believed they had the motive of requiring money to support themselves. Their computer skills and knowledge would provide both the means and the opportunity to carry out the crime and he was now beginning to doubt his initial assessment of the innocence of the woman.

On reflection, he guessed her late husband's reputation was well known, at least locally, so she may have contemplated becoming a suspect if anything came out. Remembering her convincing performances when questioned in the field and later at the station, he was aware she had time to rehearse both and had cleverly diverted suspicion away from herself.

His sandwich arrived just as he decided he would try to persuade his superior to allow him to obtain a warrant to confiscate and examine the computers of both Eleanor McLoughlin and Patrick Doherty.

There was a spring in his step as Joe took the stairs two at a time, eager to talk to the station commander about his

progress. Knocking on the man's door, without waiting for an answer, he pushed it open.

'Ah, Joe, glad you are back,' his superior said, 'Got an urgent case for you, and I'm afraid you're going to have to drop everything else to deal with it right now. Apparently, there's been an arson attack in a flat over a shop. One person is already dead and two more in hospital with life-threatening injuries. Looks like we're looking at least manslaughter, if not murder, plus attempted murder. Get onto it right away and keep me informed. We need a quick result on this, Joe.'

CHAPTER 51

Bank manager Geoffrey Wilkinson had played a good round of golf in the morning, winning a few pounds in the process, and celebrated by having a few drinks at the golf club. Two glasses of wine accompanying the roast which his wife had prepared brought on a combination of being slightly inebriated and feeling a little tired. For the first time in a long time, it also made him feel amorous and, as he helped his wife to clear away and load the dishwasher, he suggested they take an afternoon siesta. The same alcohol that created the desire had the effect on performance, but also eliminated inhibitions, causing him to suggest it might be nice if Glenda demonstrated some of her sex toys.

Reluctant at first, she had also drunk two glasses of wine, so was persuaded to bring out her little bag of goodies from its hiding place behind some coats in her built-in wardrobe. Already naked, she tentatively stroked herself with the black vibrator, feeling very self-conscious as he watched. As she twisted the end of the contraption, resulting in the low-pitched hum as it vibrated against her inner thighs, she started to relax, closed her eyes and drifted off to her own fantasy land, where the vibrator was connected to the well-built West Indian.

Her husband's eyes travelled backwards and forwards, from between her legs to her face, the former trembling

slightly, whilst he noticed her bite her lower lip and flare her nostrils. The trembling of her legs increased as she slipped the vibrator all the way inside her, using the fingers of her other hand to press her clitoris against the vibration.

She forgot about the attention of the onlooker as the sensations, beginning deep in her inner self, transferred to her brain causing a low animal growl to leave her lips as she soared into a shuddering climax such as her husband had never witnessed before.

Watching the spectacle had excited him sufficiently to cause a firm erection and Glenda did not resist as he encouraged her to remove the vibrator and replace it with his own phallus. He laboured over her body for quite a considerable time, and it took both verbal and physical urging from her before he eventually ejaculated, following which he rolled away from her, and within minutes was fast asleep.

CHAPTER 52

Eleanor was shaking as she put down the telephone, went to the small cabinet where she kept her decanter of sherry and poured herself a large glassful, despite it being only ten on a Monday morning.

The call was from the local surgery, asking her to attend an appointment the following day in order to discuss the result of her tests which had been received. Her mind could only accept that such an early appointment did not mean good news, and already she was beginning to fear the worst, head spinning, as she wondered how her son could possibly manage without her. Immediately, she chided herself, knowing Ahmed was perfectly capable of looking after Alexander if and when something happened to her. She also realised she was jumping to perhaps the wrong conclusion, recalling the words of the doctor at the clinic who reminded her that the majority of cases of cancer diagnosed early could be dealt with or at least contained. Unfortunately, like the vast majority of people, Eleanor viewed the diagnosis of the disease as a sentence of death.

Chief Inspector Smith's visit had disturbed her and, together with the forthcoming visit to the surgery, had suddenly made her feel very vulnerable. Without trying to seem irrational, she sensed danger and, with her first concern being the wellbeing of her son, considered the

idea of suggesting that Alexander and Ahmed should visit Ahmed's homeland. She had selfish feelings in that if she was to cope with the cancer threat, she would prefer to tackle it without having to concern Alexander. It also occurred to her that if Smith did continue his investigations, it might be very difficult for them to use Gerald's money which they had found. Having traced back through the files, they discovered some payments in respect of the mortgage on the house had been made using the Swiss account. They had now used the money to pay off the arrears and were investigating ways of buying the house outright without drawing attention to themselves.

Following research carried out by Alexander, the trio had already decided they could use their fictitious charity to buy the property as an investment. This allowed them to remain in occupancy, to care for the property and be rewarded for doing so. Eleanor never ceased to wonder at the way in which her son's fertile mind worked and how much information he soaked up by surfing the internet. He seemed to have an ability to grasp the nub of lengthy, complicated information and she could only assume his ability had developed from the genes inherited from his father.

The three of them had already discussed, and agreed, that Ahmed should be allowed to send a small allowance to his family in Bangladesh, but Eleanor received a shock when she suggested they make the long trip there. Naively, she was unaware that, not only would their union not be recognised in Ahmed's home country, but the situation was the same throughout the vast majority of Asia, even including Singapore and Hong Kong.

A stunned Eleanor had to confess her fears about the investigations being carried out by the police, although did

not mention her concern about the cancer tests. She allocated the young men the task of finding out which counties, outside Europe, would offer the three of them safe entry, and also allow the purchase of property by foreigners. Meanwhile, she checked her telephone list for the number of Ebenezer Cohen, past landlord when she was first married and, to her knowledge, still a shareholder in the computer business. Wary of using Theodore Farquharson, she wanted Ebenezer to introduce her to a discreet estate agent and also a solicitor, capable and willing to handle a sale to an overseas charity.

She made an effort with her appearance for the trip to London to meet up with the property man, not wishing to risk saying what she wanted on the telephone. Meeting in the coffee lounge of one of the larger hotels in Park Lane, the greeting between the old friends, business partners and lovers was enthusiastic and friendly as they hugged and kissed.

Over a light lunch, Eleanor poured her heart out to the still single, still overweight, Ebenezer, even owning up about the cancer scare and the police investigations. When offered the choice of risking being seen by Jack or Christine by going to Golder's Green, Eleanor declined and agreed she would meet two of Ebenezer's friends later in the day at the same hotel venue.

They passed away the intervening time by drinking gallons of coffee as they reminisced about past times, but also happenings since their last meeting. He was intrigued to hear about her dog walking experiences, and explained he had lost one of his to old age so just had the one left, which was also very old and no longer in need of long walks. She showed him photographs of Marilyn and Rags, and some of the dogs forming her dog walking chores, not yet wishing to give up the duties in case it drew attention to her newfound wealth.

Ebenezer's friends both offered to assist and the solicitor, when learning about the difficulties of Alexander and Ahmed, reminded her of the many advantages of the tolerant UK, but suggested they investigate Cape Verde where same sex marriage was recognised. He did warn against unscrupulous property agents and offered to locate a reliable and honest firm of solicitors on the islands, if required.

It was a happier Eleanor who boarded the train at Euston for her homeward journey.

CHAPTER 53

Javendra Bhattacharya had lulled himself into a state of false security, but was rudely awakened by a call from a cricketer colleague who had received a request for a donation to a charity in return for silence regarding a visit to Javendra's hotel during a sex and drugs orgy. The request mentioned very young girls and the cricketer, who had a wife and family back home, wanted to know what the hell was going on and how the story had surfaced.

Michael O'Flanagan suffered the consequential outburst from the Indian who passed on the same question. When pressed, Michael admitted he was investigating the financial affairs of the dog walker who, so far, was the only suspect but had to admit that, to date, he had no real evidence against her and everything was circumstantial. As soon as her name cropped up, Michael had used available credit check organisations to discover she had financial difficulties which provided a possible motive. Both his colleague, Cedric, and the Indian himself had confirmed her late husband's computer skills, which may have been inherited or passed on to his son. Michael had considered breaking into the house, but the presence of the dogs had negated that idea and he was certainly not going to use strong armed tactics against a woman and her disabled son. He had considered a possible direct approach, correctly claiming to represent a

client and asking a few leading questions but considered the folly: 'I have a client who is being blackmailed by somebody using computer knowledge. Do you know anything about it?'

He then thought his silly notion had provided him with a possible solution, and although speaking to himself, the excitement was certainly there as he exclaimed, 'Eureka.'

Overcoming her initial feeling of panic at the ring of the doorbell, Eleanor opened the door to see Colonel Foster-Clarkson accompanied by a younger man who she had never seen before. Curiosity and fear came to her as she quickly tried to calculate the purpose of their visit, wondering if it was something to do with the colonel's political position. The elderly man smiled as he greeted her.

'Good morning, dear lady. Would it be possible for you to spare a few minutes for my friend and myself. This is Michael O'Flanagan and he runs my security business, which you and I have discussed a few times, and we could possibly do with your assistance.'

Immediately on guard, but not wanting to be rude, she felt she had no option but to invite them in.

Not wanting to extend their visit, she decided against offering drinks, feigning a forthcoming visit to the shops as a reason for explaining she had not too much time and pressing them to advise the purpose of their visit.

Michael opened a bag which he had brought in, removed a laptop computer, and inquired if her son could be of any help in an investigation which he was carrying out.

He explained he was representing clients who were victims of cyber computer blackmail and had heard her son was something of a computer expert. He wondered if he

could possibly examine the laptop to see if there were any viruses which were allowing access.

Suffering internal turmoil, she was sure the pair could hear her beating heart as he explained about how the blackmailers had somehow got into people's computers and extracted information which they used to extort money out of their victims, going on at quite some length to explain as much as he knew, but also to provide himself and Cedric with an opportunity to view her reaction.

Even more on her guard, but desperately trying to keep calm, Eleanor quickly calculated this could be either genuine or, more likely, some kind of trap to discover their involvement. Deciding cooperation would be the best tack, she explained Alexander would not be up to undertake the task immediately and it would take some time, so they would need to leave the machine with them. They had no problem with that, all agreeing the colonel would contact Eleanor in two or three days' time to see if anything had been achieved.

The two men took their leave and drove away quickly, before discussing their visit and the reaction of the woman when the colonel was the first to speak.

'So, what did you think?'

'I thought she was certainly very nervous and guarded, although never having met her before I'm not sure of the kind of person I'm dealing with. You obviously know her much better, so what did you think?'

'This is the first time I've met her on home ground. Usually, I've seen her either out in the fields or on the rare occasions when she has come to the house to see about the dogs.' Then he smiled as he added, 'Apart from one occasion when I have to admit that, like several others at the time,

I was treated to a view of her splendid bosom when she appeared in a fashion show at the local cricket club. Did you learn anything?'

'I think the feedback will tell us more,' his colleague answered. 'It should give us an idea how clever the youngster is. Apparently, the professor has been a little challenging. In addition to putting in some information which can be found quite easily, he has inserted two programs which would require more expertise to find them.

'In my opinion, whoever is carrying out this work is exceedingly talented, appears to know computers inside out and has covered their backs. The wording of the threats has been very clever, the website for the charity is extremely impressive and could well have secured lots of voluntary funding without having to resort to blackmail. Unfortunately, we only know of the limited number of incidents, which all appear to be local, and there may be hundreds of others with absolutely no link whatsoever to your dog walker.'

Alexander spent two hours examining the laptop, finding there were a few viruses and several bits of spyware, one particularly very good but which he decided would have had to have had the cooperation of the owner, unless the person who remotely installed it was very adept. There was no way he could find out if the software developed by his father was on the machine, apart from using his own computer to access the laptop. Aware that by doing this, there was a possibility the owners could trace its activities, he decided against taking the risk.

Having a phenomenal memory for the kind of detail which he was investigating, he felt that, whilst he had previously had access to a considerable amount of

information on the machine, it was somehow not quite familiar. The problem which he faced was that he was unaware of the knowledge, experience and cleverness of his adversaries and did not want to show his hand. Talking the situation through with his mother and Ahmed, it was agreed that he would produce a list of the various problems and Eleanor would telephone Michael O'Flanagan to ask what action they wanted him to take. Did they wish to delete the problems or not?

It took her three attempts before she was able to talk to Michael, then read out to him details of the findings which Alexander had prepared. She was advised that, at this stage, they did not require her to delete any of the information, could she please put their findings on an email, and would it be convenient for Alexander to outline what would be needed to be done to delete the unrequired spyware and other items. Of course, they could raise an invoice for the time. It was also arranged that the colonel would call and collect the laptop some time, but Eleanor was surprised at the lack of urgency, increasing her worry of a possible trap.

The doctor had a female nurse with him as Eleanor entered the consultation room, responding to her name being shown on the electronic board in the waiting room of the surgery. His smile was faint and forced as he invited her to sit down and her heart sank as his demeanour suggested she was not going to hear good news. He did not beat about the bush, quickly explaining that she had several cancers in her lower abdomen and she tried to concentrate as the words cervical, kidney and bowel spilled out of his mouth. As though deliberately determined to give her the full broadside, pre-empting that he was not going to lie to her, he talked about

a lifespan of weeks and months, as opposed to months and years.

The nurse had put together a selection of leaflets on the various diseases, which she popped into a small bag, handing it to the patient. The doctor talked about possible treatments, suggesting this was something Eleanor herself would have to decide upon, and advised her to give the matter some thought over the next forty-eight hours or so, before making any kind of decision. He did explain that, whilst the treatment would only suffice to delay matters, there were also side effects from this, not to mention attendance at the hospital to undertake possible chemotherapy or radiotherapy.

For a while, Eleanor found herself unable to move and actually struggled to speak, despite being offered a glass of water by the kindly nurse. Whilst her eyes watered, she managed to control herself from breaking down as all sorts of thoughts, feelings and emotions spun around in her head. She was not sure how long she was in the consulting room, and her brain was in a fog as she made her way to the surgery's car park, collected the Golf and drove away, without knowing exactly where she was going.

Eleanor found herself sitting in the corner of a bar in a country pub, glass of red wine in front of her with what seemed a mountain of leaflets on cancer on the table, yet could not remember arriving at the pub, let alone driving there. She was still numb from her meeting with the doctor, trying to take in the meaning of weeks or months, as opposed to months or years, the difference that various treatment would make, and how having that treatment would affect her life, either by interfering with it as a nuisance or extending it. She had accepted the fact that any extension would only be

short and might well be counterbalanced by the loss of time in having to undertake the treatment.

As always, her first consideration was her son, thankful he now had Ahmed to take care of him, but her next problem would be to ascertain how to break the news to the pair of them, and then manage whatever period of her life was left.

The doctor had suggested that of the cancers in her body, the cervical one could have been caused by sexual relationships, and she had Javendra Bhattacharya in the frame as the culprit for that, with possible revenge at the forefront of her mind. The doctor had not been clear, or maybe didn't even know, where the cancer had started, only that it had spread very quickly.

Taking a notebook out of her handbag, she started to list things to be done:

Accommodation for Ahmed and Alexander

Selling of the house?

Ahmed learning to drive

Bills for services to have changed names

Home for Marilyn and Rags

Finalise dog walking contracts

She paused for a short while, thinking what other things to add, then simply wrote the words: *Javendra Bhattacharya.*

In addition to getting back at the Indian, she also contemplated on what she could do to somehow punish

Colonel Foster-Clarkson for not contributing to her son's wellbeing, after the initial two thousand pounds which he claimed to make on account until monies were released. They had eased up on pursuing him because of his illness and also the interference of Chief Inspector Smith, although the latter seemed to have gone quiet after his visit to the house.

After taking a sip of her wine, for the first time, Eleanor started paying attention to the medical book and put to one side the leaflet entitled 'Are You Worried About Cancer?' instead selecting 'Making Treatment Decisions' which she started to thumb through, but quickly discarded it on finding it did not actually list available treatments.

Most of her early morning walk had been in a daze, thoughts filled with the events of the previous day and an evening during which Alexander, Ahmed and herself discussed the future. It had been a torturous, tentative and guarded exchange, with Eleanor deciding not to confide in them regarding her illness, but to open up about their position in respect to their underhanded extortion activities coming to light. Having decided treatment was pointless, apart from painkillers and realistically it earned her little extra time, she had decided to forego any. Instead, she would use whatever time she had left to put into operation the plans to ensure the future of the two boys.

With the combination of the suspicions of the colonel's security man, coupled with those of Chief Inspector Smith, Eleanor convinced the pair their future would be safer abroad, and they should investigate Cape Verde as a possible option, sooner rather than later. She tasked the pair with the job of investigating suitable developers or agents, and arranging inspection visits during which they could visit two or three

of the islands to view suitable accommodation. In order to avoid rousing suspicion, she emphasised the accommodation would require to cater for all of them, including the dogs, emphasis on speed being important, for both the visit and subsequent move. She also suggested they should work with someone who either had property available immediately or who could provide some kind of temporary accommodation until it was. Ebenezer's friend had provided details of a trusted lawyer, a partner in a reputable legal firm, with close ties to a company in the UK.

All three fell in love with the area as they watched videos showing the lovely beaches, lush vegetation, beautiful blue ocean and the mixed culture, which represented a meeting of Africa and Europe, the Portuguese influence still visible. Whilst medical facilities and medicines were limited, realistically Alexander was not dependent upon any specialist drugs and most things could be obtained by internet shopping. They would just need to be careful of holding sufficient stocks to allow for delivery. Deciding they had a budget suitably high enough, the three agreed a detached villa would be ideal, but if it was not a bungalow there needed to be sufficient room on the ground floor to incorporate a bedroom and all the other facilities required by Alexander and his husband. They also agreed it should be sited on some complex with available facilities, enabling easy transportation around the site by Alexander's wheelchair. Internet access was vital, accessibility to an airport much less so.

Within two days, they had everything arranged, including a very detailed brief of the type of accommodation and facilities required. Three of the islands had developments

which would fit the bill and contacts were made to arrange for meetings with estate agents and solicitors.

Eleanor McLoughlin kept two diaries in addition to recording appointments on her mobile phone. The first diary was an appointment one, conveniently listing every hour of the day, into which she could enter her dog walking engagements.

The second one she only used intermittently to record particular events. Every meeting she had had with the accountant, Hugh Barker, was recorded, including hotels where they had spent the evening or night and restaurants where they'd had lunch together. She also went into quite a bit of detail about their sexual activities and she recorded similar events of her experiences with the Indian and his wife Carolyn. Occasionally, she had made a note if she had met any of her victims during her dog walking.

Eleanor now went through her second diary and transferred the majority of the information across to the first one. She enlarged, considerably, notes concerning the time spent with Carolyn and the boys in the caravan park in Lincolnshire, particularly mentioning the information which she had learned about the tablets. Details of Carolyn's background were also included as she recorded information provided about the Indian's wife having to provide sexual favours for all and sundry, and at his bidding. She enlarged upon the incident when the dogs and Ahmed had joined forces to prevent Javendra from harming his wife further after the initial attack.

When she had completed her task, Eleanor tore off the front and back hardcover of the second diary and meticulously used her small shredder to dispose of every single page, carefully emptying the shredder into the outside recycling bin.

Eleanor realised she had to plan very carefully if she was to make her ideas work. She was determined to make the Indian pay and, in some ways, was sorry the death sentence no longer applied. She also wanted to involve the colonel and make his life as intolerable as possible. Finally, she had to make sure the dogs were looked after and she therefore needed to arrange for someone to find them soon after the event. She had selected Hugh Barker to do this, as yet unknown to him. In order to provide the evidence, she had to use emails but also aware that if they weren't opened in time, her plans would be scuppered, and so she would have to follow up the emails by telephone in order to ensure they had been read and understood.

The email to the colonel was short and to the point:

Dear Colonel

I wonder if it would be possible for you to call round tomorrow evening at 6:30 p.m.

Do not want to put more in an email but thanks to work done by Alexander, I believe we may possibly know who is trying to get money from you.

For Javendra, she told him she felt a little guilty at not completing her task with his wife, and that by the time he ceased the agreed formal transfers into her account, he had overpaid her by several hundred pounds. He would understand that she would prefer to pay him in cash so could he call round at 7:30 the same evening.

Despite his wealth, she was sure the money would be sufficient to tempt him but decided to add a PS:

I've really missed you and have recently treated myself to a black laced thong, which I'm sure you will appreciate, and will wear for the occasion.

The same thong was referred to in her email to Hugh Barker, advising him Alexander and Ahmed were away and she would have a bottle of wine ready at 8:30.

Foster-Clarkson looked at the tempting crystal glass containing the single malt whiskey, experiencing inner turmoil at the thought of the pleasure it would bring, at odds with his diet. Today was one of four out of seven each week when he abstained from alcohol of any kind. It had not been easy to achieve, particularly in view of his official engagements, but with the assistance of his wife, apart from the occasional mishap, he had been very good. Common sense won this time.

'I'm sorry, dear lady, since my illness, I have to follow a strict diet,' he advised as, with tremendous will power, he took hold of the glass and put it to one side.

'I'm sorry too, Colonel,' she said. 'Perhaps you can top up my sherry glass whilst I get you a drink of water.'

And, without giving him time to protest, Eleanor rose to her feet and headed to the kitchen, delighted to get back with the water to find he had obviously used the decanter to top up her glass.

She settled herself, took a small sip of the replenished sherry, then leaned forwards, providing him with a view of her cleavage as she addressed him.

'Don't ask me how I know, but Alexander worked very hard to find this out, and I think that inside this envelope is

the name of your blackmailer,' she said handing over a plain white envelope with his name on the front of it.

'Please don't open it now.' She put her hand over his. 'I have my accountant calling in a few minutes, but please feel free to give me a call tomorrow if you do want to discuss the matter further.'

Reluctantly, he put the envelope in his pocket, rose, swallowed a quick gulp from the glass of water she had brought and took his leave.

As soon as he had gone, she carefully lifted the glass containing the whiskey, carried it into the kitchen and poured most of the contents down the sink, swilling them away by running the cold tap, but left sufficient in the glass to identify the whiskey.

Leaving the glass on one of the work surfaces, she returned to the lounge, taking out an additional sherry glass. She put a small amount in, drank enough out of her own to reduce the contents to just a drop and awaited the arrival of the Indian.

The ploy differed slightly as she asked him to top her glass up whilst she went to the toilet and, therefore, missed him quickly sprinkling powder into her sherry, stirring it with his finger.

He was furious when advised he could not stay long, looking forward to a bout of sexually activity, and even more angry when, handing him an envelope, she explained she had to use some of the cash for an emergency. Before he had time to open the envelope to view just how much she had used, they were interrupted by the ringing of her landline, triggered by her surreptitiously pressing the speed dial button on her mobile.

The noise also set the dogs barking from an adjoining room and he raged inwardly as he listened to her side of the conversation.

'All right, Hugh, I'll see you in a few minutes. The door will be open, so come straight in.'

Before the few minutes had passed, she regretted making Javendra leave as, grabbing her forcibly, he kissed her fiercely, tongue invading her mouth, fingers painfully squeezing her breasts. She clutched at his hair, went weak at the knees then, as her nipples burned, the realisation he had doctored her drink angered her sufficiently to provide the strength to push him away.

'You have to go. He will be here in a minute.'

Realising she did not have much time to finalise her preparations, Eleanor went to her laptop and emailed a short message to Alexander.

Am frightened. I think it might be better if you stay there a little longer.

Love to Ahmed

Closing the machine, she went to a cupboard in the kitchen from where she took a surgical specimen bottle containing a dark liquid. She had filled it from a bottle, which she had used to steal the weed killer from the garden shed of the colonel. At the time, she planned to use it to dispose of weeds on the patio, but changed her mind when the instructions warned of danger to pets. The bottle had been disposed of in a council bin a hundred yards from her house after the remainder of the contents had been poured down the toilet and flushed away. Carefully pouring the liquid into

her own sherry glass, she replaced the cap, went outside and placed it in her own rubbish bin, carefully burying it beneath other litter.

Returning to the lounge, she tore at the front of her thin dress, buttons popping, then ripped at her bra, exposing a breast.

Drinking most of the contents of her glass, but leaving a small amount, she replaced it on the table, took hold of the neck of the decanter and, with all of her strength, swung it in an arc to crash into her temple. Still conscious as she hit the floor, she realised that much of the sherry from the vessel had spilled on to her dress, some was seeping into the carpet and there was a sticky substance matting her hair. She thought she could hear the telephone ringing, then stars flashed in front of her eyes and Eleanor McLoughlin knew no more.

CHAPTER 54

Chief Inspector Joseph Smith watched patiently as the photographer took pictures of the woman from all angles, one shapely breast exposed for all to see, although the owner of it would no longer care who viewed her dishevelled state. A collection of people in overalls worked on taking fingerprints from the items on the table, in addition to what appeared to be the murder weapon: a heavy crystal decanter. Thick matted blood combined with sherry to make a horrible stain on the carpet.

The body had been discovered by the local postman who had been alerted by the frantic barking of the dogs following his ringing the bell to deliver the mail. One item was a package containing a large holiday brochure which would not fit through the letterbox, so he had tried the door to find it unlocked, letting himself in to find the horrific sight. Locating the dogs in a utility room, he had let the frantic animals out into the back garden, then dialled 999, advising both police and ambulance service. A uniformed constable had taken his statement, but as the man was still there, Joseph asked him to repeat his story. It was his regular round and he had met the woman and her dogs on a few occasions.

'You get used to dogs in this job, Chief Inspector, and I could tell they were distressed so decided to try the door.'

'What time was that?'

'About seven thirty.'

Smith calculated the man to be in his forties, quite sharp and calm, and he advised Joe he had been a postman for over ten years, loved his job due to being outdoors, being his own boss and with much less stress than his previous position as sales manager of a double glazing company. He admitted to Joe he had suffered some kind of breakdown in order to explain the change in career, and also advised this was his third discovery of a dead person, but the previous two had been very elderly, living on their own.

'Did you realise she was dead?'

'You cannot judge by looking, but I thought she was, which is why I went to the dogs, who were howling, then I called the police and ambulance, and felt for a pulse as I was doing so. There was no sign of her breathing, and when the medics arrived, they thought she had been dead for some time.'

Checking he had provided the constable with his details, the postman was allowed to leave, although Joe was not sure if he would be completing his round or not.

A uniformed sergeant approached Joe, advised him the house telephone had been flashing to indicate a voicemail message, and suggested the detective listen to it, which he did.

A man's voice spoke.

'Sorry, darling, can't make tonight after all. Henrietta is stuck at school with some problem with her car and I have to go and rescue her. Will try and see you tomorrow.'

As Joe started to instruct the sergeant to trace the caller, he was advised the man would do so, but was certain it was an accountant called Hugh Barker, husband of Henrietta Barker, head of year at the local academy.

'He is well known in the village and in the town and so is his wife.' Joe was advised then, sensing gossip, the sergeant

added, 'Does not sound like they planned to talk about accounts, does it, sir?'

Joe sought out who was in charge of the forensic team to see if he could get any idea of the time of death. As expected, he was told he would have to wait, but it was likely to be less than twelve hours. He was also advised the team had collected three sets of prints on the decanter, two sets on one wine glass, three on another and two on a whiskey tumbler, which contained traces of a single malt, and which had been left in the kitchen unwashed.

Within forty-eight hours, Hugh Barker had been interviewed and allowed to leave, but warned he would be required to assist in enquiries, whilst the local mayor, Colonel Cedric Foster-Clarkson and Indian cricketer Javendra Bhattacharya were still at the station 'helping police with their enquiries'. Neither had denied visiting the victim on the night of her death, both were adamant she had been alive and well when they left, although were evasive about the reasons for their visit. Both had confirmed Eleanor had been expecting the accountant. All three had submitted to having their fingerprints taken, with those of the mayor and the Indian found on the decanter. Without advising them it was being viewed as the murder weapon, both recalled having been asked to handle the item in order to top the woman's drink up.

When questioned about the reasons for their visits, the Indian vaguely referred to 'financial arrangements' in respect of some work which he had given to the woman in the past relating to a personal matter. The colonel claimed she had requested to see him to ask for some advice on a 'personal matter'. Joe was certain both were lying.

Having brought the victim's laptop in and set a young constable loose on it, Joe was aware of the reasons why she had asked them to her home, but did not challenge the lies. Instead, he advised both men they would have to remain at the station and faced the ignominy of being locked in the cells.

If both men had been telling the truth about timing, it seemed to confirm that the Indian had arrived at the house after the colonel left and that he had, therefore, been the last to see the woman alive. In view of this, the colonel was released after the statutory twenty-four hours, but Joseph decided to apply for an extension in respect of the Indian, much to the man's disgust and anger. The pathologist had telephoned the detective advising she had discovered fragments of dark hair under the fingernails of the woman, so the Indian was requested to provide a DNA sample.

According to the times provided by both men, Joe was satisfied Eleanor was alive when the colonel left, so felt that, at present, he had no option but to release the man, although not happy about the fact he had been lied to. He decided he would teach the man a lesson, and also frighten him a little by keeping him as long as possible.

Foster-Clarkson was shaking with a combination of anger and fear as he waited for his wife to collect him from the police station, having been curtly advised there was no transport available to give him a lift home. He had spent the night in a cell, was unshaven, feeling quite dirty and was unusually sharp with his wife who he believed had taken much longer than required to make the journey to the town, brushing aside her excuses about having to see to the dogs and get changed before she could leave. Thankfully, he had advised Penelope prior to visiting the woman, explaining she

347

wanted to speak to him about some personal matters in his capacity as a councillor.

'Does this have anything to do with Sergeant Ellis?'

'No, I told you, she wanted advice on any help she could obtain regarding her financial situation.'

Despite not being reassured, his wife decided he was in no mood for further questioning, but remained very concerned that her husband had something to do with a murder, no matter how remotely.

CHAPTER 55

The pathologist was a severe-looking woman, Joe estimating her age to be somewhere in her mid-fifties. She had a curved nose on which perched glasses, which she had an infuriating habit of pushing onto the top of her head. The loose-fitting overalls disguised whatever figure she possessed but she appeared to be fairly lean as far as he could tell.

'I thought it would be better to meet here and talk personally rather than discuss on the phone, or simply email a report to you, although I have a report which you can take away. There are lots of complications in this case.'

They were seated in the staff canteen at police county headquarters, coffee cups on the table before them.

'Like what?' the detective asked.

'Where do I start?'

Clearly enjoying being the centre of his attention, she wanted to set the pace and offer the information a little at a time in order to keep her audience of one intrigued. Joe realised he would learn things in her time.

'Why not try the beginning?'

'If only we knew where that was,' came the curt reply, then began her complicated explanation. 'To start with, she was riddled with cancer.'

Joe whistled slowly under his breath and waited for her to continue.

'She also recently had an abortion.'

Realising he knew of two possible fathers, Joe asked the question, 'Is there any way of telling who the father was?'

'Absolutely none, unless we can find out where it took place and, even then, they may not have kept a record.'

'What about the cancer?' he asked. 'How bad was it, and how long would she be likely to live?'

'All around the bottom of her abdomen,' the woman advised him. 'Cervical, kidney, liver, you name it. As for how long… weeks, not months. There's something else. Well, two things actually,' the woman went on, hesitating as though she wished to be prompted.

Joe duly replied. 'And they are?'

'There were two different substances in the glass of sherry, which she had obviously drunk on the evening. The first of these was what is known as a date rape drug, which is reputed to heighten sexual desire and experience, so I'm told,' she quickly added, seeming to indicate sexual experiences were not her line.

He sat quietly waiting for the second revelation and was not made to wait long.

'She was also poisoned.'

'Christ,' was all he could think of. 'What with?'

'The actual liquid which she consumed is used as a weed killer, but it contains quite a powerful poison.'

'Was it enough to kill her without the blow to the head?'

'Most definitely.'

The detective sat quietly, thoughtfully, before asking the next question.

'Would the blow to the head on its own have killed her?'

She stared at him. 'Possibly, probably, but not certainly.'

His mind raced around in circles at this information. He had already virtually discounted two suspects, but now there was a possibility he might have to bring them back into the frame. The accountant could have covered his tracks very well, could easily have seen her other male visitors, and the call from his mobile phone, which left a message, could be made from anywhere, including just a few yards away from her house. He had an additional motive now with the news about the abortion.

'Excuse me,' he apologised to the pathologist as he fished his mobile out of his pocket, 'I need to make a call.'

He telephoned his office and asked the constable to check the file, find out who the dead woman's general practitioner was and arrange for him to see her or him as soon as possible.

The one thing that had been really bothering Joe was why Eleanor had arranged to meet up with the accountant that evening. From information which he had put together, he thought it was some kind of safety net if the other visitors created problems. Well, at least one of them had, if not both.

He thanked the woman for her assistance, retrieved his car and set off back to his own office. Another thought struck him on the way back to town and he pulled over to make a further call, this time to get warrants to search the premises of Colonel Foster-Clarkson, Javendra Bhattacharya and Hugh Barker to see if they could find any traces of the weed killer.

The detective now had the problem of having three possible suspects and considered the options. In respect of motive, means and opportunity, the Indian was top of his list as he could be a possible father of the embryo removed from the victim prior to the murder. Getting rid of the baby, without his knowledge and agreement, could well

have triggered sufficient anger in him, particularly if she had taunted him with the information on the evening in question. There was no doubt he also had the means, and the opportunity, being a strong man alone with the woman in her house, and capable of killing her with his bare hands, let alone using the heavy decanter. There was also a possibility he had been a blackmail victim, always assuming it was the dog walker responsible for those activities.

Local mayor, Colonel Cedric Foster-Clarkson, appeared not to have a motive, possibly unable to have been the father of the child and, so far, there was no evidence of any blackmail attempts, either successful or otherwise. Like Javendra, he did have means and opportunity and possibly even more means than the Indian if he had taken with him, on that evening, a quantity of the weed killer.

Accountant Hugh Barker may well have had the motive in respect of also being a possible father of the aborted child but, at the present time, there was no evidence to suggest the man turned up at the house on the evening of the murder, having previously left a message advising he was unable to do so. His wife had confirmed the problems with her car, and that her husband had collected her from the school.

Back at the station, a flash of inspiration caused Joe to reach into the second drawer down of his desk and bring out a pile of business cards held together with a green elastic band. Flicking through, he came across the card of Michael O'Flanagan, recalling his visit to enquire about possible blackmail victims. Joe decided it was time to pay the security man a visit.

It was the young Polish girl who advised Michael the detective chief inspector wished to see him, was already in reception and insisted on an immediate audience. In his

business, Michael had been trained by Foster-Clarkson to be cooperative with the police, whenever possible, and always when it suited. Already aware of the murder of Eleanor McLoughlin, it was not difficult to assume this was the purpose of the detective's visit, so made a point of going out to greet the man personally and ushering him into his office.

'Good morning, Chief Inspector, have you been offered coffee?'

Joe hadn't and advised his preference of white with no sugar as he took his seat opposite the head of the security firm.

Whilst waiting for the coffee to arrive, the policeman clarified Michael had, indeed, learned about the murder of the dog walker, advising Michael he would like his assistance, if possible.

Both men took their time. Joe took a sip of the coffee before Michael opened the sparring.

'So, Chief Inspector, how do you think I can help?'

'To start with, it would be very helpful if you could let me have the name, or names, of the people who you were representing in the blackmail investigations.'

'You know I cannot do that.'

'On what basis?'

'Client confidentiality,' Michael answered.

Detective Chief Inspector Joseph Smith slowly and deliberately took a mouthful of the coffee, placed the mug on the coaster advertising a well-known beer product situated on the desk, looked around at the steel filing cabinets, then addressed Michael.

'Mr O'Flanagan, this has become quite a high-profile murder investigation. My superiors are after a quick result and expect me to deliver that. I already have three suspects,

so a lot of progress has already been made and there is no reason why this cannot be put to bed in a very short time. If your client is not one of the suspects, then you have nothing to worry about, but if he is, you could be guilty of withholding vital evidence.'

Looking round at the filing cabinets again, Joe continued, 'If you do not cooperate, before I reach ground floor level of this building I will have telephoned my office to arrange for a warrant to move all of the filing cabinets and computers from your nice office on the basis they may contain evidence in a murder case. In addition to the widespread coverage in the local press, this case is also being followed quite closely by the nationals, who are requesting updates on a regular basis.'

As he took another mouthful of coffee, his eyes retained contact with those of the man on the other side of the desk.

Michael O'Flanagan was aware of the devastation that would be caused to his business should such a situation be reported and very quickly made up his mind what he was required to do.

'Chief Inspector, I'm sure you're aware that, if it became public knowledge that I had provided the police with details of an important client, it would be very damaging for my discreet business.'

Whilst speaking the words, Michael took one of several pens in the immaculately kept desk tidy, took a pad from one of his drawers, on which he wrote a name, then turned it round so the policeman could read it. Joe did not need to make a note of it as he read the name of the Indian. The man was already on his list of suspects.

'Thank you. So, what kind of hold did the blackmailer have over him?'

Michael felt cornered now, but realised he had no option other than to continue his cooperation, with no doubt the chief inspector was quite prepared to carry out his initial threat, which would, in effect, close down his business. At the same time, he was reluctant to provide information which the police did not already have, so tried to cover his backside.

'What information do you already have, Chief Inspector?'

'Well, we know he owns a hotel, and believe he runs some kind of money lending business for the Asian community, and that he was having an affair with the deceased. I guess she could be blackmailing him about the latter, as he was married, although from what I hear, is not very good to his wife. Now, can I ask you a question? Were there any instances of anyone accessing his computer?'

Whilst Michael did his utmost to avoid any kind of confession, Joe saw the answer in the younger man's eyes, confident he had struck the right chord. Before giving the security man time to reply, Joe carried on.

'Someone has been carrying out a very complicated cyber-crime, and if your client has been a victim, then there is a possibility he suspected Eleanor McLoughlin as the culprit.'

Michael O'Flanagan suddenly felt very threatened, not only providing evidence that might be used to prosecute his client for murder, but which would also involve his own organisation to stand up in court and confirm that evidence. There had never been any doubt in Michael's mind that the company dealt with clients who did not always comply fully with the law, but this situation was new to him if he had to support the law against a client. His other concern was, although his business partner had not yet been mentioned, that also may become an issue. Aware that Cedric was helping

the police with inquiries, he could not believe him capable of the crime, whereas he had experienced the frustration, temper and anger of the Asian, whose personality was volatile, to say the least.

Over the next half an hour, he enlightened the policeman on enquiries which he had conducted, including details of the inspection of Javendra Bhattacharya's computer. Ready for the inevitable question regarding the colonel, Michael went to great lengths to fill in the history of the relationship with him, emphasising his kindness regarding his cleft lip, kindness to his mother, educating the youngster and bringing him into the business. Joe recognised the sincerity and truthfulness in the monologue, but really had to put the man under pressure.

'Was the colonel being blackmailed?'

Having opened the floodgates, Michael felt he really had no option but to carry on.

'Apparently, it was a very minor discretion, which happened many years ago, but which might be embarrassing in his position as mayor. To be honest, Chief Inspector, Cedric did not even enlighten me as to what it was. I do know he was brought up in a Barnardo's home which, to some snobbish people, would count against him, although Cedric always seemed proud of his accomplishments despite his humble start. I can understand it may be something which he would not share with the members of his local Conservative Association, some of who might be embarrassed.'

'Well, I can see that, whilst it could be awkward, it really would not be reason to run the mayor out of town. Can you think of anything else?' the detective asked.

'No. Cedric mentioned it just casually when we were discussing the case of Bhattacharya.'

'Did he tell you if he had paid money or not?'

'No. I mean he didn't tell me, but I rather got the impression he hadn't paid.'

Thoughtfully weighing up the information which he had just learned, Joe was not convinced Colonel Foster-Clarkson would allow himself to be blackmailed about being brought up in a Barnardo's home. In fact, he could use it as a character reference as someone who, from humble beginnings, had made his way in the world.

'Can you think of anything else which he would prefer not to be general knowledge?' Joe asked.

'No. As you will have gathered, my mother and I think the absolute world of Cedric, and God knows where I would have been without his intervention. We're very close and he has been, to my knowledge, pretty open about his life, although I'm aware he was the sole survivor of an ambush in Africa, which almost cost him his own life. That's all I know about his distant past, and I'm not aware of any kind of indiscretion since he started up this business.

'Just in case you're not aware, we do have clients who have diplomatic immunity, and others who operate nightclubs in the city, for who we provide bouncers and other security staff. Not everybody is in favour of this kind of business but, again, I can't think of any reason for blackmail.'

'What about his wife?'

'Don't know much about her, apart from previously being married to an MP and that they appear to be happy together.'

Tempted, but turning down the offer to be taken for lunch, Joe settled for the much lighter ham sandwich and pint of bitter in the station bar before catching his train back. The meeting had served to strengthen the motives of the Indian, particularly if he suspected Eleanor of being the

blackmailer. He believed that, in the main, Michael had been open and reasonably honest with him, but clearly idolised his benefactor and would certainly have chosen to safeguard his friend instead of his client.

Hugh Barker was the first to be called back by Joe, who found the man very evasive, nervous and guarded as the questions were put to him. He denied being blackmailed, initially denied having an affair with the woman until, consulting Eleanor's diary, the detective listed dates, times and places of their meetings. The man explained his earlier lie, excusing himself for being a respected member of the local community, prominent in the business world, leading a respectable life with his wife and family. The wind was taken out of his sails when Joe questioned him about the thong which Eleanor had indicated she was going to wear when asking him to visit and news of the abortion shocked him into a very subdued silence.

He was adamant he had not visited Eleanor on the night of the murder, citing his wife and two of her colleagues as an alibi and whilst Joe was aware it could have taken only minutes to carry out the crime, he had no evidence to confirm the presence of the man during the fateful evening.

A search of his house failed to produce any trace of the weed killer, which had been used, and Joseph Smith was convinced the complete shock displayed when the man was advised of Eleanor's abortion certainly removed one possible motive for the accountant wishing to end her life.

Barker was allowed to leave without any charge, but warned he may be requested to return for further questioning.

If his time at the police station had been uncomfortable, then the grilling which he had to endure from Henrietta was even more so.

The colonel was next.

'Why did you go and see her that evening?' Joe enquired as he and a young detective sat opposite the man in a sparse interview room at the station.

Foster-Clarkson hesitated, not sure what information the policeman already possessed, which had led him to find out of his visit to the woman on the evening of her death. He had already agreed to have his fingerprints taken, which confirmed they matched one of the sets on the whiskey tumbler, the wine glass and the decanter now regarded as the murder weapon.

'She asked to see me on a personal matter,' he eventually answered.

'What kind of personal matter?'

'I'm sorry. I am, was, her local councillor and Mrs McLoughlin has had a few problems for some time since the lady unfortunately lost her husband.'

'What kind of problems?' the detective persisted.

'Well, financial to start with. She was trying to bring up her son, who is very disabled and which cannot have been easy for her.'

'Did you have a drink of whiskey?'

'No.'

'Your fingerprints are on the whiskey glass.'

'I know. She offered me a whiskey, and I have to confess to being sorely tempted, Chief Inspector, but since a fairly recent heart problem, I have to watch my diet, and that particular day was on my list of being alcohol free. I seem to remember moving the glass to one side, while she went to get me a drink of water.'

'Did you put anything in her glass?'

'Sherry. She asked me to top her glass up whilst she went for the water, which is also how my fingerprints appeared on the decanter from which I poured the sherry.'

'Did you put anything else in her drink?'

'No.'

Reaching under the table, Joe produced a can of weed killer, which had been found in the greenhouse at the home of the colonel.

'This was found at your house. What do you use it for?'

'It's very good for controlling weeds in the greenhouse. When I initially bought it, I thought I could use it on the patio as well, but it's dangerous to animals and, as we have dogs, I had to find an alternative solution.'

'Did you have any of this with you on the night when you visited Eleanor McLoughlin?'

'Good heavens, no. Why should I? Weed killer is hardly something one carries around with them.'

'Unless they plan to murder someone with it.' The detective looked the man straight in the eye. 'Did you spike her drink when she went to get the water for you?'

'What is this all about, Chief Inspector?' the man asked indignantly.

'Eleanor McLoughlin was poisoned and this is what was found in her sherry.'

As Joe watched the man intently, his shoulders drooped and colour drained out of his face as he weakly murmured, 'I think, Chief Inspector, it would be inappropriate for me to answer any more questions without the presence of my solicitor.'

Using the same approach as he had used with the mayor, the first question fired at Javendra Bhattacharya was identical.

'Why did you go and see her that evening?'

Unlike the other two, the Indian insisted on having a solicitor present before agreeing to answer any questions.

'It was about a business transaction. We made an arrangement and when it ended, she had to refund me an overpayment which had been made for her services and asked me to call round and collect it.'

The Indian became extremely guarded at Joe's next question.

'Why would she insist on wearing a thong in order to pay you money? I suggest to you that your visit was for other reasons, that you expected to have sex with the woman and tried to force yourself on her. When she refused, you became angry, struck her with the decanter and killed her.'

'No.'

Joe looked at Eleanor's diary and then asked the man where he was on the date which showed they had spent the afternoon in a hotel room together.

'I don't remember.'

'Well, let me prompt your memory, Mr Bhattacharya. According to the lady's diary, she spent the afternoon with you at a hotel after you had made an agreement for her to help you on a project regarding your wife. How many other occasions did you and Mrs McLoughlin meet and have sex?'

The solicitor intervened on behalf of his client.

'What has that got to do with the matter in question, Chief Inspector? My client is quite a handsome man, well known in many fields, and it is easy to see how an older woman, and a widow at that, would be attracted to him. My client admits to not being very proud about the fact he was unable to resist the temptation of this woman, but that

does not make him a murderer and what could his motive possibly be?'

Joe ignored him as he spoke again to the Indian,

'Was it true Mrs McLoughlin was helping out with some problem which you had with your wife? Was it also true that in the presence of Mrs McLoughlin, her son and another witness, you viciously attacked your wife on a caravan park in Lincolnshire? According to her diary, it was only the intervention of her dogs and her son's carer, which saved your wife from further punishment.'

'No comment.'

'Is your wife a drug addict?'

'No comment.'

'Is that what Mrs McLoughlin was helping you with?'

'No comment.'

'Did you put something in her drink that night?'

'No comment.'

'Did you make her have an abortion?'

Expecting yet another 'no comment' response, Joe was taken aback a little as the Indian leaned forwards in his seat and glared at him threateningly.

'I don't know what you're talking about. I know nothing about any abortion and if that bitch got pregnant then it has nothing to do with me.'

Joe sensed a man beginning to lose his cool and went on the attack.

'Did she tell you about the baby when she was resisting your advances? That would have really brought shame on you, wouldn't it? A man of your standing, not only having an affair with an older woman, a friend of your wife's, but to find out she was carrying your child. Did you already know or did she tell you on that night? We know you were there

and, according to our witnesses, you were the last person to see her alive.'

'No.'

'You put something in her drink, didn't you?'

'No.'

'That's something you do on a regular basis, isn't it? You even use it to get your own wife in the mood to subject herself to your sexual advances.'

'No.'

Joe totally ignored the solicitor, who tried to intervene as he continued relentlessly.

'How many other girls have you taken advantage of this way? I can assure you that our intention is to make many more enquiries, Mr Bhattacharya. Meanwhile, I'm afraid you're going to have to remain at the station and we'll be having further discussions later.'

When the hair, found in Eleanor's fingernails, proved by DNA to belong to Javendra Bhattacharya, Chief Inspector Joseph Smith decided he had sufficient evidence to arrest the man on suspicion of murder, and successfully objected when the man's solicitor, proclaiming his client's innocence, suggested he be allowed out on bail.

CHAPTER 56

Alexander and Ahmed were seated on the patio of the villa, which they had been allocated during their viewing visit. Alexander's face glistened due to the copious amount of sun cream which his partner had plastered on his face. Under strict instructions from Eleanor, the Bangladeshi had renewed Alexander's protection from the sun every hour or so, ensuring his face, neck and bare arms were covered in the cream. They had also been provided with baseball caps, courtesy of their hosts, the developers of the site, whose name and logo featured on the front of the head wear.

No longer strong, the evening sun shone much less brightly, but the temperature was still very warm, although not quite as searing as the middle of the day. During the day, which had been tiring, they had been shown around four properties, but had also been taken on a tour around the area, enabling them to get a feel for the place. The complex itself fitted all the requirements laid down by Eleanor, complete with three different restaurants, an entertainment area, supermarket, souvenir shop, play areas for children, several small shops offering clothing and shoes, a launderette which offered services, including ironing and sewing, and a takeaway offering ready cooked local dishes.

The day had been marred by the receipt of an email from Alexander's mother, advising them she was frightened and

also suggesting they should not hurry back to England, but explore the possibilities of obtaining an extension to their visa, which they had obtained on arrival.

Ahmed was aware that, in many ways, his younger partner was much cleverer than himself, and also more world-wise, particularly in respect of the operation which he had been carrying out in collaboration with his mother in order to extract money from individuals to fund their lifestyle. The necessity of this had been reduced by the young man's ability in obtaining access to the huge fortune, which Alexander had discovered had been left by his father. The Bangladeshi realised he had now become totally dependent upon mother and son for his own financial security, appreciating this fact, whilst being totally dedicated to caring for Alexander. Cape Verde would be the icing on the cake and he was delighted with the plans to move there, although sad that, due to their relationship, he could not return to the country of his birth. They were both young, however, so there was a possibility things could change in the future. Meanwhile, the climate was not too different from that at home, and in some ways a little more tolerable. Furthermore, at least on the complex, there was no evidence of as much poverty as existed back home.

Glancing at his watch, Ahmed realised there was still over an hour to wait for the time when they had decided to have dinner, having been treated by their hosts to a very filling lunch consisting of local food, some of which Alexander had balked at, although with persuasion by his husband had tried some of the local fish.

Levering himself up from the rattan chair, he crossed to check on the fruit juice which was fixed close enough for Alexander to drink through a straw and realised it needed topping up. Taking the bottle from its holder, he planted a kiss

on the lips of the younger man and entered the villa, through the French windows, to complete his task of refreshing the drink. He was still inside when he heard a vehicle pull up at the front of the villa and heard the doorbell ring. Opening the door, he stood in shock and fear as he saw two black men in khaki drill police uniform asking to see Alexander.

It took a while for the pair of them to fully understand Eleanor was dead and the local police had been made aware someone was being held on suspicion of her murder. One of the policemen asked them if they would require any assistance in arranging flights back home immediately but, with a laboured effort, it was Alexander who advised them they wanted time to think about the situation and not make any hasty decisions until they knew more about the situation. They were provided with the telephone number and email address of Chief Inspector Smith who was in charge of the case and who was prepared to give them any information required.

The pair were utterly stunned and did not speak for several minutes after the police had driven off in their Land Rover, having provided details of how they could be contacted if their services were required.

It was Alexander who broke the silence.

'Mother said she was frightened. It was almost as though she expected something like this to happen. She also said we should not hurry back, hinting we may also be in danger.'

'What should we do?' Ahmed asked him.

'Go and have dinner,' replied the younger man, amazing Ahmed with his calmness as he slowly added, 'If Mother is dead, then we can do nothing to help her. She gave you a book with contact names in. I think we should talk to the solicitor whose name and telephone number are in there and also to

this detective man, but not before we talk things over. And we can do that whilst we are eating. What do you say?'

Ahmed thought very carefully about exactly what he could say but, flabbergasted at the demeanour of the other and aware of damage caused to Alexander's brain, wondered if this explained the lack of emotion.

Eventually, he decided the only sensible reply was, 'Of course, you're right.'

Joseph Smith replaced the telephone following a lengthy conversation with Ahmed, much time being taken with the Bangladeshi having to confer with Alexander. Aware of the email message sent to the pair by Eleanor, he was not too surprised to learn they had no plans to return home immediately, but they would be happy to talk to him if he wanted to visit the islands. Being a great believer in face-to-face discussions, enabling a reading of body language in addition to the eyes which would display all sorts of emotions, Joe decided his first ever visit to Cape Verde would be completely justified. Approaching the uniformed chief inspector in charge of the station, he obtained agreement for a young constable, very adept at taking statements, to accompany him, having emphasised the importance of interrogating the son and son-in-law of the deceased.

Collecting the tickets at the airport, which had been booked on their behalf, the flight was only fifteen minutes late taking off, with Joe utilising the five-hour trip to update the constable on the case. Eager to please and thrilled to be operating in civilian clothes in a murder case, the constable enthusiastically scribbled down lots of notes as he listened to the experienced senior officer. Like many colleagues of his age, he viewed the CID as a goal at which to aim for in

his career development and was determined to make a good impression on this opportunity to work alongside a man with a tremendous reputation.

They had managed to secure rooms in a hotel near the complex, but decided against hiring a car, instead taking a taxi from the airport and another taxi from the hotel to the villa where the pair was staying, having contacted Ahmed on the mobile number which he had provided.

Joe expressed his sympathy to the pair before beginning the questioning. Although they claimed not to know anyone who would have reason to murder Eleanor, Ahmed in particular showed a distinct disliking of the Indian, Javendra Bhattacharya. He advised the policeman of the incident at the caravan park in Lincolnshire, when they had witnessed the man striking his own wife, explaining why she had been on the holiday with them. Alexander joined in the conversation, when required, slowing down proceedings, which Joe did not mind, believing he needed to get the young man's story in his own words. The reduction in speed also suited the young constable, who had struggled taking down the notes of the excitable and fast speaking Bangladeshi. In his laboured tones, Alexander told the policeman there was something he did not like about Colonel Foster-Clarkson calling to see her with another man asking help about some laptop.

'I am not sure what it was all about, but they asked me to look for some kind of spyware that was on the machine. There were a few things, mostly advertising.' The young man paused and then added, 'My mother also said something about it being strange that the colonel was not left-handed.'

'How did you manage financially? You live in a large house and the upkeep must be quite expensive.'

The pair looked at one another, and it was Alexander, in his laborious way, who chose to answer the question.

'I am not sure of the full details, but I believe my father left some kind of legacy, or insurance, that took care of lots of the expenses,' he advised the detective.

So far, Joe had been surprised at the lack of emotion shown by the young man, who was now an orphan, but was not sure how anyone with Alexander's condition would react. In an attempt to find out if the son of the computer wizard was aware of things going on, he asked him bluntly, 'Do you know if your mother was blackmailing anyone?'

The eyes were deadpan as the young man in the wheelchair returned his gaze.

'Blackmail? How could she blackmail them and what about? As far as I know, Mr Javendra paid my mother to train his wife in how to behave in public. Apparently, she was a drug addict from a very deprived background, and Mr Javendra was a little ashamed of her at times and wanted my mother to teach her manners.

'Carolyn, that is Mr Javendra's wife, is a really nice lady and we had a lovely time when we took her on holiday. That ended suddenly when Mr Javendra hit her because she had sold her watch in order to get drugs. Although she wanted to stay with us, he insisted she travelled home with him. It was not very convenient for us as we all had to squeeze into my mother's car, including the dogs.'

The mention of these prompted Alexander to ask if the dogs were all right, and who was looking after them. He was assured they had been taken into kennels and both were fit and well.

The chief inspector apologised for taking up their time, repeated his earlier condolences and advised them they

would like to talk with them again the following day, after carrying out further local enquiries, and arranged to do so at around lunchtime.

'So, Constable, what did you think?'

'Well, sir,' the young man replied, feeling an important part of the investigation, 'I think the carer was very nervous. I was watching him whilst you were questioning the son. Also, I would say he absolutely loathes this Javendra guy, although I think that might be something to do with the differences between Bangladesh and India. In any event, if you don't mind me saying so, sir, the Indian sounds a right bastard with a temper that could possibly break and make him do something like this.'

Impressed with the young man's observations, Joe asked him, 'Wouldn't you have expected to see more grief in a young man who, having already lost his father, suddenly discovered his mother had been murdered?'

'He's had some time to get used to the idea, but yes, you're right. I would have expected more emotion. In fact, it was his carer who seemed angrier.'

'You're right about Ahmed being his carer, Constable, but he's also his husband. Apparently, they went through a marriage service a short time ago. Don't be surprised,' he added as he saw the look of amazement on the young policeman's face, 'This is our modern society and also, just because someone is disabled, does not mean they can't have relationships with others just the same as anyone else.'

Having learned from the developers and agents that Alexander and Ahmed were here to look at buying property, Joe Smith was surprised, but his surprise turned to amazement when he

found out the costs of the villas, which they had been viewing so far. Having had access to the woman's bank account, he was aware it did not contain anywhere near sufficient funds to meet the almost quarter of a million that would be required to buy some of the villas which they had viewed.

He was of the opinion that both the Indian and the colonel would have access to that kind of sum, which started Joseph thinking along different lines. Deciding to try and throw Alexander off balance, as soon as the polite greetings were over, he fired a direct question at the youngster, looking straight into his eyes as he did so.

'Were you aware your mother was having an affair with Javendra Bhattacharya?'

The shock on the young man's face gave him his answer, before the slow and simple reply 'No' escaped his lips.

Feeling guilty and cruel, Joe pressed on whilst the other was off balance.

'Did you know your mother had an abortion recently?'

The response was identical and, for a fraction of a second, Joe regretted his own line of questioning, totally convinced the young man knew nothing about either situation. He pondered his next words extremely carefully, felt he had to ask it, and softened his voice considerably as he did so.

'Alexander, I really hate to ask you this, but did you know your mother was quite ill?'

The energy drained out of the young man in the wheelchair, his body slumped and he took his time answering.

'No. How ill? What was wrong with her?'

There were tears in the young man's eyes now, and Chief Inspector Smith felt that sometimes his job could be absolutely terrible as he looked at the youngster, took a deep breath and advised him.

'I'm afraid she had cancer and therefore not long to live.'

There was an awful, uncomfortable silence which was broken by Ahmed.

'But we were looking for property here, big enough for all of us. Why should she want to do that if she knew she was going to die?'

'Good question, Ahmed, and one that is really bothering me. Perhaps she was frightened for both of you and wanted to see the pair of you settled here before she left. I can only say what the medical people have advised me that, unfortunately, Eleanor only had a maximum of a few months to live and it was more likely to be just weeks. Alexander and Ahmed, I'm afraid I have to ask this question. I understand you've been looking at properties at over two hundred thousand pounds. Have you any idea how this money would be raised?'

Alexander was still slumped in his wheelchair, totally deflated, so it was the Bangladeshi who provided the answer.

'As Alexander mentioned, his father left quite a legacy, but it was tied up in a trust fund based overseas somewhere. From what I'm told, Chief Inspector, Alexander's father was some kind of computer genius and made a lot of money as personal computers and the internet developed. He saw the sense in investing this overseas and set up a trust fund to care for his family in future years.'

Joseph looked at the young man, glanced at Alexander and asked the question.

'If that was the case, could one of you explain to me why Eleanor had to take work as a dog walker and also that she put her house on the market?'

Ahmed glanced at his husband, who still showed no interest in joining in the conversation, so decided to carry on as spokesman for the pair.

'That is easily explained, Chief Inspector. When Alexander's father died, the police took away his laptop, which was only returned to the family recently. Apparently, there had been some mix up in administration, which could have saved my mother-in-law a lot of grief had it been sorted out earlier. It was only when the laptop was returned that we were able to make contact with the banks running the finances of the trust fund. Up until that time, Eleanor had expected to have to sell the house, but thankfully this was no longer necessary when we traced the funds.'

The words were delivered with anger as Ahmed hesitated, looked at Alexander whose expression suggested they should be reasonably open, and so continued.

'In fact, the fund was able to pay off the mortgage on the house which solved our problems.'

Joe thought for a moment about money laundering and all sorts of other complications, but did not want to muddy the waters with that at this stage as his heart was reaching out to the two young men who had been looking forward to a bright future, but who had now lost their nearest and dearest.

'Why Cape Verde? Why did you not go back to your own country?'

The Bangladeshi smiled faintly.

'I am afraid, Chief Inspector, my country, along with most of the Asian continent, do not believe in same sex marriage, let alone condone formalised relationships between two people. The world still has a long way to go.' He added in a subdued tone, 'And I'm afraid we were not prepared to live a life of pretence back in Bangladesh, which would have left us open to possible arrest and imprisonment. That would have badly affected the lives of my family out there, and we were not prepared to risk that.'

'Will you return to England?' asked the policeman. 'Your mother's body will not be released for a time, but there will be the funeral arrangements to be made.'

'Eleanor told us she was frightened and look what's happened to her.' Again, Ahmed looked at Alexander before continuing. 'Naturally, we will want to come back for the actual funeral and to arrange for things to be sent from the house, but I'm sure you'll understand that we will want to make our visit as short as possible, and may even ask you for some kind of protection by the police. From what you have explained, my mother-in-law met a very violent death, and there is no way I would want to risk Alexander coming to any kind of harm whatsoever.'

Believing there was nothing else to be learned, Chief Inspector Smith thanked the young men for their cooperation, held out his hand to receive a firm handshake from Ahmed, gently touched Alexander's hand and ushered the constable outside in order to walk to the entrance area of the complex and order a taxi back to the hotel.

It was some time before Alexander came out of his morose mood in order for them to discuss and decide what to do.

Ahmed's first telephone conversation was with solicitor Richard Fothergill. After receiving condolences, he asked the man if he would attend to matters on their behalf, explaining that, whilst he and Alexander would be returning for the funeral, they had received a warning from Eleanor before her death and they believed it was in their best interest to remain in Cape Verde. He told the solicitor they were going to try to stay there long term, and would be applying for permanent citizenship. He also advised that the house would be either sold or rented out, and he was planning to contact

Fay at Theodore Farquharson's estate agency to make the arrangements. He asked the solicitor if he would be kind enough, when they had a date for the body to be released, to make the funeral arrangements on their behalf, and agreed that any necessary documentation would be signed if the solicitor could email it across to them.

On Ahmed's next call, Fay was even more sympathetic as he asked her to make arrangements for letting the property out on their behalf, asked what agreement she would need, and requested she send a copy over so they could sign. He informed her he had contacted Richard Fothergill, about handling the legal affairs, and he would locate and organise for her to have a key.

His third call was to the solicitor in Cape Verde explaining the situation and asking him if he could progress their application to gain permanent citizenship or, at least, authority to stay on the island for the foreseeable future.

When Ahmed had finished, Alexander looked at him in a new light. In the past, whilst he had not been left out of matters, Ahmed had never taken central stage, and there was a look of pride in his eyes as Alexander told his husband how clever and efficient he was.

'Well, I always told you and your mother that I would look after you.' He kissed the young man, fully on the lips as he teasingly added, 'Let's go and eat soon and I'll look after you in other ways later.'

CHAPTER 57

Richard Fothergill had to advise the mayor that he never handled criminal cases, but he was aware that one of the larger companies in town had a criminal lawyer as one of their partners, and offered to introduce Cedric to the man in question. Quinton Davenport was a hard-bitten forty-five-year-old who spent most of his time being paid to get up early in the morning and attend court to arrange the freedom of drunks, petty thieves and occasionally middle-aged lady shoplifters. To be involved in a murder case was very appealing and he jumped at the opportunity to take on the local mayor as a client.

At the request of Foster-Clarkson, after the original introduction by Richard Fothergill, Quinton met his client on a one-to-one basis. The man seemed to have convinced himself that the arrest of the Indian for murder had let him off the hook, and that the forthcoming appointment with Chief Inspector Smith would be just routine, following which the mayor could expect to carry on with his normal life. So far, his political colleagues, at least to his face, had emphasised their individual and collective support, expressing surprise that he had even been any kind of suspect in the first place and wondered why he was still being pursued.

Quinton sat quietly beside his client as Joseph Smith deliberately kept them waiting, whilst he read through a few

of the papers in the file in front of him, before commencing his questioning.

'Now, Colonel, last time we spoke we discussed the weed killer and I told you Mrs McLoughlin had consumed enough of that particular brand to kill her. As you are aware, we found a quantity at your house, but we did not find trace of any at Mrs McLoughlin's residence. Do you think you could have any explanation for that?'

'No.'

'You could have taken some with you and put it in her sherry while she went to get a glass of water for you.'

'Why would I want to do that?'

'In order to kill her. Why did you want to kill her, Mr Foster-Clarkson?'

'Chief Inspector,' Quinton Davenport intervened, 'My client has advised you several times he had no reason to kill the lady in question, and that she was alive and well when he left. I also understand you are presently holding someone who has been charged with her murder, so I really do not see why you are pursuing this line of questioning with my client.'

Foster-Clarkson looked at his lawyer with gratitude and newfound confidence.

'Even if I accept that Mrs McLoughlin was alive when Colonel Foster-Clarkson left her, it did not mean she was well as she could have already drunk, what turned out to be, poison.'

'But what possible reason could my client have for wanting this lady dead? I understand from him that she sometimes helped him out, looking after his dogs whilst his wife and he were away, and he tells me they were grateful for that, particularly at a time when my client was ill in hospital. He assures me his relationship with Mrs McLoughlin has always

been friendly, but very professional, so there's no reason why he should want to cause her any harm whatsoever.'

Recalling a comment made by Alexander during his visit to Cape Verde, Joseph Smith leaned forwards in his chair and stared straight into the clear blue eyes of Cedric Foster-Clarkson as he quietly asked, 'Why aren't you left-handed?'

Foster-Clarkson paled and his hands shook as he extracted a small white vial of liquid from his pocket, removed the top and sprayed a small amount into his mouth.

His lawyer, taken completely by surprise, immediately asked for a recess, so he could have private discussions with his client, checking the recording machine which had been switched on at the start of the interview was turned off, before the two detectives left the room.

'What was that all about, sir?' the young detective asked as he accompanied the chief inspector to his office.

'Do you know, I really don't have the foggiest idea. But my guess is that, from the reaction, we have stumbled upon something that is, somehow, very important, and we need to know exactly what that something is. The spray the colonel used was something that is used by people who have angina. Apparently, it can stop the clotting of blood, which can be dangerous, and we know the colonel recently had a heart attack. He is a pretty cool customer, so the left-handed remark really must have struck home in some way.'

Joseph asked the young detective to close the door as soon as he reached his office, took his mobile telephone out of his pocket, scrolled down to where Ahmed's number was stored in the memory and pressed the call button.

As soon as the Bangladeshi answered, Joseph checked to make sure they were in their own accommodation and could

not be overheard, before he asked the Asian to put his mobile on speaker mode. Aware he was probably breaking some kind of police regulation, he advised the pair he was in the process of interviewing the colonel in respect of Eleanor's death, had raised the question of being left-handed, and asked if Alexander could expound on his earlier statement. He waited as he heard the other two discussing the matter, then it was Ahmed who suggested the detective ask the colonel what he knew about someone called Sergeant Ellis.

CHAPTER 58

Joseph Smith did not like funerals. He had attended many over the years, the majority to sympathise with victims of sudden death, either accidental or other means, as a show of respect for the family of the deceased. In the case of Eleanor McLoughlin, he was actually on duty, alongside two other plain clothes men, with Joseph himself deciding to stick close to Alexander and Ahmed. All three policemen were armed, and Joseph had warned them there was an outside possibility someone may want to harm Alexander, Ahmed or both. Whilst Javendra Bhattacharya was still in custody, Colonel Foster-Clarkson was out on bail, both men having been charged with Eleanor's murder. Their job was not made any easier by the throngs of people who turned out, either to pay their respects or out of morbid curiosity, but the whole village population seemed to be there, and there were many standing at the back of the church during the service.

The coroner had taken some time to release the body in view of the complicated situation surrounding her death, and it had been six weeks since his visit to Cape Verde. The two young men had arrived the previous day, being met at the airport by their solicitor, accompanied by a plain clothes policeman who escorted the group to a hotel in the town. The policeman stayed with them until relieved at midnight by a uniformed constable, who had then spent the night outside

their hotel room door. Their evening meal was taken in the room, and the only people admitted were the solicitor and Fay from the estate agency.

On the morning of the funeral, again driven by the solicitor, they had an armed bodyguard as they were taken to the chapel of rest to where Eleanor's body had been moved in order to allow them to pay their own personal respects.

Following the church service, the hearse and a single car were driven to the crematorium in town, followed by several private vehicles. The wake to celebrate her life was held in the function room of the Conservative Club, and had been organised by Peggy, wife of the solicitor. Again, the place was packed, taking advantage of a really good spread of a finger buffet, which Peggy had organised, the cost of which had been agreed with Alexander. The young man was constantly surrounded by sympathisers, with Ahmed never far from his side, and by the time everyone had eventually drifted away, the pair were exhausted.

Allowing them to travel back to the hotel, Joe advised he would like to see them for half an hour or so the following morning before they caught their flight back to their new home. As far as he could understand, everything had been organised in respect of sending any additional belongings they needed, and which Fay had been looking after since the house was let out three weeks earlier.

Joseph sat at his desk at the police station, took a sip of tea and opened the file on the murder of Eleanor McLoughlin, and also the one on the blackmailing case.

Following his visit to Cape Verde, he was convinced Eleanor, her son and his husband had an incredibly open relationship and that, in the main, she took them into her

confidence in all matters. The only exceptions seemed to be those of her abortion and her illness, which he thought were understandable. It was his sincere belief she had wanted to see the pair settled in Cape Verde during the short time which she had left to live. The mystery which he had yet to fathom out was why she had taken the risk of inviting people to her home. He still did not want to believe she was capable of being the blackmailer, but was also convinced the trio were suitably equipped, and capable, of carrying out the very detailed operation and that, until recently, they had the motive of requiring money.

There was also the mystery of why she wanted to meet the accountant as Joe had no knowledge he was being blackmailed. The original email had referred to her wanting to show him a new thong, which was tempting enough, but then the same temptation had been used on the Indian. If that was the case, then why did she change her mind and, presumably, resist the advances of Javendra, although she had also used the excuse of repaying money, which would be a good incentive for the Indian to visit.

On cross examination, the accountant, although admitting to the affair, had claimed he had only visited Eleanor on one occasion in her own home, when nothing intimate had taken place. Joseph was aware Eleanor had telephoned the accountant to check he had received her email and to remind him of the visit, so she certainly seemed very eager to see him. If she had initially planned to have sex with the Indian, then why did she want to ensure Hugh Barker put in an appearance? As he flicked through the papers, he came across the statement of the postman, was about to turn it over, but stopped and read it again.

'It was the dogs,' he said aloud.

She wanted the accountant to take care of the dogs, but why? There was no way she knew she was going to be murdered, but then he paused in his thoughts... or was there?

The pathologist had been adamant the poison was sufficient to kill her, whereas a blow on the head might not necessarily be fatal. Surely, Joe mused, both the colonel and the Indian were strong enough to have hit her hard enough to kill her. Certainly, he had seen the Indian in a temper, confirmed by both Ahmed and Alexander, and had he lashed out with the heavy decanter, it would certainly have been with sufficient force to break the woman's skull. For his age, Foster-Clarkson was still relatively fit, so presumably also strong enough to deliver the right kind of blow. The fingerprints of both the suspects, plus the victim, were on the decanter but they were also on the wine glass which had contained the poison, which was definitely capable of killing her.

It had been several years since Joe had changed his own insurance policy, but he seemed to remember he had to agree to a clause which reduced the amount payable in the case of suicide. He also seemed to remember a different clause, covering things such as a violent death and wondered if the policy of Eleanor McLoughlin had also included a similar condition.

Casting his thoughts over events for some time, he thought the woman had been making plans for her own death, ensuring her son and his partner would be safe, and he also knew she had made arrangements for the animals, following her death, to be cared for in local kennels, with arrangements for payment to be made in her will.

The only problem with her death happening suddenly would be if the dogs were not found for some time, and Chief Inspector Joseph Smith was beginning to believe accountant

Hugh Barker had been chosen to discover them. Thankfully, although that plan had not worked, the postman came to the rescue as, fortunately, there were letters to be delivered to the house that day. At the time, Joe noticed the holiday brochure, which required the postman to ring the bell and a vague thought entered his brain. What if she wanted to pin the murder on the Indian, but needed an alternative plan if he did not show. From his own experience, he knew holiday companies utilised the internet and only sent hard copies of brochures on request. Why would Eleanor McLoughlin ask for a holiday brochure if she planned to move abroad? He could think of one very good reason, which was to make sure the postman had to call just in case the accountant did not.

Joseph Smith was now convinced Eleanor McLoughlin had planned her own murder, decided who would be blamed as her killer and had even selected a reserve should anything go wrong.

He considered the two suspects. The first was a manipulating groomer of underage girls for the use of any men who were prepared to pay the price, sometimes just the cost of a cheap hotel room. Alcohol and drugs were used to guarantee the cooperation of the girls, one who had been used to ensure his legal stay in the country. He was also a cruel, ruthless wife beater who, according to her diary, had used drugs to have his way with the dog walker.

The mayor was a fraud and had, at worst, possibly killed his friend, perhaps humanely, but then fooled hundreds of people into trusting him, receiving money and status built on lies.

He was also totally convinced that, if he mentioned his theory to anybody, they would believe he had lost his touch. Whilst he believed he had come up with a logical possibility,

could he persuade anyone else to agree with him? He had no way of proving what was in the mind of a woman who was now dead.

Putting the papers back in the correct order, Joseph placed them back in the file which he returned to the filing cabinet, turned out the light in his office and left the building.

The story of the murder had been picked up by the national newspapers, possibly due to the unusual twist of two separate suspects using differing methods to carry out the crime. Both had sufficiently high profiles to attract considerable interest. Initially believed to have been acting independently, Detective Chief Inspector Joseph Smith had cleverly linked the pair. By putting pressure on Michael O'Flanagan, Joe had discovered Javendra Bhattacharya was a client of the security company in which Foster-Clarkson had an interest. The detective had no doubt the two men had sufficient funds to employ the finest legal representation and that, when the trial eventually occurred, it would again hit the headlines.

Theodore Farquharson did not care about any of this. He had read the report in the local paper, which had referred to the possibility of blackmail being a motive for the killing, and had immediately ceased the payments which he had been making to the charity. Unknown to him, his actions had been mirrored by bank manager Geoffrey Wilkinson, sales agent Jackson Blanchford and the deputy head, Henrietta Barker.

Theodore was also ignorant of the fact he was not the only one to be greeted with an email received from his earlier tormentors.

As our good work is continuing to benefit the young people in Africa, we are disappointed that your

donations have not been received recently. We trust this is an oversight, and that they will quickly resume, but will be preparing to forward copies of our documents as previously advised.

Regards

PS. Did you really think it was over?

ABOUT THE AUTHOR

Accepting the challenge of writing at an age when most people have retired, John draws on his comprehensive and varied experiences in life since, in his words, escaping from a mining village in D. H. Lawrence's territory which took him to the far-flung jungles of Malaya and Borneo during an RAF career. Civilian life enabled him to continue travelling throughout Europe, America and Asia.

A late career change made him passionate in his understanding of the trials, needs and attitudes of people with severe physical and mental challenges. Dedication to his cause resulted in several awards, with the one he is most proud of being the Queen's Award for volunteering, following his charity work.

Ingram Content Group UK Ltd.
Milton Keynes UK
UKHW011904270723
425908UK00001B/5

9 781805 411260